Return on

We Come Unseen

Other books by the author

ERSKINE CHILDERS

HOW THE ENGLISH MADE THE ALPS

We Come Unseen

The Untold Story of Britain's Cold War Submariners

'To win one hundred battles is not the acme of skill. To subdue the enemy without fighting, that is the acme of skill.'

Sun Tzu

JIM RING

JOHN MURRAY
Albemarle Street, London

© Jim Ring 2001

First published in 2001
by John Murray (Publishers) Ltd,
50 Albemarle Street, London W1S 4BD

The moral right of the author has been asserted

A catalogue record for this book is available from the British Library

ISBN 0-7195-5690 2

Typeset in Garamond MT 12/14 pt
by Servis Filmsetting Limited, Manchester

Printed and bound in Great Britain by
St Edmundsbury Press, Bury St Edmunds, Suffolk

For Kate

Contents

Contents

CRIMSON TIDE

Illustrations

The author and publishers would like to thank the following for permission to reproduce illustrations: Plates 1, 5, 7 and 23, © Hulton Getty; 2, 3, 4, 9, 10, 12, 13, 14, 15, 16, 17, 20 and 21, Royal Navy Submarine Museum, Gosport; 6, John Moore; 8, Martin Macpherson; 11, James Taylor; 18 and 22, Crown Copyright; and 19, Toby Elliott. Plate 24 is from the author's collection.

Preface

The best books breed other books. This one was inspired by two paperbacks I read as a teenager. The first was Takashi Nagai's *We of Nagasaki*, a survivor's account of the bombing of the capital of the western province of Kyushu a few days after Hiroshima, on 9 August 1945. With its all too vivid account of the initial impact of the atom bomb and the subsequent effects of radiation exposure, it brought home to me the shadow under which the world was living in the nuclear age. The second was Edward Young's autobiographical account of his service during the Second World War as a submarine commander in the Mediterranean and the Far East, *One of Our Submarines*. This intensely English, quietly understated and at the same time curiously romantic tale of the submarine fraternity gave me an enduring fascination for these craft and the men who crew them.

It was a little while after I read these two books that their themes coalesced in the form of the British nuclear deterrent submarines of the Polaris force, the first of which – *Resolution* – was commissioned in 1968. Here were underwater machines capable of inflicting the damage of the bombs that fell on Hiroshima and Nagasaki many times over. Yet it was not for another thirty years that I was properly to get to know a British submarine commander, and by then the Cold War was over. Commander Simon Anderson was the sometime commanding officer of *Conqueror*, the submarine that in the hands of Commander Chris Wreford-Brown had sunk the Argentinian cruiser *General Belgrano* in the Falklands conflict. It was of Anderson that I enquired whether there were any tales of British submarines in the

Second World War that still merited telling. Anderson replied: 'Why not write about us?'

At first the barriers seemed insuperable. The essence of a submarine is stealth, and secrecy is inbred in the submarine culture. The same is equally true of nuclear weapons, the nuclear propulsion systems used by most of the submarines capable of carrying nuclear weapons, and the defence establishment more generally. Moreover, if the Cold War was history, it was only very recent history, and in some respects the conflict still endured. I very quickly realized that it would be impossible to write an authoritative and detailed operational account of the activities of British submarines during the Cold War for some years to come, especially if I was to rely – as I have – on written sources already in the public domain.

At the same time, however, it gradually became apparent that another book, in some respects perhaps a more interesting one, could be written. Preliminary interviews conducted over a period of more than a year proved a point that should in any case have been obvious to a reader of *One of Our Submarines* – or indeed its German fictional and cinematic equivalent *Das Boot*. That is, that the men who command these machines are at least as interesting as the craft themselves.

The idea accordingly germinated of following the service careers of a manageable number of officers who achieved submarine command. To do so I chose five members of the Dartmouth class of 1963: Toby Elliott, Roger Lane-Nott, Martin Macpherson, James Taylor and Chris Wreford-Brown; and one member – Jeff Tall – from the following year.

There are various limitations to such an approach, most obviously the way in which the story largely excludes all but the six officers on whom it focuses. There were a fair number of others who achieved submarine command during the Cold War, from the class of 1963 alone: Jonathan Boyle (now Viscount Dungarvan), Paul Branscombe, Johnny Clarke, Dan Conley, Nick Crews, Dai Evans, Mike Gregory, Phil Higgins, Mike Jones, Neil Robertson, Chris Roddis and Dick Strange. I believe those who I chose are nevertheless reasonably representative of their generation, and Roger Lane-Nott even goes so far as to say 'the names are interchangeable'.

By definition, though, the six are less representative of earlier and later generations, but this is hardly to suggest that these people did not play their part in suppressing the Soviet threat. John Moore therefore represents those who had served in the Royal Navy during the Second World War and who went on to command submarines in the early years of the Cold War. Sir Sandy Woodward and Sir Toby Frere represent the next generation down. As to the generation younger than the class of '63, the general problems of security were compounded by many of the best of that group still being serving officers. Nevertheless, they are represented by a weapons specialist, Marcus Fitzgerald, whom Toby Elliott characteristically describes as a 'damned fine officer'; and Geoff McCready, CO of *Upholder*, the first of what was intended to be a new generation of British diesel-electric submarines. Moreover, the approach does not prevent me covering where these men took their submarines, when, and for what purpose, although certain patrols and certain details have necessarily been omitted. Its principal intention, however, is to provide some insight into the variety of men who commanded our nuclear submarines in an age – now largely departed – when nuclear war was a hideously real possibility. As an American recently said to me, 'I always thought that submarine commanders were seven feet tall and built of high-grade steel.' I had long presumed the same.

It may seem odd in a democratic age to focus so exclusively on the commanders of these vessels, largely to the exclusion of their officers and crew. Certainly when I went to sea myself in the Trafalgar-class attack submarine *Talent*, I was most struck by the sense of CO, officers and crew working together as a cohesive unit. Similarly, Chris Wreford-Brown told me that 'There is no way *Conqueror* would have had her success in 1982 without the professionalism of the ship's company and in particular the three Heads of Department'. A submarine, though, even today, depends upon and reflects the character of its commanding officer to a remarkable degree. As William Guy Carr wrote in his account of British submarines during the First World War:

In surface vessels there are several factors which may bring success – in spite of the commanding officer. A ship may be a good shooting ship; an excellent chief of staff, mistakes on the part of the enemy, assistance from other vessels are some of the factors. In submarines none of these counts. One man only, the commanding officer, can see, and he only with one eye. No one can help him. Germany had some four hundred submarine captains during the war, but over sixty per cent of the damage was accomplished by but twenty-two of these four hundred officers. The inference is obvious. The one and great difficulty is to find a sufficiency of officers . . . who will rise superior to the incidental intricacies of these complicated vessels, who will make their opportunities and take advantage of them when found under conditions of hardship and acute discomfort.

Hence, as Carr puts it, the 'overwhelming importance in submarine matters of the character and abilities of those who command them'. Although the technology associated with the nuclear submarine has seen a limited devolution of responsibility down the chain of command, the point remains essentially valid.

An outsider suffers some very obvious disadvantages in writing such a book, but I hope that any resulting deficiencies have been at least partly overcome by the three years I have spent in England, the United States and the former Soviet Union, interviewing Cold War submariners. At the same time, I hope that my perspective is of interest to the general reader, for I have looked at and discussed issues that seem interesting from a human point of view rather than a technical or technological one; and I have tried to avoid what strike me as the more tiresome literary conventions of military history. Inevitably the result is not a portrait of submariners as they see themselves or even as they might wish to be seen, but a layman's perspective on a very particular and unusual group of men.

This book is their story.

Burnham Overy Staithe,
February 2001

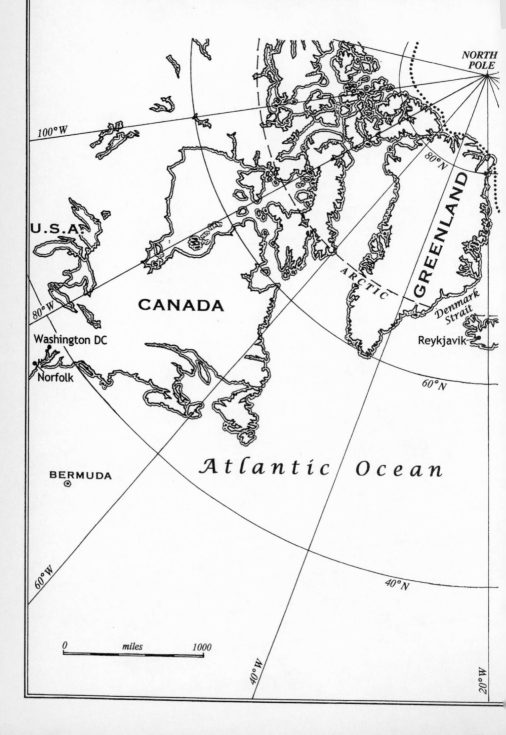

THE NORTH ATLA

NTIC AND ARCTIC

Arctic Ocean

Kara Sea

Novaya Zemlya

Barents Sea

Kola Peninsula

Kola Inlet

Bear Island

Murmansk

White Sea

Polyarnny

SOVIET UNION

Norwegian Sea

CIRCLE

60° E

Moscow

GIUK Gap

ICELAND

Leningrad

Baltic Sea

40° E

Black Sea

UNITED KINGDOM

Faslane

London

Portsmouth

Devonport

Mediterranean Sea

Suez Canal

Strait of Gibraltar

20° E

0°

·········· Approximate extent of polar icecap

THE SOUTH ATLANTIC, 1982

BRAZIL

ARGENTINA

URUGUAY

Buenos
Aires

Montevideo

CHILE

ASCENSION ISLAND
(3,800 miles)

Comodoro Rivadavia

FALKLAND ISLANDS

SOUTH GEORGIA
(900 miles)

Rio
Gallegos

Rio
Grande

*Burdwood
Bank*

200-mile total exclusion zone
(TEZ)

0   miles   500

Absolute Beginners

'Remember that joining as a midshipman is bound to be awe-inspiring. Everyone about you seems so authoritative and important . . . and you realise that no-one seems to care a hang whether you are there or not. The reason is that your talents, if any, are undiscovered.'

Captain Eric Bush, *How to Become a Naval Officer*, 1963

Prologue

'There used to be a school of historical thought which held that the course of human history was determined largely by political and economic factors rather than by the characters and actions of individuals. My own experience during the last war has emphasised to me the immense, and in some cases decisive influence exerted on the course of events by individuals.'

Air Chief Marshal Sir Arthur Tedder, preface to Hugh Trevor-Roper, *The Last Days of Hitler*, 1952

Wednesday, 17 September 1963, was a grey, blustery day, as much autumn as late summer. Squalls raced across the river towards the small Devon port of Dartmouth, and clouds loured over the grey seas of the Channel. High above the river, the Britannia Royal Naval College stood out, bleak and austere in the rain. Designed by Sir Aston Webb, architect of the façade of Buckingham Palace and of the Admiralty Arch at the other end of the Mall, the College had been executed in his finest imperial manner, a huge neo-classical structure symbolizing the Royal Navy as it approached the height of its power. Across the River Dart, a train drew slowly into the terminus of Kingswear. It was an express from Paddington, and from it descended three hundred or so passengers.

To a local their identity was obvious enough. They were the autumn intake of naval cadets for the College, the institution on which much of the prosperity of the town depended. Superficially, they were indistinguishable from their predecessors, that year or any other. Dressed in regulation tweed jackets, grey flannels and trilbys, they might have been public schoolboys in any part of the country, their gait the eager one of youth, their faces unmarked by experience. Indeed, although they were a few years older, they might almost have been their predecessors of precisely a century before, when the first naval cadets at Dartmouth had been trained on board the old Napoleonic three-deckers *Britannia* and *Hindoostan*. The successors of Drake, Grenville, Cook, Hawke and Nelson, these youths had gone on to command the fleet in the days of empire when the Royal Navy was by far and away the largest in the world. They had seen the transition from wooden hulls to those of steel, from the power of sail to that of steam, from muzzle-loading cannon to the breech-loader and the gun turret. They were the men whose sea-chests in 1914 had been packed at four hours' notice and who had been sent straight to sea, many of them to die under the command of Jellicoe and Beatty at Jutland. A generation later their successors had cornered the *Graf Spee* in Montevideo, drowned aboard *Royal Oak* and *Hood*, and conducted the extraordinary evacuation of Dunkirk. They had sunk the *Bismarck* and the *Scharnhorst*, disabled *Tirpitz* in Alten fiord, destroyed the heart of the Italian navy at Cape Matapan. They had escorted hundreds of convoys of merchantmen, and had won the battle against Admiral Dönitz's U-boats in the Atlantic. They had extracted tens of thousands from Crete, masterminded the Normandy landings, and – in the Far East – seen the great battleships *Prince of Wales* and *Repulse* die at the hand of Japanese bombers.

It was, then, a fine tradition that had formed men from the Dartmouth cadets. Yet of the class of '63 still more would be asked, for this was the generation that would bear the burden of the Royal Navy's nuclear age. These men were among the first to go to sea with the responsibility for firing Polaris, Britain's nuclear deterrent; and among the first whose submarines had to track down and show their ability to destroy their Soviet opposite numbers. It is known that British submarines spent almost forty years fighting the Cold War in the North Atlantic, and that their duties occasionally took them further north into the Norwegian, Arctic and Barents Seas and to the naval bases of the Soviet Union where they played cat and mouse with their Red Banner Fleet counterparts. The full truth is more dramatic. As one of the great submariners of his generation, Admiral Sir John Coward, later remarked, 'There was a war. And we won it.'

The cadets of the class of '63 were less nondescript teenagers than they seemed. The Navy has never been careless in its selection process, even though the qualities thought desirable have changed over the years. In the Georgian Navy birth and connections were the requirements, seamanship being of less account. The interest in and influence of its senior officers on the selection process began to be eroded in 1815, when the Admiralty started to examine those aspiring to the rank of midshipman, and by the end of the century this applied to all ranks. Even after the Second World War, though, tradition still played a part. In his memoirs, Denis Healey, who as Secretary of State for Defence between 1964 and 1970 worked closely with the Navy on the development of Polaris, recalled: 'Even in my time the Navy recruited many of its successful officers from families scattered round the great naval ports of the South Coast, which had provided Admirals for generations.' Breeding apart, the academic demands were now for five GCE passes, two of them at A-level. The requirements of personality and physical fitness were more demanding. Those who had taken their seats at Paddington had already passed preliminary screening followed by the Admiralty Interview Board at the shore establishment HMS *Sultan* in Gosport.

'Sir,' ran the invitation from the Board, 'I am commanded by My Lords Commissioners of the Admiralty to inform you that you have been selected to appear before the Admiralty Interview Board to undergo tests of personal qualities.' The word 'interview' was misleading. Candidates were required to present themselves promptly at 1600 at *Sultan*. They were advised to get their hair cut and put on their best clothes. If they smoked they should remove the tell-tale stains with pumice. Duly registered, they were set a series of short examination papers on subjects ranging from mathematics and English to naval history. Then they broke for dinner, in the course of which they were expected to display good manners. They had to be in bed by 2230. The following morning they were sent to the gym. There candidates formed groups of six or eight, each taking it in turn to be leader. An obstacle course was set up, representing – say – a ravine. Each candidate had to lead his team across the chasm to safety; or as a team member to co-operate intelligently with the leader. The members of the Board were looking for 'officer-like qualities'. Writing in 1963, Captain Eric Bush remarked in his primer, *How to Become a Naval Officer*: 'They are looking for the boy who tends to lead and can also tackle a difficult situation without getting in a flap. They are sorting out the doers from the talkers. They are noticing the young man who seems to lose heart.' Then came the debate, to test the candidate's ability to articulate ideas and present them persuasively.

One of the candidates early in 1963 was a Queen's Medallist from Pangbourne College, R. C. Lane-Nott. He was asked to talk on capital punishment, the abolition of which was high on the political agenda of the Prime Minister, Harold Macmillan. After lunch came an interview with a psychologist. According to Captain Bush, 'he wishes to know your background, thoughts, hopes, fears ambitions, tastes . . . he will find out the real reason why you want to join the navy, and whether there is a reasonable chance of your being happy there'. Another candidate, T.D. Elliott, was a Cranbrookian whose father had commanded a submarine during and after the Second World War. Soon Elliott was discussing the relationship between father and son. The psychologist took a similar tack with the Rugbeian C.L.Wreford-Brown, whose father was one of the senior lecturers at Dartmouth. Finally came the Board interview itself. This was chaired by an Admiral, and attended by all those who had overseen the candidates during their twenty-four-hour examination. 'You may', wrote Captain Bush, 'be asked everything or anything.' Admiral Sir John ('Jackie') Fisher, by far the greatest naval figure of the Edwardian age, told the painter Augustus John that his interview comprised reciting the Lord's Prayer and drinking a glass of sherry. Three-quarters of a century later, M.D. Macpherson, whose father had been a Major in the Royal Marines, his grandfather a Rear-Admiral, noted on his application form an enthusiasm for home-brewed beer. The Board chairman had a similar interest. Twenty-five minutes of the half-hour interview were devoted to the subject. Macpherson proved himself articulate and well informed. J.B. Taylor, the son of an Edinburgh veterinary surgeon, was also asked if he liked beer. Nervous after failing to do justice to himself in the gym, he felt this was a subject on which he could speak with authority.

A few days later, letters were dispatched to all the candidates. More than two-thirds of them had failed. Toby Elliott, Roger Lane-Nott, Chris Wreford-Brown, Martin Macpherson and James Taylor were regarded as suitable raw material. With the exception of Wreford-Brown, all were accepted as Supplementary List officers, the short-service category which committed them to ten years' active service and five on the reserve. Wreford-Brown, better qualified academically, was on the General List, with a long-service commission.

Getting off the train, the three hundred cadets were met by the College drill instructors and herded on to the ferry to cross to the west bank of the Dart. Then they were marshalled into three columns and marched up the hill. There, on the parade ground, they were told to which of the six divisions of the intake they had been allocated: Drake, Blake, Exmouth, Hawke, St Vincent or Grenville. They were also asked if they smoked, those that did being entitled to a duty-free allowance. Naval careers that would place unprecedented demands on these young men and their contemporaries had begun.

Chapter 1

Goodbye to Berlin

'With the defeat of the Reich and pending the emergence of the Asiatic, the African, and perhaps the South American nationalisms, there will remain in the world only two great powers capable of confronting one another – the United States and the Soviet Union. The laws of history and geography will compel these two powers to a trial of strength, either military or in the field of economics and ideology.'

Adolf Hitler, April 1945

At the time of the birth of the class of '63 a meeting took place that marked the beginning of a series of events that would greatly affect their lives.

The last conference of the Allied war leaders opened on 17 July 1945. Since the previous such encounter, at Yalta in the Crimea, President Franklin D. Roosevelt had died. In his stead was the former Vice-President Harry S. Truman. Marshal Josef Stalin represented the Soviet Union, the Prime Minister Winston Churchill, Great Britain. The Three Powers met at Potsdam, not far from the ruins of Berlin, to settle the shape of the post-war world. They would deliberate over the war in the Far East and agree plans for the invasion of Malaya, the Dutch East Indies and Japan. Following the end of the war in Europe two months earlier, they would also try to resolve the future of the Continent, and in particular of Germany. The latter was an issue fraught with uncertainty, and indeed trepidation. In the course of the previous few months, British, French and American forces from the west and Stalin's Red Army from the east had raced to be the first in Berlin. Enthusiasm to defeat the Nazis was clearly coupled with ambitions to dominate the future of the whole of Europe.

In a sense, this was inevitable. The wartime alliance had, on both sides, been a marriage of convenience brought about by Hitler's invasion of the USSR in 1941. Once the enemy in Europe had been defeated, it was scarcely surprising that ideology should reassert itself. The United States had broken off diplomatic relations with Russia at the time of the Bolshevik Revolution in 1917, not recognizing the authority of the Soviet government until 1933. Britain had gone further, providing military support for the White Russian forces opposing the revolution to the tune of £100 million. Churchill had once remarked of Lenin and Trotsky that they had 'driven man from the civilization of the twentieth century into a barbarism worse than the Stone Age'. Stalin took the Marxist-Leninist line that the capitalist world was an intrinsically corrupt society that owed its wealth to the exploitation of the masses.

Beyond ideological disagreement, it was also significant that Europe in 1945 was in chaos. Much of Germany was quite literally in ruins. The countries to its west and east through which the Nazis had fought their rearguard action against the Allies were similarly devastated. Much of Europe's industrial and communications infrastructure – factories, roads, railways, canals – had been destroyed, and millions were now refugees. Even the populations of the victorious countries were exhausted by the struggle. Above all, though, there was a vacuum of power in Europe. Marxist theory taught that the collapse of capitalism was inevitable. The economic turmoil of the 1930s in the West had lent credence to such a theory, and there had been flourishing Communist parties in many Western countries. During the course of the war the cause of national unity had led to the formation of a number of national governments representing all the major parties. With the war over, however, the political direction that the Continent would follow was far from certain. Underlying Potsdam was the issue of the very survival of European democracy.

Yet even as the conference began, it was overtaken by outside events. From Los Alamos in New Mexico came news of the successful trial of the first atomic bomb. Truman and Churchill took the decision to use the weapon. Stalin was then informed – spies had already told him of its existence and kept him informed of progress – and an ultimatum was sent to the Japanese on 26 July. Then, that same day, the results of the General Election in Britain led to Churchill's resignation, and his replacement by the new Labour Prime Minister, Clement Attlee. With the new Prime Minister in Britain's negotiating seat, the conference confirmed one critical decision made at Yalta: the division of Germany and Berlin into four zones, each zone to be ruled by one of the Three Powers and France, pending a final decision on the country's long-term future. Other matters led only to argument. No clear agreement was reached on the nature of the regimes to be established in eastern Europe, and in particular in Poland, the nominal cause of the Second World War. The summit closed on 2 August.

Three days later, the American B-29 Superfortress *Enola Gay* dropped an atomic bomb on Hiroshima. It had the power of 13,000 tons of TNT and produced such searing temperatures that it incinerated human beings instantly, leaving only scorch marks on the pavement where they had strolled. A Japanese newspaper reporter, arriving at what remained of the railway station, recorded what he saw: 'There was a sweeping view, right to the mountains, north, south and east; the city had vanished.' On 9 August, Stalin's forces attacked Japan, and a second bomb was dropped on Nagasaki. An estimated 110,000 were killed immediately in the two bombings, and many more later died as a result of burns and radiation. Then, on 11 August 1945, Japan surrendered.

This train of events was profoundly disturbing. No sooner had the threat of Hitler been removed than a new enemy seemed to have emerged, one known to be in the process of developing the weapon that had just redefined the meaning of war. Stalin, calling together his nuclear scientists within days of Nagasaki, had instructed: 'A single demand of you, comrades. Provide us with atomic weapons in the shortest possible time. You know that Hiroshima has shaken the whole world. The balance has been destroyed. Provide the bomb – it will remove a great danger from us.' The following month Attlee wrote despairingly to Truman, 'I ought to direct all our people to live like troglodytes, underground as being the only hope of survival, and that by no means certain.'

The world had been turned upside down, and the survival of democracy, great cities and even nations seemed under question.

As the post-war age unfolded, so too did the Communist threat. The Soviets, frustrated over the division of power in Germany, gradually established a buffer zone between themselves and the West; and irrespective of the wishes of their peoples, one by one the governments of eastern Europe began to fall to Soviet control. The Americans, hitherto inclined to view the Soviets as allies, were soon to change their view. In February 1946 George Kennan, a diplomat based in Moscow, dispatched a telegram to the State Department. In it he analysed Soviet intentions. Kennan believed that the Soviet Union constituted 'a political force committed fanatically to the belief that with the US there can be no permanent modus vivendi; that it is desirable and necessary that the internal harmony of our society be disrupted, our traditional way of life destroyed, the international authority of our state broken, if Soviet power is to be secure'. In short, the Soviet Union was bent on world domination and the destruction of capitalism. A month later, on 5 March 1946, in a speech at Fulton, Missouri, Churchill expressed a similar view publicly: 'A shadow has fallen upon the scenes so lately lighted by the Allied victory. Nobody knows what Soviet Russia and its Communist international organization intend to do in the immediate future, or what are the limits, if any, for their expansive and proselytizing tendencies . . . from Stettin in the Baltic to Trieste in the Adriatic, an iron curtain has descended across the continent.'

In response to the Soviet threat, the American President enunciated the Truman Doctrine, the American policy of resisting the advance of Communism. On 12 March 1947, Truman told Congress, 'At the present moment in world history nearly every nation must choose between alternative ways of life . . . It must be the policy of the United States to support free peoples who are resisting attempts to subjection by armed minorities or outside pressure.' Then, following the fall of Czechoslovakia to the Communists in February 1948, the Western powers proposed a series of measures to strengthen their position in West Berlin, consolidating the three

Western zones into one and launching a new currency. Stalin was duly informed by spies in the Foreign Office in London. On 24 June 1948, all road, rail and canal traffic between the isolated Allied zone of the city and the remainder of West Germany, a hundred miles away, was stopped. Stalin's intention was clear: to force the Allies out of Berlin. Nor was this all. As Ernest Bevin, Britain's Foreign Secretary, put it: 'The abandonment of Berlin would mean the loss of Western Europe.'

With Berlin now symbolizing the new confrontation between East and West, Churchill proposed threatening to use the atomic bomb against Soviet cities. Across the Atlantic, President Truman was lobbied by his Secretary of Defense James Forrestal to put the growing American stockpile of atomic weapons to use. As it was, the idea of an 'air bridge' to West Berlin was formulated and put into action. In a masterpiece of political will and logistical endeavour, through the bitter winter of 1948/9 British and American planes brought in two and half million tons of food, fuel and other essentials to keep the city alive.

By the time the siege was raised in May 1949, the North Atlantic Treaty Organization (Nato) had been formed. Together, the United States, Britain, France, the Benelux countries, Canada, Denmark, Iceland, Norway and Portugal constructed a defensive alliance against the Soviet threat. 'In this pact,' said Truman, 'it is hoped to create a shield against aggression and the fear of aggression.' Simultaneously, the Marshall Plan swung into action, an enormous package of financial assistance from the United States intended to discourage the growth of Communism in Europe. Offered to the whole of the Continent, it was predictably rejected by the Soviets and their associated states as a capitalist plot. That same month, in response to the formation of the new West German state, a consolidation of the Western zones in the form of the Federal Republic, the German Democratic Republic was set up by Stalin in the east. Europe was now divided into two camps.

Then, shortly before the end of August, an American B-29 bomber on a high-level exercise over the North Pacific detected unusual levels of radioactivity drifting away from a remote part of the Soviet Union. Stalin's demand for a nuclear weapon had been met, and the Western monopoly of the atom bomb was at an end.

As President Kennedy later stated, henceforth, 'every man, woman and child would live under a nuclear sword of Damocles, hanging by the slenderest of threads, capable of being cut at any moment by accident, miscalculation or madness.'

The Cold War, a phrase first used in 1947, had begun. The class of '63 were approaching school age.

*

Hitherto the focus of the new conflict had been Europe, yet Asia too was in chaos.

In Indonesia the Dutch were using force to try to restore their pre-war empire; in Indo-China the French were doing the same; in Malaya in 1948 the Communist Party launched a campaign to drive out the British; and, above all, in China, the civil war between Communists and Nationalists was reaching its climax. In October 1949, with Stalin's help, the Communists triumphed, Mao Zedong proclaiming a People's Republic. The Nationalists, who had been supported by the United States, fled to Taiwan, where their leader Chiang Kai-shek established the Republic of China. Then, in December 1949, Mao visited Stalin in Moscow. Two months later the pair signed the first Sino-Soviet treaty of friendship, alliance and mutual assistance. In doing so they created the spectre of a huge aggressive Communist bloc, bent on the imposition of Communism not just in Europe but throughout the globe.

Western fears of Communist aggression in Asia were soon borne out in Korea, where on 25 June 1950 Soviet-armed North Korean troops crossed the 38th Parallel, marched south and seized the southern capital of Seoul. Truman, smarting from the loss of China to Communism, was incensed, and at once ordered American troops to be dispatched to the South, and requested and received the blessing of the Security Council of the newly formed United Nations. So began a war that was to involve sixteen nations under the banner of the UN. On 15 September, UN troops under the command of General Douglas MacArthur landed behind enemy lines at Inchon. Soon the North Koreans were retreating. Then, on 28 November, 200,000 Chinese troops crossed the Yalu river from Manchuria into North Korea in support of their fellow Communists. Two days later,

Truman indicated at a press conference that the use of atomic bombs was under 'active consideration'.

The class of '63 had just started primary school.

As the war in Korea rumbled on, there were changes in Britain. In the General Election of 1951 Churchill was returned to office, with Anthony Eden once more Foreign Secretary.

This heralded a review of Britain's approach to the Cold War. A formal decision to develop a British atomic bomb had come in January 1947, partly in response to the US McMahon Act of 1946 that prohibited the transfer of America's atomic secrets beyond her shores. Partly, too, it reflected the thinking that the existence of atomic bombs had created a situation in which total war was inconceivable, and that it was the duty of governments to prevent it. Paradoxically, the means of doing so was increasingly believed to lie in possession of the bomb, for it was thought that no hostile power would dare to use weapons of such destructive capability if retaliation was likely. This was the essential principle of deterrence, later encapsulated in the telling acronym, Mutual Assured Destruction or MAD. Soon afterwards came the decision to develop a force of jet bombers for the RAF to deliver the weapons.

Visiting Truman in Washington in January 1952, Churchill was shown a series of new American weapons and delivery systems. Besides the original atomic bomber, the B-29, the B-36 had entered service in 1948, the B-47 in 1950, and plans for the giant B-52 were well advanced. These planes would provide the backbone of what would become the world's largest strategic bomber force, Strategic Air Command. Since atomic weapons had, through refinement, become much smaller and lighter – 1,000 pounds as opposed to the 9,000-pounder dropped on Hiroshima – the United States was also developing nuclear-tipped missiles. The first long-range missile, Vanguard, was in development; so too were shorter-range missiles called Thor and Jupiter. Fired from land bases, such missiles would in due course become the second element of America's defence. The US had plans, too, for high-altitude spy planes and spy satellites that might eventually encircle the globe.

It was clear to Churchill that if Britain was to retain what remained of her global prestige and her bargaining power with the United

States, she too should develop such capabilities. That October, the first British atomic bomb was successfully exploded off the Australian coast. A month later, the US detonated the hydrogen bomb, an immensely powerful device one thousand times more destructive than that dropped on Hiroshima. Soon Britain would develop her own hydrogen bombs, which Churchill would call 'the ultimate deterrent'. The V-bomber force to deliver them – Valiants, Victors and Vulcans – was due to come into service in 1955.

In Korea, an armistice was eventually signed in November 1953, ending a conflict that had resulted in stalemate between East and West. A conference of world leaders was set for April 1954, with a view to creating an independent, unified Korea. Also on the agenda was Indo-China, the region that would provide the next crisis in the Cold War.

Since 1946 the French had been fighting to re-establish control in the region against the Chinese-backed Communist forces of Ho Chi Minh. From 1950, in accordance with the Truman Doctrine, they had been receiving American support. Under Truman's successor, Eisenhower, the support was maintained. 'You have a row of dominoes set up,' said Eisenhower on 7 April 1954. 'You knock over the first one, and what will happen to the last one is the certainty that it will go very quickly . . . Asia, after all, has already lost some 450 million of its peoples to Communist dictatorship, and we simply can't afford greater losses.' As the conference approached, the weakness of the French military position was such that the Americans began to talk of united action by the Western powers. Then, days before the conference opened, it became apparent that the French were heading for defeat at one of their main bases in Vietnam, Dien Bien Phu. In response, the Americans envisaged collective military action by Britain, France, the Philippines and themselves in Indo-China itself, perhaps also in China. Eisenhower was urged by his staff to use atomic bombs, a Pentagon study group suggesting that 'Three tactical A-bombs, properly employed, would be sufficient to smash the Vietminh effort there.' When the Vietminh captured Dien Bien Phu on 7 May, twenty-four hours before the conference began, a crisis was at hand. All-out war between East and West seemed in prospect.

As it was, a temporary compromise was found in partition. The old French empire was abolished, and the independent states of Laos, Cambodia and Vietnam created in its stead. Vietnam was divided at the 17th Parallel. The North became Communist, the South a democratic republic, and the seeds were planted for American involvement in the region. The State Department announced that 'in the cases of nations now divided against their will, we shall continue to seek to achieve unity'. The same doctrine applied to Korea. Here, too, it proved impossible for East and West to agree on unification. Partition would continue. Eden, with some justice, wrote that 'if it [the conference] had broken up . . . we would have had World War Three by now'. Less than a year later, in April 1955, he became Prime Minister after continued ill health forced Churchill to resign.

*

Stalin had died in 1953, giving rise to hopes of an improvement in international relations. The new Soviet leader Nikita Khrushchev, though, showed no signs of taking a more constructive line on East-West relations; indeed, the creation on 14 May 1955 of the Warsaw Pact, linking the USSR with the eastern states of Europe in a military alliance, completed the dualities of East versus West, Communism versus capitalism, Nato versus Warsaw. Of the Soviet satellites, only Yugoslavia under Tito maintained a degree of independence. There were, though, internal rumblings elsewhere in Eastern Europe. In the new year of 1956 it was apparent that Hungary was in the throes of internal revolt, spurred on by Khrushchev's denunciation of Stalin at the Twentieth Congress of the Soviet Communist Party. A group of Hungarian intellectuals began agitating for the end of the Communist regime.

There was also a growing crisis in the Middle East. In June 1952, Colonel Gamal Abdel Nasser had come to power in Egypt. Although the British protectorate there had ended in 1922, the United Kingdom nevertheless retained the right to garrison the Canal zone, for the Canal provided a direct shipping link with the Gulf and the Far East. On 25 July 1956, Nasser announced the Canal's nationalization. In the face of this emergency, an international conference was called of the twenty-two countries using the Canal.

Simultaneously Anglo-French preparations were made for military action. The carrier *Bulwark*, together with Valiant bombers based in Malta, Libya, Aden and Bahrain, were put on alert. By September the situation had escalated. On the 15th Harold Macmillan, formerly Foreign Secretary, now Chancellor of the Exchequer, wrote, 'We *must*, by one means or another win this struggle . . . *without oil and without profit from oil* neither the UK nor Western Europe can survive.' Nasser rejected an American plan for international management of the Canal and took the decision to obtain arms from the Soviets. Britain and France – the Canal's principal shareholders – hatched a plot to use the young state of Israel to attack Egypt.

Then, on 23 October, the world's attention was distracted by the outbreak of revolution in the Hungarian capital of Budapest. Student demonstrators demanded free elections and Hungarian withdrawal from the Warsaw Pact. For a short while Khrushchev allowed the struggle to remain an internal matter: then he unleashed his forces. On October 29 the Hungarian leader Imre Nagy told his people, 'Today at daybreak, Soviet troops attacked our capital with the obvious intent of overthrowing the lawful democratic Hungarian government.' The next day, 1,500 miles away, Israel invaded Egypt and made for the Canal. British planes bombed Cairo and Port Said. On 5 November British forces landed in the Canal zone, provoking a tremendous international outcry, not least from the Americans and the United Nations. The UN General Assembly condemned British action by 64 votes to 5, and Khrushchev threatened rocket attacks on London and Paris. On 8 November a ceasefire was declared. Simultaneously in Hungary, under the assault of 75,000 Soviet troops and 2,500 tanks, the revolt collapsed. A month later, on 22 December, the last Anglo-French forces withdrew from Suez. And 9 January 1957, Eden resigned, to be replaced by Harold Macmillan.

It had been a momentous autumn. The Soviets had very effectively asserted themselves on the original Cold War front in Europe, and the West had shown itself hopelessly divided in the new theatre of the Middle East. That year the class of '63 were progressing from primary to secondary school, and Buddy Holly sang 'Peggy Sue'.

The political catastrophe at Suez caused a re-evaluation of Britain's place in the world. Within a dozen years of Potsdam, it was clear that

Britain was no longer a leading player in world events, that there were no longer Three Powers, only two – the Soviet Union and the United States. Despite the fact that Britain's own hydrogen bomb would shortly be detonated, the sheer economics of staying in the nuclear race made the shaping of an appropriate British defence strategy increasingly problematic. Would the country be best advised to collaborate with other Western European countries on nuclear development rather than going it alone, or should she do so in collaboration with the Americans? At the same time popular resistance to the whole idea of the nuclear deterrent was growing, soon to be expressed in the Campaign for Nuclear Disarmament, whose slogan became 'Ban the Bomb'.

In 1957 Harold Macmillan instigated a Defence Review, led by the new Defence Secretary Duncan Sandys. This, while considerably reducing the country's defence commitments and ending conscription, placed fresh emphasis on Britain's nuclear deterrent and the system for delivering it. Although the RAF V-bomber force was now in service, improving Soviet air defences meant that an Intermediate Range Ballistic Missile (IRBM) called Blue Streak was also being developed, missiles having the advantage of being far less vulnerable to enemy defence systems than bombers. In the meantime, the British proposed to the Americans that they should station sixty Thor IRBMs in Britain. These missiles would complement the shorter-range Jupiters stationed in Turkey, and would be targeted at the Soviet Union's western cities. The offer was originally made by Sandys in January 1957, then repeated by Macmillan at his first meeting with Eisenhower in Bermuda in March, on which occasion it was accepted.

Then, on 4 October, the Soviets launched the Sputnik satellite, the first man-made object to be successfully put into orbit around the earth. The satellite was harmless in itself, but it had been launched by the SS-6 Sapwood, an intercontinental rocket with a range of more than 6,000 miles that was just as capable of boosting a nuclear warhead into space. The age of the Inter-Continental Ballistic Missile, the ICBM, had arrived – and the Americans had been wrong-footed. Though their own ICBM programme had started in June 1954, the Vanguard missile had proved unreliable. As if in confirmation of this fact, on 6 December 1957 a Vanguard blew up on launch.

In Britain, the headline ran, 'Oh what a Flopnik'. Now it was American rather than Soviet cities that were threatened.

The propaganda value of Sputnik was immense. Macmillan compared its impact on the American psyche with that of Pearl Harbor, leading as it did to the notion of a 'missile gap' between the two superpowers. Although both East and West were busily developing spy networks, spy planes and spy satellites, hard intelligence about Soviet capabilities was thin on the ground. In its absence it was speculated that by 1961 the Soviets would be in possession of 1,000 ICBMs, whilst the US that year would supposedly muster only 70. In fact, the figures for Soviet missiles were enormously exaggerated, but paranoia about a missile gap stimulated the development of Submarine Launched Ballistic Missiles – SLBMs – that would form the third and final element of America's strategic defence force. American concerns about the growing Soviet threat also stimulated Eisenhower's offer to Macmillan to try to persuade Congress to end the restrictions imposed by the McMahon Act on the sharing of atomic secrets. This, and the offer to station US missiles on British soil made the previous March in Bermuda, did much to restore harmony between the two allies after Suez.

It was just as well, for within a year another crisis was to arise over Berlin.

The contrast between the Federal Republic and its eastern counterpart, the German Democratic Republic (GDR), was now startling. Under Konrad Adenauer, West Germany had been rapidly rebuilt both physically and economically, and West Berlin had become a bustling cosmopolitan city. East Germany and East Berlin, under the dead hand of totalitarian leaders, remained impoverished, and every year tens of thousands of East Germans fled to the West. In 1958 no fewer than 144,000 voted with their feet in favour of capitalism, and most were young and skilled. They escaped through Berlin, for though the frontier between the two parts of the divided country was heavily guarded, movement between the sectors in Berlin was almost unrestricted. This drain of population was not only humiliating for Khrushchev, it also created a serious labour shortage in the GDR. On 27 November 1958 Khrushchev issued an ultimatum demanding the withdrawal of Western forces from Berlin. They would be given six months to leave the city.

The crisis in Berlin dragged on through 1959 and into 1960, with Khruschchev repeatedly extending the deadline but still demanding the departure of Nato troops. In May 1960 Khrushchev, Eisenhower and Macmillan were set to meet in Paris. Days before the summit opened, an American U-2 spy plane was shot down by the Soviets and its pilot, Gary Powers, captured. On arriving at the summit, Khrushchev at once demanded an apology from Eisenhower. The American President refused, and the summit collapsed. The Berlin crisis continued, exacerbated by ever larger numbers of East Germans fleeing their homes for the West. In April 1961 the Soviets scored a propaganda coup by putting the first man, Yuri Gagarin, into space. By July 1961, though, 30,000 were leaving Berlin each month. Then, in the early hours of 13 August, a barbed-wire fence was erected by East German workers, dividing the city in two. Three days later a concrete wall followed.

The erection of the Berlin Wall profoundly affected the imagination of the Western world. Then, on 27 October 1961, American and Soviet tanks faced each other off, muzzle to muzzle, at one of the crossing-points in the Wall, Check-Point Charlie. The stand-off lasted sixteen hours. By now Eisenhower had been succeeded as President by John F. Kennedy. One of his first pledges was to upstage the Soviets' lead in space by landing a man on the moon before the decade was out. Soon, too, he made plain his resolve over West Berlin, describing it as 'the great testing place of Western courage and will, a focal point where our solemn commitments and . . . Soviet ambitions now meet in basic confrontation'.

With the class of '63 now sixth-formers, the scene was set for the worst crisis yet in the Cold War.

*

A revolution on the Caribbean island of Cuba in 1958 had led to the establishment of the regime of Fidel Castro the following year. In a country where 1 per cent of the population owned 33 per cent of the land, social reform was inevitable. At first, though, the movement seemed more nationalist in inspiration than Communist, and not until a year later did Castro sign trade agreements with the USSR. Then, in September 1960, Castro and Khrushchev met at the United

Nations and embraced as fellow revolutionaries. Not surprisingly, the United States viewed this new Marxist-Leninist outpost within a hundred miles of its eastern seaboard with considerable misgivings, and the confiscation and ruin of a number of American companies operating in Cuba did little to reassure it. With anti-Castro feeling fanned by the American press, a plan was formulated by Eisenhower for Castro to be toppled, and a band of 1,500 Cuban exiles were trained and armed for the purpose. When Kennedy succeeded Eisenhower, he approved the mission, and on 17 April 1961 the force landed on the southern coast of Cuba in the Bay of Pigs. The landing did not, however, go according to plan. Within three days the invasion was crushed and America humiliated.

Thereafter Kennedy ordered U-2 reconnaisance flights over the island to provide regular updates of military activity. In September 1962 these indicated a build-up of Soviet war *matériel*. At first this comprised SAM anti-aircraft missiles and MiG aircraft, both of which could be regarded as defensive. On 11 September, the Soviets, in response to American requests, declared that no offensive missiles would be placed on Cuba. Then, on 14 October, a further U-2 flight positively identified nuclear missiles capable of reaching Texas, Arkansas and Oklahoma. These would arrive with the minimum of warning, and defence against them was virtually impossible. To Harold Macmillan, Russian motives were obvious: Khrushchev was attempting to provoke US intervention in Cuba in order to set a precedent for Soviet intervention in the running sore of Berlin. On 22 October 1962, Kennedy broadcast the U-2 flight's findings to the world. His declaration of intent culminated with the announcement of a blockade of the island, and an appeal to the Soviet leader. 'I call upon Chairman Khrushchev to halt and eliminate this clandestine, reckless, provocative threat to world peace and to stable relations between our two nations. I call upon him further to abandon this course of world domination.'

The crisis deepened. On the 22nd, US forces all over the world were put on a state of alert known as DEFCON 3. This involved preparing ICBMs for launch, dispatching submarines armed with nuclear missiles – SLBMs – to sea, and scattering the strategic bomber force to airfields that were unlikely to be hit. In Britain, the 60 Thor missiles and 180-strong V-bomber force – representing about a third of the Western deterrent – were also put on high alert. The next day the Soviet Union followed suit. On the 24th the Americans imposed DEFCON 2, one stage below operational deployment. By now, a small armada of Soviet cargo ships carrying missiles was approaching Cuba, supported by submarines, and the United States dispatched a fleet of 180 warships to the Caribbean. Kennedy's orders were that Soviet ships breaking the blockade should be sunk. The strategic bomber force, loaded with atomic weapons, was ordered into the air. Bombing of the Cuban missile bases was planned, and the United Nations General Assembly was asked to censure the Soviets for threatening nuclear war. Robert Kennedy, the President's brother and Attorney-General in the administration, later recalled, 'We were on the edge of a precipice with no way off.'

For six days the world teetered on the brink of nuclear war. With both administrations split between hawks and doves, the outcome was genuinely uncertain. Only on the 24th, when some of the Soviet ships stopped in their tracks, did it seem that common sense might prevail. Others, though, continued, and on the 26th an American reconnaissance plane was shot down over Cuba. It was then that the idea of a quid pro quo emerged, focusing on the Nato missiles in Turkey targeted at the Soviet Union. On the 27th it appeared that six of the Soviet missile launchers in Cuba were now operational. Then, and only then, was a deal struck. On 28 October, Khrushchev agreed to remove the missiles from Cuba. In return, Kennedy agreed not to invade the island. He also agreed to remove the Jupiter IRBMs from Turkey, providing the agreement was kept secret. In his memoirs Khrushchev wrote, 'The two most powerful nations in the world had been squared off against each other, each with its finger on the button.'

*

Scarcely was the Cuban missile crisis over than, for Macmillan at least, another arose. He had been in close contact with Kennedy over Cuba, and was set to meet the President in the Bahamas just before Christmas. Of the various issues on the agenda, the most important was the fast-advancing technology of nuclear war. With the V-bomber force increasingly vulnerable, Britain had concentrated on the development of the land-based IRBM Blue Streak, and the air-launched equivalent, Blue Steel. Originally budgeted at £200 million, by 1958 they seemed likely to cost three times as much. At the same time, however, land-based missiles fired from identifiable bases were now regarded as being unduly vulnerable to ground attack. A deterrent against a first-strike attack was not a deterrent if it could not survive that attack. In early 1960 both projects were abandoned.

At a summit in March 1960, Macmillan had therefore persuaded Eisenhower to let the British have Skybolt, an American air-launched missile. The alternative was the Submarine Launched Ballistic Missile or SLBM, Polaris. A striking development, this missile could be launched from a platform – a submarine – that was very difficult to detect or destroy. Macmillan rejected Polaris on the grounds that no British submarine was designed to carry such weapons, but he did agree to let the Americans base their own Polaris submarines at Holy Loch on the west coast of Scotland, and to establish an early-warning system for Soviet missiles in North Yorkshire as part of a chain that also included sites at Clear in Alaska and Thule in Greenland. This system would give a three-minute warning of a missile strike. However, the summit agreement was compromised both by the arrival of the new Kennedy administration and by the new defence thinking that had been stimulated by the continuing Berlin crisis. Both placed less emphasis on nuclear retaliation, more on a build-up of conventional forces to counteract the Soviet threat. As a result, the Americans decided to cancel Skybolt. Britain was now left with an increasingly vulnerable retaliatory force, and risked being forced out of the nuclear club altogether.

Macmillan was furious at this volte-face. Talks in the Bahamas in December 1962 accordingly began on a less than friendly footing, and Macmillan, his Foreign Secretary Peter Thorneycroft and his Chief Scientific Adviser Sir Solly Zuckerman thought little would come of them. Initially Macmillan was offered an air-launched missile called Hound Dog. This he was obliged to reject on the grounds that it could not be fitted to the V-bombers. Eventually, after three days' hard bargaining, the Prime Minister was offered and accepted Polaris, agreeing that Britain would build five of her own missile submarines as launch platforms. She would also develop her own nuclear warheads. The extent of the independence of this new

deterrent was debatable, for it was agreed that the nuclear submarines should be attached to Nato except when there were 'vital
national interests' at stake. Moreover, the acquisition of Polaris
obliged Britain to develop appropriate submarines with great rapid-
ity. To Macmillan, though, it seemed the only way in which the
country could retain a credible nuclear deterrent after the phasing
out of the V-bomber force.

The Bahamas agreement was not popular with the RAF. It pointed
out that the Navy had no experience of handling nuclear weapons,
that it had no submarines suitable for such missiles, and that its only
nuclear-powered craft, the new submarine *Dreadnought*, was an
unknown quantity. A former Chief of Air Staff wrote of the 'really
appalling thought that a couple of ministers and a zoologist [Solly
Zuckerman] can skip off to the Bahamas and, without a single
member of the Chiefs of Staff Committee present, commit to a military monstrosity on the purely political issue of nuclear independence – which anyway is a myth'. Nevertheless, what was bad news
for the RAF was good news for the Navy. Its submarine branch, decimated in the immediate aftermath of the war and thereafter only
gradually redeveloped, was now to become the principal vehicle of
the country's nuclear deterrent.

*

The following summer, on 29 June 1963, the President and the Prime
Minister met once again in London. Kennedy was on his way back
from Berlin, where he had addressed a crowd of a quarter of a
million people. Against the backdrop of the Wall, he made what
became one of the most famous speeches of the Cold War, one that
summarized the issues that had been developing since Hitler's defeat:

> There are many people in the world today who really don't
> understand, or say they don't, what is the great issue between
> the free world and the Communist world. Let them come to
> Berlin. There are some who say that Communism is the way of
> the future. Let them come to Berlin. And there are some who
> say in Europe and elsewhere we can work with the
> Communists. Let them come to Berlin. And there are even a

few who say that it is true that Communism is an evil system, but it permits us to make economic progress. *Lasst sie nach Berlin kommen.* Let them come to Berlin . . . Freedom is indivisible, and when one man is enslaved, all are not free. When all are free, and we look forward to that day, when this city will be joined as one, and this country, and this great continent of Europe, in a peaceful and hopeful globe, when that day finally comes, as it will, the people of West Berlin can take sober satisfaction in the fact that they were in the front line for almost two decades. All free men, wherever they may live, are citizens of Berlin, and therefore as a free man, I take pride in the words *Ich bin ein Berliner.*

The class of '63 were now making preparations for their first term at Dartmouth. Berliners aside, it was they who would in the future man the front line, a front line that marked the margins of the free world, and ultimately of mankind.

Chapter 2
'No occupation for a gentleman'

'Submariners themselves were regarded as not quite the thing – smelt
a bit, behaved not too well, drank too much. They were regarded as
a sort of dirty habit in tins.'

Sandy Woodward, *One Hundred Days*, 1992

The Dartmouth regime into which cadets Elliott, Lane-Nott,
Macpherson, Taylor and Wreford-Brown were initiated was
spartan. Most of the youths slept in twenty-four-bunk dormitories,
in which there was little privacy. They were turned out at 0615 (0730
on Sundays), and had to be in by 2100. In the intervening hours
they followed a strict regime, with everything happening precisely
at a set time and place. The first six weeks were designed to toughen
them up. There was a good deal of parade-ground work to accus-
tom them to obeying orders, a lot of physical training, and practical seamanship taught in the hundred-odd boats at the College's
disposal on the River Dart. There was no leave at all during this
period, and when it was completed, the cadets still had to be in bed
by 2230.

Then came grounding in the professional branches of the Navy,
principally those of engineering, navigation, gunnery and seamanship, together with lectures in science, naval history and English. The
'officer-like qualities' – known as 'Oily-Qs' – identified by the
Admiralty Board were tested. 'Several activities', wrote Captain Bush
in *How to Become a Naval Officer*, 'are designed to put the cadet under
stress.' Sailing and canoeing were treated less as leisure pursuits than

as physically demanding sports. Night marches were a favourite exercise. Martin Macpherson remembers being woken at 0200 in the morning, driven by lorry into the heart of Dartmoor, and left with his group to find their way back to the College. Sixty miles in two days was a typical exercise.

Macpherson himself thought little of this. Like a number of the intake he had been schooled at Sherborne, and he found the regime comparable to the one he had enjoyed the year before at school. Chris Wreford-Brown was a talented pentathlete and – in an establishment in which athletic prowess was highly regarded – also took the course in his stride. Roger Lane-Nott excelled at rugby.

A Devonian called John Jeffrey ('Jeff') Tall, part of the intake of the following year, found the experience entirely different. The 21-year-old son of an RAF warrant officer, he had turned down a place at Sheffield University before joining the Navy – largely to escape from the boredom of working in the Midland Bank in Lincoln. Plunged into the public-school atmosphere of Dartmouth, he was thoroughly unsettled and found it difficult to mix. Like a surprising number of the cadets, too, he had little interest in boats and the sea. His divisional chief petty officer helped ease the situation, taking him out of the dormitory and putting him in a two-bed 'cabin' where he was befriended by his room-mate; and he would soon win the respect of his contemporaries as a gifted cricketer and rugby player. It was, though, a difficult induction.

Rest and recreation were on the agenda too. The College ran a number of clubs, ranging from gliding and climbing to rough shooting. There was also a motoring club, which attracted the attentions of Roger Lane-Nott, like many submariners a man with a taste for speed. James Taylor was a first-class shot and soon found himself representing Dartmouth with the rifle.

More universal, however, was the appeal of the traditional 'run ashore'. The essence of naval life was a period of hard work, hard discipline and relative constraint at sea, punctuated by periods of relief when the ship found its port. Not all took their 'run ashore' quite as seriously as one Second World War submariner. 'Shrimp' Simpson, commanding officer of the Tenth Submarine Flotilla based at Malta in 1941–2, wrote in his autobiography of one of his commanders:

Teddy Woodward found that it suited him best to play the game of war in reverse. The pace he set himself during rest periods in Malta would have put most men in hospital. He would arrive at Lazaretto from the rigours of leave in Malta's 'watering holes', which seemed never closed to Woodward, looking pale and in need of a complete rest. Sailing on patrol was an escape from the dangers ashore . . . On return to port, usually with the Jolly Roger flying, Woodward, bursting with health, would confide to me an address where he could be found on leave and then set out bravely to meet the dangers and demands of yet another holiday.

The Navy in the 1960s was still was a deeply traditional institution, its sons intent on following the service's traditions. In Dartmouth, well supplied with pubs, each Division had one established by custom as its own. Eight pints of beer and a fluffy omelette constituted the ideal run ashore, a combination that could be had for the price of a pound. Some of the cadets went further afield. Toby Elliott had an elderly Morris Minor convertible that, in the days before the breathalyser, he used to visit some of the unspoilt country pubs in which the Dart valley abounded. On one of these occasions the convertible became permanently open when a passenger decided to take the roof down as the car was travelling downhill at sixty miles an hour. There was also a dance hall in Plymouth. This was one of the various sources of local girls, few of whom, according to Macpherson, 'you would want to take home to mother'.

One evening in that first term, a divisional officer chalked up an announcement that met the cadets as they queued for supper. The political stability that had characterized their youth had been ebbing for some time. The previous June the long-standing Conservative government had found itself besieged by scandal. The Secretary of State for War, John Profumo, had been obliged to resign over his involvement with a call girl who was also sleeping with a Russian diplomat. Then, in October 1963, Macmillan had resigned on grounds of ill-health and had been replaced by Alec Douglas-Home. Few thought the former Foreign Secretary would remain in office for long. Now came altogether more disturbing news. The date was

22 November. Kennedy had been assassinated. Shocking in itself – for the President's role in defusing the Cuban missile crisis was still vividly imprinted on the public's imagination – this was also a dramatic reminder of the responsibilities that the cadets were being trained to face.

With some of the basics of military discipline, seamanship and naval custom now instilled in the cadets, the Dartmouth regime then prescribed a period of sea training. Cadets were required to live and work as able seamen, the basic manpower of the Navy, and so grasp from a practical perspective the essentials of their profession. At the same time they would be introduced to some of the duties of junior officers: storing the ship for a voyage, ensuring the full complement of crew was on board, leaving harbour, route-planning and basic navigation, watch-keeping, signalling and all the multitude of activities that make up the safe and efficient management of a ship at sea.

Chris Wreford-Brown was in the first contingent to depart on a cruise, escaping the English winter in *Torquay*. She was one of the College's three Type 12 frigates, a 340-foot design of 2,150 tons. That January, *Torquay* took Wreford-Brown and his fellow cadets to the West Indies. For many it was their first trip abroad, their first experience of the tropics, and their first taste of rum. The islands were still remote, almost entirely unspoilt and – for visitors at least – an earthly paradise of crystalline seas, golden beaches and luxuriant vegetation in which the Protestant work ethic was distinctly absent. The itinerary included Barbados, St Lucia, St Vincent, Grenada and Trinidad and Tobago, and ended in Bermuda. For Wreford-Brown, not an obvious romantic, it was an experience he would never forget.

After Easter, the second contingent in *Tenby* – another Type 12 frigate – and *Torquay* set out on a cruise of Scandinavian cities. Their first major port of call was Copenhagen. Then the flotilla turned east into the Baltic and visited Turku, before retracing their tracks to Göteborg. The final leg of the cruise followed the coast of Norway north to Bergen.

Martin Macpherson was Senior Cadet in *Torquay*. James Taylor, Roger Lane-Nott and Toby Elliott were on board *Tenby*. None found the work particularly exacting, be it polishing the frigates' bright-work or scrubbing their decks. All, too, were determined to take advantage of the cruise's social side. Steaming into Copenhagen, *Tenby* was signalled by the SS *Dannebrog*, the Danish Royal yacht. Was Mr Elliott on board? Would he care to dine in the *Dannebrog*? The invitation had been prompted by Elliott's father, who was the British naval attaché in Stockholm. The prospect of a gawky teenager dining aboard the Royal yacht appealed to the ship's company's sense of humour, and they were not slow to take advantage of the situation. On board *Torquay*, Macpherson had unwisely assumed that the curfew of 2300 when the ship was in port could hardly apply to the Senior Cadet. As it happened, the ship's padre liked to play a game that involved getting out of one of the portholes in the ward-room and returning through another. On the evening on which Macpherson ventured ashore, the padre got stuck and was abandoned by his dining companions. He was, nonetheless, ideally placed to spot Macpherson on his return in the early hours. The Senior Cadet had his leave stopped. Taylor, a fluent Russian speaker, got into an argument with a Russian admiral and his wife at a reception at the British Embassy. 'She somehow suggested there were no significant political differences between the Soviets and ourselves,' recalled Taylor. 'I merely pointed out that there were.' He had forgotten Captain Bush's advice: 'It is very important that a naval officer, who is at all times an ambassador of the British people, should be able to recognise different nationalities and be aware of their idiosyncrasies.' Taylor was told that his conduct had been 'noticed'.

The flotilla returned to Dartmouth at the end of July 1964. The Beatles were conquering America, where the new President, Lyndon B. Johnson, had taken the country definitively into Vietnam; and *Dr Strangelove*, Stanley Kubrick's satire on the build-up to a nuclear holocaust, was playing in cinemas across the country. The class of '63 were now promoted midshipmen, which entitled them to sew two white patches into their collars. With the exception of Wreford-Brown, their days at the College were over.

'Dartmouth', says Taylor, 'got you fit, got you smart, and stiffened your spine.' A cadet of a slightly earlier vintage believed its influence to be rather more profound. In *One Hundred Days*, John 'Sandy' Woodward writes of Dartmouth as 'the first stage of the Navy's long-term inductive training, which teaches a man how to fit in, which indoctrinates him, brainwashes him some would say, into the ways of the Senior Service, with lessons that will last a lifetime.'

*

By reputation, the midshipman's lot was not a particularly enviable one. Midshipmen were nicknamed 'snotties', because the buttons on the sleeves of their uniform jackets supposedly discouraged the habit of wiping their noses. They were the lowest form of life aboard a ship, the universal dogsbody. According to the biographer of Caspar John, who as First Sea Lord took the passing-out parade at Dartmouth in 1963, 'They were never allowed to say: "I don't know" when interrogated by a senior officer. In answer to such questions as to how to wash a ship's side, raise a sail, fire off a gun, tow another ship, snotty had to reply, "Sir, I will go and find out." But if snotty *did* know the answer, he was considered above his station. He ought *not* to know . . . they were kept down at all times.' Captain Bush was similarly discouraging. 'Remember that joining as a midshipman is bound to be awe-inspiring. Everyone about you seems so authoritative and important . . . and you realise that no-one seems to care a hang whether you are there or not. The reason is that your talents, if any, are undiscovered.'

Martin Macpherson had a taste of this on his first posting, to *Glasserton*, a 130-ton minesweeper based at the Royal Naval base, Portland. Macpherson's personal dictum, 'Just enough, just in time,' had seen him through Sherborne and seemed equally applicable to the Navy. Relieving the officer-of-the-watch on *Glasserton*'s bridge a few minutes late, he noticed the beady eye of the captain resting on him, but thought no more about it. When the end of his own watch came, he made to leave the bridge. 'Where do you think you're going?' the CO asked. Far from being dismissed, Macpherson was obliged to keep two further watches.

Roger Lane-Nott was similarly disconcerted in Singapore, where he and Toby Elliott had both been posted midshipmen on the commando carrier *Bulwark*. Lane-Nott was told at the shortest of notice that he would have to make a speech on behalf of wives and girl-friends at a ceremonial mess dinner. *Bulwark*'s wardroom was equipped for the tropics with a large revolving fan. His fellow officers encouraged him to stand on the table to make himself heard and then contrived that he should walk backwards into its slowly revolving blades. He ended up in a heap on the floor. Chris Wreford-Brown was posted to *Tiger*, a teak-decked 9,550-ton cruiser that in 1966 would play host to the first of two abortive summits on the independence of Southern Rhodesia. During Wreford-Brown's year with her, *Tiger* led a taskforce on a goodwill tour around South America and visited West Africa, Scandinavia and the Mediterranean as well as several ports in the United States. He remembers being reprimanded for keeping his CO awake by pounding back and forth across the teak deck as he kept watch in harbour above the officer's cabin. James Taylor, whose first six months as midshipman were spent in the mine-sweeper *Letterston*, was reproved for displaying far too much of the dour Scot.

At home, thirteen years of Conservative rule finally ended in October, when Harold Wilson formed the first Labour government since that of Attlee. That same month there were also changes within the Soviet Union, where the defence programme was placing a severe strain on the economy. On 14 October, Khrushchev was forced to resign, partly because of his mishandling of the Cuban missile crisis. He was replaced as First Secretary of the Communist Party by Leonid Brezhnev. Two days later, on 16 October, the Chinese exploded their first atomic bomb. Then, on 24 January 1965, Winston Churchill died. The passing of a man who had fought at Omdurman, who had risen to be the greatest of Britain's wartime leaders in her darkest hour, and who had taken Britain into the nuclear age, marked the end of an era.

As these events unfolded, the midshipmen began to mature into their new roles, grasping the responsibilities that were offered. Taylor was posted to the destroyer *Wakeful*, on fishery protection duties in the Dover Straits and the North Sea. Soon he was acting as officer-of-the-watch. In *One Hundred Days*, his future Flag Officer Submarines, Sandy Woodward, recalled the thrill of his own first stint as officer-of-the-watch on a similar vessel 'racing through the night, sometimes feeling the sea thump against the hull, knowing that the safety of the ship and her company rested temporarily on my shoulders alone. I know now that the Captain himself was at about

three seconds' notice to take over if I got it wrong. But I felt myself
in sole command of this destroyer. It was a very heady experience –
I was not yet twenty.'

Beyond the pleasures of the wardroom, *Bulwark* offered comparable professional challenges for Lane-Nott and Elliott. Britain in 1964
still had rather more than the vestiges of a world-wide navy protecting the remnants of its pre-war empire, and *Bulwark*'s duties included
patrolling off Borneo and the Malaccan and Singapore Straits. Two
years before, a rebellion had broken out in Brunei on the north coast
of Borneo. Though it had been quashed by British forces, the rebels
had escaped across the border into Indonesian Kalimantan. There
they were supported by the President of Indonesia, Achmad
Sukarno, who on 20 January 1963 declared a policy of 'confrontation'
with the fledgling Malaysian Federation of Malaya, Singapore, British
North Borneo and Sarawak. Confrontation took the form of incursions from Kalimantan.

With what amounted to a state of war in the region, there was
plenty to occupy a couple of ambitious young officers. Lane-Nott set
up a ship's newspaper, available by breakfast every morning. Elliott
got himself taken along on helicopter missions skimming the jungle
tree-tops along the thousand-mile border between Malaysia and
Indonesian Borneo. Both also managed to get their watch-keeper's
certificates at an unusually early age. These indicated that they were
competent to be in charge on a moment-by-moment basis of the
730-foot, 20,330-ton ship while she executed her duties.

Jeff Tall soon found himself in the 360-ton minesweeper *Iveston*
and was at once given a lesson on the qualities that make a naval
officer. The first thing he saw on joining the ship at Birkenhead was
half a dozen women emerging from the ship's forward hatch, closely
followed by the coxswain, the senior petty officer. Tall was told to
identify himself and was then asked what he had seen. Sensibly he
replied, 'Absolutely nothing.' Wreford-Brown, completing his year in
Tiger, found himself running liberty boats, second-in-command of
firing the cruiser's 6-inch guns and – on his second visit to the West
Indies – supervising the transfer from shore to ship of sailors rendered unconscious by the local rum.

In June 1965, just as the class of '63 completed their year as midshipmen, the Rolling Stones were enjoying their first US hit. In

Vietnam the first American ground troops had already arrived, and the United States was well on the way to becoming engaged in a full-scale war. That summer, the class of '63 were automatically promoted sub-lieutenants, their degree of seniority depending on their midshipman's assessment and final written exams. Now they had to begin to decide which branch of the Navy they wished to specialize in. All would choose submarines.

*

As his midshipman's experience in a large vessel, Martin Macpherson had spent the first six months of 1965 in the submarine depot ship *Adamant* at Devonport. There he found himself messing with the officers of the dozen submarines that formed the Second Submarine Squadron, and he was introduced to an entrancing new world.

To an outsider, the appeal of submarines was hard to fathom. Edward Young, later to write *One of Our Submarines*, had considerable misgivings about the craft before he embarked on his underwater career early in the Second World War. 'In my imagination I saw submarines as dark, cold, damp, oily and cramped, full of intricate machinery. Chances of survival at the time seemed small; death when it came would come coldly, unpleasantly, and the recent loss of *Thetis* in trials in Liverpool Bay was still fresh in everyone's memory.'

A quarter of a century on, not much had changed. The British submarines then in service were either the types in which Young had actually served during the Second World War, or their linear descendants. They were small, drawing no more than two and a half thousand tons, with a complement of sixty or seventy men. They still used diesels for surface running and electric motors when submerged; and they were therefore not particularly fast on the surface and generally still slower when submerged. They were oily and uncomfortable, so much so that no submariner submitted his smart naval uniform to their rigours, merely cold- and warm-weather variants on gardening clothes. And they were potentially dangerous. The loss of the brand-new *Thetis* with all but four of her hands in June 1939 had shocked the nation. The loss of *Affray*, her crew of sixty and the officers' training class of fifteen on exercise in the Channel in 1951 had been a further reminder of the vulnerability of these craft. So, too, had been the disappearance on 10 April 1963 of the nuclear-powered USS *Thresher*. Her entire complement of 129 perished during a deep dive manoeuvre. There had also been various accidents in the big Soviet submarine fleet, rumours of which reached the West. These included one nuclear-powered vessel that lost pressure in its reactor's cooling system, as a result of which twelve of the crew died from severe radiation exposure. The submarine was subsequently nicknamed 'Hiroshima'.

To others, though, submarines had an extraordinary magic, the essence of which was their chameleon-like ability to transform themselves from surface ship to underwater vessel and back again. Young, apprehensive at the prospect of his first dive, was in practice thrilled by the experience. 'I could not get over the feeling of excitement at being so comfortably below the surface, the great length of the ship now invisible to the world, her weight so finely adjusted between positive and negative buoyancy that she rode as delicately and majestically as an airship in the air.' Perhaps, too, their attraction lay in the property of invisibility that the seas conferred, enabling them to approach their target covertly, a property captured in one of two mottoes of the British submarine service, 'We Come Unseen'.

The idea of a submersible boat dates back almost to the Middle Ages, a time at which the imagination of the idea's inventors well outstripped the available technology. The industrial revolution brought the notion within the realms of practicality, and relatively successful experiments with such craft were conducted in the last years of the nineteenth century. The Royal Navy, though, regarded them with distaste. In 1900, Viscount Goschen, the First Lord of the Admiralty, declared: 'The Admiralty are not prepared to take any steps with regard to the submarine because this vessel is only the weapon of the weaker nation.' Behind such lofty self-assurance lay a sentiment expressed forcibly by the Controller of the Navy, Admiral Sir Arthur Wilson. The craft were 'underwater, under-hand, and damned un-English. We cannot stop invention in this direction, but we can avoid doing anything to encourage it.' Reality, though, was soon to dawn, pragmatism gradually undermining concerns about the morality of the weapon. The following year the Navy acquired the first of what would always be known as 'submarine boats'. This was a nine-man, 63-foot craft called *Holland I*, powered by electric motors underwater, petrol on the surface. In 1905, on the western shores of Portsmouth harbour looking south to the Isle of Wight and the Martello towers that symbolized an earlier age in British maritime power, Fort Blockhouse was established as the base for the submarine branch. With the backing of the First Sea Lord 'Jackie' Fisher, and subsequently the First Lord of the Admiralty, Winston Churchill, a credible force had by 1914 been assembled.

During the course of the Great War, British submarines of half a dozen classes were in operation. Typically these were small craft, displacing only a few hundred tons and using what had become the established power combination of diesel engines and electric motors. They were armed with three or four torpedoes, and they carried no more than twenty-five to thirty men. In the Baltic, they were used to restrict the passage of iron-ore ships between Germany and Sweden, and to snipe at the German fleet. Here Max Horton, who had already made his name by becoming the first CO to sink an enemy ship, the German cruiser *Hela*, was particularly active in *E9*. In Turkish waters British submarines swept through the Dardanelles into the Sea of Marmara. *E14* was the third boat to attempt the passage but only the first to return, a feat for which her commander was given the Victoria Cross – one of six to be given to submariners during the conflict. *E11*, under Martin Dunbar Nasmith, also penetrated the Dardanelles and admirably fulfilled his commander's instructions to 'go and run amok in Marmara'. Of even greater significance to the submarine's future was the conduct of the German U-boats. Their campaign against merchant shipping in the Atlantic came perilously close to severing Britain's lines of communications.

Conditions on board such craft – British or German – nevertheless remained primitive. The men largely lacked privacy and slept where they could on the deck, relieved themselves in buckets, endured an atmosphere thick with diesel fumes, and cooked on little more than hotplates. In his classic novel about the U-boats of the Second World War, *Das Boot*, Lothar-Gunther Buchheim stated his belief that 'The designers . . . have simply built their machines into this war tube and have persuaded themselves that, given the most sophisticated deployment of the jungle of pipes and huge propulsion engines, there would necessarily be enough nooks and crannies left over for the crew.' Still, while the lords and masters of the great Dreadnought battleships regarded the submarine branch as providing 'no occupation for a gentleman', its own members began to think of themselves as an élite. Serving in submarines became known as 'the Trade'.

Between the wars little happened in submarine development to make those in naval circles suppose that the craft might one day supplant the battleship as the capital ship of the world's navies. In any event, the ambitions of the naval nations were much restricted by two treaties, one of 1930, one of 1935, which placed tonnage limits on both submarine fleets as a whole and on individual craft. The outbreak of the Second World War, though, saw ten classes of British submarine ready for action. These still combined the use of diesels with electric motors, and they therefore remained surface vessels capable of diving for only as long as battery power was sustained – typically for a maximum of twenty-four hours. They could, however, dive rather deeper than their predecessors, and they were rather more habitable by virtue of such innovations as bunks, galleys, lavatories and a primitive form of air-conditioning. Even so, they remained small and slow, effective weapons only if they could ensure that they were in an attacking position when the enemy appeared. Critically, although they could attack slow-moving merchant vessels, they lacked anything like the speed of the capital ships they were sometimes called upon either to protect or to destroy. For that reason they were known as 'weapons of position' or, more graphically, 'slightly mobile, intelligent mines'.

Despite these limitations, British submarines had some notable successes in the North Sea and, once again, in the Mediterranean. Working out of Malta, Gibraltar and Alexandria, their chief strategic achievement was to help cut off the supply routes to the Axis powers in North Africa. In particular a legend grew up around the Tenth Submarine Flotilla in Malta, a force that not only managed to keep the island in essential supplies but also deprived General Rommel of war *matériel* in the build-up to what Churchill would call 'the end of the beginning' – the battle of El Alamein. The 'Fighting Tenth' bred a number of outstanding COs, who would prove role models for the next generation of commanders, notably M.D. Wanklyn, Ben Bryant and J. 'Tubby' Linton. Equally dramatic were the activities of Admiral Dönitz's U-boat forces that, in the spring of 1941, came extremely close to cutting Britain's transatlantic lifeline. Once again the importance of the quality of the COs was emphasized, since 5 per cent of U-boat commanders accounted for no less than 75 per cent of Allied tonnage sunk.

Despite the heavy losses incurred by all submarine services during the Second World War, it was clear that the submarine was a potent fighting machine, and after the war the world's navies began to seek ways to enhance its capabilities and reduce its vulnerabilities. By far the most important requirement was for a source of power that did not use oxygen, something that in effect tied the submarine to the surface. It was this that nuclear power would theoretically achieve, and its advent would mean that designers could dispense with diesel-electric power and create a craft with an underwater endurance limited – it was always said – by the crew rather than the vessel. While Britain led the way in developing nuclear reactors for civil purposes, the United States was the pioneer in the military field. The first nuclear-propelled submarine, commissioned in 1954, was the 4,040-ton USS *Nautilus*. In the US Navy she was known as an SSN, a Submarine Nuclear. Six years later, the conjunction of nuclear power with nuclear-armed Polaris ballistic missiles appeared in the form of the 6,888-ton USS *George Washington*, an SSBN or Submarine Ballistic Nuclear. The transformation of the submarine from a weapon of position to the world's principal capital ship, capable of destroying cities, was now complete.

This was the weapon that came to the Royal Navy when Macmillan acquired Polaris at Nassau. In 1963, the SSN *Dreadnought*, the Navy's first nuclear-powered submarine, was commissioned. The nuclear-armed SSBN *Resolution*, the first of what came to be called the Polaris fleet, was already on the drawing-board. At last the Cinderella days of the submarine service were over. Macpherson recalled the atmosphere that these developments generated: 'In *Adamant* as a midshipman I saw the COs of the twelve or so boats, all under twenty-nine. Money was being thrown at the service, and there was a tremendous buzz about it. I saw the opportunity to get a command very young, and people were falling over themselves to do the first patrols in the Polaris boats. It was a very special club and I wanted to join it.'

*

Macpherson was the first of his Dartmouth year to take the submarine officers' training course at HMS *Dolphin*, the submarine branch's first base at Fort Blockhouse. Its most prominent feature was the great tower of the tank used to train submariners to escape from stricken vessels.

Macpherson's course, running from 6 September to 29 October 1965, was relatively basic. It aimed to turn out officers who were sufficiently familiar with the principal features and characteristics of submarines to act safely as junior members of the watch-keeping team. To do so they needed to understand the principles of submersion; how the submarine could be dived by admitting water to its ballast tanks and surfaced by evacuating them with compressed air; how it was driven on the surface by diesel engines, and under water by electric motors; and how regularly it was necessary to surface to charge the motors' batteries. Here, officers learned of the snorkel, the device perfected by the Germans towards the end of the war that enabled the craft to draw air for its diesels at periscope depth, thus avoiding the need for regular surfacing. They learned how the craft could be navigated under water, visually by use of the periscope at shallow depths, aurally by sound waves or sonar deeper down. They learned, too, how those waves could be used to detect other craft, both surfaced and submerged. They were taught something of the submarine's weapons systems: the gun mounted just forward of the conning-tower, and the torpedoes located in tubes in the bow and sometimes the stern of the boat. They learned about the electrical and hydraulic systems of the boat, and of its handling characteristics on the surface and under water, and how it was controlled like an aircraft with a control column or columns to guide depth and direction. Above all they learned of the fragility of their under-water refuge: the incapacity of the pressure hull to withstand the forces of depths of more than a few hundred feet; the terror of fire under the surface of the sea, and accordingly the paramount importance of safety in all submarine operations. As Sandy

Woodward wrote in *One Hundred Days*, submarines are 'no place for the careless'.

Although much of this was taught in the classroom or in full-size mock-ups of parts of a submarine, *Dolphin* was also the base for the First Submarine Squadron, whose fourteen submarines provided one or two for training purposes. These enabled the trainees to be put through their paces, diving and surfacing the ship in the crowded waters around the Isle of Wight, guiding the craft through the narrow entrance to Portsmouth harbour where the tide can flow fiercely, and taking turns at periscope watch-keeping. Their initial experience of the periscope differed little from that of Edward Young years before in just these waters:

> At first I had difficulty in seeing anything, until I found exactly the right angle for my eyes. Then I saw, far more clearly than I expected, a flurry of tumbling grey-green sea. It looked rougher than it really was, because I was seeing it from so close to the surface. Occasionally a wave sprang towards me and engulfed me in a smother of bubbling foam, and then the top lens broke through again, momentarily blurred, like a windscreen in heavy rain, until the water drained off and left it suddenly clear again. It was surprising how wide the field of vision was. I pushed the periscope round and saw land, the Isle of Wight, and immediately identified the Needles. 'Now I'm going to show you something,' said the Captain. 'Keep on looking and watch carefully. Can you see the Needles? You're in low power at the moment. Now watch.' And he put his hand over my right hand, gave the handle a sharp half-turn towards me, and the Needles suddenly appeared astonishingly clear. The field of vision had narrowed, but I could see every detail of those rocks as though they were less than a mile away. I was fascinated by this remarkable toy and could have gone on looking through it all day. I had never realised that a submerged submarine could see so much of the outside world, or see it in such clarity and detail.

There was also the matter of the escape-tower. Should a submarine become disabled and prevented from rising to the surface, its crew needed to be able to escape by swimming to the surface. Part of the basic training was accordingly an ascent from a depth of 100 feet in the tank built at Fort Blockhouse for just this purpose. Trainees were required to make free ascents from depths gradually increasing up to the full 100 feet. To survive this, it was necessary for the swimmer to exhale continuously through the course of the ascent, lest the diminishing pressure cause the lungs to expand and burst. Trainees undertook this initiation with varying degrees of enthusiasm. Macpherson, an all-round athlete, tough, and certainly not lacking in physical courage, thought it thoroughly unpleasant. Wreford-Brown, a strong swimmer, thought it 'great fun'. James Taylor thought it wonderful.

Having passed the course, the next step was to be appointed junior officer in one of the forty submarines then in commission. In November 1965 Macpherson was sent out to join the Seventh Submarine Squadron, based in Singapore, the CO of which was Commander John Moore.

Born in 1921 and, like Macpherson, educated at Sherborne, Moore had conceived an ambition to become a submariner at the age of 12. Eventually joining up just as war broke out, he first served as a midshipman aboard the great battleship *Rodney*. By 1944 he had qualified as a submariner and five years later he had his own command, the Second World War T-boat *Totem*. In 1960 he was appointed commanding officer of the Seventh, which operated all over the Pacific. Well-built and with a commanding manner, Moore was highly intelligent, well read and possessed of firm views on how his force should be run. In due course he had at his disposal six A-class submarines and two more modern designs, a Porpoise and an Oberon. Macpherson's own boat was *Ambush*. Designed during the war, she was a patrol submarine of 265 feet, still fairly small at about 1,600 tons, and capable of 18 knots on the surface. She had a crew of sixty-five men.

At the time, the Seventh Squadron's role was to support British and Commonwealth forces involved in the Borneo confrontation, in which Roger Lane-Nott and Toby Elliott had seen action as midship-men. Keeping the Indonesian forces at bay involved a good deal of Special Forces work behind enemy lines. The Squadron's submarines were accordingly used for delivering these forces to their initial destination, and picking them up at the patrol's conclusion. These were taxing missions, requiring work close in-shore, in poorly charted waters. Where the threat of Indonesian observation was regarded as small, the submarines would surface a mile or so offshore, and the Special Forces would use inflatable boats to land. However, to avoid compromising the lives of the commandos, Moore developed more covert methods. One of these involved the men leaving the submarine when it was fully submerged. To do so they entered a lock-out chamber from within the craft. The chamber would then be locked and flooded, and an outer hatch opened to the sea. Macpherson remembers that the procedure was unpopular. The lock-out chamber was located in the wardroom, and its use interrupted meals. Another of Moore's ideas might have graced one of the James Bond films starring Sean Connery that were now hitting the cinema screens in Britain. An electric torpedo, its warhead removed, was modified so as to enable it to be steered by a diver with a set of handlebars, thus providing the commandos with express transit from ship to shore.

If such missions were demanding, Macpherson found that work in the Far East had its lighter moments. Although the A-boats had been designed for use in the tropics, the extent to which they were adapted for this use was limited. The air-conditioning system in particular was primitive and unreliable, ventilation poor. With water temperatures hovering at the 80 degree mark, at sea sarongs and sandals were the only possible wear on board, though in the engine-room even the sarongs had to be abandoned lest they get caught up in the fast-moving, clattering machinery. In harbour the boats followed a regime known as tropical routine. This involved a 0600 start and a noon finish. Some COs, perhaps less dedicated to their careers or duties, sometimes contrived to start at 0800 and still finish at noon, an arrangement known as 'modified tropical routine'. Thereafter, the day could be spent as the individual felt fit. Macpherson bought himself an MG sports car and a speedboat, and played the role of dashing young submarine officer to the hilt.

Macpherson was joined as a submariner in the summer of 1966 by Toby Elliott and James Taylor. Both were on the same qualifying course, run at *Dolphin* between April and June of that year. That spring Harold Wilson had been returned to Downing Street with a substantial majority, a Soviet spacecraft had orbited the moon, and the film of John Le Carré's *The Spy Who Came in from the Cold* had just been released.

The son of a submariner, Elliott had been brought up in Hong Kong and Malta. At the time he was growing up, these two famous naval bases still retained much of their pre-war character, and in Malta in particular memories of the heroic defence of the island in 1942 were still fresh. It was there as a 4-year-old that Elliott first went to sea in the submarine *Trenchant*, then commanded by his father. At the same age, he was struck by the habits of the Maltese nuns and informed his parents that he wanted to become one. Told that his sex disqualified him, he settled for the Navy – its uniform seemed equally smart. As for submarines, his background gave him a natural interest in the craft, and his boyhood was spent in the company of young submarine officers. Carefree and high-spirited, they were a group to which to aspire, the occupation an obvious one for a patriot and – contrary to the views of some – a gentleman.

Much later, when attached to *Bulwark* in Singapore, Elliott had had an opportunity to get some experience of the boats engaged in the Borneo confrontation. John Moore had had one of his A-class boats adapted for intelligence-gathering purposes by the installation of high-performance sensors that could pick up radio transmissions. Elliott spent one of his first patrols sitting on the bottom of a harbour listening to radio traffic. He found the camaraderie of the small craft, the responsibilities thrust on its young officers and men, and the excitement of the missions overwhelming. He was hooked.

A few years before Elliott attended the course at *Dolphin*, the American Second World War underwater ace George Grider had summarized the culture of submarining in his autobiography:

The very nature of the submarine service produced an intimacy and an esprit de corps, and a spirit of romantic adventure unmatched by the other branches, and virtually forgotten in the massive manoeuverings of modern war. In a sense, we inherited the mantle of mystery, glamour and freedom of action worn by the airmen of WW1. We were small, so small that every man aboard a submarine knew every man by his first name, so small a service that transfers, joint shore leaves, and overlapping friendships tied us all together . . . I remember a night when I was standing on the bridge of my own submarine, the *Flasher*, plowing through the calm sea with a moon shining, scanning the horizon in company with a lookout for a sight of the enemy, when I was struck with the almost mystical conviction that every man below was my brother. The words from *Henry V* came back to me; 'For he today that sheds his blood with me shall be my brother.' It was a feeling that I think all of us shared. To this day, when I see a man wearing a submarine pin, I stop him and wring his hand.

James Taylor, perhaps the most intellectual of the group and with a natural gift for languages, had been brought up in Edinburgh and schooled at George Watson's College. There he enjoyed participating in the school's Combined Cadet Force, using it as an opportunity to develop his shooting. Family holidays were often taken on the Mull of Kintyre, close to submarine exercise areas. One day in 1957, the young Taylor saw one of these mysterious black craft entering harbour at Campbeltown on the south-east tip of Kintyre. 'It was my road to Damascus,' he recalls. 'They were mysterious, exciting, dangerous and – I thought – heroic. I was absolutely captivated by them.' Like Elliott, he had joined the Navy specifically to get into submarines. Following his naval apprenticeship in *Letterston* and *Wakeful* – not to mention his scrape with the Russian admiral and his wife in Copenhagen – he arrived at *Dolphin* in his Morris Minor in April 1966 to take the submariners' course. 'It was a wonderful moment,' he remembers. 'I'd made it.'

A hard worker when motivated, Taylor breezed through the training. Elliott won the Max Horton prize for the best candidate on the course, named after the commander of *E9* in the First World War who had risen to become C-in-C Western Approaches in the Second, and who had overseen the defeat of the U-boats. The training tank, though, Elliott found an ordeal – in his words, 'absolute murder'. Taylor was then appointed torpedo and casing officer in *Token*. Based at *Dolphin*, this was one of the T-class boats that had been the Navy's mainstay during the war. Elliott was sent to the 2,410-ton *Porpoise* as navigating officer.

Porpoise, 295 feet long and carrying a crew of seventy-two, was one of eight diesel-electric submarines that were the first new class to be designed and built since the war and that reflected the changing role of the craft in modern warfare. Hitherto, the submarine had been used principally to torpedo merchant shipping. By now, however, it was becoming clear that the submarine, particularly if nuclear-powered and nuclear-armed, was developing into the modern capital ship. It was equally clear that a weapon had to be developed to counter it. Since submarines were no longer obliged to surface to recharge their batteries, they could no longer be located by radar from a maritime patrol aircraft. They could, though, be found by using sonar. While this can be and is fitted to surface ships, the noise that the ship itself makes in pushing through the surface of the water limits its useful-ness. A submarine, especially at low speeds, makes far less 'self-noise' and is therefore a better platform for sonar. In other words, the best vessel to find and destroy a modern submarine is another submarine. As such, the Porpoise class were called Submarine Killers, or SSKs.

Among Elliott's memories of his first patrols in *Porpoise* was an intelligence-gathering mission that took the boat up to Bear Island, a couple of hundred miles north of Norway in the Arctic Ocean. This was one of a number of geographical bottlenecks where it was easy to pick up passing Soviet submarines of the élite Northern Fleet as they departed their bases around Murmansk. There, amidst a Russian fishing-fleet, the submarine drifted with the radio mast extended, the whole crew listening to the 1966 football World Cup final in which England beat Germany 4–2.

After his uncomfortable induction into the idiosyncrasies of naval life, Jeff Tall had soon found his feet, particularly in *Iveston*. The mine-sweeper was commanded by a former submariner, Mark Ruddle, who had failed the notoriously tough submarine commanding officers' qualifying course, invariably known as 'Perisher'. A good judge of men, Ruddle soon got to know and like the tough, short, blue-eyed Devonian, with his natural skill in handling men. He saw, too, where Tall's future in the Navy might lie; and where – clearly – it would not. 'One thing you'll never be is a silk handkerchief navi-gator – you're perfect for boats.'

Tall, largely ignorant of the submarine branch, took him at his word. He was briefly seconded to *Opossum*, one of the new SSK Oberon-class boats. An improved version of the Porpoises, of which thirteen were eventually built, *Opossum* epitomized the style of the branch in the mid-1960s. The wardroom, comprising a mixture of British, Canadians and Australians, was convivial and much interested in beer and women. The men were known to each other largely by nicknames, and they welcomed intelligent officers who were keen to learn. Despite having to sleep on the deck curled around the wardroom table, Tall was thrilled. 'That', he remarked, 'was home.' He left *Iveston* with his midshipman's passing-out certificate and with a strong recommendation for submarines. In September 1966, newly married, he joined the autumn submarine officers' course at *Dolphin*.

Among his fellow students was Roger Lane-Nott, whose progression to *Dolphin* had been rather smoother. The former Queen's Gold Medallist had excelled himself in *Bulwark*, was highly ambitious, and was clearly marked out for success. Like Martin Macpherson, he was much interested in the possibilities of early command that the diesel-electric boats still offered, and even more in the unique capabilities of the submarine. 'I loved the whole concept of trying to outwit people from under the water, and I loved the level of involvement that submarines seemed to demand. It wasn't a service. It was a service within a service.' Like his fellow midshipman in *Bulwark*, Toby Elliott, he had used the proximity of John Moore's Seventh Submarine Squadron in Singapore to get some experience in submarines, in his case aboard *Andrew*, another of the six A-boats at John Moore's disposal. In his temporary capacity, Lane-Nott found himself sleeping in the passageway outside the wardroom with his feet in the pantry. One morning a kettle was left on the stove in the pantry and it boiled over, badly scalding his feet. The rest of the boat was equally primitive – its Type 186 sonar demanded that the boat itself rather than its sonar describe a circle when searching for contacts. Lane-Nott's mentor was a navigator of the old-fashioned school. 'If he wasn't shouting at you, you knew you were doing OK.' Like Jeff Tall in *Opossum*, Lane-Nott was captivated and volunteered for submarines.

Tall did so well on his training course at *Dolphin* that he was jocularly accused of cheating. He was then appointed to the 1,300-ton Second World War *Thermopylae*, a sister-ship to Taylor's *Token*, based at *Dolphin*. Since his wife was now pregnant with their first child, this had the merit of convenience. In the early months of 1967, with the Beatles' *Sergeant Pepper* often playing in the wardroom, the boat would provide Tall with a solid apprenticeship in submarining.

Macpherson, Elliott, Taylor, Tall and Lane-Nott were in due course joined by Chris Wreford-Brown. Committed to a full naval career from his first days at Dartmouth, he had followed the more comprehensive and detailed course set for General List officers. Following his midshipman's spell in *Tiger*, he returned to Dartmouth for a second year of academic studies. While his Supplementary List contemporaries were learning on the job, at Dartmouth and subsequently at Portsmouth he was schooled more thoroughly in the disciplines of gunnery, navigation, the torpedo and anti-submarine warfare. At the same time he represented the service in the modern pentathalon. Self-contained and serious-minded, he was beginning to be marked out by his superiors as a coming man. As yet, though, there was little to call him to the world of submarines. He had seen the SSN *Dreadnought* coming in to Gibraltar in 1965, and had been struck by her size and speed. Yet he had not been tempted to arrange any submarine experience, and his next career move was to spend a year in a small ship. This turned out to be *Glasserton*, in which Martin Macpherson had served. It was a good choice. Wreford-Brown was appointed navigator and correspondence officer. The old minesweeper was kept busy running out of Portland to the Western Approaches, and he soon found himself embroiled in all the day-to-day duties of a junior officer. These ranged from taking charge of the ship for the entire course of a watch to paying her crew once a fortnight – in cash. An enthusiastic swimmer, he also became the ship's diving officer, responsible for regularly checking the ship's bottom for limpet mines. If at any time this seemed excessively cautious, the Six-Day War that erupted between Egypt and Israel on 5 June 1967 persuaded him otherwise.

Wreford-Brown enjoyed the challenges and intimacy of a small ship, and soon began to appreciate that he might continue to do so in submarines, where the advantages of a small community were combined with opportunities for early responsibility and command. Despite the fact that, in his own words, he had no burning ambition to join the submarine branch, he volunteered. On 21 August 1968 he began training at *Dolphin*. On the same day Warsaw Pact tanks rolled into Czechoslovakia, acting in accordance with the Brezhnev Doctrine that permitted forcible intervention by members of the Pact in the affairs of those regarded as acting in a way contrary to the Communist ethos. Alexander Dubček's experiment in democracy, what the Czech leader had called 'socialism with a human face', was doomed.

During the course at *Dolphin* Wreford-Brown got engaged to a West Country girl he had been courting. As a result, when he completed the course ten weeks later, he contrived an appointment to the A-boat *Acheron*, attached to the Second Submarine Squadron based in Devonport.

Chapter 3

'God grant the weapon never be used'

'It is a submarine as big as a cruiser, as expensive as an aircraft carrier, and potentially as destructive as a squadron of V-bombers. It requires men of that calibre to man it. See that you do not fail in this respect.'
Captain Michael Henry, 1968

Wednesday, 15 February 1968, marked the beginning of a new epoch for the Royal Navy. At Cape Kennedy on the eastern seaboard of the United States, at 1115 Eastern Standard Time, the United Kingdom's first nuclear deterrent submarine, the SSBN *Resolution*, launched her first Polaris missile. Within minutes Rear-Admiral Levering Smith, in charge of the programme on the American side, signalled to *Resolution*'s CO Michael Henry that the shot had been a success. Just over five years after the beginning of the Polaris project, Britain's submarine nuclear deterrent had become a reality. It was a milestone, too, for the class of '63.

The story of Polaris — the missile and the submarines to which it gave its name — began in the aftermath of the Second World War when its victors began to look at ways of developing the submarine. For this to be done, the limits to the time it could spend under water, its range and its limited submersed speed all needed to be tackled. The last problem was the first to be solved, the United States Navy leading the way with developments of its diesel-electric fleet under what was called the Greater Underwater Propulsive Power pro-gramme. Historically, submarines had been long, slender vessels, with a length-to-beam ratio in the order of 12 to 1. Hydrodynamic research suggested that shorter, fatter shapes would prove easier to push through the water. This led eventually to a broad-beamed craft shaped in cross-section like a tear-drop, epitomized by the *Albacore*, a research submarine commissioned on 5 December 1953, which achieved the remarkable underwater speed of 33 knots.

A bigger problem was the absence of a power source that could work for long periods under the sea. This negated the submarine's very name, making it a surface vessel that could submerge periodically rather than an underwater craft that would occasionally surface. The Germans, at the forefront of submarine technology, had been experimenting with various systems towards the end of the war, particularly with a propellant called High Test Peroxide or HTP which, providing its own source of oxygen, showed some potential in addressing the problem of underwater motive power. The propulsive system, named after its inventor Professor Helmut Walter, was installed in experimental craft. At the end of the war the design was captured by the Allies, who soon busied themselves with its development.

Britain took the lead. One of the German Type XXVI Walter craft, *U1407*, had been scuttled in Cuxhaven in 1945. Raised by the Navy and renamed *Meteorite*, she was used for trials after the war and then as the basis for two small, 1,000-ton experimental submarines, *Excalibur* and *Explorer*. Commissioned respectively in 1956 and 1958, they were built at Barrow-in-Furness by Vickers, the firm that had constructed the first Holland boats more than fifty years previously. Though capable of very high speeds – 27 knots – for short periods under water, the craft proved temperamental, not to say dangerous. HTP decomposes continuously, and in so doing it gives off oxygen. If confined in a vessel, it will explode, and it reacts spontaneously with materials such as steel, brass and wood. The propulsion system employed HTP by forcing it to decompose by means of a catalyst, the resulting oxygen and steam being passed into a combustion chamber, mixed with kerosene and used to drive a turbine. This process was called 'fizzing'. In *The Submariners*, John Winton, engineer officer aboard *Explorer* on the occasion of a visit to the submarine depot ship *Adamant*, recalls:

> To the unwary bystander *Explorer* 'fizzing' in harbour was like a preview of doomsday. The exhaust gases, emerging at sonic

speeds, towered above the submarine in great plumes of pearly-grey smoke, accompanied by an appalling roar which shook windows a hundred yards away, stampeded cattle, and caused passing motorists to swerve off the road. When *Explorer* first 'fizzed' after joining the squadron, *Adamant*'s horrified officer of the watch called out the fire and emergency services and summoned the local brigade, being convinced that *Explorer* had become a fiery holocaust from end to end.

Unsurprisingly, *Explorer* was often called 'Exploder'. The Soviets, too, had been experimenting with HTP: a 1,500-ton, 250-foot craft, designated *Whale* by Nato, was completed at much the same time as her British counterparts. The Soviets' small Quebec-class coastal defence submarines also used an HTP unit on one of their three pro-peller shafts. However, none of these vessels proved satisfactory, as a crew member of one of the HTP boats was well aware when he remarked, 'I think the best thing we can do with peroxide is to try to get it adopted by potential enemies.'

Across the Atlantic, the US Navy was having rather more success with nuclear power. A nuclear bomb is an example of uncontrolled nuclear fission. By controlling and regulating the process, however, immense amounts of energy can be derived from a plant that can be relatively small – the size of a domestic dustbin – and which con-sumes no oxygen. The energy is used to heat water into steam that drives turbines in the manner of a conventional coal-fired or oil-burning ship. Hyman G. Rickover, a slightly built Ukrainian immi-grant and a cantankerous man invariably at odds with authority, was the remarkable figure who masterminded the American nuclear propulsion programme. Born in 1900, he had begun work on the project in 1946, and was repeatedly passed over for promotion until it became clear that nuclear propulsion would work. The SSN *Nautilus* was the proof of success, commissioned by the US Navy on 30 September 1954 as the world's first nuclear-powered subma-rine. On 17 January 1955 her captain made the famous signal 'Under way on nuclear power', and the dawning of the submarine age was most dramatically demonstrated by her voyage under the polar ice-cap that took her from Pearl Harbor to Portland, Dorset, in the summer of 1958.

At the same time, British efforts to produce such a craft were continuing apace. Although plans for a nuclear-powered British SSN had been drafted shortly after the war, it was not until 1957 that the project got properly under way. The 4,000-ton, 265-foot *Dreadnought* took her name from a series of famous ships, particularly the great battleship that had revolutionized naval practice in the years immediately before the Great War. Her existence owed much to the vision, charm and persistence of the professional head of the Royal Navy, the First Sea Lord, Earl Mountbatten. It was he who had convinced the then Chancellor of the Exchequer Derick Heathcoat Amory of the viability of such a submarine, using a scale model of the craft specially produced for the purpose. Then, when her construction was under way, it was he who had pulled off an even greater coup. The development of *Dreadnought*'s nuclear propulsion system at Dounreay in Caithness was proving problematic, largely because of the use of gas as a coolant. Indeed, it was such a problem that her projected launch date seemed severely compromised. Mountbatten persuaded Rickover to hasten *Dreadnought*'s completion by providing her with an American nuclear power-plant, a water-cooled Westinghouse S5W. Actively hostile to the British and particularly to their nuclear aspirations, Rickover was nonetheless utterly charmed by Queen Victoria's grandson. As one of Mountbatten's staff officers, Denys Wyatt, remarked, 'Rickover didn't give a damn whether we as a country got the submarine or not, but he did care whether Lord Mountbatten got one or not.'

Launched by the Queen on 21 October 1960, the anniversary of the Battle of Trafalgar, *Dreadnought* was already conducting her sea trials when the Nassau agreement between Kennedy and Macmillan was finalized. This not only gave impetus to the project but also provided the additional dimension of nuclear weapons. With the V-bomber force regarded as increasingly obsolete, in the immediate aftermath of Nassau it became apparent that the seaborne deterrent had to be made operational as soon as possible. The government's requirement was simply expressed: 'To deploy on station the first Royal Navy Ballistic Missile Submarine with its missiles, and with full support, in July 1968, and thereafter the remainder at six-monthly intervals.'

As Macmillan's party flew home from Nassau just before

Christmas 1962, it was agreed that an entirely new organization would have to be set up to manage the project, rather than doing so within the confines of the Admiralty's existing ship design and building programme. The then First Sea Lord, Caspar John, was asked to find someone to lead a group to be called the Polaris Executive. Of the three names in the hat, he chose the operational head of the British submarine force, Flag Officer Submarines (or FOS/M) Rear-Admiral Hugh Mackenzie, a distinguished wartime submarine commander. In his autobiography, Mackenzie wrote:

> I received the surprise of my life on Friday 28 December 1962; that morning in my capacity as Flag-Officer Submarines I had attended a meeting in the Admiralty not directly connected with Polaris. Returning to Gosport on my way home, I was informed that the First Sea Lord wanted to speak to me on the telephone, on the 'scrambler'; repairing to my office I was connected, whereupon a conversation on the lines of the following took place: –
>
> *1SL*   'You're fully in the picture about Polaris, well I want you to head the organisation we are setting up at the Admiralty to run the thing through.'
>
> *FOS/M (doubtfully)*   'Yes, Sir.'
>
> *1SL*   'Come and have lunch with me on Monday at one o'clock, at White's in St James's and give me your answer then: you can have the weekend to think it over.'
>
> *FOS/M*   'Yes, thank you, Sir.'
>
> *1SL*   'I tell you here and now that if you say "no", I'll twist your arm until you b....y well scream.'
>
> *FOS/M (after a pause)*   'Right, Sir, I'll see you on Monday.'

Mackenzie accepted.

The day after the lunch at White's, 1 January 1963, he found himself 'in an empty room on the ground floor of North Block of the Admiralty building; empty, that is, except for a chair and a large desk, on which sat a telephone not yet connected; no staff, no paper-work;

it was, to say the least, an unusual and perplexing situation.' To achieve the operational status of the deterrent within the five years allotted, he had to design, build and successfully commission five submarines capable of launching the American missile system; to oversee the development of the British nuclear warheads; to create a base from which the boats would be run; and to recruit and train the personnel to operate them safely and professionally.

As it turned out, Mackenzie was a masterly choice. He had outstanding skills of leadership, delegation and organization. Very rapidly, he got the project under way. The most urgent task was to settle the basic design of the submarine. For this, the SSN *Dreadnought* provided only a limited starting-point. She was designed to carry the American S5W power-plant rather than the British counterpart still in development, and her primary role was to track and destroy other submarines, be they other attack craft or ballistic missile boats. For this she was armed with six 21-inch torpedo tubes or could alternatively carry 42 mines. She could not carry nuclear missiles. The first issue was addressed by basing the design for the new submarines on the first of the all-British nuclear-powered SSNs. This was *Valiant*, then under construction at Barrow. The Polaris missiles were accommodated by taking another leaf out of the Americans' book. To create the first SSBN, *George Washington*, they had taken one of their attack submarines actually under construction, cut it in half, and inserted a 130-foot plug between the two halves. In this the missiles were located. Exactly the same was done with the design of *Valiant*, so creating the germ of the SSBN *Resolution*. The missile hangar gave her a length of 425 feet – as much as that of a six-coach train – and at 8,500 tons she would be the largest submarine in the world.

The Executive then got down to settle some of the more detailed requirements of the Resolution class, airily summarized in *The Impact of Polaris* by the head of the submarine design team, Jack Daniel, as 'the maintenance of constant depth firing readiness when launching 16 missiles weighing 20 tons apiece in rapid succession, guaranteed command signal reception, and a fundamental submarine requirement, the provision of sufficient main ballast tankage to provide an acceptable reserve of buoyancy. And of course maximum silence at all times.' By the autumn of 1963 – just as the Dartmouth year was beginning – the design had been approved. The shipyard appointed to lead the programme was Vickers at Barrow, which was to build the first and the third of the four submarines actually on order; Cammell Lairds at Birkenhead were to construct the second and the fourth boats. On 26 February 1964, on schedule, the keel of *Resolution* was formally laid. Mackenzie commented: 'It was a momentous, even historic moment . . . it had been achieved on time and was an encouraging augury for the future.'

*

With a General Election now looming, however, the political auguries were less promising. The Labour Party, well stocked with members of CND, had from the first publicly opposed the Nassau agreement, and in its manifesto it was committed to its renegotiation. This was taken by the public to mean that Labour might go so far as to abandon the nuclear deterrent altogether and cancel the Polaris programme. Although some members of the Shadow Cabinet were said to be equivocal on the matter, Jack Daniel took the issue sufficiently seriously to hedge his bets. There were rumours abroad of reversing the *Valiant*-into-*Resolution* equation, that is turning the Polaris craft back into an attack submarine. As he later recalled, 'ever mindful of employment . . . I took the Polaris design and removed the missile system and re-jigged the remainder to produce a balanced SSN design with a minimum waste of ordered materials and equipment. The resulting design was about 30 feet longer than *Valiant*.' This he tactfully named *Harold Wilson*.

Eight days after Labour took power on 13 October 1964, Mackenzie found himself presenting the whole Polaris programme to all the relevant new ministers. Principal among them was the new Secretary of State for Defence, Denis Healey.

From Mackenzie's point of view, Wilson's appointment of Healey to the defence portfolio was singularly fortunate. A Yorkshireman educated at Balliol College, Oxford, Healey had served with distinction during the war as a Major in the Royal Engineers. He was intellectually gifted and – in the words of his autobiography *The Time of My Life* – 'since the fifties had been working on both sides of the Atlantic . . . trying to understand the unprecedented problems created for strategy and diplomacy by nuclear weapons'. Duly briefed, Healey soon shifted the debate from one of cancellation to the exact number of Polaris boats that should be built.

Although the Nassau agreement had suggested that Britain would build five boats, only four were actually on order. For the British deterrent to be credible, it was obvious that one Polaris submarine had to be at sea at all times. However, the boats also had to undergo routine maintenance and longer periods of refit, and they had to be refuelled from time to time. It was for this reason that Mackenzie thought that four was a tenable number, though this would only be workable by following the American system of having two crews for each submarine – the established practice for aircraft, but unusual at sea. However, even this crewing arrangement 'made no allowance for possible accident or major breakdown in any of the submarines. Because of the overriding importance of maintaining at all times the absolute credibility of the deterrent, I was convinced the plan [to have only four boats] was basically unsound.' He continued, 'Equally important, I believed that it would impose, in peace time, an unnecessarily high degree of stress and strain on sea-going crews and base staff alike; I sensed a lack of appreciation of the fact that to ensure a submarine-borne deterrent remained totally credible at all times, it required that, for week upon week when at sea, the crew were in all respects equivalent to being on patrol under conditions of war.' Mackenzie therefore argued in favour of the full complement of five boats. Each of these would cost about £40 million, and this did not include a number of associated costs such as research and development, training, short- or long-term maintenance, or the establishment of a base.

As Christmas 1964 approached, while the class of '63 were beginning to get to grips with the rank of midshipman, the debate over the number of boats to be built raged in the corridors of the Ministry of Defence. It came to a head at a meeting of the Defence Council in January 1965. With Healey in the chair, Mackenzie reiterated his arguments. The matter then rose to Cabinet level with a meeting of its Defence and Overseas Policy Committee. Here Healey's chief opponent was the Chancellor of the Exchequer, George Brown. The Chancellor was by no means unsympathetic to the claims of CND. Indeed, in his memoirs Healey writes that Brown was at first inclined to cancel the Polaris programme altogether, but later maintained that we should limit the number of submarines to three. He argued that since this would not allow Britain to maintain at least one submarine permanently on station, a force of three submarines could not be regarded as an independent deterrent. Michael Stewart [the Foreign Secretary] drily remarked that this reminded him of a debate he attended in the Fulham Co-operative Society in the 'thirties: they had been discussing whether for the first time the Co-op should sell wine – an idea which shocked the good methodists on the committee. It was finally agreed that they should sell wine, on the strict condition that it should not be a good wine.

The Treasury duly demanded that the force should be limited to three. Healey, mindful of Mackenzie's briefing, argued for a minimum of four. Common sense – and Denis Healey – prevailed. The fifth boat, *Ramillies*, was never built.

'It was a relief', wrote Mackenzie, 'to have a firm decision at last . . . everybody could now concentrate on bringing the four-boat programme to successful fruition.'

By 1966, the industry of the Polaris team was beginning to show conspicuous results. Work was progressing on a base for both the SSBN Polaris submarines and their cousins, the attack boats of the SSN Valiant class. The submarine command's home, HMS *Dolphin* in Portsmouth harbour, was regarded as too small and too close to a major population centre to be suitable, and the surrounding waters were too shallow for the large, nuclear-powered submarines. As a temporary measure, two submarine depot ships, *Maidstone* and *Adamant*, were sent up to Faslane in Scotland. Situated on the Gareloch, a northern spur of the Firth of Clyde, Faslane had been a minor submarine base for some years, and it had already been settled that *Maidstone* would be located there to play host to the SSN *Dreadnought*, thus forming the nucleus of the Third Submarine Squadron. For the SSBNs it also seemed attractive. The surrounding waters were deep, and once the boats exited the Rhu Narrows they could take several alternative routes to the open sea, thus diminishing the chances of detection. Finally, given public sensitivity about nuclear matters, it was satisfactorily remote. In due course Faslane would become the Clyde submarine base, HMS *Neptune*, a purpose-built town created for the Navy's nuclear submarine programme, and it would host both the Third Squadron and the four Polaris submarines forming the Tenth.

Progress was also being made on a missile training centre, where the crews could be taught the intricacies of the missiles they would fire, thus obviating the need to send them to the United States. On 30 June 1966 – again on time – the Royal Naval Polaris School was opened. A general nuclear training programme was also being set up by the manning and training staff officer to the Executive. The programme was intended to find replacement crews for *Dreadnought*, and for the Polaris boats themselves. Following the American pattern it had been settled that each SSBN would have two crews, called Port and Starboard. The command communication system was also established, to liaise closely with central submarine command at Northwood in Middlesex; and it was from here that the SSBNs would be controlled. Finally, given the number of submarine movements soon to become commonplace, Faslane and the base for the Polaris missiles established at nearby Coulport were placed under the umbrella of a directorate called Commodore Clyde.

Work on the submarines themselves was also advancing. In July, the first all-British SSN, *Valiant*, was commissioned. On 25 September, the first of the Polaris boats, *Resolution*, was launched by the Queen Mother. And by the end of the year *Valiant's* sibling, *Warspite*, had successfully completed her contractor's sea trials, the principal milestone between the fitting-out and the commissioning of a boat. Soon both *Warspite* and *Valiant* would be set to work developing or testing the SSBNs' power-plant and tactical weapons (principally torpodoes).

Inevitably, there were hiccups. Faslane became a focus for the Campaign for Nuclear Disarmament, and the launch of the submarines was habitually disrupted by protesters. There was also persistent debate in the press as to whether the deterrent was really independent. *The Times*, in its coverage of the launch of *Resolution*, pointed out that the forty-first American SSBN had been launched eight weeks previously. 'There is an obvious disparity in scales between the two countries . . . the facts suggest that, technically speaking, the whole British Polaris programme is, and always will be,

linked to the American Polaris effort.' Cammell Lairds, with no previous experience of building nuclear submarines, soon lagged
behind Vickers, so much so that their own first SSBN, *Renown*, was
launched after Vickers' second, *Repulse*. And even the launch of
Repulse on 4 November 1967 was not without complications. The
attendant tugs failed to secure the powerless hull sufficiently quickly,
and she went aground. When the tide went out she was left high and
dry on the Walney Channel sands – an incident Toby Elliott remembers seeing on the television news in a bar at Twickenham. In *The
Impact of Polaris*, Jack Daniel recalled, 'It so happened that we had
some time earlier looked into the stability of grounded submarines
intact and progressively flooded in the context of escape, and I knew
that she would sit there safely upright until the next tide floated her
off. I quite enjoyed the launch lunch. Some didn't.'

Most serious of all was the discovery of hairline welding cracks in
Dreadnought's pressure hull, which might at depth have resulted in the
collapse of the hull and the loss of the submarine and crew. With the
terrible example of the USS *Thresher* still vivid, Mackenzie was
obliged to order ultrasonic testing of all the welds in all the submarines that were being built. This, he recalled, was immensely disrup-
tive to the schedule, and cracks were duly found in several of the
other hulls – notably *Valiant*'s and *Resolution*'s. These were welded
over. Nevertheless, the overall timetable was still kept.

At the end of 1964, Michael Henry had been told that he was to
command the first of *Resolution*'s two crews. Born in 1928, he had
joined the Navy in 1942 and had spent most of his career in submarines, rising to command first the 990-ton *Seraph* and then the larger
1,300-ton *Triumph*. He was bright, confident and an accomplished
ship-handler, and he had made a good impression in US Navy circles
during a staff posting in Washington. In 1965 he was sent on nuclear
training, first at the Royal Naval College, Greenwich, then at its
American equivalent in Dam Neck on the Virginian coast. This gave
him the opportunity to ride on several of the American SSBNs, the
force that had pioneered the Polaris deterrent patrols in 1960. By the
spring of 1966 he was in Barrow, overseeing the completion of
Resolution and the preliminary training of her crew. Following her successful launch, the reactor core, the boat's nuclear fuel, was loaded in

January 1967. Her sea trials were successfully completed that summer, largely in the Clyde, where she was closely observed by a Soviet intelligence-gathering trawler. By Christmas, the boat and crew were ready for their final official inspection. During its course, wrote Henry subsequently, 'I had the thrill of throwing 8,500 tons of deterrent submarine around the water like an attack submarine, in the course of a dummy attack.' Finally, on 15 February 1968, came the demonstration and shake-down operation off Cape Kennedy that was to see the first firing of her missiles.

The first submarine of the Polaris project had been completed on time and, even more remarkably, to budget. Shortly after *Resolution* was commissioned, Mackenzie completed his term as Polaris Executive. 'It was sad to leave such a wonderful team which, against all odds, had achieved so much; but I felt that, with the first of my submarines operational, it was the right moment to hand over to my successor a "going concern", full of confidence with its tail up.'

On 14 June 1968, Britain's first SSBN Polaris submarine, armed with her sixteen Polaris missiles, left Faslane on her first patrol. Her departure was not announced, and she left at a time at which merchant shipping activity was at its peak, so as to minimize the chances of detection. Attached to Nato as the submarine was – technically to the Supreme Allied Commander Europe – she joined a force of thirty-four United States Navy SSBNs assigned to the Atlantic Fleet. A year later, RAF Strike Command handed over responsibility for Britain's strategic deterrent to the Navy.

*

In the interim Lieutenant Toby Elliott, winner of the Max Horton prize, had further distinguished himself in his first submarine, the SSK *Porpoise*. He was smart, ambitious, attentive to his duties, and full of high spirits ashore. Early in 1967, he was told that he was to undergo nuclear training. Despite the rapid expansion of the submarine service that the arrival of the nuclear boats required, for young officers this was by no means an inevitable progression. As communications officer in the Port crew, he would take *Repulse*, the second of the Polaris submarines to be commissioned, on her first patrol.

Theoretical training was then run from the splendour of the Royal Naval College in Greenwich. Designed by Sir Christopher Wren as a naval hospital, its construction had been overseen by Nicholas Hawksmoor and Sir John Vanbrugh, and it remains one of the few Palladian glories of London. In these surroundings Elliott and his fellow students were introduced to the mysteries of nuclear power.

Nuclear fission, they learned, occurs when the nucleus of an atom of uranium is split in two after being struck by a sub-atomic particle such as a neutron. This causes the release of large amounts of heat, of fissile products such as gamma rays, and of several more neutrons. Those neutrons in turn collide with other uranium atoms, creating more heat and more neutrons. A series of reactions of this kind is then established, generating a continuous supply of nuclear energy. The device in which such a reaction can be started, sustained and controlled is the nuclear reactor. The first had been constructed and run in a University of Chicago squash court in 1943, and one of its descendants called Jason had since been set up for training purposes at Greenwich.

Fission only happens when the naturally occurring neutrons found in an isotope of uranium, U-235, are slowed to a small proportion of their normal speed. This is achieved in the reactor by the introduction of what is called a moderating element, such as water or graphite. The students learned that the process can then be controlled by the use of materials that absorb the slow-moving neutrons. These normally take the form of rods of cadmium or boron. Withdrawing them from the reactor core starts the chain reaction, the point at which the reactor goes critical, as it is termed. Reintroducing the rods slows and then stops the process. The vast amounts of heat generated by the fission process are extracted from the reactor by running a coolant through the core, sometimes water, sometimes liquid metal. This is used to heat water, producing steam to drive turbines.

Without a coolant, the core will melt, with catastrophic results. And without due screening, the highly radioactive gamma rays will cause the death of anyone in the reactor's proximity for any significant period of time. In an emergency the reactor can be SCRAMed. This is the picturesque term derived from the Safety Control Reactor Axe Man who, in the Chicago experiment, had been responsible for

cutting the ropes suspending the rods over the reactor core if anything looked like going wrong. The term survives, although the rods
are now removed mechanically, 'unless', remarks Sandy Woodward,
'the submarine is heeled more than 45° – when they tend to fall out!'

All this was regarded as sobering stuff by the submariners,
although the course tutors themselves – generally civilian nuclear
physicists – were thought to make the whole business more complicated than it really was. Stripped of its mystique, the reactor, thought
Elliott, was little more than a kettle; and the tiresome process of
starting up the tiny Jason was the traditional punishment for minor
infringements. Besides, Greenwich at the time was still regarded as
one of the best clubs in London, and London itself in the Swinging
Sixties represented, as Elliott put it, 'birds, booze and fun'.

Once Elliott had completed the course, he was posted to Barrow,
where *Repulse* was being built. There, like *Resolution*'s CO Mike
Henry – albeit at a more junior level – he was responsible both for
overseeing the boat's completion and for the initial training of the
crew. This simple statement covers a multitude of tasks, graphically
described by James Taylor as 'transforming a heap of metal and a
bunch of people who don't know one another into an efficient
fighting machine'. To Elliott, the heap of metal was certainly a
remarkable one. *Repulse* was far larger than the 2,000-ton diesel-
electrics with which he was familiar, and she looked different. When
she first visited Devonport she was described in *The Times* as 'this
killer whale in our midst', and there certainly was something dis-
turbingly reptilian about her, her black hull looking more like skin
than plating. The crew of thirteen officers and one hundred and
thirty ratings nevertheless had to turn itself into a machine, as
Elliott puts it 'one hundred and forty three people acting as one'.
This, to the layman one of the most striking achievements of these
vessels when at sea, was the culmination of months of training.

Then, after the launch of *Repulse* in September 1967, Elliott was
posted to the Royal Naval Polaris School in Faslane, at the time no
more than a series of Portakabins on what was still a building site.
Familiar with the submarine and her power plant, he now had to
learn about her principal weapon. Martin Macpherson, recently promoted lieutenant, was hard on his heels. He was also up for nuclear

training, and would be posted to the Starboard crew of *Repulse*. Soon Roger Lane-Nott, too, would undertake the nuclear general course.

*

The Polaris missile was a descendant of the Nazis' V2 rocket, one of the wonder-weapons that Hitler thought would change the course of the Second World War. Developed by the rocket genius Wernher von Braun, the Führer's missile had a range of 200 miles and a maximum altitude of 50 miles, was impossible to intercept and – travelling faster than the speed of sound – came without warning. Both the V2 and the V1, a cruise missile, were at the time considered revolutionary, and they attracted a great deal of interest from the Allies. In the closing days of the war, both the British and the Americans, and the Soviets captured missiles and missile engineers. Subsequently, the opposing ideologies invested a great deal of time, trouble and money in missile technology. The Americans scored an early first with various developments of the V1, one of which was the nuclear-tipped Regulus. Then, in 1957, the Soviets launched the Sputnik satellite into space using a long-range ballistic missile. This was the development that so alarmed the Eisenhower administration, prompting the notion of a 'missile gap' between East and West, and the deployment in England of the nuclear-armed Thor IRBM missiles, and of the smaller Jupiters in Italy and Turkey, which in turn led to the Cuban missile crisis.

The events in Cuba in 1962, however, had demonstrated the vulnerability of land-based missiles to surveillance and therefore to pre-emptive attack, and it was for this reason that both sides had started to develop Submarine Launched Ballistic Missiles or SLBMs. These had three distinct advantages over land-based missiles. First, as Admiral Arleigh Burke, the American Chief of Naval Operations, had once pointed out to Lord Mountbatten – and as was now pointed out to Lieutenant Elliott – virtually three-quarters of the world's surface is sea; half of the world's population live within fifty miles of the sea; and of all the cities with more than a million inhabitants, the vast majority are seaports. This means that a submarine, even with a short-range missile, has the majority of the world's population within its reach. Second, as a submarine at sea is very difficult to detect and therefore to destroy, the credibility of its threat is far greater. Third, the location of the deterrent away from its mother country makes that target and its inhabitants less legitimate for its enemies, theoretically at least.

Pursuing this thinking, the Americans successfully fired a modified V1 – actually Regulus – from the diesel-electric submarine *Cusk* on 12 February 1947, thus establishing the fact that a submarine was a viable platform for launching missiles. Regulus was subsequently used operationally in submarines. Then, in 1955, the Soviets launched the first SLBM. This was the SS-N-G Sark, fitted in 1958 on the diesel-electric Whiskey- and Zulu-class boats. However, the missile had to be fired from the surface, and it had a range of only 350 miles. If it was to be used for deterrent purposes, it would oblige the Soviets to patrol perilously close to the American seaboard. The US response was Polaris, the weapon that *George Washington* had taken to sea on her first deterrent patrol in 1960. Started in 1955 under the dynamic leadership of Admiral William Rayborn, the development of Polaris became the US Navy's top priority, eventually involving 100,000 people working at 30,000 different companies, and requiring 7,000 test firings to perfect it. Of its kind, it was an extraordinary device, small enough to be deployed in a submarine, and – using solid fuel – relatively safe. In its first A1 operational variant it was capable of shooting its one-megaton warhead a thousand nautical miles, to an accuracy measurable in yards.

While Elliott was at the Polaris School in Faslane it had been agreed that the British missile boats would be fitted with the A3 variant, with a range of 2,500 miles. This was the missile that Captain Henry had fired off Cape Kennedy on 15 February 1968. Like its Soviet equivalents, in the first phase of its flight the missile would burst from the sea, and its rocket motor would then rapidly accelerate the missile on its pre-set course, before stopping and dropping away. In the second phase, the missile payload of warhead and guidance system would coast at supersonic speed above the earth's atmosphere. Then, gradually, as gravity reasserted itself, the missile would enter its terminal phase, plunging down towards its target zone as its nuclear warhead self-armed, and exploding two thousand feet above its target.

Seven months after Henry's successful firing, on 28 September,

Harold Wilson was told that Soviet missiles aimed at Britain had 20,000 times the explosive force of the Hiroshima bomb. Among the targets were Bomber Command in High Wycombe and the Ministry of Defence in Whitehall, a stone's throw from Downing Street. A few years earlier a group of British experts had been assembled to prepare reports on the likely effect of nuclear attacks on Britain, the Soviet Union and North America. Called the Joint Inter-Service Group for the Study of All-out Warfare (JIGSAW), it posited an attack on 113 British cities with a population of over 50,000 using one-megaton weapons. It concluded that more than 90 per cent of the entire population would be killed. Wilson was also told that *Resolution*'s sixteen Polaris missiles and their manifold US Navy counterparts were targeted at all the great Soviet cities. JIGSAW studies concluded that the fact that Soviet cities were much farther apart than British centres of population meant that three-megaton weapons would be necessary at about 250 sites to kill 80 per cent of the population. Wilson's reaction to these figures and to the possible use of Polaris is not on record. However, Rear-Admiral Mackenzie was well aware of the missile's destructive capability when he wrote on the occasion of the commissioning of *Resolution* a prayer that began, 'Give us the will, but never the wish, to obey the order to fire. God grant the weapon never be used.'

*

Elliott completed his Polaris course shortly after *Resolution* set out on her first patrol, just as Chris Wreford-Brown was beginning his sub-marine officers' training course at *Dolphin*, and just as Warsaw Pact tanks were rolling into Czechoslovakia. James Taylor, now navigator of his second submarine, *Walrus*, believed the crushing of the Prague uprising signalled that 'the next war was busily brewing'.

Walrus was one of the modern Porpoise-class SSK designs. Her CO was Lieutenant-Commander Colin Grant, another of the Navy's pre-nuclear generation. Tall, heavily built and red-bearded, he was a first-class submariner, a bon viveur, and a man who was convinced that excessive physical exercise dulled the brain. He proved a fine tutor for Taylor, schooling him well in the professional and social duties of a submariner. Part of the Third Submarine Squadron based on the depot ship *Maidstone* in Faslane (HMS *Neptune* was as yet unfinished), Grant and his officers regarded the Gareloch as dreary. The boat's principal role was to patrol the seas of the Western Isles, where Taylor had first been inspired to join the submarine service. There she conducted torpedo trials, undertaking development work on the troublesome Mark 24 Tigerfish weapon, a design intended to home in on its target by active guidance from the firing submarine, ordered at the beginning of the decade as a replacement for the Second World War Mark 8 torpedo. As often as he could, Grant contrived that the boat should weekend not at Faslane but at Campbeltown on the Mull of Kintyre, where the weekly *ceilidh* at the Territorial Army hall at least provided some form of entertainment.

By now *Walrus* was getting rather too long in the tooth for operational work, so it was decided that she should go on a tour to countries interested in buying British arms. This took her via the Azores to the West Indies, down to Colombia, and back up to Key West, the south-eastern tip of Florida. There, Taylor's cocktail-party charm again came to the fore. The Asian expression of the Cold War, Vietnam, was now at its height. On being asked by an American serviceman: 'Why aren't you guys in Vietnam?' Taylor replied: 'Because the Vietcong haven't invited us.'

When *Walrus* was paid off, Taylor was posted to the SSK *Otter*. As befitted the more casual ethos of the age, and indeed the submarine culture of the time, Taylor did not view this simply as a good career move: '*Otter* had a marvellous and well-justified reputation as a party animal, and we used to play Jimi Hendrix's "Star-Spangled Banner" as a sort of theme-tune.' Nevertheless, he was doing his job sufficiently well to be asked to transfer from the Supplementary to the General List. Just married, he had his future to consider. So he made it a condition of the transfer that he should be allowed to undertake the Russian interpreter's course at the Army's School of Languages.

Jeff Tall, too, was cutting his teeth on conventional submarines. The Second World War *Thermopylae*, in which he was fourth hand, was kept busy running out of Portland acting as 'clockwork mouse': that is, as a target boat on which more sophisticated submarines and frigates could practise their anti-submarine techniques. The regular rhythm of day-running – taking the boat on daily trips, berthing by night – out of Portland harbour, the rigours of diving and surfacing the old boat, and the navigational demands of working closely with other ships soon taught him the basics of safe submarine operation. He also learned something about man management from the poor example of others. One of the boat's senior officers was fond of throwing his weight around, and was quite prepared to stop an officer's leave if there was – say – a typing mistake in a signal. Tall and his Electrical Officer, Lieutenant – later Vice-Admiral – Malcolm Rutherford, finally had enough of the man one day when he told Tall that his weekend leave was cancelled because of a similarly minor lapse. At the time, the three were sitting round the wardroom table. Turning to Tall, Rutherford – the duty officer for the weekend – asked him to shut the door. Tall did so, and Rutherford then knocked the senior officer out. Tall left for his weekend's leave, wondering if his and Rutherford's naval careers had ended. Returning the following Monday, he re-encountered the senior officer with some trepidation, but the matter was never mentioned again.

Soon Tall was posted to *Finwhale*, another SSK of the Porpoise class belonging first to Faslane's Third Submarine Squadron and subsequently to Singapore's Seventh Submarine Squadron. He spent three years in this submarine, rising to be its First Lieutenant under the command of Lieutenant (later Rear-Admiral) Sam Salt. Just as Toby Elliott was setting out on his first deterrent patrol in *Repulse*, Tall was told that he, too, was to be selected for nuclear training. Chris Wreford-Brown had recently received similar news. It was the summer of 1969, the summer of Woodstock, and the summer when Neil Armstrong and Edwin 'Buzz' Aldrin walked on the moon. The class of '63 had come of age.

Chapter 4
The Triumph of Admiral Gorshkov

'The creation at the will of the Party of a new Soviet Navy and its emergence on to the ocean expanses have fundamentally altered the relative strength of the forces and the situation in this sphere of opposition. In the person of our modern Navy, the Soviet armed forces have acquired a powerful instrument of defence in the oceanic areas, a formidable force for the deterrence of aggression, which is constantly ready to deliver punishing retaliatory blows and to disrupt the plans of the imperialists.'

Admiral S.G. Gorshkov, *Navies in War and Peace*, 1972

While the 1960s had seen dramatic developments in Western submarine capability in general, and British capability in particular, the Soviet Union had been far from idle. Indeed, under a politically adroit and strategically acute commander-in-chief, Admiral Sergei Gorshkov, the Soviet Navy was turning itself into an all too credible threat.

Born in 1910, Gorshkov was educated at Frunze, the Soviet equivalent of Dartmouth, and spent the early years of his career in the Soviet Pacific Fleet. This was the time of Stalin's great purges that decimated the ranks of senior officers. Promotion for junior officers was as a consequence swift, and Gorshkov reached flag rank after only ten years in the Navy. Posted to the Black Sea in 1941, he was a key figure in the rearguard action against the Germans at Odessa that left the port virtually inoperable when the Soviets eventually evacuated it. He was then seconded to the 4th Ukrainian Front as naval deputy to the 47th Army, where he was fortunate enough to meet not only the future General Secretary of the Communist Party Nikita Khrushchev but also his protégé Leonid Brezhnev, who was subsequently to lead the Party. In September 1944, Gorshkov was promoted vice-admiral, the following year squadron-commander of the Black Sea Fleet. In 1951 he became the Fleet's Commander-in-Chief, in 1955 Deputy C-in-C of the entire Soviet Navy. Then, in January 1956, he replaced Admiral N.M. Kuznetsov as Commander-in-Chief. He was only 45.

Gorshkov's timing could scarcely have been better. In 1945, Stalin had instigated a massive programme of naval expansion. Despite its enormous coastline, the Soviet Union has relatively few ports, and fewer still that are not ice-bound in the winter months and that can be used all the year round. Partly as a consequence of this, Soviet naval achievements in the Second World War had been modest, and the fleet in 1945 was outdated and its crews demoralized.

Stalin set out to change all this. The main thrust of his naval programme was focused on submarines, of which he ordered the extraordinary number of 1,200, their design to be based principally on the latest German designs captured after the war. Although this new submarine force could be regarded as defensive, the US Chief of Naval Operations, Chester Nimitz, thought otherwise. In 1946, he suggested that the Soviets were intending 'to neutralise Britain by blockade, bombardment and invasion, and were aiming to launch submarine raids against American coastal cities'. As well as the submarines, new cruiser and destroyer designs were put in hand and, like the Americans, the Soviets also pursued the Nazi lead in missiles.

Since the death of Stalin in 1953, however, the programme had lost much of its impetus, and only a third of the submarines planned under Stalin's programme were ever completed. Khrushchev's belligerent attitude towards the Cold War provided a new fillip to naval expansion. In particular he was an enthusiast of submarines, writing in his memoirs, 'A submarine doesn't make much of an impression. There aren't many people on board, and the craft itself looks like a floating cigar. But a submarine is still the supreme naval weapon nowadays, and I'm proud of the role I played in reassessing the direction in which our navy was going and introducing submarines as the basis of our sea power.' Of the surface fleet warships he was dismissive.

'Our naval commanders thought they were beautiful and liked to show them off to foreigners.'

A year before Gorshkov's elevation to Commander-in-Chief, the first Soviet ballistic missile designed for use in a submarine had been launched. By 1956, the first Soviet ballistic missile submarine, a Zulu-class diesel-electric, was at sea. This carried the SS-N-1 ballistic missile, with a range of 150 kilometres, capable of being launched only when the submarine was on the surface. Two years later the Golf class appeared, which could carry three missiles. Designated by Nato SS-N-4, these missiles had a range of 650 kilometres. By 1967 there were thirty-five examples of the two classes at sea. They were followed by the first nuclear-powered missile boats, the Hotel-class SSBNs, of which there were to be nine. At first these submarines carried the SS-N-4 system, but this was replaced in due course by the SS-N-5, the first Soviet missile that could be launched from a submerged submarine. Then came two nuclear-powered cousins: five submarines of the Echo class, armed with cruise missiles and called by Nato SSGNs (G standing for guided missile); and fifteen SSN November-class attack boats. By comparison, the American SSBN *George Washington* was the first of a class of forty-one similar boats, and carried Polaris with a range of 2,600 kilometres; and she was paired with four SSNs of the Skate class, five of the Skipjacks, followed by fourteen of the Thresher class – to be reduced to thirteen after the loss of the lead boat on 10 April 1963.

However, though the Soviet force was formidable enough on paper, it had a number of limitations. The first was geographic. The very sizeable force had to be split between four fleets – Pacific, Black Sea, Baltic and Northern – none of which could realistically provide support for another. Furthermore, each of the four fleets could reach the high seas only by passing through bottlenecks or choke-points outside Soviet control. Submarines of the Northern Fleet were obliged to pass through the Greenland-Iceland-UK (GIUK) gap on the way to the Atlantic; those of the Baltic Fleet had to negotiate the Kattegat and the Skagerrak between Denmark and Sweden; the Black Sea Fleet had to pass through the Dardanelles and under the bridge linking the two halves of Istanbul; the Pacific Fleet had to transit either the Korea, the Tsugaru or the La Pérouse Strait.

Second, the modest range of the missiles that these early ballistic missile submarines carried meant that, if they were to act as a realistic deterrent, they had to patrol relatively close to the European or American seaboard. This in turn required long periods of transit to and from the patrol areas, and a large number of craft. Third, like both the British and the American early attempts at nuclear propulsion, Soviet boats were exceptionally noisy, which meant that they were fairly easy to detect. Fourth, they had relatively poor sonar systems. This was particularly significant as far as the Soviet SSNs were concerned, for they were therefore unable easily to detect the quieter second-generation Western boats that formed the Nato SSBN force: the George Washington and – later – the British Resolution classes.

There were human problems, too. The sheer size of the Soviet submarine construction programme inevitably placed enormous demands on training and manpower, and the quality of the crews in the boats generally fell below Western standards. All the ratings were conscripts, and they were drawn from all over the USSR. In addition to the challenges of submarine training, there were therefore also basic language barriers to overcome. Similarly, the number of command posts meant that the officers were less carefully screened than their counterparts in the West. (Indeed, the Soviet submarine service as a whole forms an interesting contrast to the Royal Navy, which appears to have benefited considerably by comprising a small élite force of volunteers who were far more closely knit than their counterparts in the much larger Soviet – and US – Navy.)

Then, too, neither of the Western navies thought it necessary to follow the Soviet practice of having a political officer, a *zampolit*, on board submarines to inculcate ideology and ensure conformity to a particular creed. Moreover, Soviet morale was not improved by the fact that the shielding used around the nuclear reactors of the boats was insubstantial, so giving rise to the joke, 'How do you tell a man is from the Northern Fleet?' 'Because he glows in the dark.' The early Soviet nuclear-powered submarines – collectively known as the HENS (Hotel/Echo/November) – emitted so much radiation that Nato seriously considered using radioactive monitoring as a means of detecting them.

Finally, in the late 1950s and early 1960s, Gorshkov was seemingly content to act as a subsidiary to the ground and strategic rocket forces of the Soviet Union: the submarine force confined itself to a defensive role protecting its own missile boats and suppressing the Western SSBN force.

Together, these factors meant that by the time of the Cuban missile crisis, however formidable the threat of Soviet land-based missiles, that of the submarine force was relatively modest.

In the next few years, though, while pursuing submarine development internally, the Soviets also took advantage of the fruits of espionage to upgrade their weaponry. As the phenomenon of the 'missile gap' that followed the launch of Sputnik suggested, accurate information on the opposition's capability was vital if appropriate plans were to be made for its neutralization. Given that neither West nor East was in the habit of issuing press releases about their latest developments in weapons technology, the gleaning of information by all sorts of means became a major feature of the Cold War. Exactly how much the Soviets extracted covertly is uncertain, but the trial in 1961 of what was dubbed the Portland spy ring made it clear that significant information was being passed.

Harry Houghton and Ethel Gee were employees of the Admiralty Underwater Weapons Research Establishment in Portland, Dorset, who, with Gordon Lonsdale and a married couple called Kroger, had conspired to obtain secret information on new submarine technology. Tipped off by a Polish intelligence officer who later defected to the West, the security service arrested Houghton and Gee on Saturday, 7 January 1961, in the act of passing a shopping bag to Lonsdale just outside the Old Vic Theatre near Waterloo. The bag contained papers on *Dreadnought*. The Krogers, friends of Lonsdale, were arrested the same day. The espionage lair of their Ruislip bungalow was then searched and found to be equipped with all the trappings of popular fiction – a radio transmitter, false passports, and objects such as a torch battery hollowed out to make a hiding-place. In the trial that followed, Lonsdale was sentenced to twenty-five years' imprisonment, the Krogers to twenty, Houghton and Gee to fifteen. In his memoirs Harold Macmillan described the Portland spy ring as 'a dangerous conspiracy to obtain important information of a highly secret character regarding modern submarine methods'. For the Soviets the principal benefit appears to have been the sonar system used on *Dreadnought* and on the remaining first-generation British SSNs, *Valiant* and *Warspite*.

Shortly afterwards, a remarkable amount of material about the US SSBN programme made its way into the public domain, not least accurate scale models of the George Washington class of SSBNs. In 1967, Soviet replacements for the HENs appeared in the form of the Charlie SSGN, the Victor SSN and a new SSBN. All were equipped with what appeared to be sonar based on the British model, while the SSBN bore such a striking resemblance to her American counterparts that she was inevitably dubbed the Yankee. There would be forty-nine of the Victor class, thirty-four Yankees, and twelve Charlies. Altogether by 1970 there were almost three hundred Soviet submarines in service, and 65,000 trainees were going through the Soviet equivalent of HMS *Dolphin* in Leningrad each year.

At the same time, in a major change of policy, Gorshkov's new navy was gradually extending its operations beyond its own waters. Its first significant operation outside Soviet waters was conducted in 1961 when two groups of ships, one from the Baltic and one from the Northern Fleet, met in the Norwegian Sea. Subsequently, each year saw a larger exercise, some taking place in the Faeroes-UK gap, some off north-west Scotland. Then came a major deployment in 1967 during the Arab-Israeli war. In a matter of days, more than seventy ships including submarines were dispatched through Turkish waters to confront the US Sixth Fleet in the Mediterranean. By the end of the decade, Soviet ships and submarines patrolled everywhere: in the Baltic, in the Barents and Norwegian Seas, on the European continental shelf, and on both the eastern and the western American seaboard. In April 1970 this naval strength was symbolized by an enormous exercise codenamed Okean 70 that involved more than two hundred warships and, unusually, combined the Northern, Baltic and Pacific fleets, together with a squadron that had been established in the Mediterranean seven years earlier off the island of Kithira. One of the purposes of the exercise was to indicate to the world that the enforced withdrawal of a Russian fleet, as had happened during the Cuban missile crisis in 1962, would not be repeated. The message was underlined that same month by the visit to the island of a Kresta I missile cruiser, two diesel-electric Foxtrots and one Echo II nuclear-powered submarine.

By then, Gorshkov had overseen a remarkable transformation in the Soviet Navy. When he had taken over as C-in-C fourteen years previously, he had been in charge of what amounted to little more than a coastal defence force, albeit one that made up in numbers for what it lacked in technology. In 1970 he presided over a large, modern fleet, perfectly capable of operations beyond home waters and certainly capable of offering a very significant threat to the West. The Soviet fleet, in 1958 the twenty-fifth largest, was now the fifth largest in the world. Like the class of '63, the Soviet Navy had come of age.

Days of Heaven

'I was just 28 when I was given my first command, which is young for peace time. During the war we had operational C.O.s of 22, but I think, on average, probably the best years of a submarine C.O.'s life are 25 to 30 – old enough to have experience, self confidence and judgement; young enough not to think too much. At 35 most men are getting too old and over cautious.'

Ben Bryant, *One Man Band*, 1958

Chapter 5

The Defence of
the Realm

'The folks in the U.S. Navy Undersea Warfare Office (N-87) call them
"Roles and Missions". Whatever you call them, these are the tasks
that are currently defined for nuclear submarines. Up until very
recently, though, just discussing them was cause for extreme discomfort (based on security regulations) on the part of the senior leadership of the handful of navies that operate SSNs.'

Tom Clancy, *Submarine*, 1993

It was ironic that the culmination of the Royal Navy's achievement
in getting the first two Polaris submarines, *Resolution* and *Repulse*, on
patrol should coincide with the dilution of much of the political will
that had created the British nuclear deterrent in the first place.

President Kennedy in his inaugural address in January 1961 had
proclaimed that the United States would 'pay any price, bear any
burden, meet any hardship, support any friend, oppose any foe to
assure the survival and the success of liberty'. Macmillan, in his
rather more understated way, had been similarly unambiguous as to
the role the West in general – and Britain in particular – had to play
in the containment of Communism. When Kennedy's mantle fell on
Lyndon B. Johnson on 22 November 1963, the new President
matched Kennedy's words with deeds, making Vietnam the Cold
War's principal battlefield. The first US bombing of the country took
place on 4 August 1964, and the first US troops landed on 8 May
1965. By the end of 1967 there were 485,000 troops in Vietnam, and
the war was costing America $20 billion a year.

By contrast, in Britain the Labour government was forced by economic circumstances in July 1967 to commit to the partial withdrawal of British armed forces east of Suez. An involuntary declaration that she was no longer a major combatant in the Cold War, it was also an acknowledgement that she no longer had an empire in the East to protect. Still, at Denis Healey's urging, Labour largely supported the Polaris programme, despite cancelling the fifth boat *Ramillies*. Moreover, the sloughing off of responsibilities in the East permitted a strategic concentration on the battle against Soviet submarines in the Atlantic, and overall defence spending between 1964 and 1970 only fell from 7 per cent to 6 per cent of GDP.

The election to the American presidency of the Republican Richard Nixon in November 1968 marked the beginning of further change. In his Presidential campaign Nixon had advocated the scaling-down of American involvement in the Vietnam War, for it now seemed clear that the war could not be won, that it was a stupendous burden on the economy, and that it had lost almost all public support. At his inaugural address on 20 January 1969, he spoke presciently of 'an era of negotiation'. As a new decade began, there seemed scope, too, for a shift in policy towards China and the Soviet Union. Though they had appeared close in the early 1950s, the two great Communist states had since had a serious falling-out.

The Chinese had publicly criticized Khrushchev's denunciation of Stalin in 1956, and had taken as an insult the Soviet leader's refusal to help develop their own atomic bomb. Then, in 1960, the Soviets abruptly withdrew their thousands of experts from China as the vitriolic exchange between Moscow and Beijing intensified. At the root of this family quarrel lay the question, who was to lead the Communist world? Competition between the Soviets and the Chinese in supplying the North Vietnamese with aid grew. In 1967 China went so far as to denounce the USSR over its failure to go to the aid of Egypt, Syria and Jordan during the Six-Day War. It was also alarmed by the invasion of Czechoslovakia the following year, fearing that the Brezhnev Doctrine – the right of the Kremlin to impose its own brand of Communism on another state – might be employed against China; and the signature by the Soviet Union, the United States and Britain of a Nuclear Non-Proliferation Treaty that same year, prohibiting the transfer of nuclear technology to other countries, seemed to indicate collusion between Moscow and Washington. By 1969, the 3,000-mile border between the Soviet Union and China had become the focus of an immense arms build-up. A million Soviet troops and 1,200 warplanes faced a million Chinese soldiers, and border clashes became increasingly frequent.

Here was an opportunity for Nixon and his National Security Adviser Henry Kissinger to exploit the Sino-Soviet split and to end the hopeless war in Vietnam. The confrontation that had characterized the era of Kennedy and Khrushchev was beginning to give way to détente, an easing of strained relationships. At the same time, the opening of arms limitation talks in 1968 had signalled a recognition that arms control was necessary. The stockpile of weapons in both the East and the West had grown enormously since the Cuban missile crisis and a further escalation looked likely to lead to bankruptcy. Arms control would not, however, involve disarmament but rather the establishment of a stable nuclear balance between the superpowers, or mutual assured destruction.

There were changes in Britain, too. In June 1970 the Conservatives under Edward Heath came to power. Heath, however, broke away from Conservative foreign policy traditions. Born in 1916, and educated at Balliol College, Oxford, he had been 23 when the Second World War broke out. During the conflict he attained the rank of Major, serving in the Heavy Anti-Aircraft Regiment. This took him into what remained of Germany in 1944–5, an experience that imbued him with a sense of what was to be his life's work: the reconstruction of Europe. As a politician he was far more concerned with Britain's relationship with Europe than with the United States, and it became one of his principal ambitions to take the country into Europe during his term of office. Indeed, a meeting between Heath and Nixon in Bermuda in December 1971 – nine years after the Kennedy/Macmillan summit in the Bahamas – was reported as marking the end of the much-vaunted 'special relationship' between America and Britain. As Kissinger later commented: 'Paradoxically, while other European leaders strove to improve their relations with us . . . Heath went in the opposite direction.'

In practice, Heath's interest in foreign policy was diluted by the demands of domestic circumstances, among them the resurgence of the Irish question in the form of civil unrest in Northern Ireland, the continuing decline of the economy, and a related series of industrial disputes. Nevertheless, he came to believe that Britain's nuclear technology should make a contribution to the European cause. In his memoirs he later wrote of his fear at the time that 'A combination of increased Soviet military strength, diminished Western vigilance and reduced American commitment could lay Western Europe wide open to Soviet domination.' He proposed to Nixon that an Anglo-French nuclear deterrent be formed, combining the Polaris boats with the new French force of five SSBN deterrent submarines, the '*force de frappe*'.

Heath's flirtation with the idea of nuclear co-operation with France was in the end to come to nothing. Of greater long-term significance, however, was the fact that the Americans now intended to replace Polaris with a more sophisticated missile. The debate as to what should replace it in Britain, whether the new American missile or a home-grown one, was to occupy the government for some time to come.

*

On 9 January 1970, Lieutenant Chris Wreford-Brown caught the night-sleeper from Euston to Glasgow, and the following morning arrived in Faslane. Security at HMS *Neptune* was elaborate, and it took him some time to reach the dockside. There lay the SSN *Warspite*, the ominous-looking black craft to which he was now posted as casing and correspondence officer. *Warspite* was the third and latest of Britain's attack submarines, named after Admiral Cunningham's flagship at the Battle of Cape Matapan in 1941. Two hundred and eighty-two feet long and capable of almost 25 knots, she had a complement of 13 officers and 90 men. It was a requirement in nuclear-powered submarines that both the CO and the First Lieutenant should have qualified as submarine commanding officers. *Warspite*'s captain was Sandy Woodward, her First Lieutenant – known as the Executive Officer on nuclear submarines – John Coward. Respectively in their late and early thirties, both were already formidable officers. Together with Wreford-Brown, they would crystallize their reputations twelve years later in the Falklands War.

Warspite was Woodward's first nuclear command. Born in Penzance in 1932, he had won a scholarship to Dartmouth, taking up his place in the early days of January 1946. Introduced to submarines by way of the depot ship *Maidstone*, he was 'volunteered' for them and undertook the usual basic training at *Dolphin*. His first boat was the Second World War *Sanguine*, based in Malta. Here he distinguished himself sufficiently to be sent to Barrow to help supervise the building of *Porpoise*, the first of the new SSK class, in 1956. He then passed the commanding officers' qualifying course, and was appointed to command the Second World War *Tireless* in December 1960. Two years later he was one of the first commanding officers to be sent for nuclear training at Greenwich. After a spell in the SSK *Grampus*, he was appointed second-in-command of the SSN *Valiant*, then being completed at Barrow under Commander Peter Herbert, who would later serve as Flag Officer Submarines during the Falklands conflict. This was succeeded by two years as Teacher, the instructor in charge of the commanding officers' qualifying course, described by Woodward as 'the job most coveted by all submariners'. Then came *Warspite*, which he joined as CO in December 1969. Reputedly the brightest man in the Navy, Woodward was inclined to question received wisdom and to do things his own way. Though not a man to suffer fools gladly, and often brusque to the point of rudeness, he would nevertheless prove an inspiration for Wreford-Brown.

Warspite's Executive Officer was quite a different character. Born in 1937, John Coward was the son of a Medway shipbroker. He was educated at Downside and Dartmouth and, like Woodward, he was not especially attracted by submarines, eventually submitting himself to the *Dolphin* course principally – he claimed – because most of his friends did. Thereafter, the camaraderie of the service and the lifestyle offered by the Far Eastern stations of Singapore and Hong Kong created a talented new advocate for submarines. Convinced by the Cuban missile crisis of the reality of the Soviet threat, by 1969 Coward was one of the service's rising stars. He was also a great reader and well versed in naval history, and prone to disguising his professionalism and aggression with an air of languid insouciance.

He liked to claim that the real test of how well a submarine was run was whether the plates at dinner were warm, and he always insisted on fresh flowers in the wardroom. His dictum, though, a quotation from Macaulay, was, 'The essence of war is violence. Moderation in war is imbecility.'

If Woodward and Coward were chalk and cheese, the pair nevertheless shared high professional standards and were clearly keen to make their mark with the country's newest SSN. They welcomed the opportunity to take the submarine, as Wreford-Brown put it, 'up north'.

Mike Henry had encountered considerable Soviet interest in *Resolution*'s sea trials in 1968. Nato were equally interested in every aspect of the Soviet Navy and its submarine fleet. In a democracy it is necessary to release at least a certain amount of information about submarine capability, not least so as to convince taxpayers that the money invested in these spectacularly expensive machines is well spent. Admiral Gorshkov was under no such obligation. Nato and its navies nevertheless needed to know the operational capabilities of the Soviet fleet so that due preparation could be made for its reception in case of war. Specifically this ranged from information about the speed, diving depth and armament of the various classes of Soviet submarine, to the range of their missiles, their ability to detect and be detected, and their habitual operating patterns. Such information might be derived from various sources – agents on the ground, spy planes or satellites, eavesdropping on signals and various other forms of electronic surveillance. Few methods, though, were more effective than actually going up and visiting the Soviet bases. Since the late 1940s, therefore, the West had dispatched submarines to the main Soviet ports: Vladivostok on the Sea of Japan, Leningrad on the Baltic, and Murmansk on the Barents Sea. As well as these general intelligence duties, such patrols could also register any sudden deployment of the Soviet submarine fleets that might signal war. By 'up north' Wreford-Brown meant the Barents Sea and the headquarters of the Northern Fleet in Murmansk.

In 1941, Edward Young had visited the Barents Sea as torpedo officer in *Sealion*. Operating in that forbidding region was fraught with difficulties:

In our patrols between the Kola inlet and North Cape we encountered no floating ice, but during the brief daylight visibility was hampered by the spray which froze on the periscope and by frequent snow storms which blotted out the land for hours on end. And on the surface in the long hours of darkness we faced the beastliness of spray which turned to ice even before it struck our faces. It froze on the gun, on the periscope standards, in the voice-pipe, and all over the bridge. Icicles hung from the jumping wire from one end of the submarine to the other, and sometimes formed so much topweight that the Captain became concerned about our stability.

The first post-war patrol of the Barents Sea was made by the American diesel-electric *Cochino*, which left Portsmouth for Murmansk in August 1949. In the company of a second US Navy submarine *Tusk*, her task was intelligence-gathering outside one of the main bases of the Soviet Northern Fleet, Polyarnny on the Kola peninsula close to Murmansk. The patrol ended in disaster when *Cochino* caught fire and ultimately sank on 26 August, a hundred miles off the Norwegian coast. Although the majority of the crew were rescued by *Tusk*, there were fatalities on both boats: one on *Cochino*, six on *Tusk*. Nine days later, the discovery by the United States that the Soviets had developed their own atomic bomb provided considerable further incentive for such intelligence-gathering missions.

In due course, a year-round routine of submarine surveillance was established by the US Navy, in both the Barents Sea and the Sea of Japan. The first British submarine to undertake a Barents Sea patrol was *Artful*, commanded by Lieutenant-Commander Roger Stone, in 1952. This was a mission in which Churchill, then Prime Minister, took a personal interest. John Moore, later to command the Seventh Submarine Squadron in Singapore, was at the time serving as a staff officer to the Third Submarine Squadron at Rothesay on the Isle of Bute. In this capacity he had the task of drafting the operation order to *Artful* outlining her mission. One afternoon Moore received a telephone call. Down the line came the unmistakable Churchillian drawl: 'Have you drafted that operations order yet?'

Before the first SSK Porpoise-class boats were commissioned in

1957, the British patrols had been conducted by T- or A-class boats dating from the Second World War. These were given special sensors for intelligence-gathering, including an antenna for picking up radio transmissions, and snorkels to enable them to recharge their batteries without surfacing. In other respects they were ill-equipped for the work. Though the diesels theoretically vented their exhaust into the sea, in practice the boats soon became permeated with fumes, and primitive air-purifiers did little to prevent the atmosphere from becoming stale. The boats also lacked a water distillation plant, so fresh water was in very short supply, and there was scarcely enough in which to shave, let alone wash.

Nor was it known what the Soviet response to incursions close to their territorial waters would be, or what their standing orders or Rules of Engagement in such circumstances were. The matter was clarified on 19 August 1957 when the US diesel-electric *Gudgeon* was detected outside Vladivostok. Soviet units kept her at bay for forty-eight hours, depth-charging her and forcing her to surface. Only in 1966 was the first British submarine apparently detected in the Murmansk area, but it is unlikely that she was the last. James Taylor recalls there being various rumours later on about British submarines returning from the Barents Sea after having been patched up in remote northern harbours. There is also more specific evidence that a Second World War T-boat and an Oberon-class boat were depth-charged. Such missions were clearly dangerous, and for that reason they were regarded as war patrols by both the Western navies involved. They were also valuable, for they collected vital intelligence, and for that reason those undertaking particularly distinguished missions were awarded decorations.

By 1970, an intensive Anglo-American intelligence-gathering mission, codenamed Holystone, was operating in the Barents Sea. The US Navy, with far more submarines at its disposal, ran the majority of the missions, while the British ran one spring and one autumn patrol. By now, nuclear-powered SSN boats were being used on such patrols, from the Americans the Thresher class, from Britain *Dreadnought* and *Valiant*. Critically, these vessels did not have to snorkel to charge their batteries, and they also enjoyed what the Royal Navy nicely described as greater levels of habitability: limitless fresh water, proper air-cleaning and air-conditioning systems, good food and greatly improved recreational facilities. A new generation of sensors, including thermal imaging devices and TV cameras, were also fitted to these boats, greatly improving their intelligence-gathering attributes; and the crew were accompanied on patrol by intelligence-gathering experts.

The patrols provided an immense challenge for ambitious submarine commanders. Woodward, his skills honed by his period as Teacher, knew exactly what he wanted to get out of his equipment and his men, and that was a great deal. During his own commanding officers' qualifying course he had been fascinated by the ability of his Teacher to know when the frigates acting as targets for the candidates had reversed course, turning back to attack the trainees' submarine. Only eventually did he realize that this was attributable to the Doppler effect, an apparent increase in the frequency of sound as its source approaches, and a similar decrease in frequency as the source moves away. Woodward applied equal attention to the various sensors on board *Warspite*, and demanded all sorts of innovations to enable him to gather information in Soviet home waters, the better to identify, track and – should it come to it – destroy his Soviet opposite numbers. Although details of these patrols cannot be given, US commanders were equally enterprising, as *Blind Man's Bluff*, an account of US Cold War submarine operations, makes plain. 'Many submarine commanders believed it was their job – and forget about the niceties of international law – to drive straight into Soviet territorial waters. Fleet commanders graded captains on how long they kept their "ears and eyes" up out of the water. The more daring the attempt, the higher the grade. This had become a contest of sorts, a test of bravado for the captains, their crew and their craft. And for most captains, these days of unfettered risk would forever mark the high-point of their careers.'

Woodward doubts whether the patrols were so overtly a test of bravado, but wrote of his own command: 'In the following eighteen months I learned another whole bookful of extraordinary things in the company of excellent people, and enjoyed myself about as much as I had as Teacher.' Fred Scourse, an engineer officer in *Warspite* who was to rise to the rank of Rear-Admiral, is more illuminating about Woodward's philosophy. 'He wanted to show we were technically and tactically superior to the opposition, and therefore dedicated his life to that.' On this particular patrol he slept for no longer than twenty-two minutes at a stretch.

Wreford-Brown was determined to make an impression on his new CO, and he went about his duties on what was for him an entirely new submarine with his customary professionalism and – he thought – efficiency. Woodward and Coward thought otherwise. 'I remember them calling me into the wardroom and telling me I wasn't doing as well as I thought I was,' says Wreford-Brown. 'That made me angry and I really got stuck in.'

He also interested himself in becoming a specialist navigator. He had long been fascinated by navigation, partly because it required accurate work carried out quickly and under pressure, and partly because he found the technological innovation that came with the nuclear boats intriguing. Now that surfacing was an option rather than a necessity, the traditional method of navigation by sextant and star-sight was replaced by the Ship Inertial Navigation System or SINS, accurate to within 300 yards after a circumnavigation of the globe. Given that a submarine starts its voyage from a fixed, known point, SINS provides its position at any given moment by measuring how far and in what direction the boat has moved since the point of departure – or indeed any other fixed point. This is achieved by devices called accelerometers that measure every movement of the submarine. The efficiency of SINS was demonstrated in 1967 when *Warspite*'s sister-ship *Valiant* steamed home from Singapore, undertaking the entire 12,000-mile voyage submerged. Still, though SINS was accurate, it was thought prudent to update or check the given position at intervals, as Wreford-Brown points out. 'With SINS 1, which *Warspite* had, you often had to work hard to make its suggested position tally with where you knew you really were.' This all lent a certain challenge to the safe navigation of a £20 million nuclear submarine in the Barents Sea, the busy Western Approaches or the Mediterranean.

Wreford-Brown accordingly contrived to get himself sent on the navigation course run at the shore base HMS *Dryad* outside Portsmouth, and qualified as a specialist navigator in August 1971. He had hoped to be returned to an SSN but instead found himself posted as navigating officer to the SSBN *Repulse*, then undergoing her first refit in Rosyth. This naval dockyard in the Firth of Forth had been established as the maintenance base for the nuclear fleet. Along with the historic naval dockyard at Chatham, Rosyth was also equipped to replace the nuclear fuel in the submarines' reactors. Martin Macpherson – also serving as navigating officer – had taken the SSBN into refit a few months previously.

*

Like Toby Elliott in *Repulse*'s Port crew, Macpherson had now spent two years on Polaris patrols, and he was keen to move on. The job had not been without its challenges, however. Each patrol had to fulfil three objectives if the credibility of the Polaris deterrent was to be maintained: to remain undetected, to maintain constant communication with the Polaris command centre at Northwood in Middlesex, and to be ready to fire the Polaris missiles at short notice and at any time. These all required work.

The crucial advantage of a submarine over an aircraft as a means of delivering weapons lies in the fact that it is intrinsically difficult to detect. Under water it is effectively invisible, and sonar, with which it can be detected, is less efficient than its surface equivalent, radar. Moreover, the range of the Polaris missiles, even in their early variants, meant that a submarine such as *Repulse* could patrol vast areas while still being within range of its target cities in the Soviet Union. Polaris command could direct the boat to the Arctic Ocean, the Barents Sea, the North Sea, the Eastern Atlantic or the Mediterranean, or further afield to the Indian or Pacific Ocean, even if in practice she was likely to be closer to home – a House of Commons expenditure committee was told in 1972 that 'there was a great advantage in operating from the British continental shelf, under the protection of Nato, where anti-submarine warfare was difficult'.

Still, while *Repulse* might have been anywhere in these seas on patrol, the Soviets knew where she started from, and almost from the outset they made significant efforts to track boats on their departure from the Clyde and thence to their patrolling grounds. This was of course merely the mirror image of the West's own activities outside Soviet bases. To counter this, one of the various tasks of the Nato SSN fleet was to track their SSBN cousins on departure, to ensure that they were free from Soviet underwater escorts. This was an elaborate operation that also involved surface units and maritime patrol aircraft, known as delousing. Similarly, quiet though the SSBNs were, *Repulse* and her three sister-boats were by no means silent. The very action of a propeller on the sea creates energy in the form of sound, and much of the machinery aboard these boats was also noisy, the main coolant pumps for the reactors particularly so. The boats were accordingly vulnerable to Soviet listening devices, be they sonar aboard submarines or surface vessels, microphones fixed on the seabed or electronic buoys (called sonobuoys) dropped from aircraft. Like their Soviet counterparts they could also be detected by a system known as Magnetic Anomaly Detection. This measures changes in the earth's magnetic field caused by the passage of an 8,000-ton lump of ferrous metal in the shape of a submarine hull. Part of the task of the Polaris boats was accordingly to listen for the opposition and to distance themselves when necessary.

Besides the submarine's own sonar, the Polaris patrols also had access to intelligence on Soviet submarine activity derived from SOSUS. This was the acronym for the Sound Surveillance System, a net of underwater listening devices that the US Navy had begun to place on the seabed off the Atlantic and Pacific coasts in the 1950s. It was later extended to the choke-points through which the Soviet submarines were obliged to pass on their way to their patrol areas, and it would ultimately ring-fence the Soviet bases entirely. SOSUS first made its mark in July 1962 when a SOSUS array off Bermuda detected a Soviet HEN-class submarine as she approached the GIUK gap. As has been discussed, at the time at which the British Polaris patrols began, Nato submarines were a good deal quieter than their Soviet equivalents, making them difficult to detect; and they had better sonar, making it easier for them to detect the opposition. But while this all made the Soviet task difficult, it was by no means impossible.

The requirement to remain in contact with base was also more difficult to fulfil than might at first appear. Clearly the deterrent was not effective unless it was susceptible to command at a military, and ultimately a political, level. Although forbidden to transmit, for it is quite easy to source such transmissions, *Repulse* needed to be able to receive messages at any and all given times. No one could predict when crises such as that over Cuba might arise that could – at worst – require an atomic response. To receive command messages by low-frequency transmission *Repulse* trailed a wire hundreds of feet long that floated on the surface. Not surprisingly, however, both this aerial and the radio receiver were susceptible to failure.

Most difficult of all was the requirement that *Repulse* be ready to fire her missiles at what was in reality fifteen minutes' notice – and at all times. This demanded the successful interlocking of a whole series of different systems and technologies. First, the message to fire had to be successfully received and authenticated. Second, in order for the missiles to hit their target accurately, *Repulse* had to know where she was within a matter of yards. Third, for the same reasons, she had to be held virtually stationary in a status known as 'hover' when the missiles were fired. Finally, the whole weapons system comprising the sixteen Polaris missiles and the process whereby they were blown from their tubes needed to be operational. This capability was constantly monitored in the course of a patrol by drills known as weapons systems readiness tests. These started with a message from Northwood that might arrive at any time during the day or night. Martin Macpherson remembers looking forward to watching the first man land on the moon, set for the early hours of 20 July 1969. Northwood had sensitively timed the drill for immediately afterwards. The delay in the landing meant that the test occurred just as the lunar module was touching down.

Within such a complex process involving highly sophisticated machinery, the potential for human or mechanical failure was relatively high. The demands placed on the mechanical and weapons' officers to keep the submarine and missiles fully operational were enormous, and running repairs – and of course maintenance – had also to be undertaken on patrol. With a limited number of British deterrent submarines available even when all four were commissioned, there was never any question of returning to port to carry out repairs before the patrol's set period was complete. Willy-nilly, the boats had to be kept at sea and at operational readiness at all times. Not surprisingly, the Admiralty set great store by the maintenance of these patrols, keeping very extensive records of each patrol's movements and sonar contacts, and for this the officers of the boats carried the ultimate responsibility.

Within the US Navy, which had anything up to a dozen Polaris boats on patrol at any one time, there was inevitably less pressure on individual vessels and their officers. US submarines sometimes took a break in mid-patrol, they transmitted outgoing signals, and they regarded their periodic detection by Soviet vessels as an acceptable quid pro quo for a rather more relaxed deterrent stance. By contrast, the Royal Navy had only one boat or occasionally two on patrol. These vessels stood in the front line of the national deterrent and constituted the centrepiece of the defence of the realm. It was of the first importance that the patrols should go undetected. As Jeff Tall remarks, the political ramifications of detection would have been 'shattering'.

*

There were, too, more human challenges. The need for the patrol to be utterly secure removed *Repulse* from daily life in a much more definitive way than normal submarine operations. For seven or eight weeks at a time the crew were almost as isolated as they would have been in space. They were thrown back upon their own resources, were highly restricted in their physical movement, and had no choice in the company they were obliged to keep. As Alastair Mars the commander of the submarine *Unbroken* during the Second World War, wrote in his memoirs:

> Once we were afloat I would come to know [the men] well enough as individual personalities, for there is not even a pretence of privacy in the shoulder-rubbing, breath-down-the-neck confines of a submarine. Within a very short space of time everyone, from the Captain to the most junior Ordinary Seaman, would know everyone else's habits, idiosyncrasies, loves, hates, birthmarks, town of origin, pre-war job, political and religious beliefs, sex life and innermost thoughts. Rhapsodise, if you like, on that happy band of brothers this made us – and to a degree you would be right – but I knew that the inevitable time would come when a man's prayer to God

would be in effect: Please let me be alone for just five minutes, and then let me see a change of face.

The same was true of the Polaris patrols but, using a number of pro-cedures adopted from American practices, much was nevertheless done to keep the crew alert and amused. The Polaris boats were orga-nized on a three-watch plan, so that each man spent eight hours out of every twenty-four on duty. During this period, apart from day-to-day duties, he would also undergo special exercises and drills. A further eight hours was spent sleeping and eating, and the rest of the time was devoted to leisure. Some spent this reading in the relative privacy of their bunks. Others devoted themselves to hobbies ranging from knitting to modelling. Roger Lane-Nott remembers a complete Scalextric set on board *Revenge*. Films were immensely popular, and the latest releases were shown. In Macpherson's time the highlights were Stanley Kubrick's *A Clockwork Orange* and Francis Ford Coppola's *The Godfather*. There were also 'family-grams'. These were the short – thirty-word – personal messages sent once a week by the family of every submariner in the crew. Though they provided a vital link with the outside world, they could still be the cause of trouble if the domestic news was unhappy. Really bad news was another matter. Each member of the crew was required, before the patrol began, to state how he wished such news to be communicated to him, whether immediately, shortly before docking, or when the patrol was over. The majority opted for just before arrival.

Officers like Macpherson were as susceptible as anyone else to worries about those left behind, but they also carried the burden of responsibility for the patrol's *raison d'être*, ultimately that of firing a series of nuclear weapons that would devastate the population – civilian and military – of the Soviet Union. Given that Nato was a defensive alliance, the deterrent was designated a 'second strike' force. This meant that it would only be used if the Soviet Union had already successfully launched its own missiles. Macpherson's views were clear-cut and typified those of his contemporaries. He would defend a democratic society against attack by a totalitarian regime. Equally, he was resolute as to the validity of the deterrent. 'I never had any great misgivings about nuclear weapons. There were three or four people I knew or had heard of who resigned when we got

Polaris. The rest of us thought it was part of the job.' In fact, as a matter of course, all nuclear submariners were interviewed by the security services on the issue of nuclear weapons, the process being known as positive vetting.

It was not for all these reasons that Macpherson was keen to move on from the Polaris patrols. Soon after the nuclear boats became operational two distinct cultures emerged within the submarine fraternity. Officers in the attack boats disliked the tedium of the Polaris patrols and the absence of the cut-and-thrust that typified many SSK and SSN operations. At its simplest this was summarized by the fact that on encountering Soviet forces, the Polaris patrols were obliged to turn away from the threat, the SSNs to turn towards it. 'If you were any good, they'd have given you a full-time job,' an SSN officer would tease his SSBN counterpart.

In reality, these were different jobs requiring different skills. Macpherson's own temperament – outgoing, convivial, forceful – was certainly more suited to the attack boats. Early on in his time aboard *Repulse* these same characteristics had nearly got him into trouble with the authorities. Just around the peninsula from Faslane was the missile base at Coulport on Loch Long, where the Polaris missiles were stored and serviced. After a particularly demanding run ashore, Macpherson overslept and arrived at the base just in time to see his submarine sailing off into the distance. He had missed the boat on her hop round to Faslane. When *Repulse* docked at HMS *Neptune*, Macpherson was standing alongside the CO of the Polaris squadron, John Fieldhouse. *Repulse*'s CO, Tony Whetstone, shouted to Fieldhouse: 'What's small, black, sheepish and standing on a jetty?' From that day on, Macpherson, of medium build and with coal-black hair, was known as 'Black Mack'.

In a masterly piece of man-management, Whetstone forbore from alluding to the incident once during the entire seven-week patrol. Then, when *Repulse* docked, he summoned Macpherson to his cabin.

'I expect you've been wondering what I'm going to do about that Coulport business,' said the Commander.

'Yes,' said Macpherson with understatement, 'as a matter of fact, I have.'

'Nothing,' replied Whetstone.

Macpherson had already been recognized as one of the more gifted submariners of his generation, and the Navy was prepared to forgive lapses among such men.

That autumn Macpherson ran the officers' training course at *Dolphin* in what was supposed to be his last job in the Navy before his short-service commission came to an end. For Macpherson, this was a turning-point. He was 25 and recently married. He enjoyed the job enormously and − disciplinary matters apart − was highly regarded by the Navy. Once a year a Board sat to consider the cases of Supplementary List officers who wished to be transferred to the General List. Macpherson applied for a transfer and was one of the few accepted. He was then sent on a lieutenant's course, and appointed as First Lieutenant to a Porpoise-class boat based at *Dolphin*, the SSK *Rorqual*.

*

For half a dozen young submariners beginning to get a firm grasp of their profession, few events were more damaging to their confidence than the sinking on the evening of 1 July 1971 of the A-boat *Artemis* while she was secured at her moorings at *Dolphin* in Haslar Creek.

On deck at the time were Chief Petty Officer David Guest and several crewmen. As the boat began to sink, all those on deck with the exception of Guest jumped clear. Guest, who was the duty senior rating, rushed below to warn the remainder of the crew and three visiting naval cadets. He found the cadets and hustled them up the conning-tower. Then he returned to discover two other ratings. The three of them managed to clear the accommodation spaces as the water cascaded in, but escape up the conning-tower proved impossible. Instead they sought refuge in the torpedo compartment, shutting the water-tight door behind them. Within sixty seconds, *Artemis* had sunk to the bottom of Haslar Creek and the three were trapped, with sufficient air for about forty-eight hours.

A rescue operation began at once but at dawn the following morning the three men managed to escape from the forward torpedo hatch and swim the twenty feet to the surface. The submarine herself was raised ninety hours later. A Board of Inquiry into the incident, headed by the Flag Officer Submarines, Vice-Admiral John

Roxburgh, opened immediately. Within four months, the officer-of-the-day was facing a court-martial at which he would receive a severe reprimand.

The story that emerged at the court-martial was thoroughly discomforting. *Artemis* had come into Portsmouth for some minor repairs. Following their completion in the naval dockyard, she was towed across the harbour and into Haslar Creek. Few craft are at their best under tow, and a ballast tank was flooded during the short passage to improve her stability. When the tow was cast off and *Artemis* moored, a number of routine jobs needed to be accomplished. For these purposes a power line was run from the shore, snaking through almost the entire length of the boat and so running through the water-tight doors that divided her into compartments. A series of hatches were also opened. The chief stoker then began the process of filling the external fuel tanks. Before doing so he should have sought the permission of an officer. This would only have been given if the submarine's trim had been checked. Had this in turn been done, it would have revealed that the boat was low in the water, a consequence of the flooding of the ballast tank during the tow. Indeed, one of *Artemis*'s open hatches was only five inches above the waterline.

The filling of the external tanks on the A-boat involved first flooding them with water. While this was being done, at about 1300, *Artemis* began to settle in the water. At 1915 water lapped over the rear escape hatch and began to pour into the compartment below. Even in such an emergency, the crew would normally have been able to isolate the compartment by closing the water-tight doors. The electric cable prevented them from doing so. It was only by good fortune that the cable did not run all the way into the torpedo compartment, where the three ratings took refuge.

Soon the signal SUBSUNK was winging its way across the oceans of the globe to the entire submarine fleet. The signal dated from the sinking of *Poseidon* in the North China Sea in June 1931, and was designed to instigate a series of procedures to deal with such an eventuality as quickly as possible.

Although the US Navy SSN *Scorpion* had sunk with all hands in 1968, it was twenty years since the Royal Navy had lost *Affray* off the Channel Islands in April 1951, fourteen years since the loss of *Sidon* and thirteen men off Portland. The shock of *Artemis*'s sinking was profound, and it was exacerbated when the circumstances of the sinking emerged in the days following the ratings' escape and the raising of the boat from the bottom of the creek. 'I simply couldn't believe that we had made such complete and utter Charlies of ourselves,' says James Taylor.

In many respects, though, the sinking of *Artemis* was a timely reminder for the submarine service. Nuclear propulsion was still a relative novelty, *Dreadnought* having been commissioned less than nine years previously. The enormous responsibilities of carrying Britain's nuclear deterrent were even newer – the Navy had only formally accepted responsibility for the deterrent three years earlier. To cope with its new task, the service had been obliged to expand rapidly. Yet these multi-million-pound strategic weapons were being operated alongside submarines that dated from the Second World War, and they were occasionally treated in a similarly cavalier manner. Defending *Artemis*'s officer-of-the-day at the court-martial, Lieutenant-Commander Michael Everett – later to command the SSBN *Renown* – spoke of the strain that the introduction of the nuclear vessels had put on the submarine command, stating that many experienced officers had been lost to the new boats. The challenge for the Navy was to adjust to the new circumstances of the nuclear age, which required much higher levels of technical ability and greater professionalism all round.

Artemis was a call to order, fortunately issued without loss of life, which forced the submarine service into a period of introspection and self-doubt. In the view of contemporaries, the service learned its lesson and emerged the stronger for it. It was in any case a period in which the programme of nuclear-powered boats was turning the submarine service on its head, forcing it to abandon many traditions. *Artemis* served as a traumatic catalyst, a wake-up call. In the view of Martin Macpherson, submarining also became less fun thereafter.

Chapter 6
First Lieutenant

'The First Lieutenant (called "Number One" by his fellow officers, and known as "Jimmy" amongst the men) is responsible to his Captain for seeing that the ship *works*. He organises the watch-keeping, allots the men their duties, trains them, looks after their health and welfare, and in general keeps his finger on all the details that are vital to the smooth running and efficient operation of the ship. In submarines the First Lieutenant has an additional respon-sibility that is literally a matter of life or death – the Trim.'

Edward Young, *One of Our Submarines*, 1952

After his nuclear training at Greenwich, Jeff Tall was posted as supply officer to the SSN *Churchill*, attached to the Third Submarine Squadron in Faslane.

Faslane was a port Tall grew to dislike. Thrown together in the rush to provide a base for the new nuclear-powered submarines, HMS *Neptune* had been formally opened on 10 August 1968 by the Queen Mother. Despite Vice-Admiral Mackenzie's efforts, the base was a not particularly happy example of 1960s architecture. Indeed so bleak was the spectacle of the houses crawling up the side of the loch that it was nicknamed 'Moon City'. This impression was exac-erbated by the weather, which provided all the rain for which the west coast of Scotland is famous, at all seasons of the year. At the same time, although some sense of community had been established, the base had all the strengths but also all the weaknesses of being prin-cipally a naval establishment. Its inhabitants (over 7,000 of them in

1972) shared a common interest and common experiences, but it was difficult to escape from the confines of what amounted to barracks life. Hierarchy, too, was all pervasive. Tall, on moving into married quarters previously occupied by an officer of a higher rank, was surprised to see a man arrive with scissors to cut off the edge of the carpet. Tall's rank did not entitle him to the luxury of 'fitted'.

Churchill, though, was more satisfactory. She was an improved version of the SSN Valiant class and she was almost new, having been completed on 15 July 1970. Displacing 4,900 tons and with a crew of ninety-nine, she was also unique in being the first operational submarine in the world to use the revolutionary pump-jet system of propulsion. As its name suggests, this device drives the submarine by ingesting water and then expelling it in a jet from the stern. With the propeller effectively cowled, and with lots of small blades rather than four or five large ones, its vital advantage lies in the fact that it avoids the propulsion noises created by conventional propellers. Though there were initially problems associated with the system, particularly in boat-handling at low speeds, its introduction would keep British SSNs one step ahead of their Soviet counterparts for some time to come. *Churchill* also had much of her machinery mounted on rafts, thereby preventing the noise it made from being transmitted to the hull and thence to the water; and sound-deadening tiles on the outer surface of the hull would appear on later boats. All three innovations were British, and they established Britain's technological lead in what was called 'quiet running'. They also permitted a satisfying sense of one-upmanship in the friendly rivalry that existed between the United States and the British submarine fleets.

After the privations of the diesel-electric submarines, *Churchill* seemed the epitome of comfort. *The Times* ran a story on the submarine under the headline, 'Luxury for all in nuclear submarine.' In prose perhaps most suited to an interior design magazine, it described the predominant colour in the junior ratings' mess as 'ivory and kashmir walnut', and noted approvingly the senior ratings' 'formica design of grey gingham', and the officers' cabin, 'panelled in grey with ash furniture'. Each of the ninety-nine officers and men had his own bunk, and there was plenty of fresh water. There was even a cinema and a library. It was all a far cry from Tall's early days in the service in *Opossum* and *Thermopylae*. Indeed, American submariners moving from diesel-electric to nuclear boats said it was like 'dying and going to heaven'.

In his role of supply officer, Tall was provided with an unforgettable insight into the technical and personnel management of a modern nuclear submarine. 'If it was on board I knew about it, and if it wasn't and should have been, you knew pretty soon. Go short on beer and the Senior Ratings' Mess will soon let you know.' Equally he was given the opportunity to develop his 'officer-like qualities'. Confronted with a rating complaining about the quality of the fresh fruit supplied, Tall was invited to inspect a pear. The rating proposed making an official complaint, a tiresome bureaucratic procedure that offered few prospects of glory for the supply officer. 'It's inedible,' the rating grumbled. Tall promptly ate it, and then declared that it wasn't. That was the last he heard of the matter.

There were also more serious issues to consider. Despite the scepticism with which most submariners viewed the nuclear physicists at Greenwich, they were well schooled there both in nuclear theory and in the practicalities of the safe management of nuclear reactors. Once actually aboard a nuclear-powered submarine, officers and crew were then rigorously drilled in the routine of operating their particular power-plant, and they carried dosimeters to measure how much radiation they actually picked up. This system was further reinforced by visits from the Nuclear Safety Inspectorate. The duties of this unit included surprise inspections aboard the nuclear submarines to ensure that reactors and ancillary systems were maintained to high standards.

The importance of such precautions was in due course dramatically illustrated to Tall. One of the most important safety procedures aboard a nuclear submarine is the reactor safety check, carried out daily. Among other things this includes a check to ensure the integrity of the cooling system that carries away heat from the core, without which the reactor would melt down. In British and American submarine reactors there are two cooling systems. The first runs through the reactor and uses water under very high pressure to prevent it from boiling. Such systems are described as pressurized water reactors. In the process, this water inevitably becomes radioactive. Accordingly, the primary system that cools the reactor is itself cooled by a separate secondary system, which uses unpressurized water. Critically, although the two systems are connected by way of a heat exchanger so that the primary can be cooled by the secondary, the water in the systems does not intermingle. Thus the radioactive water is restricted to a relatively small closed circuit and cannot reach the turbines actually driving the boat, which for obvious reasons cannot be effectively treated to prevent the egress of radioactivity. Nevertheless, from time to time leaks in the system do occur. The most hazardous are those between the primary and the secondary systems, which are capable of contaminating the submarine. On one of Tall's first patrols in *Churchill* in the North Atlantic he was asked by one of the duty engineers for permission to run the daily safety check. It was 2300, and Tall was just about to go off duty. He gave his permission, and then went to the wardroom for a cup of coffee before turning in. Moments later he heard a buzzer going that alerted the engineer officer to a problem. It appeared that just such a leak had occurred. The standing orders for such a situation demanded that the reactor be immediately and completely shut down: in other words a full SCRAM. This was precisely what happened on *Churchill.* 'There was a thump,' says Tall, 'and the whole boat shook as the control rods dropped home.'

At the best of times, the total loss of power in a submarine is a difficult situation to manage. Nuclear submarines have back-up battery power, but this is of limited capacity, and a modern SSN uses a vast amount of energy. *Churchill,* like all her class, also had two small back-up diesel engines to be used in just such an eventuality. This, though, meant taking the boat up to periscope depth so that the diesels could draw in air from the surface to burn their fuel. *Churchill* rose to periscope depth to find that it was blowing a gale, with Force 10 winds and high rolling seas. SSN submarines are designed principally to run quickly and smoothly under water, and are not at their best in such circumstances. Lacking the keel of a yacht, in heavy weather they roll horribly: hence the old submariner's saying, 'Happiness is six hundred feet in a Force 10.' Tall continued:

An SSN is just not designed to spend hours at periscope depth. You've got to keep your snort mast above twenty-foot waves with the boat running at about 6 knots and rolling between 10°

and 15° – it's just a battle with the elements. Getting about the boat was tricky, cooking was impossible and you certainly wouldn't risk even boiling a kettle.

As it turned out, the alarm was false, and there was no leak between the two systems. Nevertheless, it took ten hours plugging against the gale to get *Churchill*'s reactor up and running again.

Tall's experience aboard *Churchill* stood him in good stead, and in 1973 he was appointed First Lieutenant of the Porpoise-class SSK *Ocelot*. After nine years in the Navy and seven in submarines, he was to be second-in-command of a submarine, with all the responsibilities that such a position brings.

The First Lieutenant is charged with ensuring that the crew and the vessel are in running order. Given the nature of submarine patrols, he is also in sole charge whenever the CO is asleep. And though it is principally the captain's job to stamp his personality – his way of doing things – on his vessel, in practice care is taken to ensure that COs and their First Lieutenants are complementary characters: experience has taught that pairs of – say – tartars or pairs of more easy-going characters tend to be unsatisfactory. This in turn means that the second-in-command has at least some opportunity to develop his own ideas as to how he will do things. The bright and ambitious ones do just that, and woe betide those members of the crew who let him down. As John Moore says, 'If the First Lieutenant says the boat is ready for sea, it is. And if it isn't, heads will roll.' Martin Macpherson takes a similar line on the difficulties of the job. 'Being First Lieutenant is really the worst job in the world, with all the responsibilities of command and none of the power. You get little thanks when the job's done well, and you collar all the blame when things go wrong.' With hindsight, Jeff Tall is inclined to take a slightly broader view, regarding the post as one element of a three-man team that really controls the submarine on a second-by-second basis: the First Lieutenant, the Coxswain and the Chief Engine Room Artificer. 'You're the triumvirate who make things happen.' In the end, though, even he found the job profoundly frustrating. 'It's a horrible job, like having sex with fourteen condoms on – all effort and no pleasure.' Nevertheless, it is a step on the ladder of promotion.

In fact, by this stage about a third of all submarine officers had either left the service or would clearly not be put forward for the greatest hurdle of all: the commanding officers' qualifying course, known as Perisher, that lay between First Lieutenant and command. Those remaining officers approaching an appropriate degree of seniority and merit were assessed by their COs using an XYZ/123 grading system. Y1 indicated that the officer was not yet ready for the course, but that he would be very good in due course. X2 was sufficient to win a place. Tall was told by his CO on *Ocelot*, Barry Wallace, that he had rated him X1 – a first-class candidate, ready now. A necessary preliminary to Perisher itself, though, was Tall's transfer from the Supplementary to the General List. When the signal marking this transfer came through, Tall was understandably puzzled to find that his name was not on it, and confronted his CO. Wallace realized that he had failed to make the special application necessary for the transfer. Rather than bluster his way out of the situation, however, he sent a signal explaining the position to the Ministry of Defence and the Flag Officer Submarines. The signal began with the unconventional phrase, 'I have fucked up.'

*

Toby Elliott, too, was approaching the rubicon of Perisher. He had enjoyed his two years in the Port crew of *Repulse* rather more than Martin Macpherson in Starboard. He had been fascinated by the process of building the SSBN, working her up to operational readiness and then embarking on the pioneer Polaris patrols; and he had also made a series of lifelong friendships. Transferred to the General List in 1969, he had left *Repulse* to become a torpedo and anti-submarine specialist at HMS *Vernon* in Portsmouth, and there he became interested in sonar. Major technological improvements had recently been made, and there was much new equipment to get to grips with. Elliott soon became sufficiently knowledgeable to be asked to teach the subject for a year at the submariners' school at *Dolphin*.

There were two systems then in use. The first was 'passive' sonar, which is simply a series of hydrophones used to detect sound emitted by a target on a variety of frequencies. Since sound travels well in water, and since the early Cold War Soviet submarines were so noisy, this was a useful tool, although it rarely allowed the range or identity of the target to be defined, merely the direction of the sound – its bearing. 'If you were lucky, you could pick up a noisy liner at something like 20 miles,' says Elliott. At the same time, though, special techniques were being developed to detect low-frequency sounds, which could be picked up over very considerable distances. These were now just beginning to be implemented. Some of the submarines were also experimenting with an American invention called towed array, a series of hydrophones attached to a line that was trailed behind the submarine. In due course this would enable sounds to be detected at a far greater distance.

The second system was active sonar, originally called ASDIC after the Anglo-French Allied Submarine Detection Committee, set up during the First World War. This works by emitting a wave of sound which, when it strikes an object, echoes back to a hydrophone. Measuring the time taken for the echo to return provides the target's range. Typically, active sonar can detect targets at a much greater distance than its passive equivalent. Indeed by 1980 a Soviet submarine undergoing trials in the Norwegian Sea could be heard by the US Navy in Bermuda. However, active sonar has two disadvantages. If it is used over a long range, it requires a vast amount of power, normally that which only a nuclear reactor can provide; and its use, creating the characteristic 'ping' so often featured in Second World War films, discloses the presence of the user.

Though both systems are simple enough in principle, in practice their use is complicated by a number of factors. The speed of sound in water varies with temperature, pressure and salinity, and these in turn vary depending on the submarine's depth, its geographical location in the water and even the time of year. This means that the same signal on a sonar read-out can mean a number of different things, depending upon these variables. As a consequence, sonar interpretation is more of an art than it is a science. A contemporary article in *The Times* reported that at *Dolphin* there were 'teaching machines to give instructions on underwater noises so that those using sensitive listening systems can distinguish between the squeaks of whales or porpoises, the odd noises that shrimps can make, or other noises from the deep, and more aggressive noises emanating from enemy submarines'.

Having been brought up to date on the most recent sonar developments, in 1972 Elliott returned to sea as First Lieutenant on *Alliance*. The last but one of the Second World War A-boats to be commissioned, she had suffered two major accidents just before Elliott joined. In the process of charging, batteries give off hydrogen, so in the enclosed space of a submarine care is taken to vent the gas from the battery spaces to prevent the risk of an explosion. One night in September 1971 while *Alliance* was charging her batteries alongside in Portland Harbour, the ventilation system failed. The subsequent explosion caused by a spark killed one man and injured fourteen. Then, following five months in dock to repair the damage, she was taken out for a test dive in February 1972. One of the First Lieutenant's most important responsibilities is the trim, the total weight of the boat that dictates its overall level of buoyancy and its distribution forward and aft of the centre of gravity. Despite indications that *Alliance* was heavy forward, the order to dive was given. In fact she was so out of trim that she plunged straight to the sea bottom, fortunately in the relatively shallow waters of Plymouth Sound. Her First Lieutenant was severely reprimanded, and Elliott was sent out to replace him.

Not surprisingly, *Alliance*'s crew had been thoroughly unsettled by these incidents, and it was a challenge for Elliott to take them in hand, restore their confidence in the boat and her leadership, and instil an appropriate degree of professionalism. Elliott, though still only 28, was beginning to relish his job. A firm disciplinarian with a strong sense of duty, he regarded himself as particularly fortunate to be approaching real levels of responsibility in the service at a time when a tremendous cross-pollination was occurring both between the nuclear and the conventional boats, and between the SSBN Polaris patrol boats and the SSN attack boats. Increasingly he felt he had been born for the job.

*

In the last year of her final commission, *Alliance* was of little value as a front-line operational boat, and in fact just keeping her running was a challenge. She spent most of the time acting as the opposition in fleet exercises in the Atlantic and the Mediterranean. These involved the submarine operating against Nato anti-submarine warfare units in set-piece exercises designed to provide the maximum of experience.

Such exercises were necessary, for by now – at Gorshkov's instigation – Soviet naval forces were deploying well beyond their home waters. In the early days of the Cold War, the Atlantic, the Gulf of Mexico, the Gulf of California, the eastern Pacific and the west coast of the United States had generally been recognized as the territory of America and her allies. By the same token, the Soviets regarded the Black Sea and the Baltic as their own. Although there had been a limited amount of maritime activity by East and West beyond these areas during the Korean War and the Cuban missile crisis, on the whole the spheres of influence were respected. Then, in May 1962, a US Navy anti-submarine force led by the carrier USS *Wasp* was deployed in the Baltic. She was ostensibly on a visit to Kiel, but her presence was also regarded as a demonstration that the Baltic constituted international waters. Shortly afterwards the Soviet Navy began deployments to the Mediterranean and – as noted earlier – from June 1964 it established a permanent anchorage off the island of Kithira close to Crete. Here, by means of a series of depot ships supplied on a regular basis, the Soviets provided themselves with what amounted to a blue-water port, removing the need to return to the Black Sea to refuel and reprovision. From this new base they also began to visit ports in the eastern Mediterranean, and they ventured out through the Straits of Gibraltar into the Atlantic. The number of ships deployed in the Mediterranean grew steadily, culminating, as has been seen, in the deployment of seventy ships during the Six-Day War in 1967.

Subsequently, the Soviet Mediterranean presence continued, with anything up to fifty ships generally at sea at once. Increasingly, too, Soviet SSN attack submarines and guided-missile SSGNs were sent to trail US SSBNs operating from a base at Rota, close to Cadiz in Spain, which together with Holy Loch and Guam in the Pacific were the only US SSBN bases outside America. At the same time, US and British submarines began to watch the Kithira anchorage and the eastern Mediterranean ports where the Soviets sometimes replenished their vessels. Given the close interest that each side was beginning to take in the other's activities, contact of one kind or another was inevitable. In December 1967 there occurred the first reported collision between a Nato submarine, the US SSBN *George C. Marshall,* and a Soviet submarine in the Mediterranean. The sea had become established as the latest arena of the Cold War, where each superpower displayed its prowess to the opposition, as if in parody of a ritualized courtship. In addition, each side carefully surveyed, photographed and monitored the other. Rivalry extended to even minor matters – Nato ships barbecued beef on their fantails and let the smoke drift down towards their Soviet counterparts, who were rarely so well fed, while US sailors in their alcohol-free ships watched the Soviets swill beer with envy.

In order to counter the Soviet threat in the Mediterranean, Nato forces were obliged to develop co-ordinated tactics. Two factors made this a difficult task. First, the SOSUS acoustic net did not then cover the Mediterranean. Second, sonar detection was difficult, particularly in the Straits of Gibraltar where cold salt water meets fresh water from the land. Nevertheless, Nato focused on developing further the standard anti-submarine techniques used against German U-boats during the war. These involved the deployment of aircraft, helicopters, surface ships and submarines, all working together to locate the enemy.

In the absence of SOSUS, it was likely to be a sonar on a submarine that first picked up a contact, be it a Soviet submarine or *Alliance* posing as such. Like SOSUS, the new sonar units on such submarines used low-frequency detectors to pick up sounds made by another submarine at a considerable distance. At this point a maritime patrol aircraft or a helicopter might be called in. Both could drop a series of sonobuoys in the area in which the contact had been made to try to narrow down the search, and aircraft might also use Magnetic Anomaly Detection with the same object, or a sensor system that can detect diesel fumes from a snorkelling submarine. Then, on the assumption that a better fix on the contact had been achieved, the local commander would call in whatever units were at his disposal to narrow the search right down and get a real trail set up. This might well take the form of another submarine. As the Royal Navy and RAF Coastal Command had discovered in the course of the Second World War, such operations require patience, tactical acumen in guessing what the opposition might do in any given circumstances, and a considerable slice of luck.

It was also the role of Nato submarines in these waters periodically to carry out surveillance exercises known as 'underwater looks', in which a submarine would approach very close to a ship's bottom so as to photograph and film such features as the propeller and fittings such as sonar domes, special sensors and ship control surfaces. It was an exercise often used against Soviet vessels, both submarines and surface ships, and it could be highly dangerous, for it sometimes required the submarine to pass as close as six feet below the vessel it was surveying. This, in a modest swell, left little margin for error. In *Submarine*, on the subject of what the US Navy calls 'underhulling', Tom Clancy comments: 'This is so difficult that captains of US submarines are almost never ordered to try it, as bumping a target can be non career-enhancing. On the other hand, successfully gathering hull shots is a sure sign that the boat's skipper has the right stuff and is worthy of promotion to a higher rank.' Woodward calls it merely 'a useful technique which is not needed very often'.

Despite such occasional excitements, Elliott in *Alliance* found these Nato exercises less riveting than his SSBN patrols, though he enjoyed running the submarine as First Lieutenant, and he was given the opportunity to hone his attacking skills under the tutelage of his CO, Lieutenant-Commander David Pender-Cudlip. It had to be admitted, too, that Mediterranean patrols did at least involve some attractive ports of call.

After a year in *Alliance*, and with the all-important recommendation for Perisher from Pender-Cudlip, Elliott was sent as third hand and torpedo and anti-submarine warfare officer to a submarine then being built in Barrow-in-Furness. *Sovereign* was one of the new class of Swiftsure attack boats that were to form the second generation of British SSNs and that had survived Denis Healey's 1966 Defence Review. Their appearance was a recognition of Britain's obligations to Nato, and of the continuing need for submarine activity in the North Atlantic to protect the SSBN force. Shorter and faster than the Dreadnought/Valiant class, and carrying five rather than six 21-inch torpedo tubes, the 4,900-ton Swiftsures had a hull form that allowed them to dive deeper than their predecessors. They were also better equipped in terms of sonar, and they were considerably quieter. And unsurprisingly, they were very much more expensive, averaging out at more than double the £20 million that each of the Valiants had cost.

Though Elliott established himself and his family at Bouth, between Coniston and Windermere, and bought his first house, he did not in the end go to sea in *Sovereign*. Her building programme was delayed by a fire caused by a welder's torch. Instead, he was selected to go on the submarine commanding officers' qualifying course, the Perisher.

*

Roger Lane-Nott had also been given his nuclear grounding on the Polaris submarines, undertaking three patrols on *Revenge*, the second of the two Polaris boats built by Cammell Lairds and the last of the four British SSBNs to be commissioned. Then, early in 1972, he was appointed navigating officer on *Conqueror*, attached to the Third Submarine Squadron in Faslane. Completed by Cammell Lairds on 9 November 1971, *Conqueror* was a sister-boat to Jeff Tall's *Churchill*, and Lane-Nott served in her under a succession of three commanding officers. The most demanding of these was Commander Chris 'Sharkey' Ward. Ward ran a very tight ship in which everyone was supposed to be up to the mark – and more. In particular he instilled in his young officers the need for responsibility. It was their job not simply to issue orders but to ensure that the task had actually been carried out. 'He was a complete tartar,' says Lane-Nott, 'but in twenty months he doubled my level of knowledge of submarine operations.'

One of Lane-Nott's more memorable experiences occurred on New Year's Eve 1972. The IRA was then running guns across the Irish Sea for use in its campaign on the mainland, and submarines were occasionally deployed to catch them red-handed. On 30 December 1972 intelligence indicated that a gun-running attempt was to be made, and *Conqueror* was scrambled. 'This was a bugger', says Lane-Nott, 'because a fair number of the crew were on leave. But we got them back, every single one, including a senior rating all the way from the Isle of Wight.' No sooner was the SSN at sea, however, than she was diverted to bigger game. There were indications from SOSUS that a Soviet submarine was in the Clyde area, a hazard for any outbound or inbound British SSBN. Like the Soviet presence in the Mediterranean that required the use in fleet exercises of *Alliance*, here was evidence that Admiral Gorshkov's arm had grown even longer. Lane-Nott refers to the period as 'the time when the Soviets started turning up on our doorstep'.

Conqueror's first job was to find the Soviet intruder. This was easier said than done. SOSUS is a passive sonar system, indicating the presence of a submarine – or at least a source of submarine-like noise – but not its precise location. Instead it indicates an area within which the target can be found, an area that might be a box a hundred miles square, sometimes more. In practice, however, the number of routes that a submarine can take through the Clyde area is limited, and in this case *Conqueror*, using her own passive sonar, found her quarry without great difficulty.

One of the curiosities of any ship is that she emanates her own distinct spectrum of sound. This is particular not simply to a class of vessel but to an individual hull, so much so that it is called a signature or fingerprint. One of the routine tasks of any Nato patrol by surface or submarine units was to record the sound signature of Soviet vessels. These were then placed in a library of such sounds, accessible by computer, so that when the submarine was again detected, it could be identified. In this case SOSUS had provisionally identified the submarine as a Soviet Victor-class SSN. *Conqueror* was eventually available to confirm this.

This was the first identified incursion of a Soviet submarine into an area close to the Clyde submarine base, and the protocol for dealing with such an incident, more specifically the Rules of Engagement for British boats, had not been formulated. *Conqueror* signalled submarine command in Northwood for orders. The duty officer could do no better than, 'Oh, chase them off, I suppose.'

This, too, was easier said than done. A surface ship can signal its aggressive intentions to another ship by training its guns on it, firing shells over or in front of it or cutting across its bows. These work because each CO can see what the other is up to. A submarine below periscope depth has no eyes, and such ears as it possesses – active and passive sonar – have distinct limitations. The sound the submarine itself makes as it forces its way through the water means that its passive sonar is useless at speeds of more than 5 or 6 knots. And without the use of active sonar, no submarine can be certain of the position of another, unless it is very close. Instead it has to work on assumptions – assumptions that are complicated by the fact that the game is three- rather than two-dimensional. Blind man's bluff is a fair comparison, although the consequences of a mistake on the part of either CO are clearly very far from entertaining.

Moreover, even at this relatively early point in the submarine Cold War, an element of brinkmanship existed between submarine commanders. Like a couple of racing-car drivers approaching a corner, the question was who would brake first. Those submarine COs who suspected they were being trailed would try all sorts of tricks to shake off the opposition, stopping dead in the water, diving or climbing abruptly, or rapidly reversing course. Given that neither submarine could see the other, it was not surprising that encounters could be very close. Submarine COs might also order the outer doors of the torpedo tubes to be opened, one of the most obvious preparatory stages in the firing process, and quite easily heard by another submarine at close range. At no stage in the Cold War was it definitively known whether Soviet submarine COs had permission to fire on their Nato opposite numbers, and if so in what circumstances. In *The Hunt for Red October*, Tom Clancy rightly concluded that, 'The submariner's trade required more than skill. It required instinct, and an artist's touch; monomaniacal confidence, and the aggressiveness of a professional boxer.'

After an encounter that Lane-Nott describes as within 500 yards – 'and that's damn close' – the Soviet intruder withdrew. The incident led to a number of changes in procedure ranging from the division of command between the Clyde and Northwood, to standing orders on encountering Soviet submarines in home waters, and to the introduction of centralized submarine operational control.

Lane-Nott now anticipated a First Lieutenant's posting. As it was, he was sent as temporary replacement to the A-boat *Aeneas*, whose own First Lieutenant had broken his jaw in an accident. Three weeks later, the usual six-monthly promotions signals came through to the A-boat's wireless office. Among them was the Perisher signal. 'The following officers have been selected for the

Commanding Officers' Qualifying Course.' Lane-Nott was on the list at the age of 29.

*

Meanwhile, Nixon and Kissinger's policy of détente was beginning to bear fruit. In February 1972, Nixon visited China, the first US president ever to do so. Already relations between the two countries had eased. US nationals were allowed to visit China, most famously a group of American table-tennis players; the twenty-one-year-old trade embargo was partially lifted; and the regular patrol by the US Seventh Fleet of the Taiwan Straits in support of Nationalist Taiwan was halted. Now Nixon met the Chinese leader Zhou Enlai to discuss American withdrawal from Vietnam and the further lifting of the trade embargo. On his return to the United States he declared, 'This was the week that changed the world.' In fact the visit had been more symbolic than practical, but it did help to lessen tensions. Moreover, the prospect of a rapprochement between the United States and China, alarming to the Soviet Union, was also a useful negotiating tool.

Three months later the President dispatched Kissinger to Moscow. In the course of secret talks with Brezhnev, progress was made on the bargaining that would culminate in America's withdrawal from Vietnam. They also discussed arms control. The Strategic Arms Limitations Talks, otherwise known as SALT, had been dragging on since 1969. In the meantime, the Soviet Union had narrowed the missile gap, and the Americans had developed an anti-ballistic missile defence system (ABM) in response to a Soviet system of questionable value set up around Moscow. On 22 May 1972, Nixon flew to Moscow. Again, he was the first US president to do so.

Though that year marked the fiftieth anniversary of the foundation of the Soviet Union, the Eastern bloc was not a workers' paradise. The economy was stagnant. The state had signally failed to provide the sort of social welfare enjoyed in the West. There was also as much unrest as might be admitted within a police state. In Lithuania and Latvia there were nationalist demonstrations. Agitation for reform in Czechoslovakia continued. And in Moscow itself a Human Rights Committee had been formed, one of its

1. On 9 August 1945 the mushroom cloud that characterizes the explosion of an atomic weapon rises high above Nagasaki. Four days earlier, a similar bomb had exploded at Hiroshima. Over 100,000 died in the two explosions that marked the beginning of the nuclear age. As President Kennedy would declare after the Soviet Union had acquired the bomb, 'every man, woman and child . . . lives under a nuclear sword of Damocles, hanging by the slenderest of threads, capable of being cut at any moment by accident, madness or miscalculation'

2. Early in the Second World War, Edward Young undertook his first dive and was astonished 'that a submerged submarine could see so much of the outside world'. A quarter of a century later, the Dartmouth class of '63 were similarly surprised. Here is the Tribal-class frigate *Ashanti* seen through the periscope of a British submarine

3. The first post-war British submarine design, the SSK Porpoise/Oberon class, was a diesel-electric superficially the descendant of vessels that had served the Royal Navy so well in the course of the Second World War. In fact, it owed much to the revolutionary German Type XXI U-boat. This is *Orpheus,* commissioned in 1960. The structure on the bow is the sonar dome

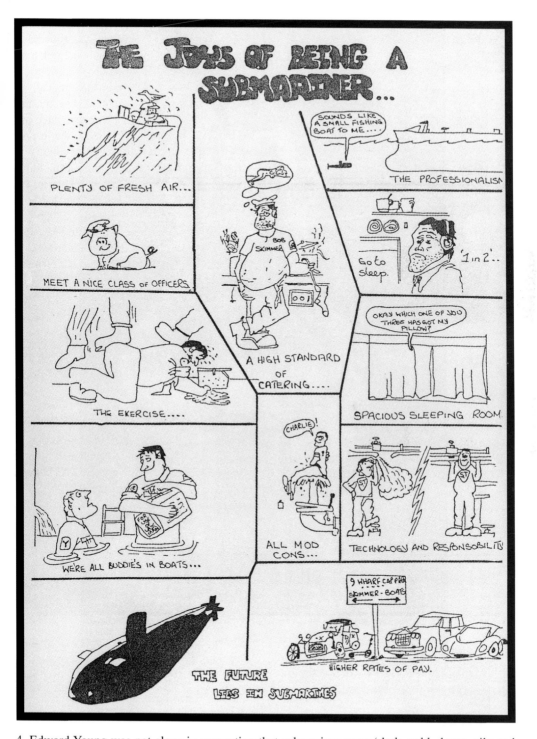

4. Edward Young was not alone in suspecting that submarines were 'dark, cold, damp, oily and cramped, full of intricate machinery'. These cartoons from *Thumper*, the magazine of the SSN *Churchill*, well summarize both the physical discomforts that submariners endure and the sense of fraternity that this inspires. James Perowne, a distinguished Cold War submariner and Flag Officer Submarines in its aftermath, remarks, 'It's not the men who make the machines, but the machines who make the men'

5. 'The two most powerful nations in the world had been squared off against one another, each with its finger on the button.' Nikita Khrushchev's words highlight how close the world came to a full-scale nuclear exchange in October 1962. Here a Soviet cargo ship carrying missiles on her deck leaves Cuba *en route* for Russia after the missile crisis was resolved. Nonetheless, the world had for six days teetered on the brink of nuclear war

6. Admiral Sergei Gorshkov, Commander-in-Chief of the Soviet Navy, 1956–85. Under his leadership, Soviet naval forces were transformed from little more than a coastal defence force to a blue-water command capable of mounting operations almost anywhere in the world. His most startling achievement lay in submarines, starting in 1956 with the first such craft in the world capable of firing a nuclear missile. Soon nuclear-powered vessels appeared, called the Hotel/Echo/November classes by the US Navy, and by 1967 no fewer than three new classes of craft were at sea – the Victor SSN, the Charlie SSGN and the Yankee SSBN

7. Military parades in Moscow's Red Square were among the more graphic and public demonstrations of Soviet power during the Cold War. Widely covered by the world's press, they provided a showcase for military developments. Nuclear missiles first appeared in the shadow of the Kremlin on 7 November 1960. This is the city's own garrison parading exactly eight years later

8. Martin Macpherson, a leading member of the class of '63, here pictured on the bridge of the Porpoise-class SSK *Rorqual*, in which he served as First Lieutenant in the run-up to his Perisher. His appearance is evidence of the demands of these boats, which encouraged neither uniforms nor shaving. In its early days submarining was regarded as 'no occupation for a gentleman'

9. The launch of the nuclear deterrent submarine, the 8,500-ton SSBN *Resolution* on 15 September 1966, represented a remarkable achievement. Britain had agreed to acquire the Polaris missile system from the United States in 1962, and had then set about building submarines to carry them, establishing a base from which they could be operated, and training officers and men to crew them. The project was completed on budget and on time. Its driving force, Vice-Admiral Hugh Mackenzie, wrote, 'God grant the weapon never be used'

10. *Warspite*, the third of Britain's nuclear-powered attack submarines and immensely more capable than the diesel-electrics she superseded. Her nuclear reactor gave her a sustained underwater speed approaching 25 knots, and since the power source did not require a source of oxygen for combustion she was a genuine submarine rather than a submersible. Under the command of Sandy Woodward, in 1970 *Warspite* undertook one of the earliest British SSN patrols to the Barents Sea. Another of the class of '63, Chris Wreford-Brown, was her casing and correspondence officer

11. James Taylor, a contemporary of Macpherson and Wreford-Brown, at the periscope of *Orpheus*, the Oberon-class boat that was his second command, in 1977. Submarine command was an ambition he had nurtured since first seeing a submarine coming into Campbeltown. 'They were mysterious, exciting, dangerous and – I thought – heroic. I was absolutely captivated by them'

12. A dramatic shot of the SSN *Dreadnought* in the Arctic. When the Soviet Union first deployed nuclear missiles on submarines, the missiles' short range obliged the craft to patrol close to the European and US seaboards. As Soviet missile technology improved, the SSBN force could withdraw into the wastes of the Pacific and the Atlantic, where they were far harder to find. By the end of the 1970s the 7,800-kilometre range of the SS-N-18 meant that they could target the major Western cities without leaving their bases. They could also retreat under the superb cover provided by the Arctic ice-cap. Martin Macpherson was sent to the Arctic in the SSN *Valiant* to discover ways of tracking and destroying them there

13. *Dreadnought,* the first of the British nuclear-powered attack submarines. Completed on 17 April 1964, she was every bit as revolutionary as the great First World War battleships with which she shared her name. In this shot from the stern, her unusually angled diving planes can be clearly seen. In 1976, Martin Macpherson was her Executive Officer when she was dispatched to the Falklands at the behest of the Foreign Secretary David Owen

14. *Dreadnought*'s controls were by no means dissimilar to those of an aircraft, two planesmen – one port, one starboard – controlling her heading, depth, and speed of ascent and descent

15. *Spartan*'s commissioning ceremony. *Spartan* was one of the six-boat Swiftsure class, the second generation of British SSN submarines. Faster than the Dreadnought/Valiants, they could dive deeper, and above all they were quieter. *Spartan* was James Taylor's first nuclear command. 'After *Orpheus*, it was a bit like getting out of a Ford Sierra and into a Formula 1 car.' Taylor saw action with *Spartan* during the Falklands conflict. Fighting alongside her were several other SSNs, including her sister-ship *Splendid,* commanded by another of the class of '63, Roger Lane-Nott

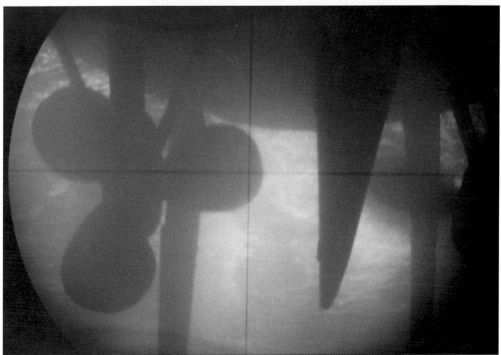

17. A bearded Chris Wreford-Brown (*far right*) brings the SSN *Conqueror* home to Faslane at the end of the Falklands War. On 2 May 1982, Wreford-Brown made history as commander of the first British submarine to fire a torpedo in anger since the Second World War. The sinking of the Argentinian cruiser *General Belgrano* was a turning-point in the war, and a vivid example of the capabilities of an SSN. The Jolly Roger was a token of this success, a tradition initiated by Max Horton during the First World War

16. (*left*) The 'under-water look', one of a series of surveillance techniques used by British Cold War submariners. This shot is of a Royal Fleet Auxiliary. Soviet surface ships and submarines were the more normal quarry. A surprising amount of information can be so garnered, dangerous though the technique is: hunter and hunted come within feet of one another

18. *Trafalgar*, the culmination of British Cold War SSN engineering and expertise. An improved version of the Swiftsures, the first boat in the class was taken out of build by Martin Macpherson and commissioned in May 1983. Her first patrol was sufficiently successful for Macpherson to be awarded the OBE. She was then taken over by another of the class of '63, Toby Elliott

19. Toby Elliott (*right*) on the bridge of *Trafalgar*. Like James Taylor, Elliott had long nurtured an ambition to join the Navy; and like Macpherson and Lane-Nott, he had served on the British SSBN Polaris boats before passing the commanding officers' qualifying course – Perisher – and being given his own command, first of the SSK *Otter,* then the SSBN *Resolution*, and finally *Trafalgar*

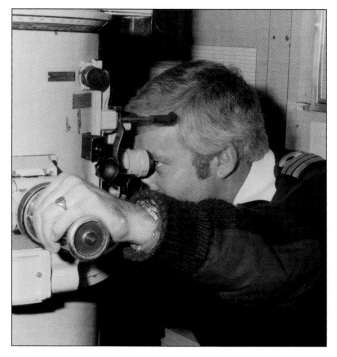

20. Jeff Tall at the periscope of his first nuclear command, the SSN *Churchill*. Edward Young wrote: 'Efficient periscope work demands a constant and deliberate act of the imagination. All the time you have to say to yourself, "At this very moment an enemy vessel may be approaching just beyond the horizon".' Although advances in technology have gradually diminished reliance on the periscope, its meticulous use is still of paramount importance

21. The replacement by the Americans of the Polaris missile system by the far more powerful Trident required both the US and the Royal Navy to develop large new submarines to accommodate the 13-metre Trident missiles. The 18,700-ton *Ohio* was laid down in 1976 and commissioned in 1981. Britain followed suit with *Vanguard*, the first of four new SSBNs. The 16,000-ton *Vanguard* displaced almost twice as much as the Polaris boats, and was laid down in 1985. This is her sister-ship *Vigilant* surfacing at a much steeper angle of ascent than normal

22. The Soviet equivalent of the NATO missile boats was the monstrous SSBN Typhoon. With a displacement of between 25,000 and 30,000 tons, this is by far and away the largest submarine ever constructed, the scale of which is suggested by the crew on the bridge. Tom Clancy took this submarine, apparently designed specifically for use in the Arctic, as his subject in *The Hunt for Red October*. This helicopter shot is taken from James Taylor's archive of his patrol of the Barents Sea in 1989

23. The fall of the Berlin Wall on 6 November 1989 was the culmination of a series of events that swept through Eastern Europe in the course of that year, and one that heralded the dissolution of the Soviet Union and the Warsaw Pact, and the end of the Cold War. Not without reason, President George Bush talked of a new world order, one from which the threat of global holocaust had very largely been lifted

24. A London reunion on 1 February 2001 of (*seated, left to right*) Jeff Tall, James Taylor, Martin Macpherson, (*standing, left to right*) Roger Lane-Nott and Toby Elliott. Together with Chris Wreford-Brown, these half dozen submariners are representative of the generation that played a significant part in the waging of the Cold War, worthy successors of Churchill's 'Few'

founders the nuclear scientist Andrei Sakharov. In the light of these inconveniences, the Kremlin viewed Nixon's visit as welcome public recognition of the status of the Soviet Union as a superpower. On 26 May 1972 Nixon and Brezhnev signed the Strategic Arms Limitation Treaty (SALT 1) and the ABM treaty, thereby placing an upper limit on the number of offensive and defensive missiles that each side could hold.

All this was a far cry from the tensions that had culminated in the Cuban missile crisis ten years earlier, and it seemed to represent a turning-point in the Cold War. In reality the two treaties froze the military balance. Each side could destroy the other but only by guaranteeing its own end. The world was still highly vulnerable to, in Kennedy's phrase, 'accident, miscalculation or madness', but at least some sort of stability had been attained, and at least some means of control over the spiralling costs of the arms race had been established.

For Nixon, however, this achievement was soon to be compromised. As the class of '63 prepared for Perisher, the American President began to face accusations that, in the build-up to the presidential elections of 1972, he had authorized the burglary of the Watergate Building, the Democratic Party's headquarters in Washington.

Chapter 7

Perisher

'For all the costs, just what does the Perisher course produce?
Arguably the world's finest quality submarine captains. Perisher is the
Royal Navy's commitment to making sure that the men who
command their submarines are as good as the boats themselves. With
only about twenty submarines in the force, they feel they *must* have
them commanded by the very best . . . it is a course unlike anything
else in any other service.'

Tom Clancy, *Submarine*, 1993

There is an established ritual surrounding admission to the élite cadre
of Royal Navy submarine commanding officers. The commanding
officers' qualifying course, or Perisher as it is known, is a five-month
ordeal that culminates at sea. Those who pass – at least one in four
fail – are called from the submarine's control-room to her wardroom.
There sits Teacher, the instructor who has guided, cajoled and
encouraged his candidates through the course. He rises to his feet,
puts on his cap and shakes the successful candidate's hand: 'Welcome
to the most exclusive club in the world.' This is the dream of almost
every man who has ever served in a submarine, what James Taylor
and his contemporaries regarded as 'the glittering prize'.

The training course for submarine commanders was originally
called the Periscope School. Started in the last year of the Great War,
it gradually evolved to focus on three areas. Its principal concern was
safety, for it was on the second-by-second decisions of the CO that
the crew's lives depended, and it was critical that his competence in

this area be beyond question. Second, the candidates had to show their ability to carry out the variety of operational tasks undertaken by submarines, from simple ship-handling tasks such as coming alongside, diving and surfacing, to more difficult jobs such as mine-laying, intelligence-gathering and Special Forces operations. Third, they needed to show in abundance the 'officer-like-qualities' that the Admiralty Interview Board was intended to identify, and which the Navy's traditions were supposed to inculcate. They needed to be men who could lead other men into battle. If they failed to display all these qualities, they could be dismissed from the course at any point, and failure was absolute. Those deemed not up to the mark were at once escorted from the vessel, and would never again be seen in a serving capacity in a submarine. Many left the Navy entirely. It was a course known to break marriages and break men, hence the term 'Perisher'.

The severity was and is justifiable. The job of submarine commander has never been one to be taken lightly. The responsibilities falling on the CO had been remarked upon from the earliest days of the service, and the experiences of two world wars had emphasized just how much depended on the qualities – or otherwise – of such men. In Lothar-Gunther Buchheim's *Das Boot*, the Commander puts it trenchantly:

> Actually we ought to be able to get along with fewer men. I keep imagining a boat that would only need a crew of two or three. Exactly like an aircraft. Basically we have all these men on board because the designers have failed to do a proper job. Most of the men are nothing but links in a chain. They fill the gaps the designers have left in the machinery. People who open and shut valves or throw switches are not what you'd call fighting men. I can't listen these days when the C-in-C U-boats tries to get everyone all excited with his advertising slogans: Attack – Defeat – Destroy – it's all pure bullshit. Who does the attacking? The Commander and no one else. The seamen don't see so much as a trace of the enemy.

The advent of first nuclear power and then nuclear arms had added significantly to the burden placed on commanding officers both in technical and in moral terms. While the gifts of some of the submarine commanders on both sides during the Second World War can

scarcely be understated, they employed technology no more sophisticated than that of the Spitfire, and weapons capable of killing at most
hundreds of men. Their successors a generation later needed to know
a good deal more than the mere principles of nuclear power; they had
to understand and operate highly sophisticated fire-control, navigational and sensor systems, and they were ultimately responsible for
weapons that could annihilate mankind. Introducing candidates to
one of these courses in 1983, Sandy Woodward – by then Flag Officer
Submarines – remarked in Jonathan Crane's book *Submarine*: 'When
you become a commanding officer, your life-style changes. Suddenly
you're taking life-and-death decisions for quite a lot of people all the
time, and you're on your own. Perhaps most of all, you're centre stage
– you have to give a command performance all the time.'

For the demands of the course itself, intended to develop such
abilities and to filter out those incapable of delivering them, he made
no apologies. 'You will find that Teacher does stress you from time
to time. It may be bloody-mindedness – that's his privilege – but it's
also deliberate. We need to know your personal limitations under
pressure. It's an unrepeatable offer, to drive yourself and your submarine to their limits. It's an opportunity for you to find yourself, and
you must use it. If you don't, you won't get through the course.' As
to failure, Woodward told the candidates that as a possibility it had
to be faced. 'It's traumatic at the time,' he conceded, 'but lots of
people have survived it.'

Each of the twice-yearly Perisher courses comprised a group of
ten to twelve men and was run by its own Teacher. The first of the
group to go through the course were Jeff Tall, James Taylor and Toby
Elliott, who took the earlier of the two courses run in 1974. Roger
Lane-Nott was on the second that year. Martin Macpherson followed
in 1975; Chris Wreford-Brown in 1976. Statistically, at least one of
them would have been expected to fail.

*

Perisher involved some theoretical classroom work, and it also
provided the candidates with glimpses into such matters as co-
ordination with RAF anti-submarine patrols and surface ships undertaking similar roles, but it was principally a practical course. It began

with the candidates developing their tactical skills in submarine simulators called Attack Trainers. One of these was based at *Dolphin*, the other at the Clyde submarine base at Faslane. Each Perisher was accordingly divided between the two locations, each with its own Teacher. The two groups subsequently joined up for the last stage of the course in the Clyde, in which they spent time in a submarine at sea.

At *Dolphin*, the simulator had changed very little since Edward Young's own Perisher, thirty years previously.

> It was built on two levels. The top floor, reached by an outside flight of steps, was the plotting-room. At the far end of it a travelling platform, with a small central turn-table to take the target model, ran out on rails through a window into the open air. The other end was occupied by a large white plastic plotting-table, marked off in squares to a scale of a thousand yards (half a sea-mile) to the inch. The plotting of the attacks, and the operating of the machinery which controlled the target's movements, were performed by a team of charming and intelligent Wrens. On shelves around the walls stood fleets of small-scale models of ships of all the warring nations: battleships, cruisers, aircraft-carriers, destroyers, submarines; liners, cargo-steamers, tankers, tramps. The lower floor of the building represented the interior of the attacking submarine. Imagine for a moment that you are a spectator in this lower room and that it is my turn to carry out the next attack.
>
> The circular white box in which I am standing represents the submarine's control-room, though in appearance it does not resemble one in the least. A periscope leads up into the plotting-room; its top window is covered for the moment because the stage is being set for the start of the attack. Out of sight upstairs, Commander Teddy Woodward, the instructor, is placing a new ship-model on the travelling target platform. As the attack develops, the target will move slowly in towards the periscope, turning on its platform in accordance with the gradually changing relative bearing of the submarine. Its movements are pre-arranged by Commander Woodward before the start of the attack, and these are automatically repeated on the plotting-table. My own tactics also will be plotted on it by the Wrens, following the orders I give up the voice-pipe.

Around me in the room below, my fellow perishers are waiting to take their turn at the various duties which, when I get a boat of my own, will be carried out by my officers. One of them stands by me to read off bearings and range-angles as I set them on the periscope, and to help me identify the target from the various ship-recognition manuals at hand. Another operates the fruit-machine, into which he will feed the information I give him about the enemy's bearing, inclination, masthead height and range-angle, and in return will translate these data into the enemy's true bearing, course, range in yards, and distance-off-track. This information in turn will be passed to the navigating officer, whose job is to chart the progress of the attack and work out the target's speed.

Suddenly a Wren's voice in the voice-pipe at my ear startles me into action.

'Control-room, control-room. You are a T-class submarine on patrol in the North Sea. Submarine's course one four five. Are you ready? *Start the attack.*' I repeat 'Start the attack' as a signal to the stop-watches, and at once order 'up periscope'. The top lens is now unmasked to represent the raising of the periscope, and looking into the eyepiece I find myself confronted with the urgent sight of the *Scharnhorst* coming straight at me, or a merchant-ship I cannot for the moment identify, or perhaps a U-boat whose angle-on-the-bow is impossible at range to judge. I must take action at once. How am I going to get into an attacking position?

The simulator course started with the exercise of attacking a single ship. The submarine had to be manoeuvred so as to be able to fire a torpedo, destroy the target and remain safe. This involved accurately estimating the speed, range and course of the target, the manoeuvring options available to the vessel, and what these then dictated to the submarine. Most important, it required judgement as to when it was necessary to dive deep prior to the attack. The submarine could only plan the attack from periscope depth and had to work on the assumption that at any moment the target might spot the periscope and turn directly towards the submarine to ram it. Provided the Perisher knew the maximum speed of the target and the time taken for the submarine to dive underneath her, he could gauge how close he could let the vessel approach before diving. To go deep, the Perisher had to order the flooding of a hypothetical 200-gallon ballast tank at the bows of the submarine called 'Q'. By way of preparation he would shout 'Stand-by Q. Stand-by Q routine.' If he hadn't done so thirty seconds before being obliged to dive, Teacher stepped in and did so himself. This was not career-enhancing. The critical problem was to maintain surveillance on the target to see how it was manoeuvring without exposing too much periscope or putting the submarine in jeopardy, something that required both experience and nerve.

An attack on a single target proceeding in an orderly fashion was fairly straightforward. Having established her range and speed, and having checked these at regular intervals using a stop-watch to judge when to raise the periscope to check her progress, the Perisher could then choose his moment to dive deeper. This became more difficult when other factors were added to the equation. Naturally enough, once the students had got the hang of the basic attack, the target started to manoeuvre, and to the single target were added one, two, three or four more – with stop-watches to match. Like a skilled bowler, targeting his deliveries just outside the stumps and forcing the batsman into the 'corridor of uncertainty' where he does not know whether he needs to play or not, Teacher juggled with the targets' courses, making it as difficult as possible for the Perisher to decide when to go deep. Each target had to be thought of as having an imaginary circle around her that moved with her, its size dictated by her own size and speed. When she crossed that circle the submarine had to go deep. A single target could skirt the edge of this circle, tantalizing the candidate and requiring him to watch minutely for changes in course. Even better, two targets might head directly towards the submarine, only to alter course just at the edge of the circle, one in each direction. At the same time as dealing with such problems and calculating when to go deep, the candidate had constantly to feed his support team details of the targets' positions so that calculations as to when and in which precise direction the torpedo salvo needed to be fired could be made, taking into account the time taken for the torpedo to reach its target and the consequent need to aim ahead of rather than at the target.

Martin Macpherson, when he came to take the course, found he had a particular knack for this sort of thing. James Taylor, on the other hand, was mildly bemused by the artificiality of the exercise and the environment in which it was conducted, pointing out that it is unusual in a real submarine to forget which way you are going: 'I had the knack. It's just that I found it impossible to forget we were in a steel drum in a brick building in Hampshire.'

The role of Teacher was critical. The term was accurate in the sense that it was Teacher's task to develop the candidates' talents and abilities over the five months in a way that would enable them to pass. Teacher, though, was also Examiner, whose duty it was to push the candidates to the limit, and to fail the inadequate and the incompetent without compunction. By definition Teachers were remarkable men. To pass Perisher was to join an élite. Teacher was an élite within an élite, and was – as Sandy Woodward has remarked – among the most coveted jobs in the submarine branch. Macpherson and Lane-Nott shared as Teacher Commander Toby Frere.

Born in 1938, the son of a publisher, Frere was educated at Eton before going to Dartmouth in 1956, an experience he found a refreshing contrast to the country's most famous school. There he joined what was still a world-wide navy, with dockyards in Gibraltar, Simonstown, Trincomalee, Singapore, Malta and Hong Kong. By 1962 he had found his way into submarines, and he was in *Astute* during her deployment as sentinel off Newfoundland during the Cuban missile crisis. He passed the commanding officers' qualifying course in 1968, and his first command was *Andrew*, followed in 1971 by the much more modern Oberon-class SSK *Odin*. He took over as Teacher in 1974. In that role he combined the manners and understatement of an English gentleman with authority, benevolence, high intelligence and tactical aggression. Cultured and well-read, he was highly regarded by his Perishers. Toby Elliott saw him as a 'fantastic example of who we'd all like to be, someone whom you could hero-worship'. Frere had taken over from Lieutenant-Commander John Lang, who had in fact led Elliott through the first half of his course. Like Roger Lane-Nott, Lang had been schooled at Pangbourne College, and he had served with P&O before transferring to the Navy. Elliott described him as 'a highly professional man, meticulous in detail, and another fine commanding officer'. He went on to make Rear-Admiral.

Equally important were the relationships established with the other Perishers. The course was not competitive in the sense that candidates were measured against one another. The standard was absolute, and on the ability of the candidates to work as a team, providing each other with mutual support, much depended. A group that developed a strong team ethos could carry its weaker members and push its leaders to greater heights. Taylor and Tall formed a mutually supportive pair under their Teacher Commander Terry Woods in 1974. The opposite was equally true, and the instances of failure in those circumstances were often high. Macpherson, when he himself became Teacher, was once obliged to fail four out of a group of five. As Roger Lane-Nott remarked, the relationship with both Teacher and the other Perishers was absolutely fundamental.

All the class of '63 got through the simulator tasks without undue difficulty.

*

Next the Perishers moved to Rothesay on the Isle of Bute, in the Firth of Clyde. Accommodated in one of the local hotels, by day the candidates would train in a submarine allocated for the purpose. Six days a week the Perishers rose at 0500 and began conducting their first attack at 0830. They seldom returned to the hotel before 2000.

The Perisher submarine was under the ultimate control of her day-to-day CO, with Teacher in charge of specific exercises. For the first time, though, the Perishers had practical command of a diesel-electric submarine and its sixty men, one or other of the candidates taking it in turn to act as captain each day. Similarly, although superficially these three weeks were merely a repetition of the simulator activity, real frigates now took the place of their symbols, with the familiar build-up from a single target to five. In the simulator both sea-state and visibility had been ideal. Now the Perishers were faced with the turbulent and volatile weather of the Western Isles, and the area in which they exercised was often full of all manner of small and larger craft that might unsettle them. Teacher was turning up the temperature and inviting the Perishers to discover their limits.

Above all, the Perishers were having to deal with the reality of a living, working submarine crewed by human beings. In the case of Taylor and Tall this was a Porpoise-class SSK, *Rorqual*, of which Martin Macpherson was First Lieutenant. The submarine had her own foibles, and her crew needed active management and leadership. In fact *Rorqual* was a boat with an unhappy reputation: an explosion aboard her in September 1966 had killed two ratings, and Macpherson described her as 'old and clapped out'. Moreover, speculation among the crew on the progress of the next generation of commanders was rife. The ratings invariably kept a book on who was going to pass, and who fail. They also influenced the outcome. As Toby Elliott remembered, 'If they didn't like you they made it very clear. You'd only got to lose your temper with them at the wrong moment, and you'd had it. My own personal philosophy was that everyone was trying damn hard to get you to pass. Not everyone thought that way.'

There were other pressures too. The long day invariably ended with a few pints in the hotel bar. Here the intention was quite consciously to encourage the Perishers to burn the candle at both ends and to see if they had the physical stamina required for command. Chris Wreford-Brown remembers being obliged to drink into the early hours of the morning. Inevitably, talk was mainly 'shop', but there was some conversation about the wider aspects of the Cold War. A bestseller in 1974 was John le Carré's *Tinker, Tailor, Soldier, Spy*. Revolving around the unmasking of a double agent at the highest level of British Intelligence, its theme was quite close to home for a group whose operational advantage – particularly in sonar – had been compromised by the activities of the Portland spy ring. Most welcomed a subject that took their minds off the ordeal of the day to come.

Failure, though, was not something on the minds of James Taylor, Martin Macpherson and Toby Elliott. 'I had been through one or two courses before', remarked Macpherson, 'and I didn't think I'd have much difficulty.' Toby Elliott was determined to enjoy the course and get through it. 'After all,' he says, 'it cost over a million pounds per student, so one had to make the most of it all.' Taylor was similarly confident. 'It's a stepped course and when I began I wasn't up to the mark. But it certainly never occurred to me that I would fail.' Taylor, indeed, who had found the artificial-ity of the Attack Trainer mildly disconcerting, was relieved to be back at sea, in familiar surroundings, and with an engaging chal-lenge. In the busy waters of the training area the targets were lined up, and once again he got into the rhythm of accurately assessing their range, providing his team – the other Perishers – with the information to produce solutions for torpedo targeting, and flood-ing the Q tank to go deep when necessary. It was, says Taylor, easy – 'Easy in that the time comes when it all seems to click. It's like speaking in a foreign language when – after you've said something – it suddenly occurs to you that you're *thinking* in the language.' A weapons officer of a slightly younger generation, Marcus Fitzgerald, remembers that there was something almost balletic about the spectacle of a good Perisher at work, the periscope shooting up at a pre-ordained bearing, held just long enough to check the target, shooting down into the periscope well, then, seconds later, shooting up again at a fresh bearing to observe the next target.

Although some of the skills could be taught, several – like the vital quality of self-confidence – could not. First, unlike a motorist who can see the condition of the road and the speed and direction of other traffic changing before his eyes, the submarine commander has to rely on periodic snap-shots of the surface world derived from the periscope. He cannot watch constantly for fear of detection. Indeed it was once calculated that a commander could use the per-iscope for no more than 5 per cent of the duration of an attack. To succeed in safely piloting his craft, let alone targeting the enemy, he has to be able to retain in his mind a clear image of the surface picture. He also has to have the tactical imagination to anticipate how this scene might have changed when he takes his next look thirty seconds, sixty seconds or a couple of minutes later. 'Imagine sticking your head out of a manhole in Piccadilly Circus, taking one swivelling look around, ducking back down into the sewer and trying to remember all you have seen,' wrote Sandy Woodward in *One Hundred Days*. 'The idea is to generate sufficiently accurate recall and timing to avoid a double-decker bus running over your head next time you pop up through the manhole.' Submariners call this the 'periscope eye'.

Second, there is the simpler issue of nerve. A number of Perishers comfortable enough in the Attack Trainer were rather less so when faced with command of several thousand tons of submarine and sixty men's lives. A 2,000-ton frigate heading straight for the boat's periscope at a combined speed of 40 miles an hour – not much less than a mile a minute – can be unnerving. Motorists may or may not have the ability to cope with comparable situations; racing drivers certainly do.

Both these qualities could be honed but they could not be taught. Those who possessed them enjoyed exercising them. Woodward comments, 'For a very few, this is heaven under water. For most it is the severest test they may ever face. For some, it is the ultimate nightmare. To be really good, you have to love it.'

Woodward also comments that the course, though relevant to the commanding officers of the Second World War, was rather less so in the 1970s. A Cold War submariner then was not going to find himself the prey of half a dozen frigates, and he certainly wouldn't have to rely on stop-watches and mental arithmetic to help him keep out of their way. The principal challenge that faced an SSBN commander was to avoid the Soviets, that of the CO of an SSN or SSK to find them. The Perishers of the time knew that the course was not strictly relevant to the experiences they were about to undergo, but they thought that it was invaluable nevertheless. 'It was a gloriously old-fashioned course,' says Taylor, 'but it taught you how to handle the boat and its men in stressful situations, and it gave you utter confidence in your ability to do so, whatever the distractions.'

Beyond the discipline of the attack, Teacher also challenged his students' competence by means of various tricks of the trade. One of Toby Frere's favourites, when an acting captain was deep into an attack, was the diversion. This might consist of the cook rushing through the control-room wielding a meat-cleaver in hot pursuit of a rating, shouting 'I'll kill you!' Verisimilitude was sometimes added by covering a finger, in the form of a sausage, with tomato sauce. The correct procedure was to invite the First Lieutenant to deal with the matter. Jeff Tall's Teacher, Terry Woods, preferred the sudden and urgent ringing of a bell. Says Taylor, 'He would ring it to indicate an error or an oversight. It was up to you, the Perisher, to identify it and correct it. But he wasn't above ringing it – and it was bloody noisy – when there was nothing wrong, just to see how confident the Perisher really was.' Equally, to the stream of information constantly coming into the control-room, some particularly alarming item – the unintentional flooding of a torpedo tube, or a fire – might be added by Teacher as what was called a 'fuck-up factor'.

There were other tests. Towards the end of his training, on a day on which the waters of the Clyde were exceptionally busy, Jeff Tall was asked by Terry Woods about the surface picture. 'What about the fisherman at red three zero?' With absolute conviction Tall replied: 'There is no fisherman.' He was right. 'If I'd put up the periscope,' says Tall, 'I'd probably have failed.' Some Perishers were unable to leave the periscope alone. On occasion the entire control-room would be cleared while such a Perisher was at the eye-piece. When he finally detached himself from it, he would find himself in the *Mary Celeste*. Conversely, the more confident would turn the tables. Martin Macpherson beguiled Toby Frere by taking a great interest in an entirely imaginary object. When Teacher put up the after periscope to investigate the 'sighting' for himself Macpherson knew he had won.

Taylor and Macpherson sailed through this part of the course; Tall and Wreford-Brown appear to have found it rather more difficult but manageable; Elliott and Lane-Nott had an altogether harder time. Elliott caught a dose of flu during the height of the period at sea, felt thoroughly ill, and found it a struggle to keep going. Similarly, Roger Lane-Nott suffered something of a crisis three weeks into the sea attack course. Frere was piling on the pressure, with more and more targets, and one of them was behaving pretty oddly. Sandy Woodward was conducting sea-trials in the destroyer *Sheffield*, driving her backwards at 15 knots. Lane-Nott also found the mental arithmetic torture. 'I got to the middle of week three and felt I wasn't doing as well as I should be. It was an agonizing period, and I put myself through a lot of self-analysis.' He talked things over with his wife and got her to throw long-division questions at him, and then he determined to ride out the storm. 'It may sound pretentious to say it,' he later commented, 'but Perisher is always said to be about understanding your own limits and – ultimately – looking into your own soul. In a sense it is.'

*

At the end of the first period of sea-training there was a formal mess dinner, at which the Perishers thanked the wardroom of the host submarine. This was rarely a sober occasion. Then there was a brief period of leave and some final classroom training before they returned to sea. Some of this last stage was spent in the Clyde, some in deeper waters. Having proved their ability to handle attacks safely, the Perishers now needed to demonstrate their judgement and leadership in three of the more straightforward submarine roles. The first was mine-laying, a task regularly undertaken by British submarines during the Second World War. The second was the sort of reconnaissance activity that Wreford-Brown had been observing in the Barents Sea in *Warspite*, though for the purposes of Perisher this normally took the form of simple still photography. Finally there were the exercises conducted with Special Forces, like those run by John Moore and the Seventh Submarine Squadron in Singapore.

All required careful planning, teamwork, properly functioning equipment, good weather and good luck. As with most submarine operations, not all of these invariably obtained. Martin Macpherson was told to lay a minefield at the entrance of Campbeltown Loch. Here the water is relatively shallow, leaving little room to manoeuvre if the unexpected should occur. In the midst of the operation, Macpherson spotted two minesweepers coming up the loch. There was insufficient water under the keel for the submarine to duck under them, and there was nowhere for her to withdraw. Macpherson was obliged to surface right in front of the minesweepers, forcing them to change course quite abruptly. 'I spent a couple of worrying days wondering whether I'd done the right thing.' His concern was exacerbated when Frere, perhaps mindful of Macpherson's imaginary sighting a few weeks previously, took him off operational duties 'to give the others a chance'. Lane-Nott was similarly on tenterhooks, not feeling confident that he had passed until the last exercise was completed: 'There was always that nagging doubt as to whether I was up to the mark.'

By this stage of the course, though, Frere and his fellow Teachers had invariably made their decisions. In the tradition of Perisher, they looked for candidates who were safe, who had a suitably aggressive spirit, and who were administratively capable, in that order. Even so, it was recognized that each submariner was an individual and that no two men would possess these qualities in the same combination or to the same degree. Different men would command their submarines and serve the Navy in different ways. 'The main cause of failure was stress,' comments Woodward. 'It was noticeable in the last couple of weeks of the periscope course as a drop-off in competence instead of continued improvement as the pressures increased. Eighty per cent of failures were of this type. Though Teacher was not necessarily doing this deliberately it was the deciding factor.'

At the end of the course, calling his Perishers one by one into the wardroom, Teacher would congratulate them and tell them of their first appointment as COs. Understated as ever, to Lane-Nott, Frere simply said, 'Congratulations, Captain. *Walrus*.' For the newly qualified commander, who at times had struggled on the course, it was a supremely exhilarating occasion, the culmination of more than ten years of hard work and dedication to the Navy. 'It was', he says, 'a life-defining moment.'

The remainder also passed and reacted to the news in different ways. Elliott, measured and self-controlled, was relieved. Tall felt much the same. Wreford-Brown regarded it very rationally as a vindication of his decision to go into submarines. Neither Taylor nor Macpherson were entirely surprised, but like the others they were prepared to regard it as good news. 'It was a magic moment,' says Taylor.

Since the course's inception more than half a century before, fewer than nine hundred officers had passed, of whom seventy-nine had lost their lives in command. Now, they were to be joined by those of the class of '63 who had made it thus far.

Chapter 8
First Command

'One's first command is always a milestone. All one's submarine career till then has been watching and learning. Now is the chance to put one's ideas into effect. It is easy to think how much better one would do it oneself and criticise others, but it is a very sobering feeling when it is all yours. I have had a number of much bigger commands since my submarining days, with hundreds of men for each man I had in my submarine, but I know no other job that is so completely yours and yours alone.'

Ben Bryant, *One Man Band*, 1958

Just over ten years into their naval careers, the newly qualified submarine commanders took on their fresh responsibilities at a time of considerable national and international uncertainty.

In October 1973, another in the series of conflicts between the client-states of East and West erupted in the Middle East. Following the débâcle of Suez that had ended Anglo-French influence in the region, the Kremlin and the White House had vied for power. Khrushchev offered assistance to the emerging Arab nations, while Eisenhower and Kennedy supported pro-Western regimes. Israel's spectacular victory over Egypt in the Six-Day War left her as the major military force in the Middle East and cemented her alliance with the United States, thus forcing the Arab nations further into the Soviet camp. Not surprisingly, ambitions then grew to reclaim the land lost in that war. On 6 October 1973, the day of the holiest of Jewish festivals, Yom Kippur, Soviet-backed troops from Egypt and

Syria attacked Israel, so threatening the détente that Nixon and Kissinger had laboriously established with Brezhnev, and which had culminated in the signing of the SALT treaty in May 1972. The invading forces enjoyed early successes against Israeli positions undermanned because of the holiday, capturing the strategic high ground of the Golan Heights and crossing the Suez Canal into Israeli-occupied Sinai. A counter-offensive was then launched, led by Israel's Seventh Brigade in the Golan. On 9 October, the Soviets began to resupply Egyptian forces with weapons that reportedly included nuclear missiles. Nixon started to supply arms to Israel on the 11th. On the 14th the greatest tank battle since the Second World War was staged in the Sinai, with Israel inflicting huge losses on the enemy. A ceasefire was called, backed by both Moscow and Washington. It held briefly, but was then broken. The Kremlin threatened direct intervention, and the White House responded by putting US forces on DEFCON 3, the highest state of alert employed since the Cuban missile crisis. This time, though, the ceasefire held, and a situation that could easily have resulted in a direct conflict between the superpowers was defused.

The war left détente looking fragile, the Middle East in a highly volatile state. Throughout the conflict, Nixon had been distracted by allegations over the Watergate break-in, and policy had been directed by Kissinger, now Secretary of State. Though a summit was held in Moscow between Nixon and Brezhnev on 27 June 1974 at which it was agreed to ban underground tests of small nuclear weapons, it was increasingly clear that the presidency of the architect of détente could not survive. On 9 August, Nixon was at last obliged to resign, and was succeeded by the Vice-President, Gerald Ford.

In Britain, Edward Heath had finally taken the country into the EEC on 1 January 1973, but domestic affairs soon came to dominate his premiership. The IRA had begun to conduct a bombing campaign on the mainland. At the same time a series of highly damaging industrial disputes arose that culminated in the miners' strike of January 1974, and the declaration of a state of emergency. Heath called an election, his campaign hinging on the question as to whether the government or the miners actually ran the country. The result was equivocal, resulting in no overall majority for either of the major parties. Heath resigned, and Harold Wilson formed his third government. The miners' strike was called off, compulsory wage restraint was stopped, and a full working week restored. The governing of the country was nevertheless bedevilled by the absence of a clear electoral mandate, and on 10 October Wilson called another election. The high taxes imposed by the new Chancellor, Denis Healey, took their toll. Labour were returned to power with a majority of only three seats.

Such domestic difficulties left little time for foreign affairs, although in its first months of power Labour did decide to adopt a British upgrade of the Polaris missile system, known as Chevaline. The Conservatives, now in Opposition, replaced Heath with the 49-year-old Margaret Thatcher. A chemistry graduate from Oxford, she had trained as a lawyer before being elected as MP for Finchley in 1959, and she was the first woman to lead the party. In a world increasingly sympathetic to female icons, that year Elton John had an enormous hit with *Goodbye Yellow Brick Road*, which included his tribute to Marilyn Monroe, 'Candle in the Wind'.

Against this backdrop, military activity at sea was intensifying. By the early 1970s, the front-line Nato submarine force comprised forty-one American SSBNs and the four British Resolution-class boats. Besides the early Skate and Skipjack SSNs of the US Navy, there were thirteen of the Thresher class, thirty-seven of the slightly larger and newer Sturgeon class, and six British boats: *Dreadnought*, *Valiant*, *Warspite*, *Churchill*, *Conqueror* and *Courageous*. The first of the British second-generation SSNs, *Swiftsure*, had been completed in April 1973; and the prototype for a new US Los Angeles class, *Glenard P. Lipscombe*, was launched the same year.

The opposition, though, was becoming an increasing threat. To strength in numbers, Gorshkov was now adding a sophistication of design that would begin to challenge the West. The *annus mirabilis* of 1967 had seen the introduction of three classes of submarine. As remarked, one of these was the Yankee SSBN, which bore such a close resemblance to the American missile boats. The second was the Charlie-class SSGN, the main armament of which was an SS-N-7 cruise missile with a range of 35 miles; the third the Victor-class SSN attack submarine. Then, in 1971, came the Delta-class SSBN. The Yankees carried sixteen SS-N-6 missiles, but these had only a modest range of 1,800 kilometres. The Deltas carried a smaller number –

twelve – of the larger SS-N-8. Critically, these had a range of more than 6,700 kilometres. This meant that rather than leaving Soviet home waters and risking detection on their way down to the Atlantic or the Pacific, these submarines could remain within home waters and still target anywhere in Europe and almost all of the United States. Soon they began to do so, lingering in the Barents Sea or the Sea of Okhotsk, sometimes protected by one or two SSNs, surface forces, patrol aircraft and mines in areas called bastions. The same year a prototype of the 14,000-ton cruise-missile class, the SSGN *Papa*, appeared. The use of titanium to construct her pressure hull gave her a remarkable diving depth, and the metal was not susceptible to Magnetic Anomaly Detection. In addition, her two reactors could drive her under water at 37 knots, which was comparable to the fastest of the Western boats. Even more alarming was the SSN Alfa class, the first of which was also completed in 1971. Likewise constructed of titanium, the 3,700-ton boat was small for a modern attack submarine. Her speed though, was astonishing, normally quoted at 45 knots, or more than 50 miles an hour. It was also believed that her diving depth of 900 metres put her beyond the reach of many Nato torpedoes. Finally, in 1972, a modification of the Victor-class SSN appeared, thirty feet longer than its predecessor, supposedly to accommodate a more sophisticated weapons system.

The proximity of Nato to Warsaw Pact forces and their increasingly close interest in each other's activities inevitably led to close calls between the opposing craft and, from time to time, to collisions. These included a clash between a US Navy SSN and a Soviet submarine in the Barents Sea in the early 1960s, one between the US SSK *Barbel* and a Soviet freighter in the Gulf of Tonkin in 1968, and a third between the US SSN *Gato* and a Soviet Hotel-class SSBN in 1969. The most violent, however, was between the USS *Tautog* and a Soviet Echo II submarine off Petropavlovsk in June 1970. By 1972 such encounters had become sufficiently frequent and serious for an agreement to be needed on how such incidents might be avoided or, when they did occur, adjudicated. The 'Incidents at Sea Agreement' was signed by the US Secretary of the Navy and his Soviet opposite number on 25 May 1972. Collisions, incursions in the opposing navy's exercise areas and other encounters nevertheless continued. By 1973 Nato had been obliged to set up three 'Standing Naval

Commands'. Comprising the Atlantic, the Mediterranean and the English Channel, these command structures enabled Nato units to exercise in these areas and improve their operational capabilities while at the same time projecting power against the observing Soviet units. Then, in November 1973, at the height of the Yom Kippur War, more than a hundred Soviet vessels, including twenty-five submarines, steamed east through the Straits of Gibraltar. Gorshkov was throwing down the gauntlet. The US Sixth Fleet, stationed at the time in the eastern Mediterranean to supply war *matériel* to Israel and hitherto unchallenged, was put on its mettle.

The newly qualified British submarine commanders would likewise now have to face a Soviet threat of unprecedented aggression and strength. Of those who passed Perisher, about a third would not receive a second command, their sea-going days effectively over. The remainder would go into the front line of the Cold War.

*

Roger Lane-Nott – at this stage still a Lieutenant – joined the first submarine he was to command at the end of 1974. This was one of the Porpoise-class diesel-electric SSK boats, *Walrus*, then being refitted in Rosyth and attached to the Third Submarine Squadron. First commissioned on 10 February 1961, she was thirteen years old.

Her new CO thought that taking over the submarine in such circumstances would provide him with the chance to set his own stamp on the boat and its crew. Taking command of an operational submarine with its own established way of doing things was a more difficult task, the crew having already settled into the *modus operandi* demanded by the previous commander. With *Walrus*, Lane-Nott could establish matters to his own satisfaction from the beginning. For a 30-year-old this was God's own job, and Lane-Nott certainly relished it. Naturally cheerful and open, he was an easy man to get on with. Professionally, though, he was a stickler. His experience with Chris 'Sharkey' Ward on the SSN *Conqueror* had led him to develop the precept, 'Don't believe it's been done unless you've seen it'. This he drove home relentlessly to *Walrus*'s wardroom which, unusually, comprised six officers all of whom held the same rank of lieutenant. He also had to work hard to ensure that *Walrus* got the attention she deserved from the shipyard. One of the Polaris boats was being refitted there at the same time, and the old diesel-electric boat with her relatively junior commanding officer was not a top priority.

In the new year of 1975, as the submarine refit reached completion, so too did the training of her crew. However, it had by now become clear that Lane-Nott's First Lieutenant was by temperament not entirely suited to submarines. Matters came to a head during *Walrus's* sea trials in the Moray Firth, and the new CO was obliged to request a replacement. Once the new officer, Lieutenant Tony Taylor, was in place, the work-up proceeded.

This comprised a series of trials and drills designed to ensure that the submarine and her crew were fit for operational patrol. It began with basic safety exercises such as the Deep Dive, which involved taking the boat down towards her operational limit of 500 feet to ensure that the hull and its various external valves remained sound. Then came the Noise Trial, in which Lane-Nott took *Walrus* up to the range off the Isle of Rona on the west coast of Scotland, where sound sensors on the seabed monitored the submarine at different speeds. During run after run, various pieces of machinery were switched on to check whether they had been sufficiently sound-proofed. Finally there were tactical exercises with surface ships, in which *Walrus* played now the hunter, now the hunted. The work-up ended with an inspection by the commander of the squadron, who spent a day on board. Even in such a short period, much can be learned about the character, morale and state of training of a boat, and the commander tried all sorts of tricks to test out the crew and her new CO. These ranged from giving surprising orders to surreptitiously changing the trim. Passing the inspection was a relief, but Lane-Nott had still not assumed the psychological burden of command. This happened during the early hours of his first operational patrol. He was sitting in the wardroom when a rating knocked on the door, came into the tiny room, and made a routine request for permission to stop draining sewage from the boat. Lane-Nott's automatic reaction was: 'Ask the captain', but he stopped himself just in time, remembering that the buck now stopped with him.

Jeff Tall had a similar moment when he brought his first command to periscope depth for the first time. This was the Oberon-class SSK

Olympus, also attached to the Third Submarine Squadron at Faslane, which he was given to drive after Perisher. 'Remember', says Tall,

> you have two and a half thousand tons and seventy men in your charge. I was in the Clyde and it's an area where you've prob- ably got something like twenty sonar contacts – fishing-boats, trawlers, ferries, yachts, tankers. You can run into any of them and end your career, at worst your life and the lives of your crew – not to mention the guys on the surface. I'd had a good look around before we went down, so I knew roughly where every- thing was, and had checked out the ferry routes and so on. And of course you apply every bit of common sense, all the tricks of the trade. But the first time you say 'half-a-head together, ten up' is quite a moment. Up you come, easing the angle at 100 feet, and grabbing the periscope as it rises up the tube. The second it breaks the surface you have the quickest of looks around to make sure you're in the clear. Then you heave one absolutely enormous sigh of relief.

*

Toby Elliott, commanding *Olympus's* sister-ship *Otter*, was also based at Faslane. Soon he found himself working with the Special Boat Squadron on special operations off the Norwegian coast. At a pre- ordained rendezvous point, an RAF C140 Hercules transport aircraft would drop a number of folding canoes, known as fol-boats. They would be followed by the SBS team, normally six to eight men, and their equipment. Landing in the near-freezing sea and getting rid of their parachutes, the swimmers would gather their equipment around them and then deploy a snagging rope about fifty feet long between them. They would then begin to activate something rather like a sophisticated rattle: two sound-generators operating on slightly different frequencies, and known as trongles. *Otter*, at periscope depth, would pick up these sounds on her sonar, locate their orien- tation, and then slowly approach at a speed of a couple of knots. Placing *Otter* carefully between the sources of the two sounds, Elliott would edge her forward on the electric motors until the extended periscope snagged the line. The men would be swept back on to the submarine's after casing. 'And remember, 'says Elliott, 'all this is taking place in complete darkness, with not much room for mistakes. Too long in the water and the marines die of hypothermia.' The boat would then surface, and the marines would scramble aboard. Subsequently they would be taken closer to the coast in *Otter* before making their own way ashore in the canoes.

James Taylor recalled that the successful rendezvous between Hercules and submarine was confirmed by no more than a 'click-click' from the aircraft radio operator in response to an identical signal from the submarine. 'I was always amazed at the readiness of people to jump off a Hercules into the sea on the basis of just a "click-click".'

Taylor had cut his teeth in *Grampus*, which he took over a week after completing Perisher in July 1974. One of the early Porpoise-class SSK boats, she suffered from a rash of defects. 'We had hideous electrical problems caused by earths, the occasional minor fire, and frequent and regular bursts in the high-pressure air system – these manifested themselves as shotgun-like blasts as the seals gave out, followed by a blast of 4,000 pounds per square inch of air draining itself into the submarine. And at maximum depth the water pissed in, especially in the engine-room.' Taylor commanded her for just ten months before she was paid off for disposal. Nevertheless he felt he learned a great deal, 'not', he says, 'just about what you could still achieve operationally in a submarine that wasn't functioning as designed, but principally what you could ask your crew to do, and what they were willing to do if they had faith in you'.

Then, in the spring of 1975, Taylor took over *Orpheus*, like *Olympus* and *Otter* attached to the Third Submarine Squadron at Faslane. *Orpheus* was an Oberon-class SSK boat and the first fitted with a purpose-built five-man chamber that allowed Special Forces to enter and exit from the submarine when it was dived in a group rather than, as hitherto, one or two at a time. The system was being developed for various purposes, including the sort of operations being conducted off the Norwegian coast by Toby Elliott. These involved the SBS team exiting the submarine under water, releasing an inflatable assault boat from the submarine's forward casing, and following it on a line up to the surface. There the boat was inflated, and its engine removed from a waterproof bag and fitted. The assault team then clambered aboard and dashed off on their mission. Not surprisingly, such operations can be risky, as was tragically demonstrated aboard *Orpheus* in January 1977.

Taylor had been detailed to conduct a training exercise with Special Forces using the new chamber. These started with harbour drills in which the submarine was tied up alongside, then progressed to static drills with the submarine sitting on the bottom in shallow water, and worked up to drills while the boat was underway. They culminated in an exercise with the Special Boat Squadron in Loch Long, the strip of water that runs north off the Firth of Clyde, a few miles west of the Gareloch. It had rained very heavily during the previous few days, and a lot of water had poured off the hillsides and into the loch. In due course this fresh water would mix with the sea water, but for a short period there were pockets of fresh water in the loch. Fresh water is less dense than sea water, and therefore also less buoyant. If a submarine hits one of these, control can be lost, rather as happens when an aircraft hits turbulence. The risk of such pockets is of course known, and standing orders for such an incident exist. Specifically, in the case of the exercises in which divers ride on the submarine's casing, these require the CO of the submarine to regain control of the vessel before returning to the surface. On the day of the training exercise, a strong wind was also blowing and the sea was choppy.

At first all went well. Taylor dived the submarine and settled her into a steady slow run up the loch at little more than a knot: any faster and the divers would be swept off the casing as they exited the diving chamber. The first diver successfully exited *Orpheus*, and stationed himself on the submarine's forward casing. His job was to check that all the equipment located there for the operation – the boats, their engines, personal kit, radios, weapons and air-bottles – worked. The air-bottles in particular were vital because the swimmers leaving the submarine carried small bottles with a capacity of only ten minutes. To reach the surface they would need to use the larger 150-cubic-foot bottles positioned on the casing, though even these had only sufficient air for a relatively short ascent. The first diver found that the air-bottles were working correctly and signalled to the remainder of the team to join him on the casing. These men, each carrying several heavy items of equipment, including weapons, joined the casing diver one by one and then plugged themselves into the air-bottles. No sooner had they done so than *Orpheus* hit a concentration of fresh water.

At once the submarine took charge and began to plunge towards the bottom of the loch, beyond the depth at which the divers could safely reach the surface. Taylor could not increase the submarine's speed by much because that would sweep the divers off the casing. Nor could he blow the submarine's main ballast tanks, because a sudden rise to the surface might injure them. Realizing what was happening, at 120 feet the casing diver inflated his lifejacket, freed himself from *Orpheus*, and broke for the surface. As Taylor fought to regain control of the submarine, two members of the team took the same decision and abandoned the boat, this time at 170 feet. Such was the weight of their equipment and the pressure at that depth that, despite their lifejackets, they were scarcely buoyant and only with immense difficulty did they reach the depth at which they became positively buoyant. Slowing their ascent to prevent the diver's sickness known as 'the bends', they eventually reached the surface. The two remaining SBS men waited until the submarine had reached 180 feet before attempting to break away, but by then it was too late. Although they had inflated their lifejackets, they were too deep and their equipment too heavy to enable them to reach the surface. Taylor, all too aware of the dilemma that faced the divers, had eventually regained control of the boat at 200 feet, and then surfaced. 'We searched for them all night,' says Taylor, 'assisted by everything Faslane could find – small craft, patrol boats, tugs, helicopters.' Their bodies were later found on the bottom of the loch by the sonar of a minehunter, standing upright on the seabed.

Taylor was exonerated of blame by a Board of Inquiry. 'We were', he says, 'pushing the envelope in what all acknowledged was a dangerous area.' Inevitably, though, it was one of those occasions when a commander of any sensitivity will blame himself. Almost a quarter of a century later, Taylor read an account of the incident in Don Camsell's *Black Water*. 'I'd forgotten', he says, 'how deep those scars were.'

*

Despite – or perhaps because of – this experience, Taylor subsequently established *Orpheus* as the maid-of-all-work for the Third Submarine Squadron.

Orpheus was a well-built and reliable boat, and unlike *Grampus* rarely troubled by major defects. To this Taylor added the personality that submarine commanders invariably impose on their commands. For it is a curious fact that – as Toby Frere puts it – a group of up to 130 men in a submarine will all take on the tone of the CO. Taylor is a tall man of commanding presence with a strong, confident manner, redolent of the traditional 'officer-like qualities' demanded by the Navy and perhaps the embodiment of the public's idea of a submarine CO. More than capable of taking a firm line when needed, he led by example, asking much of himself. As far as discipline was concerned, he was disinclined to be dictatorial. To anyone who stepped out of line he would say, 'If you do that again, I'll chuck you overboard on a wet night.' Those concerned were never quite sure if he was joking. What was quite clear, though, was who was in command.

Tactically, too, Taylor was acute. In the summer of 1977 *Orpheus* was deployed to the Mediterranean, where a series of varied patrols culminated in a major exercise codenamed Dawn Patrol, in which Nato forces divided themselves into two, and attacked each other. In such an exercise each would normally have an aircraft-carrier group in its midst, the carrier's role in time of war being to attack the support bases of the Soviets' principal fleets.

Although it was gratifying to attack and 'sink' supporting ships such as tankers and transports early on in the exercise, the carrier was the prize. In this instance the ship was the *John F. Kennedy*, the US Navy's largest fossil-fuel powered carrier, a 1,000-foot, 87,000-ton monster commissioned in 1968. Taylor had already detected the carrier's attendant SSN submarine operating well away from her charge and had simulated a successful torpedo attack. Now the area was flooded with anti-submarine aircraft, *Orpheus*'s battery was low, and every time Taylor brought her up to snorkel, the radar intercept equipment told him he was about to be detected by airborne radar. Then, during an attempt at snorkeling in the very early hours, Taylor's signals monitor picked up a radar emission that he failed to recognize at first. Trying again, he identified it as a US Navy aircraft weather radar, which was odd because the bearing seemed to be changing very little, whereas normally one would expect airborne radar to move rapidly. It was Taylor himself who realized that the signal might be coming from an aircraft on the deck of the carrier.

There were no sonar contacts, so if the carrier was there she was moving only slowly, thereby reducing her sound signature to avoid detection. Backing his hunch, Taylor took *Orpheus* down below periscope depth and raced along the bearing of the radar. Going back up to periscope depth again, he found the noise from the radar getting stronger but heard nothing else. Again he went deep and sprinted. Then, returning to periscope depth once more, on a clear starlit night he was rewarded by the sight of the *Kennedy*. She was less than a mile away, proceeding at about 5 knots, with no navigation lights, no sonar emissions, no radar and no escorts. Using the skills that he had developed during Perisher, Taylor then proceeded to get into an attacking position and 'fired' a full salvo of Mark 8 torpedoes from inside a mile. 'The radar was from an aircraft on *JFK*'s deck,' says Taylor. 'No doubt a technician was readying the aircraft for a sortie, or testing after routine maintenance. Whatever it was, it was a fatal error.'

In lighter moments, Taylor divided his time between Ben Bryant's submariner's 'bible', *Submarine Command*, the *Shooting Times* and Alexander Solzhenitsyn's *Cancer Ward*.

After his time as navigator in the SSBN *Repulse*, Chris Wreford-Brown was appointed First Lieutenant of the Oberon-class SSK *Onslaught*, attached to *Dolphin* as part of the First Submarine Squadron. The submarine carried a variety of special surveillance equipment and spent each summer in the Mediterranean gathering intelligence on the Soviet Navy. During her 1976 patrol under the command of Peter Lindley, she spent two months surveying the activities of the Soviet fleet in its various anchorages, including the principal one at Kithira and a secondary one in the Bay of Salum on the Egyptian coast. By day the submarine operated within sight of the anchored ships, monitoring their activity through the periscope, listening to their communications, radar and sonar, and conducting underwater investigations to gain further intelligence on targets of special interest. At night she withdrew outside visual range to snort in order to recharge her batteries, though her sensors continued to monitor the Soviet ships. Wreford-Brown recalls that several of the special operators aboard the submarine were extremely large. As they were all in the same six-hour watch, the officer responsible for the trim had to move water around the submarine to compensate for the redistribution of weight when they came aft from their sleeping quarters in the fore-ends to their watch-keeping space amidships.

The patrol was highly successful, obtaining considerable high-grade intelligence, for which Lindley was awarded the MBE. It also provided an ideal opportunity for Chris Wreford-Brown to hone his skills and prepare for command. He then heard that Lindley was to be replaced by a new CO. This proved to be Martin Macpherson, fresh from Perisher.

Eager to impress his new commanding officer, Wreford-Brown presented Macpherson with an exacting programme for the first few days of his command, which involved seven days continuously at sea. Macpherson, certainly in the eyes of Wreford-Brown, was keen enough to make his mark from the start. Nevertheless, while accepting the need to get acquainted with his new vessel and her crew, Macpherson had envisaged a rather different itinerary. A few days at sea would be fine, but the weekend was to be spent in Falmouth. It began with a party in the wardroom on the Friday night. Then the officers piled into a car and spent the remainder of the weekend exploring Cornish pubs and Cornish beer. They returned to *Onslaught* ten minutes before she was due to sail, with the officer-of-the-day getting restive on the casing.

This all suited Wreford-Brown, who was by no means averse to a run ashore. Macpherson, though, soon established himself as a fine replacement for Lindley. He was a thoroughgoing professional at sea and an outstanding manager of men, and he also possessed an intuitive tactical awareness of the dynamics of submarine operations in crowded waters. Two stories Macpherson tells against himself nevertheless illustrate the challenges facing the young commanders.

In August 1975, *Onslaught* was on a Nato exercise involving the brand-new nuclear-powered carrier USS *Nimitz* and her battle-group. *Nimitz* was huge, at 97,000 tons the biggest warship ever built. She measured 252 feet across her beam and she was capable of accommodating ninety aircraft. Her theoretical destruction would be a fine feather in the cap of an ambitious young submarine commander – just as Taylor's theoretical sinking of *Kennedy* had been. The challenge was to penetrate her screening escorts, including an SSN. It was a typical Atlantic summer's day with a moderate wind – Force 3–4 – and a gentle swell, the bright sun glinting on the waves. As far as Macpherson was concerned, there should not have been anything else apart from the Nato force in the area. This, though, was the time of increasing surveillance of Nato exercises by the Soviets. Just as Macpherson was approaching *Nimitz*, a Soviet Krivak-class destroyer appeared on the scene, a modern gas-turbine-powered 3,670-tonner capable of 34 knots. This, thundering almost straight towards him at a range of less than a mile, was the first thing Macpherson saw when he put up the periscope. 'It had simply never crossed my mind that she'd be there.'

The second incident was an even closer call. Early in 1976 Macpherson was conducting an exercise off Portland Bill with a frigate. These waters are busy, and there are always a lot of sonar contacts around. Dusk was approaching, and Macpherson was thinking of calling it a day. He decided, however, to take one more look at the frigate. As he did so, he was profoundly disoriented to discover that absolutely nothing could be seen through the periscope except pitch darkness. Could the ship's chronometer be wrong? Could he somehow have lost twelve hours? In seconds, though, the answer became apparent. *Onslaught* was so close to a black-hulled tanker that the hull filled the entire periscope frame. Memories of Perisher came flooding back as Macpherson prepared to dive in a hurry: 'Stand by Q routine. Full ahead together. Flood Q' – 'It was one of those things you practise on Perisher, so I knew just what to do. But it was a frightening moment.'

Such incidents were endemic to the submarine service, particularly during the Cold War, and were in a literal sense occupational hazards. As far as the squadron commanders were concerned, what mattered was not the incidents themselves but how the young COs coped with them. As Roger Lane-Nott says, 'Submarines are fragile and dangerous things. When something goes wrong, everyone turns to the captain. If you let uncertainty show, it goes right round the boat. If you don't know what to do you've got to damn well pretend you do.' The way in which commanders dealt with the inevitable emergencies of command distinguished the adequate and acceptable from the outstanding. To only a few did command and the presence it requires come naturally.

It was also in *Onslaught* that Macpherson had his first meeting with a Soviet submarine. By this time the core of Nato anti-submarine activity had been long established as the erection of barriers in the bottlenecks between the Soviets' principal bases and their patrol areas. These included the gap between Bear Island and the northern tip of Europe, North Cape; the Greenland-Iceland-UK gap; and the Kattegat between Denmark and Sweden. In each area a SOSUS chain was installed that provided long-range warning of approaching submarines. Once a threat had been identified, it was then shadowed either by another submarine or by a maritime patrol aircraft. Typically, submarines were used in forward areas such as the Barents Sea, and aircraft were employed closer to their home bases in the UK.

Macpherson was off North Cape when he received a signal that SOSUS had picked up a contact in his area. He at once gave the order for silent running, the set of procedures that minimizes the amount of sound that the submarine makes to reduce the risk of counter-detection. The submarine is slowed down to 3 or 4 knots, at which speed diesel-electrics make very little noise, all non-essential machinery is switched off, and routine operations like cooking that can be noisy are postponed. Macpherson then set off gingerly on a bearing that took the submarine towards the contact. Sure enough, in due course *Onslaught*'s sonar operator picked up signs of a Soviet submarine. Gradually, the two vessels converged and Macpherson was able to pick up her acoustic signature and so identify her as a Yankee-class SSBN. For the young CO, it was a first. 'In a sense it was easy,' says Macpherson. 'I knew he was coming down and I knew where to look. But it was the first time I really got an idea of what Cold War submarining was about. You spend all that time being trained for the job, and all that time talking about these encounters in the bar. But the first time it happens is an exciting – in some respects a frightening – experience. You worry about the men in your own boat and about the others.' Jeff Tall agrees. 'It's a worrying business. Not only are you carrying the weight of your own ship, but also the guy you're prosecuting.'

It was Macpherson who recommended Wreford-Brown for Perisher, which he undertook in the first five months of 1976. Having passed the course, he was given the SSK *Opossum*, which he joined as CO in July. He found her a relaxed and confident boat, which was just as well, for he was at once dispatched to the Baltic.

For a new CO, taking the twelve-year-old craft across the North Sea, through the Kiel Canal and into the tideless Baltic was an experience. The aim of the deployment was to establish what operating conditions were like in the Baltic in preparation for longer submerged operations by another Royal Navy SSK the following year. The different salinity of the Baltic makes trimming a submarine difficult, while sonar conditions are very poor, and *Opossum* was under almost constant surveillance from various units of the Soviet Baltic Fleet.

The deployment also included a visit to the town of Karlskrona, the home port of the Swedish submarine service, where the ship's company were well looked after in an excellent run ashore. For Wreford-Brown, one of the more exciting moments of his command came when some sixth sense told him to grab the periscope from the officer-of-the-watch. Taking a rapid all-round look, he at once spotted a Soviet Foxtrot-class diesel-electric bearing down on *Opossum* on a reciprocal course. Manoeuvring to get off track he watched it pass close down the port side with relief.

There are plenty of tales about such experiences, which most submariners attribute to working in such close proximity to the machine – or rather inside it. 'I think subconsciously you get so used to all the sounds of the boat that when something changes you automatically go on alert,' says Toby Elliott. He himself had a similar experience to Wreford-Brown's when on patrol in the Straits of Gibraltar. The submarine was on the surface and he was asleep in his cabin. He woke up suddenly, convinced that something was wrong, walked into the control-room and checked her position. All was in order. He then climbed the ladder up though the conning-tower to the bridge. It was balmy night, with just a rating and an officer keeping watch. Ahead and all around, the shore lights shone brightly, and there was a pleasant scented breeze. But right ahead and very close were the lights of a large tanker. He had to react rapidly to avoid being run down. For Elliott, the moral of the story is clear. 'If you sense that something is wrong you have to get up and find out what it is, no matter how tired you are. You may be wrong and there will be nothing, but once in a while, more often than you might think, there is.'

Despite such occupational hazards, these were halcyon days for all the new submarine commanders. The responsibility that they carried as 30-year-olds was in many respects astonishing, bearing little relation to anything their contemporaries might carry in the civilian world. In the Army, the equivalent rank to naval Lieutenant is that of Captain, in the RAF that of Flight Lieutenant. Both ranks are demanding, but in neither is the responsibility for the lives of men quite so direct. For those who possessed the qualities needed to join the exclusive club of submarine commanders, such responsibility was to be relished. Moreover, the robust, simple and relatively cheap diesel-electric boats encouraged them to take risks and learn their trade in a way that later generations, with only nuclear boats on which to learn, would be denied. The nuclear submarines were stupendously expensive and – given public sensitivities about nuclear matters – politically sensitive pieces of equipment. No one took any risks that were avoidable in these vessels. Yet the confident and effective command of such a craft demands that both man and machine are pushed very hard, this especially so in time of war. Woodward had remarked of Perisher that the course enabled candidates to discover their own limits by pushing them to the edge. The diesel-electric commands did the same job even more thoroughly. Taylor, Tall, Elliott, Lane-Nott, Macpherson and Wreford-Brown had the immeasurable benefit of learning the skills of command on the older, conventionally powered submarines. They were virtually the last generation to do so.

*

On the global stage changes were afoot. The new American President Gerald Ford met Brezhnev in Vladivostok in November 1974 and agreed a framework for a new arms-limitation agreement which would include setting limits on the number of warheads in each nuclear arsenal. Though there were to be delays in this second round of SALT negotiations, the Kremlin was in a confident mood. New trading links were established with Europe and in August 1975

Brezhnev and Ford signed the Final Act of the Conference on Security and Co-operation in Europe. This agreement, which dealt with security in Europe, the encouragement of trade and cultural links and industrial and scientific co-operation, and humanitarian issues, marked the high point of détente. East and West had, it seemed, learnt to co-exist peacefully, at least in Europe.

Elsewhere, however, the superpowers continued to challenge one another through surrogates. In 1975 in Vietnam, Saigon finally fell to Communism. In Africa, too, as the European colonial powers withdrew and dozens of new states declared their independence, fresh opportunities for superpower rivalry arose. Angola, engulfed in a civil war after independence, fell to Cuban-backed Marxists, and it would not be long before a similar crisis arose in the Horn of Africa.

By then, there was a new incumbent in the White House. Jimmy Carter, in his inaugural address, had spoken of his 'ultimate goal of the elimination of all nuclear weapons'. The crisis in the Horn of Africa, however, soon began to unhinge any hopes of progress in the SALT talks that were still under way. Proposals for deeper arms cuts than those agreed by Brezhnev and Ford in 1974 were rejected as unrealistic. Simultaneously, the Carter administration began to send supportive messages to dissidents like Andrei Sakharov, and the US State Department publicly announced its support for Charter 77, a human rights document drafted in Czechoslovakia. This was regarded as unjustifiable interference in Soviet internal affairs. Then the Soviets began to replace the old SS-4 and SS-5 intermediate-range missiles based in Eastern Europe with the more powerful and reliable SS-20, each capable of carrying three independently targeted warheads. To European leaders, it seemed as if the Soviet Union, already asserting itself aggressively in Africa, was now developing the means to wage a limited nuclear war in Europe. If Europe alone was hit during such a war, would the United States hazard its own population by responding in kind? Nato linked American with European defence; this Soviet deployment seemed an attempt to divide them. In Britain, where James Callaghan had replaced Harold Wilson after his surprise resignation on 16 March 1976, the government took a similar view. Détente, if not dead, seemed to be dying.

Chapter 9
Commander

'Say not the struggle naught availeth,
The labour and the wounds are vain,
The enemy faints not, nor faileth,
And as things have been, things remain.'

Arthur Hugh Clough, 1855

Following his spell as CO of *Onslaught*, towards the end of 1976 Martin Macpherson was appointed First Lieutenant to the very first of the British SSNs, *Dreadnought*. That she was a hybrid, comprising a British hull and an American Westinghouse S5W power-plant, he already knew. What he had not properly appreciated was the extent to which this manifested itself in practical terms. In the boat's forward sections, British engineering principles and practices obtained. In the stern, American principles and practices ruled. The transition was symbolized by a 'Check-Point Charlie' plaque, named after the famous Berlin crossing-point between East and West. This made *Dreadnought* like no other British submarine; and her eighty-eight-man crew, rather than being relatively rapidly rotated, tended to stay for years. Some had been in the boat since her commissioning on 17 April 1964 and had grown old tending her many idiosyncrasies. The consequence was an unusually happy ship, a community in its own right, proud of running the first and still among the fastest of Britain's nuclear-powered submarines.

Under the captaincy of Commander Hugh Michell, *Dreadnought* embarked on a series of patrols in 1977 that were intended to culminate in a voyage to Australia. This would involve passing through the

Suez Canal, now cleared of the detritus left over from the Yom Kippur War. It would be the first time a nuclear-powered vessel had passed through the Canal, the scene of Britain's national humiliation almost precisely twenty-one years previously. According to Macpherson, there was some uncertainty at the Foreign Office as to how, in diplomatic terms, the passage should be handled. In the end it was decided to say nothing. As it turned out, the Egyptian officials at Port Said, at the northern end of the Canal, knew precisely what *Dreadnought* was, and refused to let her enter the waterway. In early December, while waiting for this issue to be resolved, the submarine received a signal that caused great excitement. It read, 'Sail immediately, go to Gibraltar and store for war.'

The Falklands, 350 miles north-east of Cape Horn, had long been the subject of a dispute between Britain and Argentina. Though the Buenos Aires government had declared its sovereignty over what it called Las Malvinas in 1820, the islands had been continuously administered and occupied by the British since 1833. Argentina periodically reasserted her claim to sovereignty in the first half of the twentieth century, but it was not until August 1964 that the issue was raised more formally at the United Nations. Britain defended her claim to sovereignty on the basis of her long occupation of the islands, and on the grounds of the principle of self-determination by the islands' people, a principle enshrined in the UN Charter. Accordingly, the following year the UN General Assembly approved a resolution for Britain and Argentina to hold talks with a view to resolving the issue peacefully.

These measured diplomatic processes were punctuated by less pacific Argentinian activity, which continued almost until the end of Isabelita Perón's regime and its replacement in March 1976 by a military junta. Earlier that year an Argentinian destroyer had fired on the British research ship *Shackleton*, construed to be within Argentinian territorial waters around the Falklands, and in December an Argentinian fishing station was discovered illegally established on the dependency of South Thule.

To David Owen, newly appointed by Callaghan as Foreign Secretary, all this clearly spelled trouble. Owen's concerns were redoubled by a proposal put to him in April 1977 by Fred Mulley,

Secretary of State for Defence. This was that the research ship *Endurance* should be withdrawn from the region. Her principal role was Antarctic research, but she was also obviously a local symbol of British power. Owen rebutted the idea by pointing out that it would 'indicate that the government's withdrawal in the Falklands and the South Atlantic was also under way'.

That summer there was a diversion by way of the Queen's Jubilee Review of the Fleet, the first since her coronation twenty-five years previously. Chris Wreford-Brown in *Opossum* was one of several diesel-electric submarines to join the line-up of 180 ships. The impression nevertheless was of a fleet much depleted since 1953, and Argentinian sabre-rattling continued. That November, the Foreign Secretary accordingly ordered a full intelligence inquiry into the threat posed by an Argentinian invasion, and the viability of sending a nuclear submarine to the area. With fresh negotiations on the future of the islands set for the end of the year, Owen felt it was essential to argue from a position of military strength and, should the islands actually be invaded, to demonstrate to the electorate that preparations for such an eventuality had been made.

The outcome was the decision to dispatch a force of two frigates and a nuclear submarine to the islands. At a meeting in late November of the service chiefs, the Rules of Engagement, the circumstances under which force might be used, were agreed. Any warship entering a zone within fifty miles of the islands could be investigated, and its identity and intentions demanded. The British force was also to be allowed to open fire 'upon those Argentine units that displayed hostile intent'.

*

Making her best speed of almost 30 knots, *Dreadnought* returned to Gibraltar. There she was stored with thirty-two live torpedoes and sufficient food, stores and spare equipment to last for four months. Knowledge of her destination was restricted to the five most senior officers, but inevitably speculation was rife. The night before her departure from Gibraltar a rating heard 'Don't Cry for me Argentina' playing on a juke-box and at once correctly guessed where she was going. The resulting gossip necessitated an MoD security inquiry.

Codenamed Operation Journeyman, the patrol began with *Dreadnought*, the two frigates *Phoebe* and *Alacrity* and a tanker ploughing down to the Falklands. The 7,000-mile voyage was largely uneventful, although *Dreadnought* – not the most reliable of boats – provided her usual cocktail of ills to keep everyone on their toes. She was also so overloaded that she was negatively buoyant and had to be kept going at a fair speed to prevent her sinking below the depth at which her hull would collapse. 'After a bit,' says Macpherson, 'we'd eaten enough to lighten the ship.'

The Falklands themselves also proved a difficult area for submarine operations. In the days of a worldwide, coal-fuelled fleet, the islands had been a significant – albeit remote – coaling-station for the Navy. In recent times, though, the area had been largely neglected. As a result, it was at best poorly surveyed and there were few charts suitable for submarines, which require detailed information on underwater topography. This deficiency was exacerbated by local sonar conditions. The waters of the South Atlantic abound in microscopic plankton. However, sonar sets designed to be operated in the North Atlantic and the seas of the European continental shelf registered such plankton as a contact. In addition, communications with Submarine Command, recently transferred from *Dolphin* to Northwood in Middlesex, proved exceptionally difficult, at best adequate, at worst virtually non-existent. Finally, the navigation instruments of both the submarine and her weapons were affected by the Coriolis force that causes water to corkscrew to the left in the southern hemisphere, to the right in the northern.

With little sign of Argentinian activity, Christmas turned into New Year, and *Dreadnought*'s crew amused themselves by making presents for one another and listening to the record-breaking *Rumours*, Fleetwood Mac's long-running hit album, on the radio. They also spent time trying to master local conditions, preparing what would turn out to be a catalogue of useful experience. *Dreadnought*'s orders were to avoid being seen by other shipping. However, when she came across the Royal Fleet Auxiliary *Cherry Leaf* on her way out of Port Stanley, Macpherson – taking his turn in command – thought this a suitable subject for an exercise in intelligence-gathering. This involved a close approach to the auxiliary. It was Macpherson's misfortune that on the steamer's bridge there was a look-out who had been aboard *Cherry Leaf* on a recent anti-submarine exercise, and who now spotted the tell-tale feather-shaped stream of water from the back of the periscope that betrayed *Dreadnought*'s presence.

Subsequently, there was a good deal of speculation as to whether *Dreadnought* deliberately exposed herself as a warning to the Argentinians, and James Callaghan later commented that he had told the head of MI6, Maurice Oldfield, that he 'would not be unhappy' if news of the boat's presence reached Buenos Aires. Macpherson is adamant that the *Cherry Leaf* sighting was indeed unintentional, and that the group's orders were for *Dreadnought* to remain undetected.

Whether or not the Argentinians knew of *Dreadnought*'s presence, the negotiations over the islands proceeded, and it was agreed that two working groups should be set up to report on sovereignty and on economic co-operation. Operation Journeyman was completed in February 1978 when the submarine returned to her home port of Faslane. She had been away for seven months, and during that time she had spent only seventeen days in harbour.

*

It was not long before a matter altogether more central to the Cold War began to occupy the British government. What was to replace the Polaris nuclear deterrent?

Lead-times in developing such weapons had always been long, and the increasingly sophisticated technology of weapons systems inevitably led to further lengthening of the period between political commitment and military deployment. Accordingly, the Polaris boats had scarcely started to patrol than plans were laid for upgrading the system. At first, these took the form of an American modification of Polaris. The first Polaris missiles had carried a single warhead capable of following a prescribed path to a single identified target. Quite early on in the life of the project the idea of multiplying the effectiveness of the missile by using several warheads was investigated and duly developed. This was known as a Multiple Re-entry Vehicle (MRV), the word re-entry referring to the return of the missile to the earth's atmosphere. The logical consequence of the MRV was the development of independently targeted warheads. This technology was termed the Multiple Independently Targeted Re-entry Vehicle, or MIRV. At the same time, the further idea of using inert decoy warheads was developed, so as to saturate Soviet missile defences with multiple targets.

The technological challenges of producing such devices were tremendous, centering on both miniaturization and the need for the missile to change speed and direction to send each warhead – live or dummy – to its target. In Britain, one of the first acts of Edward Heath's government in 1970 had been to approve the development of a British counterpart of this system, and in 1974 Harold Wilson had endorsed the decision. By 1978 the system known as Chevaline was well advanced, although its cost had quadrupled. In its operational form it had two live warheads and three dummies. All five were housed in metal balloons and – to confuse defences further – there were also empty balloons. Heavier than the original warhead system, Chevaline had a shorter range than Polaris and accordingly restricted the area in which the missile boats could patrol. This in turn made them – at least theoretically – easier to detect. The system was scheduled to go into service in 1982.

This, though, was no more than a temporary measure. While pursuing the SALT talks, both the United States and the USSR were continuing with the development of weapons systems. The American equivalent to Chevaline, named Poseidon, entered service in 1971 and was installed on the thirty-one 7,485-ton Lafayette-class SSBNs that had joined the American SSBN fleet between 1963 and 1967, and that had initially been armed with Polaris. Like the British missile, Poseidon had its limitations, most obviously in the size of its payload. As an MIRV system it had ten warheads, but each with the explosive power of only 40 kilotons, less than twice the power of the bomb dropped on Nagasaki. In its early days the system was also very unreliable. The Nixon administration had accordingly set in train the development of an entirely new submarine missile system.

Inevitably, this was the brainchild of Admiral Rickover, the force behind the entire US nuclear submarine programme. Though he was by now a septuagenarian, Rickover remained a man of vision, foreseeing a submarine that would be sufficiently large to carry a missile with a range three times that of Polaris. The laws of geometry in turn dictated that such a submarine would be capable of covering not three times the area of the Polaris boats, but five – that is fifteen million square miles rather than three million. This in turn would make it proportionally more difficult to find. The new missile was known as Trident and it had an immense range – in its original form 7,400 kilometres – as well the capacity to carry eight 100-kiloton warheads. At the time the whole system was the most expensive weapons system ever conceived, and it was scarcely surprising that Congress baulked at the cost. Its hand was forced by the Soviet Union's deployment of its own long-range, submarine-launched missiles: first the 6,700-kilometre SS-N-8; then, in 1976, the 7,800-kilometre SS-N-18. These missiles were fitted respectively to the Delta I and Delta II SSBNs, the latter carrying sixteen rather than just twelve missiles. On 10 April 1976, under President Carter's new Democratic administration, the first of the new Trident-carrying Ohio-class boats was laid down. These 18,000-ton machines would be almost 600 feet long and would each carry a reactor capable of generating 35,000 horsepower, that is twice as powerful as that of *Dreadnought*.

Given the history of Britain's own Polaris deterrent, it was inevitable that the acquisition of Trident should be one of the options for sustaining the country's nuclear force. Once it became apparent that Carter was irrevocably committed to Trident, tentative talks on the subject were held between the Ministry of Defence and the Pentagon. Nothing had been resolved by the time David Owen took over at the Foreign Office. The issue was a matter of some sensitivity for the Labour Party which had always been so ambivalent about nuclear weapons. Like Denis Healey, Owen was personally committed to the deterrent, but he recoiled at the cost of Trident, particularly given the parlous state of Britain's economy. He accordingly advocated the new US Tomahawk cruise missile as a cheaper and more flexible alternative. The new missile was a descendant of the United States' first successful cruise missile, Regulus. Tomahawk, though, was such a masterpiece of miniaturization that it could be fired from a standard 21-inch submarine torpedo tube, as well as from surface ships and aircraft. It could also be armed with either conventional high-explosive or a nuclear payload. By comparison with a ballistic missile, however, its range was limited to 2,500 kilometres, it was more vulnerable to local defence, and its payload of 200 kilotons was relatively small. Though subsequent conflicts such as the Gulf War have shown it to be a formidable weapon, the Ministry of Defence nevertheless argued the case for the more sophisticated and far more powerful Trident, and in the end this view prevailed.

In January 1979, therefore, on the Caribbean island of Guadeloupe, Callaghan formally asked Carter about the possibility of acquiring the system, while at the same time agreeing to the siting of a new generation of ground-launched missiles in Britain in response to the Soviets' installation of their own SS-20s. The President raised no objections, Owen commenting that 'Jim used his friendship with Jimmy Carter over Trident in much the same way that Harold Macmillan had used his personal relationship with President Kennedy over Polaris'. At Heathrow on his return from that meeting the Prime Minister unwisely countered questions about the public-sector strikes that were engulfing the country with a response that appeared in the headlines as: 'Crisis? What crisis?' That spring he was forced to call an election in which he faced the new Conservative leader Margaret Thatcher.

At the time Martin Macpherson was in Barrow-in-Furness. Coming out of the shipyard one day he was confronted by the sight of Denis Healey addressing members of Vickers' workforce. Despite the secret negotiations with Carter, in its election manifesto Labour was taking the line that Polaris would not be replaced. Barrow had long been a safe Labour seat, and the Chancellor told his audience that although the government would not order Trident, he would ensure that other naval work would be channelled in the dockyard's direction. This was not a line the Vickers men found credible. The Conservatives had pledged that they would buy Trident. On 3 May Barrow voted for a Conservative MP, and the country as a whole voted for Mrs Thatcher, Britain's first female Prime Minister. Macpherson wryly recalls remarking at the time, 'What do we want a woman for? She'd be useless on defence.'

*

With the replacement of the deterrent still undecided, the existing Polaris patrols continued. Toby Elliott, having spent two years acquiring the art of command in the SSK *Otter*, had done sufficiently well to be posted to the Port crew of the SSBN *Renown*. Like Macpherson, he followed the position of CO with that of Executive

Officer, a routine career path for his generation, though he had hoped to be given command of an SSN – not to mention an opportunity to escape from the Clyde. *Renown* was the first of the two SSBNs built by Cammell Lairds in Birkenhead, and in Elliott's view she had not been completed 'to such a fine standard of finish' as her Barrow siblings. She also had a reputation for being accident-prone – a reputation that her CO, Commander Michael Everett, was keen to lose.

One of the many curiosities about ships in general and submarines in particular is the way in which they acquire reputations that are very difficult to change. The received wisdom is that those vessels that start well continue in that vein, and vice versa. It was for this reason that a great deal of trouble was taken to ensure that the COs responsible for taking the boats out of their building yards, through their sea trials and into operational service were of the highest calibre, particularly when it came to the building of a crew or – in the case of the Polaris boats – crews. The first of the Polaris submarines, *Resolution*, had got off to a bad start because of friction between the Port and Starboard crews. By contrast, *Renown*'s problems were of a technical nature, partly stemming from a collision early on in her first commission, which had resulted in her CO and navigator being court-martialled. Quite what the submarine hit was never publicly revealed, but she was certainly damaged. The navigator was exonerated, the CO reprimanded for hazarding his ship.

For Elliott the posting was therefore something of a double-edged sword, to be approached with caution. '*Renown*', he says, 'gave us quite a few problems and wrecked the careers of a number of COs. Simply keeping her operational was difficult enough, never mind avoiding detection by the Soviets. A patrol felt like a technical endurance test from start to finish.'

Two years later, after four deterrent patrols, Elliott was posted Staff Officer Operations to the Second Submarine Squadron at Devonport, which had been established as a base for nuclear boats in the early 1970s to take the pressure off Faslane. Elliott's new job gave him a change of perspective, from that of a submariner in charge of a single boat to a clear overall picture of the Cold War at sea. It also required him to put into practice a philosophy of submarine operations summarized by a contemporary CO, Richard Sharp, who had a considerable influence on the thinking of his contemporaries: 'Any operation, be it overt or covert, must contain an underlying element of threat, such as to make the use of force an unattractive option.' The Soviets, in short, needed to be kept on the back foot.

Then, in 1979, Elliott was promoted to the rank of Commander. This was a significant step in so far as it is the first rank at which sheer ability counts for far more than length of service or the passing of technical exams. At the same time, now aged 35 and married with three children, Elliott was given his own Polaris command in the form of the first of the British SSBNs, *Resolution*. This meant a return to Faslane, not a particularly attractive posting for a man with a family. For Elliott, though, long schooled in the proudest of the Navy's traditions, it was a tremendous moment, perhaps the greatest of his career. An intensely patriotic man, he felt he had fulfilled his promise.

After taking his first command, the SSK *Olympus*, into refit in 1976, Jeff Tall had a short spell in command of the SSK *Finwhale* when he relieved a CO who had injured himself. Still a Lieutenant, he then spent a couple of years as Elliott's opposite number on the Starboard crew of *Renown*. As a fellow Executive Officer, he had formed an excellent working relationship with Elliott, and he was delighted to hear of his friend's promotion. He was also happy enough to see a Conservative government back in power, not least because the Navy now got a pay-rise. Finally, he was pleased to hear that he had been appointed as an exchange officer on the staff of the Commander of the US Third Fleet. Based in Pearl Harbor, Hawaii, he was to serve as Undersea Warfare Officer, in the rank of Lieutenant-Commander.

Leaving aside the pleasures of the climate, Hawaii was an unusual posting in that it gave Tall an insight into Western operations in the Pacific where there had been very little British naval activity since the withdrawal of Britain's forces east of Suez. Tall's job entailed co-ordinating fleet exercises that were dominated by the huge US Pacific fleet but that also involved Japanese, Australian and Canadian units. Force of personality and a degree of diplomacy were necessary in this particular posting, as well as tactical gifts. Almost to his own surprise, Tall realized he had a talent for this sort of task, so much so that he regarded it as a turning-point in his career. He also formed an excellent relationship with his superior on the US Pacific command, Admiral Kinnaird McKee. On several occasions McKee backed Tall's judgement when the issue was too close to call and it was a backing worth having. According to *Blind Man's Bluff*, McKee was one of the stars of the Anglo-American surveillance operations in the Barents Sea. He had made his name in 1967, when CO of the SSN *Dace*, by photographing a Soviet nuclear-powered icebreaker under tow and taking radioactive air samples that were indicative of a reactor incident. Then, in 1968, he had taken the first photographs of, and collected the first sound signatures from, two of the second-generation Soviet nuclear-powered submarines that had made their début the previous year: a Charlie SSGN and a Victor SSN. Detected by the Soviets, he had escaped by taking *Dace* under the Arctic ice, outracing 'a group of Soviet surface patrols pinging wildly with active sonar'. Here was a fine mentor for Tall, whose talents and Southern charm he relished. Lacking the supreme self-confidence of some of his contemporaries, Tall found that these incidents gave him faith in himself. He had come a long way since Dartmouth.

Elliott was one of those submariners who took a good deal of interest in the political situation. Like most of his contemporaries from Dartmouth, he welcomed the return of the Conservatives to power, hoped they would sort out the economy, and presumed they would honour their pledge to buy Trident. Looking abroad, he had heard the rumblings of trouble in Eastern Europe. In Poland, criticism of the regime and of increasingly chronic shortages was becoming more public. The return to his homeland of the first-ever Polish-born Pope in June 1979 culminated in a rally attended by half a million people in Warsaw. Soon strikes spread across the country and the strikers, forming a group known as Solidarity, began to make political demands.

Elliott had also followed the chequered course of the second phase of the SALT talks with interest. In June 1979, Carter and Brezhnev met in Vienna to sign the SALT II treaty. It effectively codified the agreement reached by Ford and Brezhnev in Vladivostok five years earlier, but it came too late to reverse the breakdown of détente. The US Congress had scarcely begun to consider the ratification of SALT II when Carter was obliged to protest to the Soviets about the presence of 3,000 combat troops in America's old *bête noir*, Cuba. In September, the head of the pro-Soviet regime in Afghanistan was overthrown. Here, on the Soviet Union's south-eastern border, the Communists were battling against Muslim fundamentalists, a situation with disturbing implications for the largely Muslim Soviet Central Asian republics. Already there were 15,000 Soviet 'advisers' in the country. As Soviet authority was increasingly threatened towards the end of the year, Brezhnev was forced to take action. On 25 December 1979, a two-day airlift into the capital Kabul began. Tanks and motorized infantry followed. By the end of the year it was apparent that the Soviets had completed the largest such operation since the invasion of Czechoslovakia in 1968. In his State of the Union address, Carter described the action as 'the most serious threat to peace since the Second World War' and threatened military reprisals, not excluding the use of nuclear weapons. In Britain, the *Daily Telegraph* described the Soviet action as 'intervention'. Martin Macpherson, recently promoted Commander, in a letter published in the same newspaper, pointed out that it was an invasion. This, together with the return of the arms race symbolized by American plans for Trident, represented further nails in the coffin of détente. For the 35-year-old submarine commanders, it looked as though the chances of having to fight in the near future were better than even. Moreover, if push came to shove, they would be fighting a force of unprecedented strength and sophistication.

*

By 1980, Admiral Gorshkov had been in charge of the Soviet Navy for almost a quarter of a century and, at the age of 70, was approaching retirement. He had been awarded the title 'Hero of the Soviet Union', and his work on enlarging and modernizing the Soviet Navy had certainly been remarkable. In 1979, Thomas B. Hayward, the US Chief of Naval Operations, told Congress that 'in the past fifteen years the Soviet Navy has steadily grown from a coastal defensive force into a blue-water navy powerful enough to challenge the US Navy in most ocean areas in the world'. Nevertheless, in some respects Gorshkov's greatest successes were yet to come.

In the submarine field this success was partly a consequence of a research and development programme second only to that of the United States. By the end of the 1970s the front-line fleet comprised the latest Delta SSBN – the third in the series – sixteen Delta Is and four Delta IIs; the third in the line of Victor SSNs, sixteen Victor Is and seven Victor IIs; and a development of the single example of the Papa-class guided-missile SSGN, the 14,000-ton Oscar.

Yet these impressive craft were equally the product of espionage by a spy-ring invariably assessed in the United States as the most damaging that had ever been unmasked. The brothers Arthur and John Walker were born in the 1930s in Scranton, Pennsylvania, and joined the US Navy in the aftermath of the Korean War. Both soon graduated to submarines, the elder – Arthur – becoming an instructor in anti-submarine warfare. He retired from the Navy in 1976, and in 1980 went to work for a major defence contractor, VSE. John graduated to nuclear submarines and spent his career on a variety of vessels. He too retired in 1976, by which time his son Michael had also joined the service. In 1970, John Walker had met Jerry Whitworth, who was to become the fourth member of the ring. A native of a tiny farming community in Oklahoma, Whitworth was born in 1939, joined the Navy in 1962, and soon became a communications specialist. John Walker was the leader of the group and may have begun selling secrets to which he personally had access before the end of the 1960s. Certainly the group as a whole was divulging material wholesale to the Soviet Union throughout the next decade, and indeed right up until their arrest in May 1985 as a result of a tip-off by John Walker's estranged wife Barbara. By then, though, the damage was done. Their motive had apparently been money.

The ring operated over such a long period, and its members were so well placed within the US Navy, that the true extent of the material divulged to the Soviet Union will not be known until – or if – Russia opens her files on such matters; or indeed until such time as its members make a complete confession. At a press conference on 11 June 1985, the Chief of Naval Operations, Rear-Admiral James D. Watkins, stated: 'We always consider the worst case. We have to assume that any sensitive information that could have been possessed was actually given to the Soviets.' On this basis it was assumed that by 1980 the Soviets knew:

- the patrol areas used by US SSBNs and SSNs, their duties and the number of vessels on station at any given time;
- performance data on US submarines, including critical issues such as speed, diving depth and armament;
- details of the command and control communications systems that might permit them to be jammed, and the codes that enabled the messages to be cracked;
- details of how Nato tracked Soviet submarines, and with what success, including SOSUS and sonar developments; and
- details of how US – and UK – submarines were quietened, the critical field of quiet-running technology in which the Soviets, hitherto, had lagged.

The progress that the Soviets had made in submarine technology during the 1970s had already led some in Nato defence circles to believe that a ring such as the Walker-Whitworth group was operating. Others argued that the West was in the habit of underestimating Soviet abilities. It had done so, after all, with both the atomic bomb and the hydrogen bomb. In due course, those favouring a conspiracy would be vindicated. Meanwhile, both US and British submariners would have to deal with the consequences of espionage at a time when the threat of war had rarely been greater.

Crimson Tide

'It is easy to forget at the end of the 'eighties that when the decade began, the prospects for world peace seemed worse than at any time since 1945.'

Denis Healey, *The Time of My Life*, 1989

Chapter 10
Up Against It

'A huge, largely land-based country like Russia does not need to build the most powerful navy in the world just to guard its own frontiers. No. The Russians are bent on world domination, and they are rapidly acquiring the means to become the most powerful imperial nation the world has seen.'

Margaret Thatcher, 1976

Despite the serious economic position in which her government found itself, Britain's new Prime Minister had few doubts about Trident. On her first day in office she discovered a minute from her predecessor James Callaghan permitting her to see the correspondence with President Carter over the replacement of the deterrent. This she thought constructive. Moreover, as part of her induction as Prime Minister she had been thoroughly briefed on the current assessment of the Soviet threat. The invasion of Afghanistan seemed the clearest possible indication that détente was at an end, and the Kremlin was also making increasingly threatening noises over Poland, where Solidarity was beginning to demand economic reform, freedom of speech and the release of political prisoners. The upgrading of the Soviet IRBM force in Europe by the introduction of 900 of the immensely powerful SS-20s was continuing, a process that appeared to be an attempt by the Soviets to decouple the defence of Europe from that of the United States, and one which threatened to turn Europe into a nuclear battlefield. The Nato response to this, to be finalized in October 1979, was what became known as the 'dual track' policy. The first was the decision to introduce 572 Pershing II IRBMs and Tomahawk cruise missiles to Western Europe; the second was to pursue talks with the Soviets with a view to getting the SS-20s removed.

With an eye to both the political and the military significance of the deterrent, Mrs Thatcher accordingly saw a good deal of sense in pursuing the option of Trident. As her biographer Hugo Young wrote, 'Possession of the independent nuclear weapon, no matter how excessively large or expensive it was, remained, of all aspects of her inheritance, the one about which she countenanced least argument.' The events of twenty years before leading up to the acquisition of Polaris were beginning to repeat themselves, albeit on a grander, more expensive and even more destructive scale. Some talked about the opening phase of a new Cold War.

On 13 July 1980, the Defence Secretary Francis Pym announced the decision on Trident to the House of Commons. Four new submarines would be built to replace the Polaris fleet, with an option for a fifth. Each would be equipped with sixteen Trident missiles. As with Polaris, although the missile system itself was American, the warheads would be British. The cost to the taxpayer was estimated at £5,000 million over fifteen years. It was a decision publicly deplored in the Soviet Union, where the official news agency Tass described it as 'militaristic hysteria on the banks of the Thames'.

The real problem, however, was whether the country could afford the weapon. The new government had pledged itself to match overall Nato spending by increasing the defence budget by 3 per cent annually, but it was by no means clear where this increase would come from. The services themselves were at loggerheads over the matter, and each was pressing so hard for a share of the budget that it was decided to replace Francis Pym with someone who it was hoped would take a firmer line. In his review the new Defence Secretary John Nott, a former Gurkha officer and career merchant banker, confirmed the government's commitment to the Trident submarine deterrent. It would not, however, come out of the general defence budget but out of that of the surface Navy.

Sandy Woodward, fast climbing up the Navy's hierarchy, was by now a director of the Naval Plans Division based at the Ministry of Defence in Whitehall. Nevertheless, he was not yet in a position to

debate government policy, though in *One Hundred Days* he rehearsed
the argument that he would have used had he been in a position to
do so:

> the Trident system, like Polaris, was a political lever and not a
> military weapon system. So my line would have been: the whole
> project is of no real interest to the Royal Navy *per se*. Trident is
> a national defence system, not a single Service requirement.
> Faced then with all three Services united against the awful pros-
> pect of having to pay for this system out of existing budgets,
> the Defence Secretary would be forced either to spread the
> costs evenly or to provide additional funds for the project.

As it was, in June 1981, Nott outlined a series of cuts that the Navy
regarded as swingeing. They included a reduction of 15 per cent in
Navy personnel, the closure of the naval dockyard at Chatham, the
decommissioning of nine destroyers and frigates and the amphibious force, the sale of the aircraft-carriers *Hermes* and *Invincible*, and
the disposal of the South Atlantic survey ship *Endurance*. Following
David Owen's lead in 1977, the Foreign Secretary Lord Carrington
at once warned Nott that the withdrawal of *Endurance* would send
undesirable signals to Argentina.

These proposals inevitably caused enormous controversy in the
Navy, and the First Sea Lord Sir Henry Leach in particular fought a
tenacious rearguard action for the retention of the aircraft-carriers.
The controversy was compounded by the more widespread debate
over Trident itself and the announcement of the decision to base
the Pershing and cruise missiles in Europe from 1983, an announcement that breathed new life into the Campaign for Nuclear
Disarmament in Britain, and indeed into anti-nuclear campaigns all
over Europe.

*

The main argument for Trident lay in the approaching obsolescence
of the existing Polaris deterrent. To date, it had done a good job. In
1980 the Chief Polaris Executive Rear-Admiral John Grove told the
Commons Defence Committee that none of the Navy's Polaris

patrols had yet been detected, while their Soviet counterparts invariably were. Nevertheless, it was also true that when Toby Elliott put to sea in the SSBN *Resolution*, the challenges he faced were of quite a different order from those encountered when the boat's first commanders had set off on patrol in 1968.

Despite the size of the Soviet submarine fleet twelve years previously, the technical abilities of the submarines tasked with seeking Nato SSBNs had not been particularly impressive. The Novembers dated back to 1957 and represented the Soviet Union's first attempt at nuclear propulsion. They were relatively slow and noisy, giving Western SSBNs plenty of time to take avoiding action. The Victors were the second-generation SSNs that had appeared in 1967. Rather larger than the Novembers and incorporating the hydrodynamic tear-drop shaped hull pioneered by the United States Navy, by Western standards these were still noisy craft. By 1978, though, Gorshkov had introduced the Victor III, which showed improvements in quietening that surprised Nato observers and fuelled the debate about a possible Soviet spy-ring operating in the West.

More alarming still were the five new titanium-hulled Alfa-class boats. The first boat of the class had undergone extensive trials in 1970 and 1971 but had suffered from severe machinery problems and had to be scrapped. The Soviets, though, persisted with the design, and by the time Elliott set to sea again in *Resolution*, the class's problems had been solved. Short and plump, with the conning-tower carefully faired into the hull, the five boats were the talk of the navies of the Western world. In 1980, Admiral Thomas Hayward, US Chief of Naval Operations, told Congress: 'The Alfa class is the most advanced example of Soviet submarine technology. It is most impressive, with advanced concepts that permit it to travel faster and dive deeper than any other submarine in the world today.' More dramatically, a headline in the *Daily Telegraph* declared, 'West Outclassed by Latest Soviet Submarines':

> Russia is now believed to have at sea four [*sic*] Alfa-class torpedo-armed nuclear submarines whose diving depth and speed would enable them to evade most Western anti-submarine weapons. They can dive to depths of 3,000 to 4,000 feet, far greater than any Western nuclear submarine – the principal anti-submarine

weapon – can attain. The underwater speed is known to be at least 40 knots, as the American Navy has been able to track them at such speed on several occasions. If the Alfa design were to be modified to carry anti-ship missiles, the task of protecting convoys would be immeasurably harder.

At the same time, Elliott in his first posting as a Polaris commander certainly had a good deal more intelligence at his disposal than his predecessors of the late 1960s had had. The SOSUS system of listening devices had been in constant development over the previous decade and was now much more widespread and sensitive. By 1981, it was publicly acknowledged that thirty-six installations existed, including those around the United Kingdom, Turkey, Japan, the Aleutians, Hawaii, Puerto Rico, Bermuda, Barbados, Canada, Norway, Iceland, the Azores, Italy, Denmark, Gibraltar, Panama, the Philippines, Guam and Diego Garcia. Equally, the improved command and communication systems associated with the establishment of submarine headquarters in Northwood, together with the development of computers, allowed rapid cross-referral of intelligence data drawn from a very wide variety of sources. Not the least important of these were satellites, of which there were now a considerable number. All this meant that Elliott could be kept far better-informed by Northwood of Soviet submarine movements than his predecessors had been.

Resolution herself was also provided with sensors that improved her knowledge of the surrounding waters to a remarkable degree. Chief among these was towed array, the device that Elliott had first learned about ten years previously when he started to specialize in sonar. Towed array consisted of a cable almost a kilometre long carrying special hydrophones and deployed by the submarine once it had sailed from its base port. Hitherto, passive sonar listening devices had allowed Western submarines to detect their relatively noisy Soviet counterparts at ranges in the order of 10,000 to 20,000 yards, depending on the noise emanating from the opposition and on sonar conditions at any given time. As Elliott says, this meant that on the early Polaris patrols 'you might not get any sort of contact for three or four days'. As the Soviets learned to produce quieter submarines, the range at which they could be detected obviously diminished, with equally obvious implications for the security of the SSBN force. The towed array system picked up the very faint and very low-frequency sounds emanating from submarines, and by doing so it once again increased the range at which the Soviets could be detected, typically by a factor of ten, sometimes by far more. In Elliott's words, 'The seas came alive for us.'

Like SOSUS, a series of towed arrays operated by a range of Nato surface and submarine vessels created a net, described as SURTASS 'Surveillance Towed Array Sensor System', that fed into the Acoustic Research Centre in California. From there SURTASS and SOSUS each fed into the US Navy's Anti-Submarine Warfare Centre command and control system, and this clearing-house then provided both a worldwide picture of submarine movements and local tactical information. On this Elliott and his fellow Nato submarine commanders – be they American, Dutch, Scandinavian, German, Italian, Greek, Turkish or Spanish – could act.

Despite these advances within both the Soviet fleet and that of Nato, it might be imagined that the greatest burden on the new SSBN commander would be the nuclear deterrent itself. A little less than a century previously, the Prime Minister William Gladstone had remarked of *Resolution*'s Victorian counterpart, the 11,880-ton battleship *Inflexible*, 'I really wonder if the human mind can bear such responsibility.' That resting on the commander of *Resolution*, with her forty-eight nuclear MIRV warheads, was infinitely greater.

Paradoxically, though, Elliott found this aspect of his burden relatively easy to cope with. He had thoroughly thought through his own position on the deterrent and felt absolutely prepared and trained for the responsibilities of nuclear command. Some COs sidestepped the issue by remarking that it was very unlikely that they would ever be called upon to fire their missiles. Not so Elliott. As CO of the Port crew of *Resolution*, his period of command coincided with a time when it seemed very likely that the Soviets would invade Poland. In the spring of 1981 there were Warsaw Pact exercises close to the Polish border; in September an amphibious landing was likewise conducted close to the border; and on 13 December martial law was imposed in Poland by the Prime Minister General Jaruzelski. These events focused Elliott's mind on the issues involved. 'If that had all led to nuclear war, and if ordered to do so, I would have started the launch sequence without compunction. I personally had every faith in the chain of command, and I was a disciplined person who was bound to that chain. As CO, I was at the end of the chain in operational terms. One had been brought up to that level of command, and it would have been my duty to do it.' It is difficult to doubt him.

Interestingly, for many SSBN COs, it was the more normal issues of ship-handling that were burdensome. The journalist Charles Douglas-Home, later to edit *The Times*, spent seven days at sea on Elliott's old submarine the SSBN *Renown* during the early days of the Polaris patrols. He wrote of the CO:

A mistake committed while he conned the submarine out of the narrow waters of the Gareloch and he would have, at a stroke, entirely wiped out the British deterrent. It would be the equivalent, when Bomber Command operated the deterrent force, of a personal misjudgement by a senior officer ground-ing hundreds of bombers. . . . it is more that kind of respon-sibility, than the thought of incinerating the inhabitants of Omsk, which weighs heavily on *Renown*'s CO.

So it was with Elliott. He had enough on his mind coping with the complexities of submarine command and the three critical require-ments of remaining undetected, staying in touch with Northwood, and being ready to fire within fifteen minutes, without worrying unduly about the ethical issues involved in precipitating a nuclear holocaust.

On 8 December 1980 Elliott heard that John Lennon had been shot dead in New York. The heady, irresponsible days of the Sixties, Greenwich, 'birds, booze and fun', had gone. While *Resolution* was at sea, it was Toby Elliott who might have to take the final decision to fire missiles that could lead to the deaths of hundreds of thousands of Russians. For Elliott, though, the deterrent was just that. It pre-vented war, and it was the factor that, in his own words, 'maintained the peace between the Warsaw Pact countries and the West'.

*

At the same time as Elliott was grappling with the problems of Polaris operational command, James Taylor, Chris Wreford-Brown and Roger Lane-Nott were coming to terms with driving SSNs.

Following his spell as CO of *Opossum* that had taken him to the Baltic, in 1980 Wreford-Brown was promoted to Commander and given a taste of the SSN *Dreadnought*. It had been discovered that the twenty-year-old submarine was suffering from reactor screening problems that needed to be examined in a fully equipped dockyard. Wreford-Brown was ordered to take her from Faslane down to Devonport. This he was obliged to do under tow, the pride of the fleet now reduced to a sorry group of submarine, escort vessel and tug. A year later, John Nott announced she would be scrapped, so saving the cost of a £70 million refit. Wreford-Brown then spent a year at the National Defence College at Latimer on a strategic studies course for all three of the services, for which the participants are specially selected. While on the course he saw some of the activities of Nato land forces on the Cold War eastern front in Germany, and he flew in the latest of the RAF maritime patrol aircraft, the Nimrod. This was all an education for someone whose horizons had been restricted to the Navy for seventeen years. As he remarks, 'It was the first time I'd had the opportunity to work with, and understand, what the other Services were up to.'

Then, in June 1981, he was appointed to command the SSN *Conqueror*, the fourth of the Valiant-class SSNs. *Conqueror* displaced 4,400 tons, carried a crew of 103, and had six 21-inch torpedo tubes that took both the old-fashioned Mark 8 free-running torpedoes and the troublesome Mark 24 Tigerfish homing torpedoes. Following CO-designate training, Wreford-Brown would take command in March 1982. It was, he says, 'a great opportunity and privilege to be given a nuclear command.'

Roger Lane-Nott had followed his first command of the SSK *Walrus* with an appointment as deputy chief operations officer, attached to the Submarine Command at *Dolphin*. His spell in this post coincided with the transfer of the Command from Gosport to Northwood, in which – increasingly highly regarded as an administrator – he played a significant part. Under the Flag Officer Submarines John Fieldhouse, Lane-Nott oversaw the establishment of a state-of-the-art communications centre and operations room suitable for the orchestration of the Third World War. Then, promoted Commander, he was posted to the SSN *Swiftsure*, the first of the second generation of British SSNs. Commissioned on 17 April 1973, she was followed by *Sovereign*, *Superb*, *Sceptre*, *Spartan* and *Splendid*. To the last of these, then still being built in Barrow, Lane-Nott was soon transferred, and he would be her first CO. Preparing himself psychologically for command, Lane-Nott – in common with most of his fellow COs – decided to make a will.

James Taylor was promoted to Commander in 1979 after his spell in *Orpheus*. He then spent a short time at the Ministry of Defence in Bath, working on submarine design and improvement, before being posted CO of *Splendid*'s sister boat *Spartan*, attached to the Second Submarine Squadron in Devonport.

For Taylor, yet to serve in a nuclear-powered boat in any capacity, command of *Spartan* marked the recognition of his record during his first two commands, *Grampus* and *Orpheus*, and reaffirmation that he was not regarded as culpable for the SBS tragedy on Loch Long. He was astonished by the machine of which he was now placed in charge. Her reactor was capable of producing 15,000 horsepower that in turn gave her a speed of 30 knots, and she had new, highly sophisticated sonar systems, including towed array, and all the latest quietening devices. Despite the advances the Soviets were undoubtedly making, this was a submarine better able to detect and better able to avoid being detected than almost any other submarine in the world. 'After *Orpheus*,' he said, 'it was a bit like getting out of a Ford Sierra and into a Formula 1 car. Here was something that could do anything, absolutely anything that a submarine of any sort could do. She was fast off the mark, very manoeuvrable, and damn quiet. I have to say I was absolutely thrilled.' Taylor then rewarded the faith of Submarine Command with a first patrol that set tongues wagging throughout the Second Submarine Squadron.

Taylor's recollection of the patrol reflects not only the excitement of the command but also its complexity.

Sailing from Devonport in January, I aimed to fit in four days or so of Independent Exercise – INDEX – in deep water west of Ireland. This would allow me to put the boat through her paces, see just how she handled, and what the limits were. It was to prove great fun, and from then on, the boat had something of a reputation for 'angles and dangles'.

But this was all to come when I slipped from Devonport, not yet having served in a nuclear-powered submarine, except for familiarization training. Six feet off the wall at Devonport, I signalled to Jeff Tall, who was standing on the jetty, 'So far, so good.' I think he knew how I felt. After INDEX, we berthed in Faslane for final storing, and to tweak a couple of minor defects, then set to sea again, attaching a 'clip-on' sonar 2024 towed array in the Clyde.

My target was a Soviet Victor, returning to the Northern Fleet from the Mediterranean. The initial information we were given from Northwood was good, and we set up patrol well to the west of the UK and gained contact. We then tracked her north, building up her track and her pattern of operations, and gaining more on her noise signature. Before too long, I had to decide whether to remain on the trail through the very difficult waters of the Gaps [the ocean front where the Atlantic and the Norwegian Sea meet] or break the trail and sprint ahead. I chose the latter, and set up patrol in the better sonar conditions north of the Gaps, hoping that we had correctly interpreted the Victor's intentions. We had.

Everything seemed set for a routine but valuable northward trail, as *Spartan* took the Victor through the Norwegian Sea. We watched him clear his stern arcs, the areas behind the submarine where – because of the noise of his own propeller – he is deaf, and which he periodically checks for a trailing submarine by changing direction; and we saw him establishing his operating pattern, all the while gaining more and more information on his noise signature.

Off Bear Island, some 200 miles north of Norway – it seemed a roundabout route to Polyarnny – we saw the Victor set about a different pattern of operations, with more frequent zigs and then a rectilinear pattern. All this indicated that the Victor was either operating with another unit, anticipating the arrival of another unit, sanitizing an area, or trying to ensure – ineffectually as it transpired – that a Soviet SSBN was not being trailed by a Nato SSN.

As *Spartan* moved in closer, we detected the signature of a Delta SSBN and observed the sanitization take place. Reckoning that the attention of the Victor would be concentrated on his Delta, I saw this as the time to move in closer still.

Good hull-mounted passive sonar contact will give you a pretty accurate range, and we had confidence in that. The depth of the other submarines remained, of course, an unknown, as were his Rules of Engagement – his instructions if he found an intruder submarine at this time. How would he react?

At this stage you have to remind yourself of the basic rule – you are there to observe, not to participate! We moved in closer still and were well rewarded by a wealth of sonar information; at about this time, all three submarines were within one square mile or so which made things pretty interesting.

At this stage, too, we knew that the Delta was not on the plot at Northwood; and that if it was outbound on patrol, it had a greater priority than the homebound Victor. Yet Northwood would still assume that I was trailing the Victor, and would allocate water – lumps of sea space – accordingly. I was not about to give away my position to the Soviets by breaking radio silence. The Victor and the Delta parted company, the Victor homebound; the Delta headed north-west, with *Spartan* on his trail.

Trailing the Delta was more tricky than it should have been. Whenever we pulled off, for example to read the VLF [Very Low Frequency radio] broadcast, we found it difficult to determine on which side of the array the contact really was. As we closed to resolve the picture it suddenly became clear that we had bagged not one but two modern, quiet, strategic missile submarines. Two Deltas were running in company up towards the marginal ice zone, the area between open water and firm ice [of the Arctic Ocean]. We stayed with them and what we pulled in over the next couple of days was pure gold.

Northwood knew nothing of this at the time, and my fear was that the water I had been allocated, up to and including the ice edge, would be 'wrapped up' – allocated to another unit –

obliging me to pull out and sprint back south. In the event, I had all the water space I needed. When the time came for me to pull out, we got a signal alerting us to the presence of a Charlie-class SSGN – an anti-ship missile firer – homebound from the Mediterranean. We set up patrol in the Norwegian Sea, and gained firm towed array contact, staying with him as long as we could before turning for home.

Taylor brought back an intelligence treasure-trove that merited the plaudits he received. A fellow CO, Robert Stevens, then driving the SSK *Odin* and later to become Teacher and Flag Officer Submarines, was an acute observer of Taylor's style. He remarked, 'It contained all the traditional Taylor elements – persistence, nerve, dash, intelligence – and sheer bloody luck!'

There was more to it than that, though. Taylor's patrol was an intrinsic part of British submarine policy to prosecute the Cold War in an aggressive manner, always seeking to show the Soviets that Britain's forces were technically and tactically superior – that they had better submarines that were better crewed and better led. Following Richard Sharp's dictum, it was intended that each operation contain 'an underlying element of threat, such as to make the use of force an unattractive option'.

*

Spartan's first patrol under Taylor's command coincided with the inauguration of a new American President in January 1981 and his first one hundred days in office.

From the outset of his presidency Ronald Reagan adopted a strident note on the Cold War. Even on the campaign trail he had identified the country's defence policy as one of 'three grave threats to our very existence'. At his first presidential press conference on 29 January he dismissed détente as a one-way street that the Soviet Union had used to pursue its own aims. He upheld the rebuttal by Congress of Carter's SALT II strategic arms agreement; and the Secretary of State Alexander Haig told the Senate Foreign Relations Committee of 'the transformation of Soviet military power from a continental and largely land army to a global offensive army fully capable of supporting an imperial policy'. Carter had begun the process of rejecting détente and had increased defence spending. Reagan, inclined to see things in black and white and fervently anti-Communist – he described the Soviet Union as an 'evil empire' – believed that the United States could afford an escalation in the arms race whereas the Soviets could not. One of his first acts in office was substantially to raise the defence budget, and during his first term as a whole US defence spending would rise by 50 per cent. Much of this would go on military equipment, not least on the giant Ohio-class Trident SSBNs, the first of which was commissioned on 11 November 1981; and on the continuing production of the Los Angeles-class SSNs, of which sixty-two were eventually commissioned. Funds were also used to support the Mujahideen resistance to the Red Army in Afghanistan.

Here was a confrontational White House that the Kremlin had scarcely seen since the days of President Johnson. Leonid Brezhnev, now an ailing old man increasingly embroiled in the quagmire of Afghanistan, was bemused; and the KGB began to advise that the United States appeared to be preparing for a first strike against the Soviet Union.

It was a little before this time that Martin Macpherson had been appointed as one of the two Teachers, tasked with taking the next generation of officers through the commanding officers' qualifying course.

Much though he had enjoyed his own Perisher six years previously, Macpherson was aware that changes would have to be made to the course. Even then there had been some debate over whether the use of frigates in training Cold War submariners to attack was really relevant. Now, with John Nott's Defence Review beginning to bite, there arose the rather starker issue of the sheer availability of ships. These maids-of-all-work were busy enough as it was, not least in fulfilling their anti-submarine warfare role in the North Atlantic. Macpherson accordingly took the lead in changing the balance of the course from an emphasis on attack work with frigates to training the new commanders to undertake other tasks, particularly those required on intelligence-gathering patrols.

At the same time, the emphasis on the Navy's nuclear programme meant that there were now not enough diesel-electric submarines for all who passed Perisher to be given the opportunity to test their novice command skills on a diesel-electric SSK. The A-boats, a legacy from the Second World War, were in the process of being decommissioned, and there were simply too few of the Porpoise- and Oberon-class submarines to go round. Although a new SSK, the Vickers 2400, was being designed, the first submarines of this class would not become operational until the end of the decade. The course had therefore also to be reformulated so as to prepare newly qualified COs for their more likely postings as Executive Officer on one of the nuclear submarines, an SSN or an SSBN.

Macpherson relished the role of Teacher, as had Sandy Woodward and Toby Frere before him. Nevertheless, Teacher was not simply there for the ride. 'As a student', wrote Woodward in *One Hundred Days*, 'you always had Teacher there to save you if things went wrong, because he always held the ultimate responsibility. Now, if things were to go wrong, the responsibility would be entirely mine.' Woodward recalls that he was quite frankly very nervous during his early months as Teacher, and that he lost a stone and a half during the first course. Macpherson seems to have undertaken the job with greater equanimity, although he admits to having to steel himself to be hard-hearted with those who were not going to make it. On one of the three courses he ran between 1980 and 1981, he was obliged to fail four out of the five candidates. Overall, though, he says, 'I enjoyed it immensely.'

He also took the opportunity traditionally afforded to Teacher – and habitually taken – to read his own Perisher report, and those of his friends and contemporaries. All, he says, made very interesting reading; and some were amusing. 'I would go to war with this officer, but not to a diplomatic reception,' wrote one Teacher of a candidate more suited to undersea life than diplomatic service. Nevertheless, the officer concerned was subsequently posted as a naval attaché with – as Macpherson says – predictable results.

*

After Teacher, Macpherson was given the job of acting as command rider. This involved providing senior support and operational advice to a submarine commander taking his vessel on a particularly demanding patrol. In Macpherson's case he was to act as rider to Commander Tom Le Marchand, who was taking the SSN *Valiant* up to the Arctic ice-pack for a joint operation with the US Navy.

During the First World War, the proximity of the Russian bases to the Arctic ice had encouraged the Russians to explore its margins, and in the 1930s the Americans had made some abortive under-ice voyages. In the Second World War, German U-boats operating out of the northern ports of Norway against the Allies' Murmansk conveys had devised the tactic of dipping under the edge of the Arctic ice-pack to escape from enemy aircraft. Once the Cold War got under way, both sides returned to the region. The pioneering American SSN *Nautilus* made her record-breaking trip underneath the ice-cap in 1958, and the SSN *Skate* surfaced at the North Pole on 17 March 1959. British submarines also made Arctic forays. The ill-fated *Artemis* was pictured in Arctic waters in *The Times* in 1964; the boat that Chris Wreford-Brown would later command, the SSK *Opossum*, was there in 1965; and the SSN *Dreadnought* reached the North Pole under Commander A.G. Kennedy on 3 March 1971.

Those voyages were not merely exploratory. Submarines are always difficult to find but they are doubly so under the ice-pack. Of the two principal methods of anti-submarine warfare, that of maritime patrol aircraft working in conjunction with surface ships is obviously impossible in a frozen sea. The alternative, of using another submarine, is only slightly more satisfactory because of the difficulties involved in operating submarines under ice.

Arctic navigation has been a problem ever since explorers first ventured into the northern wastes. The poles of the earth have peculiar magnetic properties that compromise navigation by compass, and even the sophisticated SINS system used in nuclear-powered submarines has to be specially adapted to work accurately close to the North Pole. The use of sonar in this region is similarly problematic, partly because of the usual difficulties involved when saline and fresh water mix; partly because of the noise made by the shifting and breaking-off of blocks of ice on the edge of the ice-zone; and partly because up-ended slabs – called keels – of ice that extend as deep as 50 metres, cause curious echoes. Communication under water is also difficult if not impossible, which is a problem if it becomes necessary to fire a missile or torpedo in anger. Finally, surfacing is always diffi-cult and generally hazardous. The polar ice-cap varies tremendously in thickness. In places it is sufficiently thin for a submarine to be able to force its way through the ice to the surface. There are also small patches of open water, known as polynyas. If a submarine can locate one of these it can surface within it, but their location, size and very existence change constantly as the ice itself shifts on the surface of the Arctic Ocean. This is critical, because although ballistic missiles can be fired from under water, they cannot be fired from under ice.

Polynyas are also of course the submarine's bolt-hole, where it can surface if things go wrong. In their absence the feeling of vulnerabil-ity inevitable in underwater operations is redoubled, the sub-mariners' lives more than ever depending on the reliability of the vessel. As James Calvert, the CO of *Skate* puts it in *Surface at the Pole*:

> All of us knew the risk inherent in taking the submarine under ice. We had mainly been concerned with the risk of major calamities – collision, fire, steam leaks, and radiation. But so dependent were we upon the intricate mechanics of our ship that even minor malfunctioning in her safety equipment could place us in grave peril. If the [nuclear] plant should suddenly shut down – for whatever reason – while we were under ice, our lives would depend upon restarting the plant before the storage battery gave out or finding an opening [a polynya] in which the *Skate* could be brought to the surface and her diesel engine operated. If we should fail, we should find a cold and airless tomb.

As Martin Macpherson remarks of such under-ice voyages, 'You just take a deep breath and go under as far as you dare.'

Yet if the problems of under-ice operation can be overcome, the rewards of an Arctic passage are considerable. A submarine that wishes to hide can tuck itself up under a keel, wind down all its noise-making machinery and be virtually impervious to detection. And even if it is found, a keel produces so many echoes that it is difficult for a homing torpedo to latch on to its target. For once the prey has the advantage over the predator.

While the Soviets possessed only short-range ballistic missiles, their submarines were obliged to patrol the Atlantic and the eastern American seaboard to target American cities, and use of the Arctic remained relatively academic. However, once they acquired longer-range missiles installed in Delta SSBNs, they were able to move some of their missile submarines closer to their home bases in the Barents Sea or the Sea of Okhotsk, in their so-called bastions. Tracking them there was difficult enough. If, however, they managed to solve the problems of operating under ice, tracking them would be far harder. In the late 1970s it became clear that they were indeed managing to operate under the ice, and that their Arctic SSBNs were also being further protected by SSNs, mines and patrol aircraft in yet more bastions.

The significance of this development cannot be overstated. Hitherto, almost all the Soviet SSBNs dispatched to target the United States or Western Europe had been tracked on SOSUS, and a very fair number of them had been trailed by Nato submarines that could – theoretically – have destroyed them before they fired their missiles. If the Soviets no longer needed to venture out of their home waters, much of Nato's advantage was lost. And if they could hide under the ice, that advantage disappeared completely. Summarizing the position a few years later, Richard Compton-Hall wrote in *Submarine Warfare*:

> Deploying in the Arctic, the fourth largest of the world's oceans and nearly landlocked, Soviet SSBNs and supporting SSNs have no need to transit through choke points, and their Arctic operating areas are necessarily much more familiar to them than to opposing Nato boats . . . Conversely, Western submarines – SSBNs (which might conceivably seek ice-cover) or anti-SSBN SSNs – have to make their long passage through the choke points of the Davis, Denmark or Bering Straits, the latter shallow and dangerous. There is a real danger of hitting the bottom or colliding with the ice projecting downwards, in places down to 200 feet and sometimes touching the bottom of the Bering Strait.

Macpherson's patrol was to develop tactics for the destruction of Soviet SSBNs in these waters. To do this a Hercules C-130 transport aircraft was flown in and landed on the ice. Specialists on board then set up what amounted to an underwater firing range by introducing a series of sonobuoys into the sea through holes in the ice. Then *Valiant* and an American SSN trailed, targeted and fired dummy torpedoes at one another. The torpedoes were retrieved by the team on the C-130, using something like a giant Bunsen burner to cut through the ice. Carefully assessed, these exercises had considerable practical value, for they began to suggest ways to restore the balance to the predator, they stimulated ideas for equipment better suited to Arctic conditions, and they evolved tactics that would work in the strange Arctic environment. The two submarines then went right up to the North Pole and surfaced there. This part of the voyage was of more symbolic value. The submarines were likely to be spotted by Soviet satellites, and photographs were taken to be released to the world's press. As Commander John Hervey, who had taken *Warspite* into these waters ten years previously, wrote, 'One aim of such patrols has been to make clear to the Russians that the Arctic is not their lake.'

It was Macpherson's first experience under the ice, and he returned somewhat sobered. The Arctic was certainly a difficult place for submarine operations, and if the Soviets were to retreat to their Arctic bastions in significant numbers, they and their missiles would be very difficult indeed to forestall. One of the films shown on the patrol was *Chariots of Fire*, Hugh Hudson's film about two British runners in the 1924 Olympics. This was stirring stuff, and it needed to be. The prognosis for the Cold War was not very bright.

*

Moreover, as if to underscore the challenges then facing Macpherson's generation, his return to Faslane coincided with an accident to another of the SSNs, *Sceptre*.

Sceptre was the third of the Swiftsure-class SSNs specially equipped for covert intelligence-gathering missions. Building on the experience of the early SSNs that had operated close to Soviet naval units in Arctic waters – like *Warspite* – they were exceptionally quiet, they were fitted with the latest sonars that included towed array, and they had an unusual range of other sensors that enabled them to pick up a variety of information about Soviet submarine operations. They were commonly known as 'special fit' or 'sneaky boats', and they were used mainly in conjunction with US SSNs in the continuing Operation Holystone. The American COs, though, were generalists for whom covert intelligence-gathering missions were only one element in a variety of duties including carrier battle group support operations and – particularly more recently – land attack missions. The British COs became specialists, and as such enjoyed a very good reputation among their US counterparts. Indeed, they were in many respects the élite of the Cold War COs.

The first of the British special-fit submarines was *Swiftsure* herself, completed on 17 April 1973. She was followed by *Superb*, completed on 13 November 1976. Under the captaincy of Geoffrey Biggs and his Executive Officer Douglas Littlejohns, she followed *Swiftsure* in rapidly establishing a reputation for aggressive and highly successful patrols. This continued when Michael Boyce – now Chief of Defence Staff – took over the boat, an equally aggressive although less flamboyant figure, and when James Perowne took command in 1981. In *Superb* Perowne estimated that he was at sea for 60 per cent of the time and in contact with the Soviets for 30 per cent of the time. An avuncular, larger-than-life figure, he was subsequently pro-moted Flag Officer Submarines and later became a full admiral. *Sceptre*, the third of the boats, was completed on 14 February 1978, and was soon fitted in to the intelligence-gathering rota. Then, in the late summer of 1981, she appears to have been involved in a colli-sion, officially with an iceberg. This incident was the subject of much press speculation, including an article in the *Daily Telegraph* coincid-ing with the sinking of the Soviet submarine *Kursk* in August 2000. It suggested that *Sceptre* had actually collided with a Soviet submarine and had been badly damaged, although apparently without causing serious injury on either British or Soviet boat.

Although Martin Macpherson and his contemporaries would not be drawn on the incident, it was clearly sufficiently serious to raise legitimate questions about the wisdom of operating in areas tradi-tionally used by the Soviets and where ice was only one of the threats to the safety of a patrolling submarine. At the time, approaching the height of the submarine Cold War, the Navy would doubtless have argued that it was its job to mark the Soviet deterrent and thereby to prepare itself as thoroughly as possible for the advent of a 'hot' war. If that entailed a degree of risk, then so be it. That was part of the job, and one of the responsibilities its submarine commanders embraced. It was a question of balancing risk against reward. Though the precise nature of the reward cannot yet be revealed, and leaving aside the acknowledged role of submarines like *Sceptre* as sentinels for surge deployment of the Soviet Northern Fleet, the extent of Anglo-American activity suggests that the intelligence derived from such patrols was of a very high value. It might, for instance, have included command and control methods used on Soviet ballistic missiles that could enable them to be jammed. This might reasonably be considered as very well worth the risk. In a letter to the Admiralty in March 1805, Nelson had written, 'If I had been censured every time I have run my ship, or the fleets under my command, into great danger, I should have long ago been out of the service, and never in the House of Peers.' His descendants justifiably felt the same. Shortly after the incident, it appears that Nato trailing procedures were reviewed, taking into account improving Soviet technologies and tactics. In many respects, for the Royal Navy's submarine service, this was a watershed.

Sceptre's CO was later relieved of command and replaced by *Superb*'s former Executive Officer, Douglas Littlejohns. Following repairs, Littlejohns took her on two Holystone patrols. At the end of this he was required to debrief the Prime Minister, and he was awarded the OBE – the same decoration as was conferred on Geoffrey Biggs, Mike Boyce and James Perowne. In Littlejohns's view, 'The British contribution to the programme far outweighed our resources – we really brought home the bacon.'

Chapter 11

The Hot War

'The diplomats and politicos have fucked up again. We are being sent
to sort it out for them. Damned if I know whether we can do it or
not. Some of us will certainly *not* get home. But the harder we all try,
the more of us will.'

> Sandy Woodward, address to ships' companies,
> South Atlantic, April 1982

On Monday, 29 March 1982, James Taylor was in the control-room
of *Spartan*, taking part in Operation Springtrain. This was the annual
Navy spring exercise, designed to work up the participating destroyers, frigates, submarines and aircraft-carriers to operational readiness
after the winter. For this purpose the eastern Atlantic was divided up
into boxes, and mock war was conducted between two different
groups of ships. In command of the operation was Sandy
Woodward, newly promoted Rear-Admiral and Flag Officer First
Flotilla. Among his subordinates, now commanding the new Type 22
frigate *Brilliant*, was Woodward's Executive Officer from his *Warspite*
days, John Coward. Both submariners had already shown outstanding gifts, and Coward himself was now promoted Captain. That
morning off Gibraltar it was grey, wet and choppy, and many of those
in *Spartan* were suffering from the after-effects of a run ashore the
previous evening. Still, the exercise overall had run smoothly enough,
and Taylor was surprised to be called to the underwater telephone
and told by Coward that he had some urgent radio traffic. Taking the
submarine up to periscope depth, Taylor was able to pick his signal.

He was to proceed to Gibraltar forthwith and *Spartan* was to be stored for war and sailed immediately. Calling together his heads of department, Taylor gave them the news. To a man they asked: 'War with whom?'

The crisis over the Falklands had at last come to a head. General Galtieri's military junta in Argentina were aware that by 1983 John Nott's Defence Review would leave Britain bereft not only of the South Atlantic research ship *Endurance* but also of her two operational aircraft-carriers, *Hermes* and *Invincible*. As Woodward was to put it, for the Argentinians 'no British carriers means no air cover, no air cover means no British surface ships, no surface ships means no British landing-force, no landing force means "No Contest"'. Although Galtieri was forced by several factors including domestic unrest to implement his invasion plans before the decommissioning of the carriers, the prospect of retaliation so far from Britain still seemed unlikely. In early March 1982, therefore, some Argentinian scrap-metal merchants landed on South Georgia, the easternmost island of the Falklands group. Though they were supposedly there to clear the remains of an old whaling station, the party at once raised the Argentinian flag. On 20 March, Mrs Thatcher agreed with the Foreign Secretary Lord Carrington that *Endurance*, on the eve of her departure from the region, should be dispatched from Port Stanley to South Georgia. The following week, intelligence reports suggested that the Falklands were genuinely threatened with invasion. Drawing on contingency plans drafted for such a situation over the previous decade, Nott ordered three SSNs to the area. One of these was James Taylor's *Spartan*. The second, at the time in Faslane, was Chris Wreford-Brown's *Conqueror*. The third was Roger Lane-Nott's sister-ship *Splendid*. He was in the North-Western Approaches trailing a Victor SSN when he was called to the radio room and told, 'There's a blue-key message for you' – one intended for the captain's eyes only. 'I'd waited my entire career for one of those. It was wonderful.'

As the three digested orders unprecedented in their naval careers, the crisis deepened. By Thursday 1 April, just as *Spartan* was clearing Gibraltar, intelligence from the South Atlantic suggested that the Argentinian fleet was at sea and capable of attacking the islands within forty-eight hours. Argentina had two major capital ships. The largest was a 15,800-ton aircraft-carrier, built by Cammell Laird and commissioned in 1945 as HMS *Venerable*. She had subsequently been sold to the Dutch, and had then been acquired by Argentina in 1968. In honour of Argentina's national day she was named *25 de Mayo* – the 25th May. The second was the *General Belgrano*, a 10,800-ton cruiser commissioned by the US Navy in 1939. A survivor of Pearl Harbor, she had been acquired by Argentina in 1951. The junta also had at its disposal six ships equipped with sea-skimming Exocet missiles, four diesel-electric submarines and more than 200 aircraft, a few of which could also carry Exocets. To counter such a force at such a distance from Great Britain was regarded in official defence circles as impossible.

That evening in Mrs Thatcher's office in the House of Commons, Nott counselled caution. Invasion was far from a certainty; diplomacy on the part of President Reagan and the US Secretary of State General Alexander Haig might turn the tide; and a taskforce – even if practicable – would possess a political momentum of its own. The meeting turned on the late arrival of the First Sea Lord, Sir Henry Leach, delayed by the police constable in the Commons' Central Lobby who objected that he came without appointment. In the face of Nott's defence cuts, Leach had political as well as military reasons to make the case for a taskforce, particularly one that would depend to such an extent on aircraft-carriers. A man of both vision and conviction, he put forward an altogether more positive interpretation of the situation, suggesting to the Prime Minister that the islands were recoverable, providing adequate air cover was available. Woodward comments, 'His conditional statement was all the PM needed. Now she could avoid not going – which would probably lose her the next election. She could go, and fail, and blame the military. She could go, and just conceivably win the next election. Easy!'

'First Sea Lord, what precisely is it that you want?' asked Mrs Thatcher.

'Prime Minister, I would like your authority to form a taskforce which would, if so required, be ready to sail for the South Atlantic at a moment's notice.'

'You have it', she replied.

Two days later, on Friday, 2 April, Argentina invaded the Falklands with a force of 11,000 men under the command of Brigadier-

General Mario Menendez. Formal approval was at once given by the Cabinet for the departure of the taskforce under the codename Operation Corporate.

*

By then *Splendid* had already joined *Spartan* in the race south. The following day Wreford-Brown's *Conqueror* cleared Faslane: under nuclear propulsion she would reach the Falklands in a matter of days. Indeed, according to the *Daily Telegraph*, another of the S-boats, *Superb*, was already there. James Perowne's 'sneaky boat' had in fact been part of the Operation Springtrain group at Gibraltar. She was then detached to pursue a pair of Soviet Victor SSNs that had been spotted operating in the Western Approaches. To the Ministry of Defence, however, it seemed convenient to suggest that she was heading south rather than north, a fact that appears to have been one of the factors that prompted Galtieri to rush ahead with the invasion, despite the fact that Britain still had her aircraft-carriers at her disposal. In February 2001, Woodward commented: 'While domestic unrest was probably the prime cause of an invasion force being prepared, a chance misunderstanding of an SSN's sailing from Gibraltar actually seems to have caused it all to happen when it did – with all the consequences of our being better equipped than we would have been only a few months later.'

*

If the dispatch of the British taskforce represented a statement of intent, the three-week voyage provided pause for thought.

The Argentinian junta now realized that their bluff had been called and that they might actually be called upon to fight. The Reagan administration in Washington saw an opportunity to reconcile the positions of two nations to which it was formally allied: to Great Britain for familiar reasons, to Argentina to emasculate the Communist influence of Cuba in South America. The President's advisers were also obliged to consider the implications of the diversion of British military activity from the Cold War theatre in the North Atlantic. For Mrs Thatcher and her Cabinet, there was time to consider the ultimate implications of her commitment on 3 April to the House of Commons 'to see the islands returned to British administration'. The operational commanders in their bunker in Northwood – the Commander-in-Chief of the Fleet Admiral Sir John Fieldhouse and the Flag Officer Submarines Sir Peter Herbert – now had to fulfil Sir Henry's promise and prediction. They had also to be mindful of the country's Nato obligations, not least with regard to the roles of the SSNs in trailing their Soviet strategic missile counterparts and in protecting Nato's own Polaris patrols.

Woodward, who had been appointed commander of the hastily assembled taskforce of twenty-seven major ships, faced rather more practical problems, much exacerbated by the very limited amount of intelligence available on the Falklands or on the Argentinian forces. Whether or not war was going to break out, he had to ponder 'from which direction should we approach which part of the Falklands? What and where are the possible landing sites? Where are the Argentinians least likely to be? Where should we deploy our special forces? Where are they likely to have stationed their submarines? How many mines could they have laid? And where would be most likely? What kind of approach tactics will their aircraft use?' He had very few answers, but he was conscious that the scales were tipped against him. The combined Argentinian forces were far from negligible. The problems of sustaining his own force at the same distance from their home base as Japan were staggering. The absence of any proper form of airborne early-warning radar was probably critical: the South Atlantic was far beyond the effective range of RAF maritime patrol aircraft, and there would therefore be little warning of enemy attack. Woodward was obliged to assess Argentina's military strength from *Jane's Fighting Ships* and its companion on fighting aircraft. And as to the strength and quality of the Argentinian garrison defending the Falklands, nobody knew.

Aboard *Conqueror*, thundering south past Ascension Island, Wreford-Brown was scarcely better prepared. He had taken command of the submarine only three weeks before sailing to the South Atlantic, and he was unfamiliar with many of her officers and crew, and with some of the technical complexities of his new vessel. Like his old CO in *Warspite*, Woodward, he was uncertain as to whether he was part of – in Mrs Thatcher's words – a diplomatic armada, or whether he might actually be called upon to fight. Vitally, too, he was venturing into seas where operations were likely to be very different from normal SSN operations in the northern hemisphere. His training had admirably equipped him for the problems of trailing Soviet submarines in the North Atlantic, the Norwegian and the Barents Sea, and periodically in the Baltic and the Mediterranean. However, he had no experience of the four Argentinian diesel-electric submarines, two of them old American craft, the others newer West German boats; nor of the general problems of navigation in an area last properly surveyed by Captain Cook, or the particular ones of operating a large submarine in the shallow rocky waters around the Falklands or on the Argentinian coastal shelf. 'We were going into the unknown. In terms of the opposition all we had was *Jane's Fighting Ships*, and it would really have been easier if we had never been up against the Russians. We had little idea of what the German submarines or a German torpedo sounded like.' Indeed, without the knowledge that *Dreadnought* had brought back in 1977 on the area's hydrography and sonar conditions, and the behaviour of weapons and navigation systems in the southern hemisphere, Wreford-Brown would have been ill-prepared.

He had, though, been given one piece of advice that he would later consider carefully. As was traditional, his Squadron Captain had wished him well before his departure on patrol, and the conversation had turned to weapons. *Conqueror* carried the modern and sophisticated wire-guided Mark 24 Tigerfish torpedo and also the traditional Second World War Mark 8. The former could be guided from the submarine towards its target and had a long range, but it had no particular reputation for reliability. The latter Woodward had described as little more than a large, motorized lump of TNT. It was, though, both powerful and dependable. These were the weapons that *Dreadnought's* visit had caused to be modified for South Atlantic use. The Squadron Captain advised, 'If it actually comes to shooting anything, I'd use the Mark 8.' Meanwhile, Wreford-Brown thought it best to prepare his men for possible conflict with drills for evading torpedo attack or containing damage in action caused by fire or flood. His fellow commanders Taylor and Lane-Nott in their rather different styles took similar precautions. They also gave daily briefings on the diplomatic and military situation. Lane-Nott remembers that the ratings divided into hawks and doves. 'The split was broadly by age, the youngsters keen to get amongst them, the older ones more restrained.'

On Easter Sunday, scarcely two weeks after the Argentinian invasion, the taskforce reached the refuelling point of Ascension Island.
Conqueror was by now approaching the Falklands. Among Wreford-
Brown's signal traffic were his Rules of Engagement. Critical in any
theatre of war, now they were doubly so. For Britain was soon to
declare a maritime exclusion zone (MEZ) that forbade foreign ships
to close within 200 miles of the Falklands. At the same time, in the
course of the submarine's voyage south, it had been decided that
Conqueror, Spartan and *Splendid* should be controlled from Northwood
rather than locally by Woodward. The decision was, Woodward
knew, a political one, for these boats were capital ships and projec-
tors of power, and environmental sensitivities surrounded their
nuclear reactors. In fact, Woodward was himself a remarkable submariner, and he was ably supported by the submarine force commander, Captain Andy Buchanan, and his deputy Jeff Tall, fresh from
his Hawaii posting as Undersea Warfare Officer and fully abreast of
the problems of co-ordinating submarine and surface units.
Together, this trio were in a considerably better position to understand the immediate tactical position and to direct submarine operations speedily – though as James Taylor rightly observed, bearing in
mind the possibility of an Argentinian assault on the taskforce, 'All
of a sudden, they might not be there.' Wreford-Brown, Taylor and
Lane-Nott were also obliged to operate on what Woodward called
the 'patch' system. This divides the sea into a series of squares, boxes
or patches, and – in general terms – usually restricts each unit to its
own area so as to avoid accidents. Both arrangements would turn out
to be, as Woodward put it, 'momentous'.

The arrival of *Spartan* off Port Stanley on 12 April enabled Britain
to announce the imposition of the MEZ. Two days later, Roger
Lane-Nott signalled Northwood that he was on his billet, between
the Falklands and the Argentinian mainland. Finally, a week after
Taylor's arrival, Wreford-Brown reached his first area of operations,
South Georgia. When news of *Spartan*'s departure from Gibraltar
had been leaked to the world's press, Mrs Thatcher recorded that 'she
was not too displeased because the submarine would take two weeks
to get to the South Atlantic, but it could begin to influence events
straightaway'. She continued, 'My instinct was that the time had
come to show the Argentinians that we meant business.'

On the shoulders of three 35-year-olds now lay the burden of showing quite what that business would mean.

*

Woodward had now established himself on board what was to be his flagship for the duration of the war, the 29,000-ton aircraft-carrier *Hermes*. He had also been fully briefed by his superior, the Commander-in-Chief Fleet Admiral Sir John Fieldhouse, and his Land Forces Deputy, Major-General Jeremy Moore. The latter would mastermind the amphibious invasion being planned as a contingency. Together, *Hermes* and the second carrier *Invincible*, each carrying highly manoeuvrable vertical take-off Sea Harrier aircraft, and various escorts and supply ships comprised the nucleus of the taskforce. Off the coast of Brazil and about 1,500 miles south of Ascension, Woodward was under loose instructions from Mrs Thatcher's War Cabinet to do no more than 'go into the Exclusion Zone and keep the Argentinians out of it'. The hope was that this would be sufficient to cause an Argentinian withdrawal.

More aggressively, a separate group of ships somewhat in advance of the main taskforce and led by the County-class destroyer *Antrim* under Captain Brian Young, was heading towards *Conqueror* and South Georgia. Simultaneously, John Coward was leading a group of destroyers and frigates, comprising *Brilliant, Sheffield, Coventry, Glasgow* and *Arrow*, towards the Falklands. As his former First Lieutenant in *Warspite*, Woodward of course knew Coward well, and remarked that he 'had in a way been waiting all his life to fight this war'. Considerably ahead of *Hermes*, Coward signalled Woodward that he was 'keen to hurry on over to Port Stanley and set about them [the Argentinians] at the earliest possible moment'. Woodward was tempted by this idea, noting in his diary that 'He could swing it, I expect . . . and it *would* get the war under way before the Args can pre-empt on the aircraft-carriers.' Ultimately, though, caution prevailed, and Woodward signalled Coward: 'Do nothing of the sort. Wait for me and stay out of trouble.' Coward was disgruntled, but his opportunity would soon arise.

In Northwood and Downing Street the recapture of South Georgia seemed an attractive prospect. Far further from the

Argentinian mainland than the Falklands themselves, the island was unlikely to be plentifully garrisoned, and its importance was symbolic rather than strategic. With the British public restless for action, and some among the Americans openly doubting British conviction, something needed to be done. Wreford-Brown in *Conqueror* was ordered to provide reconnaissance for the *Antrim* group, checking for an Argentinian naval presence in the island's vicinity. He ventured as close inshore as he thought prudent in the shallow waters, and by a periscope reconnaissance established that the coast was clear. He then withdrew north-west to a position from which he could support a British landing. *Antrim* closed on South Georgia in the appalling weather characteristic of the on South Atlantic autumn, and landed a party of SAS by helicopter high on the island's Fortuna glacier in a snowstorm. Conditions there proved so bad that the team was obliged to signal to be withdrawn. First one, then a second Wessex helicopter crash-landed in the attempt. The SAS and the stranded airmen were successfully rescued by a third, an extraordinary feat for which the pilot, Lieutenant-Commander Ian Stanley, received a DSO.

The following day, 23 April, an SBS expedition was scarcely more successful, and it too had to be rescued. Meanwhile, it seemed that the Argentinians had become aware of the British presence off South Georgia and that an Argentinian Hercules transport aircraft had overflown the island. Intelligence now suggested that an Argentinian submarine was also in the area. Wreford-Brown was ordered to locate the boat, and in the meantime *Antrim* was obliged to withdraw. With no major assault possible without more helicopters, it was time to send for reinforcements. These were provided by John Coward, who steamed through terrible weather to deliver *Brilliant*'s two Lynx helicopters.

On Sunday, 25 April, one of *Antrim*'s helicopters picked up a radar contact close to the main Argentinian base at Grytviken on South Georgia. Three of *Antrim*'s frigates launched their Wasp helicopters, *Brilliant* one of her Lynx, to discover the forty-year-old Argentinian submarine *Santa Fe* on the surface trying to make her escape after delivering troop reinforcements. Attacked with torpedoes, depth-charges and the Lynx's machine guns, within seconds she was badly damaged and turned back to beach herself. With the enemy in disarray, a naval bombardment of the Argentinian positions was begun, and an ad hoc force of seventy-five SAS and SBS was put together on *Antrim*. At 1445 the first of these were helicoptered ashore. By 1715 the Argentinian commander Captain Alfredo Astiz had surrendered.

Though victory had been adroitly snatched from the jaws of defeat on South Georgia, Woodward now had the infinitely more difficult issue of the Falklands themselves to tackle. The junta had rejected Alexander Haig's latest peace proposals, and the main task-force led by Woodward's own flagship was fast approaching the operational area.

*

James Taylor had already observed the Argentinian landing-ship *Cabo San Antonio* and one other vessel laying mines off Stanley, but his Rules of Engagement had prevented him from attempting to sink them. Next he was directed north-east to locate the *25 de Mayo*. *Splendid* was given the same mission. Capable of covering 500 miles a day, the *25 de Mayo* was a mobile airfield, thought to be carrying A4 Skyhawk fighter-bombers and possibly Exocet-equipped Super Etendards. She was a formidable threat to a taskforce that would be obliged to abandon the whole operation if either of the British carriers was badly damaged. On 23 April, Roger Lane-Nott had found the carrier some way south of her Puerto Belgrano base, a few miles off the Argentinian coast. She was well outside the MEZ, and Lane-Nott was therefore debarred from attacking her. Vividly aware of her capabilities, however, he immediately signalled for the Rules of Engagement to be relaxed. On the advice of the Attorney-General Michael Havers, Mrs Thatcher was obliged to refuse on the grounds that the carrier was only just outside Argentinian territorial waters. 'It was an extremely frustrating moment,' commented Lane-Nott. 'I really thought I had her.'

As a consequence, though, the mood in Northwood stiffened. A new concept, a total exclusion zone (TEZ), applying equally to ships and aircraft, was announced. With it came new Rules of Engagement that permitted the taskforce to 'open fire on any combat ship or aircraft in the TEZ identified as Argentinian'. Woodward duly prepared to enforce the new zone. Northwood divided it up into four quadrants, and the three submarines were ordered to patrol them. Given her location off South Georgia, Wreford-Brown's *Conqueror* was allocated the south-west and the south-east, *Spartan* the north-west, *Splendid* the north-east. As directed by Northwood, none was allowed to enter another area except 'in hot pursuit' of the opposition.

By 28 April the submarines were in position. The following day Woodward's group closed to within 500 miles of the TEZ. On 30 April, the taskforce commander was 'formally given leave to proceed inside the TEZ and start the process of recapturing the Falkland Islands'. In Mrs Thatcher's Churchillian words, the day marked 'the end of the beginning of the campaign to regain the Falklands'.

For Woodward and the three submarine commanders the pace now quickened. The taskforce commander was approaching the Falklands from the north-east so as to maximize his ships' distance from the Argentinian mainland air bases. American satellite intelligence suggested that the *25 de Mayo* was once again venturing more or less due east off Puerto Belgrano. To the south-west of the islands Wreford-Brown was patrolling off the Burdwood Bank, a patch of relatively shallow water about 70 miles wide and 200 miles long in which large submarines cannot operate at any significant speed. That day he made a sonar contact about 50 miles east of the island of Los Estados, the easternmost tip of Argentina. In the evening he followed the bearing, and late the next morning he sighted the cruiser *General Belgrano* and her two Exocet-armed escorts *Hipolito Bouchard* and *Piedra Buena*. When so informed, Woodward took the view – shared by Northwood – that he was threatened with a pincer movement by the two Argentinian battle-groups. To neutralize it he could remove one or both pincers. His preference at the time was for the carrier, principally because of the threat of her aircraft. 'My hope was to keep *Conqueror* in close touch with the *Belgrano* group to the south, to shadow the carrier and her escorts to the north with one of the S Boats [*Splendid* or *Spartan*] up there. Upon word from London, I would expect to make our presence felt, preferably by removing the carrier, and almost as important the aircraft she carried, from the Argentinian Order of Battle.'

Woodward was busy. That day – effectively the first of the war – the SAS and SBS conducted raids on the Falklands, an RAF Vulcan bombed the runway of the Falklands capital Port Stanley, Sea

Harriers from *Invincible* and *Hermes* carried out their first raids, and a naval bombardment of Argentinian positions on West Falkland was begun. Although Wreford-Brown's trail of the *Belgrano* group was compromised by damage to his communications mast in the foul weather of the previous week, *Conqueror* had few problems staying deep below and several miles astern of his contact: 'They steamed steadily south-eastwards and then east, avoiding the TEZ by about 25 miles and conducting a fairly simple zig-zag, but heading towards the Burdwood Bank.' Further north, things were altogether less satisfactory for Taylor and Lane-Nott.

Splendid had enjoyed a coup on 26 April when she spotted two of the Argentinian Type 42 destroyers, *Santissima Trinidad* and *Hercules*, accompanying three Exocet frigates. The group was moving south down the coast towards the port of Comodoro Rivadavia, and Lane-Nott was able to shadow the ships for twenty-four hours. It seemed as though they were the carrier's escort. Then, much to his chagrin, he was ordered by Northwood to abandon the trail in favour of the pursuit of the aircraft-carrier itself, supposedly to the north. 'I couldn't understand why they wanted me off the escort when – by definition – in due course the carrier would join them or vice versa.' Moreover, in the absence of airborne radar, Lane-Nott had relatively little precise information to go on. He was looking for an admittedly fairly large ship in an infinitely larger sea. Taylor's position was scarcely better. He had already once had an Argentinian ship within range of his torpedoes. Now he too had been given Northwood's best estimate of the carrier's position and ordered to find her. Twice, though, Northwood had diverted him to seek much less important or threatening targets in the form of Argentinian submarines. The carrier, furthermore, was on the move. She had located the British taskforce and – early on May Day – had begun to close on it. When fresh satellite intelligence of *25 de Mayo*'s position came through, both Lane-Nott and Taylor were signalled. Communications now and throughout the campaign were spasmodic. *Splendid* did not immediately pick up the signal, and *Spartan* – although closest to the estimated position – realized at once that the carrier was in *Splendid*'s patch. Certainly not technically 'in hot pursuit', Taylor felt debarred from the area and enormously frustrated. This was the consequence of the adoption of the North

Atlantic 'patrol' system and of keeping tactical control of the SSN force so far from the theatre of operations.

In the light of *Splendid*'s and *Spartan*'s failure to find the carrier, Woodward ordered his Sea Harriers to try to do so. At 0330 the following morning – 2 May – he was alerted to the fact that one of the Harrier pilots had found what appeared to be the *25 de Mayo* 200 miles north-west. Woodward at once concluded – correctly – that the carrier was planning a dawn raid. 'We could expect a swift thirty-bomber attack on *Hermes* and *Invincible* at first light . . . he might also have Exocet-armed Super Etendards to add to our problems.' This, though, was only the first half of the problem, the *Belgrano* group representing the second. 'To take the worst possible case,' wrote Woodward, '*Belgrano* and her escorts could now set off towards us and, steaming through the dark, launch an Exocet attack on us from one direction just as we were preparing to receive a missile and bomb strike from the other.' In these circumstances Woodward and his team, in the half-light of dawn, were obliged to consider their options. Withdrawal, as Woodward remarked, was 'scarcely in the traditions of the Royal Navy'. The only other real choice was 'to take out one claw of the pincer'. The carrier was not an option because neither *Splendid* nor *Spartan* were in touch with her. Therefore it had to be the *Belgrano*, though Woodward later remarked, 'I am obliged to say that if *Spartan* had still been in touch with *25 de Mayo* I would have recommended in the strongest possible terms to the C-in-C that we take them both out that night.' The decision taken, two problems still remained. The first was that the *Belgrano* might head more determinedly and directly for *Hermes* and *Invincible*, taking a course across the Burdwood Bank where it was too shallow for *Conqueror* to follow at any speed. The second was that Wreford-Brown's Rules of Engagement still permitted him to attack only within the TEZ that the old cruiser was then skirting. As Woodward at once realized, it was essential that action be taken quickly, and he started the process of getting the Rules of Engagement changed in a hurry.

On board *Conqueror*, Wreford-Brown had been resting in his bunk, turning over in his mind very similar matters. He was ignorant as to the precise disposition and threat offered by *25 de Mayo*, but he knew that his was the only boat in touch with enemy units, he was aware of the constraint of the Rules of Engagement, and he was concerned that the *Belgrano* might head across the Burdwood Bank. Acting on the assumption that he would in fact be called upon to attack, he settled the matter of his weapons. On reflection, he decided to take his Squadron Captain's advice and use the Mark 8s. At least he knew where he was with them. This in turn dictated that *Conqueror* would have to approach to within little more than a mile of the *Belgrano*, and place herself on the cruiser's beam to provide the largest possible target for the unguided weapon, though this manoeuvre would make the submarine that much more vulnerable to counter-attack from the *Belgrano*'s escorts.

At 0800 on Sunday, 2 May, just as the Chief of Defence Staff Sir Terence Lewin was contriving to get the War Cabinet to change the Rules of Engagement, the *Belgrano* group altered course to the west. *Conqueror* followed closely and spent the rest of the morning keeping up with the cruiser while simultaneously trying to keep in touch with Northwood. As the latter required the submarine to steam relatively slowly at periscope depth, *Conqueror* was forced to fall well behind her target. In the early afternoon, when – after several failures – Wreford-Brown at last picked up the signal permitting him to attack, he was seven miles adrift. At once he set about getting into an attacking position. He chose the port beam of the cruiser, the two escorts both being off the starboard beam. To get there he ran deep at 18 knots for periods of fifteen or twenty minutes, then came up to periscope depth to take a visual fix on his target, repeating the exercise five or six times. It was Perisher all over again. 'Listening later to the tape of the attack, it was remarkable how like an ordinary attack it was,' wrote Wreford-Brown. 'It sounded like a good attack in the Attack Teacher at Faslane, everything tidy, no excitement. I'm not an emotional chap and had been concentrating the whole time on getting into a good position.'

The day was now getting on, visibility declining. By 1830 he was close enough for a final approach, and *Conqueror*'s control-room was beginning to get crowded. In the bows of the boat, in the torpedo space, the hands were making ready three of the Mark 8 torpedoes. Tension was high as Wreford-Brown once again ordered *Conqueror* up to periscope depth. By now the control-room was packed, men standing between the chart tables, the computers and the weapons controls, all bathed in the eerie half-light that minimized the adjustment that Wreford-Brown's eyes would have to make when he applied them to the periscope eyepiece. Grabbing the handles of the periscope as it shot upwards, he snatched a final look at the cruiser, an ungainly slab of grey against grey autumnal seas and a dreary grey sky. He shouted her bearing – three-three-five – and her range – fourteen eighty yards – to the Fire Control Officer. Hesitating only briefly, he found himself peculiarly calm, and then he called to the officer: 'Shoot.'

First one, then the second, then the third torpedo shot out of their tubes and accelerated away. *General Belgrano* steamed on. Forty-seven seconds later the first, then the second of the torpedoes hit the cruiser. 'I distinctly recall', wrote Wreford-Brown later, 'seeing an orange fireball in line with the main mast – just aft of the centre of the target – and shortly after the second explosion I thought I saw a spout of water, smoke and debris from forward.' Within an hour the *Belgrano* had sunk, taking with her 368 of her thousand-odd crew. *Conqueror*, meanwhile, went deep and fled south-east. Three salvoes of depth-charges were launched by the *Belgrano*'s escorts, but by the time the submarine was five miles away they had lost the trail.

The sinking of the *Belgrano* was the first occasion since the Second World War on which a British submarine had fired a torpedo in anger. It had been a textbook operation, successfully taking out one claw of the pincer, and it excited the professional admiration of Taylor and Lane-Nott as well as Woodward. Commented Lane-Nott, 'I would have been extremely proud to have done the attack that well.' As it so happened there was insufficient wind for the heavily loaded aircraft on board *25 de Mayo* to attempt the dawn raid on *Hermes* and *Invincible*. The carrier returned to port and remained there for the rest of the war.

Within forty-eight hours, however, the reality of the Argentinian Exocet threat manifested itself. Woodward had sailed the taskforce into the south-eastern sector of the TEZ in preparation for the insertion of SAS and SBS reconnaissance parties on to the islands. In the absence of any airborne radar that could provide early warning of the approach of Argentinian aircraft from the mainland, *Glasgow*, *Coventry* and *Sheffield* were placed 20 miles 'up-threat' to act as sentinels. The last, a Type 42 destroyer, was commanded by another submariner, 'Sam' Salt. At 1440 on 4 May, *Sheffield* was hit by an Exocet fired from an Argentinian Super Etendard on a sortie from Rio

Grande. Twenty men were killed and a similar number injured, and the Navy lost its first ship in action since the Second World War.

The loss of *Sheffield* had an enormous impact on the taskforce, for it brought home the reality of war and in an instant dispersed some of the complacency that had hitherto prevailed both at home and within the taskforce. The ability of the taskforce and its principal ships to defend themselves seemed now very much open to question. So by extension was the viability of the whole operation to recover the Falklands. Martin Macpherson, a frustrated observer of the action back in Britain, was not surprised by the turn of events. 'Given the Argentinians' strengths, it wasn't exactly unexpected.' Naturally though, he was saddened by the loss of life; and *Sheffield*'s CO Sam Salt was an old friend. Jeff Tall, in *Hermes*, agreed that it was predictable but was nevertheless shocked. 'Once *Sheffield* went it was clear we were in for a nasty little war. Things got serious.' Woodward agrees that from then on 'We laboured under the . . . impression that "there is something wrong with our ships".' He also points out, though, that it was a false impression. 'At the back of my mind I felt at the same time that *Sheffield* should have been able to deal with the Exocet – a view confirmed some months later. A critically important member of Sam's team had left his post without permission at the vital moment.'

It was with a view to containing the airborne threat that on 7 May the TEZ was extended to the international limit of 12 miles from Argentina's coast. This in turn permitted Northwood to order *Spartan*, *Splendid* and *Conqueror* considerably closer to the Argentinian mainland. Their initial task was to bottle up the *25 de Mayo*. At the same time it was apparent to Northwood that it would be preferable to destroy the Argentinian aircraft on the ground at their bases rather than in the air. A successful attack by the SAS on Pebble Island which saw the destruction of eleven enemy aircraft served to offer the promise that a similar operation against the air bases on the Argentinian mainland might be mounted. For this purpose the covert landing by submarine of Special Forces – SAS and SBS – might be required. As large nuclear-powered craft, however, *Spartan*, *Splendid* and *Conqueror* were not ideal for the task. For this purpose the slower Oberon-class SSK *Onyx*, driven by Lieutenant-Commander Andrew Johnson, was dispatched from Portsmouth on a voyage that would take more than a month. *Onyx*'s departure was by no means a secret, and of this period of the campaign Mrs Thatcher carefully wrote in her memoirs, 'There was some concern (entirely misplaced) that we were preparing an attack on the Argentinian mainland: whether or not such attacks would have made any military sense, we saw from the beginning that they would cause too much political damage to our position to be anything other than counter-productive.' Meanwhile, *Onyx* nosed her way slowly south.

For Woodward the situation in the days immediately following the destruction of *Sheffield* scarcely improved. It had been hoped that the demonstration of force in the South Atlantic would be sufficient to secure Argentinian withdrawal from the islands. Clearly, this was not to be the case, and on 8 May the full Cabinet took the decision to dispatch Major-General Moore's amphibious landing-force south from Ascension. The fleet of twenty-one ships included the requisitioned P&O liner *Canberra* and the container ship *Atlantic Conveyor*. On 12 May the liner *Queen Elizabeth II*, carrying reinforcements of 5 Brigade, cleared Southampton.

Though the agreed precondition for the landing of troops – air superiority – had not been achieved and the enemy's airforce and of course its aircraft-carrier remained intact, the government and the service chiefs determined to embark upon a landing in the Falklands and defy the Argentinians to do their worst on the day.

*

Woodward had already agreed that the landing should take place at San Carlos on the north-western corner of East Falkland. Now, with the South Atlantic winter approaching, diplomatic pressure on Britain increasing and the ship-borne troops fast losing combat-readiness, he was obliged to hurry. Woodward's days had been drearily filled with further bombardment of Argentinian positions and the repelling of a few rather half-hearted sorties of the Argentinian airforce's Daggers. The only bright spot was a particularly imaginative piece of submarine hunting from John Coward. In the absence of depth-charges he had beer barrels full of high-explosive strapped beneath his Lynx helicopters, and with these he subjected what was thought to be the Argentinian SSK *Santa Luis* to attack for twenty-six hours. She took no further part in the conflict.

In the early hours of Tuesday, 18 May, Woodward made the rendezvous with Major-General Moore's fleet. Later the same day he was
given the go-ahead for the landing by the Cabinet. All the taskforce
commander could now do was attempt to minimize the dangers of
the landing. With this in mind the role of the nuclear submarines was
reviewed. *Sheffield* had been sunk in British territorial waters. 'Perhaps,'
wrote Mrs Thatcher, mindful of *Spartan*'s and *Splendid*'s lost opportunities, 'we should send out submarines to sink Argentinian ships in
their harbours.' Given the continuing threat posed by the *25 de Mayo*,
critical during the period of disembarkation at San Carlos, this was a
perfectly sensible layman's suggestion but militarily quite impractical.
To the further disappointment of Lane-Nott and Taylor, the
Attorney-General also thought the scheme questionable under international law. With Wreford-Brown in *Conqueror* now patrolling to the
north-west of the Falklands, guarding the taskforce from the threat
posed by the remaining Argentinian submarine, *Spartan* and *Splendid*
were deployed seaward of the coastal air bases of San Antonio and
Rio Gallegos. There, as the final preparations were being made for
the San Carlos landings, they were to operate as pickets, using their
sensors and visual sighting to provide notice of Argentinian air
sorties. For Taylor in *Spartan*, this part of the operation emphasized
the peculiar abstraction from reality of submarine warfare. They were
so near the Argentinian coast yet so far: only he and his fellow watch-
keepers would ever see it. This was further underscored by the relative domestic comfort that the nuclear submariners enjoyed, a tiny
self-contained British community living and working within a few
thousand yards of the hostile coastline, while on the radio Abba
blasted out their latest hit.

With Andy Johnson's *Onyx* still on her way south from Ascension
Island, they were joined by a fourth SSN, Commander Tom Le
Marchand's *Valiant*. This was the boat in which Martin Macpherson
had accompanied Le Marchand to the North Pole the previous year.
With the demise of *Dreadnought*, *Valiant* was now the oldest SSN in the
fleet, and she was dispatched to picket the most southerly of the bases
at Rio Grande. Operating these submarines in very shallow waters
required good ship-handling skills, and the relatively clear coastal
waters made the SSNs vulnerable to visual detection. *Valiant* herself
was bombed, though probably unintentionally and fortunately

without damage, by an aircraft offloading its bombs before landing. So too was *Spartan*, off Comodoro Rivadavia, again probably unintentionally. Chris Craig, CO of one of the taskforce's Type 21 frigates, *Alacrity*, wrote of the surveillance operation in *Call for Fire*: 'Such notice would enable us to shorten our readiness at appropriate times and significantly reduce the potential for surprise attack, even though we had just lost one of our three air-defence destroyers. The early warning that the submarines provided by watching the enemy's doorstep saved the lives of many men. That the achievements of *Valiant*, *Splendid* and others were not recognized more emphatically after the war, I found a travesty.'

The landings at San Carlos began in the early hours of 21 May. Woodward was all too aware of the day's importance: 'I suppose I knew that on the morning of 21 May 1982 the Royal Navy would be required to fight its first major action since the end of the Second World War.'

The irony was that, given the requirement to protect *Hermes*, *Invincible* and their invaluable Sea Harriers from the fate of *Sheffield*, Woodward was obliged to sit out the fight. Too far away from San Carlos to use short-wave radio and thereby maintain tactical control of the battle, he had to cede control to the Harrier pilots and the commanders of the principal frigates and destroyers.

Dawn that day saw *Antrim*, together with four older frigates *Plymouth*, *Argonaut*, *Ardent* and *Yarmouth*, fairly and squarely in San Carlos Water. They were to protect the bridgehead being established in San Carlos itself. Woodward's first line of defence, comprising *Brilliant* and *Broadsword*, was 'up-threat'. In the course of the first major attack of the day in what was to become known as 'bomb alley', *Antrim* was hit by a thousand-pounder delivered by an Argentinian Dagger. Although this failed to explode, several fires broke out on board the destroyer, and *Antrim* was at once forced to relinquish the critical role of controlling and directing the Harriers against the incoming Argentinian sorties. John Coward in *Brilliant* immediately took over this role, Woodward's aviation controllers advising him: 'Now you be very careful of our aircraft.' Coward replied, 'Of course we'll be very careful. Don't worry.' And, as Woodward wrote, 'fairly typical for that ship, they finished with a flourish: "We know what we're bloody well doing."'

Coward's basic plan was 'to position *Brilliant* bang in the middle of the entrance to the bay and treat the entire operation like a pheasant shoot'. There were five further raids. The first two were seen off without major incident. The third, though, irretrievably damaged the Leander-class frigate *Argonaut* and saw *Ardent* hit by three bombs, two of which exploded. Cannon shells from one of the Daggers in the sortie also smashed straight through *Brilliant*'s operations room and a metal splinter hit the vitally important aircraft director in the back. Finding he could still talk, Lieutenant-Commander Lee Hulme pressed on. Woodward commented, 'When you fight for John Coward, minor problems like that tend to fade into the background.' The fourth raid saw *Ardent* hit by seven more bombs, and soon the order was given to abandon ship. There were twenty-five dead.

When the final attack of the day was driven off, it was apparent that the forces ashore had suffered no casualties. The Navy, though, had *Ardent* sinking, *Argonaut* and *Antrim* badly damaged, and both *Broadsword* and *Brilliant* hit by cannon fire. The Argentinians had launched over fifty sorties and had lost sixteen aircraft. Of *Brilliant*'s role in directing the Harriers, Woodward wrote that 'but for them, at least eight more Arg bombers would probably have got through to the ships'.

During the following three days the pace scarcely abated. While the land forces slowly consolidated their position, with five battalions of Marines and Paras dug in on the shores of the bay, seven more Argentinian aircraft were shot down for the considerable loss of the Type 21 frigate *Antelope*.

Woodward then braced himself for Argentina's National Day – the 25th – on which something more than a gesture might be anticipated. Perhaps, he pondered, the day would see the return of Admiral Anaya's navy, of which nothing had been heard since the loss of the *General Belgrano*. 'It would be a fine, daredevil counter-stroke for them to play – bringing out their carrier *25 de Mayo* and launching a co-ordinated attack on *Hermes* and *Invincible* to celebrate such an important day. Win *or* lose, it would go down in their history books as their finest hour.' Putting himself in the position of his opposite number, he argued that the Admiral would send the aircraft-carrier south to attack *Hermes* and *Invincible* with her Exocet-carrying Super Etendards from the least expected quarter. Woodward's solution was to try to get one of the submarines sent south with orders to sink the carrier if she came within range. He signalled Northwood, and accordingly suggested that Chris Wreford-Brown might care to add to his tally. Northwood disagreed, feeling the scenario Woodward had sketched was unlikely. Woodward wrote furiously in his diary, 'There's just fuck-all flexibility there.'

As it was, Northwood was proved right. The *25 de Mayo* stayed in harbour and left the celebrations to the airforce. Captain Bill Canning's *Broadsword* and David Hart-Dyke's *Coventry* formed the westernmost picket line for San Carlos that day. At 1700 six Skyhawks were spotted taking off from Rio Gallegos by James Taylor in *Spartan*. An hour later they attacked *Broadsword*, hitting her with one bomb that failed to explode. *Coventry* was hit by three, all of which did explode, killing nineteen men. Soon she would capsize. Then, half an hour later, *Hermes'* battlegroup was attacked by two of the Exocet-carrying Super Etendards and one of these hit the *Atlantic Conveyor*, destroying both the ship and the three Chinook heavy-load helicopters aboard her that were supposed to transport the landing-force across 40 miles of terrible terrain to Port Stanley. 'The marines', remarked Woodward, 'will have to walk.' It had been quite a day.

The following forty-eight hours proved quiet, poor weather discouraging Argentinian sorties, while the Marines and the Paras consolidated their bridgehead. Then, on 27 May, 2 Para set out for the settlement of Goose Green, a strategically insignificant target that was won at the cost of the life of the regiment's commanding officer, Colonel 'H' Jones. It was for this sacrifice that he was posthumously awarded the Victoria Cross.

That same day *Onyx* finally arrived in the operational area after a voyage which had in itself been a considerable test of endurance for Johnson and his crew. '*Onyx* is at the front door,' Jeff Tall remembers being told by one of his communications colleagues. 'She needs an escort.' Two days later she was joined by the fifth and final SSN *Courageous*, sister-ship to *Conqueror*, driven by Commander Rupert Best, a burly rugby player. *Courageous* was to replace Lane-Nott's *Splendid*. The latter had already spent nearly two months on patrol and one of her generators was causing serious problems. *Courageous* was equipped with the Sub-Harpoon missile, a weapon that enabled her to target surface ships at a range of up to 70 miles. Best was another submariner keen to get the *25 de Mayo* in his sights.

With their spirits lifted by the speed and heroism of the Goose Green victory, the British land forces drove through largely demoralized Argentinian positions towards Port Stanley over the next few days with ruthless efficiency, though they met with some heavy fighting.

Here, as in the campaign from the beginning, Special Forces were to play a critical part, and in doing so they provided Andy Johnson's *Onyx* with a role she was well equipped to fulfil. Smaller and more manoeuvrable than her nuclear cousins, she had been intended to be used to put Special Forces ashore, possibly on the Argentinian mainland. By the time of her arrival this was regarded as unnecessary. She could nevertheless be used for just such a purpose around the Falklands themselves. On 30 May she embarked an SBS unit of sixteen men and subsequently disembarked them close to Port Stanley from a hatch in the conning-tower, using the same procedures that James Taylor had been developing in *Orpheus* on his ill-fated exercise on Loch Long. Although the operation was carried out successfully, the perils of operating in such waters became all too apparent when *Onyx* hit an uncharted rock. The collision damaged two of her torpedo bow tubes and actually jammed one of the torpedoes in its tube. It could have been much worse.

*

As British forces pressed on towards the high ground that surrounds Port Stanley, the reinforcements that had arrived aboard the liner *Queen Elizabeth II* were gradually being ferried to two new operational areas from which it was planned that the main assault on the Argentinian positions around Port Stanley should be launched. Given the loss of *Atlantic Conveyor* and her Chinooks, these needed to be considerably closer to the capital than San Carlos. The first area chosen was Teal Inlet leading off the northern coast of East Falkland. The second was Bluff Cove, on the Atlantic side of that island. For this purpose various amphibious warfare vessels were employed, including 6,000-ton LSLs (Landing Ship Logistic), each capable of transporting up to 500 troops ashore. The Teal Inlet operation was successful, and Woodward was persuaded by the commanders of the amphibious operation that the same trick could be pulled off at Bluff Cove. The plan was for a 'mini D-Day' on 6 June, something Woodward now says 'was totally against all my instincts'.

In the end two of the LSLs, *Sir Galahad* and *Sir Tristram*, were loaded with Welsh Guardsmen and sailed initially to Port Fitzroy, sixteen miles from Bluff Cove. The ships were spotted by Argentinians on the high ground overlooking the bay, and Port Stanley was duly warned. The Argentinian Southern Command ordered an immediate sortie of six Daggers from Rio Grande and eight Skyhawks from Rio Gallegos. Tom Le Marchand's *Valiant*, acting as picket off Rio Grande, was able to warn of the Daggers' imminent arrival, but the warning did not reach *Sir Galahad*. As it was, David Pentreath's *Plymouth*, an elderly Type 12 frigate, bore the brunt of the attack, being badly damaged by four bombs.

In *One Hundred Days*, Woodward records John Coward as remarking: 'Of course *Plymouth* was always going to cop it. She did not really have the right kit to fight these kinds of action. But I'll never forget her in Carlos Water when we were under such serious attack – she just steamed round and round the other ships in a gesture to the Args of total defiance. She had comparatively little to fight with – just guns and an old Sea Cat – but she gave it everything. Pentreath? Bravest chap I've seen. Of course, I knew that one day we'd steam into Carlos Water and *Plymouth* would be not much more than a cloud of black smoke. And one day she was.'

Meanwhile the Skyhawks attacked *Sir Galahad* and *Sir Tristram*, bombing both. Fifty Welsh Guardsmen were killed on *Sir Galahad*, and a similar number wounded or badly burned. Woodward was understandably distraught, and blamed himself for not countermanding what he knew to be a risky landing. 'In war, you have to take risks, and sometimes they go sour on you.'

Yet Bluff Cove was to be the last significant reverse of Woodward's war. Three days later the final battle for Port Stanley began, Mrs Thatcher moving her entire operation to Northwood for the purpose. There followed the bitter fights on Tumbledown and Wireless Ridge that constituted the toughest engagements of the war. With those strongholds in British hands, only the promontory of Sapper Hill remained. On 14 June, just sixty-four days after James Taylor had first set eyes on the Argentinian garrison at Stanley, General Menendez surrendered. On returning to Downing Street from Northwood, Mrs Thatcher was greeted by a vast crowd singing 'Rule Britannia'.

Over the following weeks, the first of the SSNs to be dispatched to the Falklands returned to their home ports, *Spartan* and *Splendid* to Devonport, *Conqueror* to Faslane. All three looked battered, although *Conqueror* proudly flew the Jolly Roger, indicative of her successful action. Haggard and long-haired after anything up to a hundred days at sea, their crews had been on reduced rations for several weeks. *Spartan* had a single chicken left in her deep freeze when she got back to Plymouth. Nevertheless, great efforts were made to entertain the senior naval officers and the families who came to welcome them home. On seeing her husband return, James Taylor's wife Elizabeth simply said to him: 'You've changed.' Woodward comments, 'I doubt she was the only one.'

*

A colonial war fought in the post-colonial era, the Falklands conflict was an historical anachronism. As close run as Waterloo, it provided Mrs Thatcher with the pivot of her prime ministerial career. Up until the spring of 1982, her position even as leader of the Conservative party was under threat. After the Falklands she never looked back. For the Argentinian junta, too, the episode was pivotal. Within a month of Menendez's surrender, the junta had been deposed.

For the submariners the war was equally critical. Though regarded as abrasive, Sandy Woodward was widely thought to have excelled. As the military historian Max Hastings remarked in *The Battle for the Falklands*, like Jellicoe at Jutland he could have lost the war in an afternoon, but by careful husbanding of the limited forces at his disposal, he brought off a triumph. He was awarded the Order of the Bath and given the posting that he had been about to take up before the Falklands blew up, that of Flag Officer Submarines. He was also the only admiral in any navy to distinguish himself in the art of war – as opposed to bureaucracy – since the Second World War. The Commander-in-Chief of the Fleet, John Fieldhouse – another submariner – was promoted to First Sea Lord. Of John Coward it was widely said that '*Brilliant* was brilliant'. He was awarded the DSO, and would in due course follow Woodward as Flag Officer Submarines. For some time his nickname had been JC. In the view of a number of submariners, the Falklands confirmed Coward's ability to walk on water.

Of the submarine commanders themselves, Tom Le Marchand, Rupert Best and Andy Johnson took pride in their achievement, and the last was awarded an MBE for his 116-day war patrol. For the sinking of the *General Belgrano*, Wreford-Brown was awarded the DSO. He regretted the loss of life on the Argentinian cruiser but regarded the task as part of his job. On his return to Faslane in early July he wrote: 'I feel we did just what we were invited to and I would have no hesitation in doing it again.' This, too, was the line taken by Admiral Fieldhouse. 'I have no doubt it was the best thing we ever did. It took the heart out of the Argentinian Navy and we only had their Air Force to deal with then. That was a very considerable advantage.' Others point out that the war for the first time graphically demonstrated the qualities of the SSN as a capital ship. This was certainly Roger Lane-Nott's analysis. 'Here we were for the first time in history, using the nuclear submarine for the first time as it was intended.'

Yet for some, James Taylor, Roger Lane-Nott himself and – aboard *Hermes* – Jeff Tall and Sandy Woodward, there was also a sense of missed opportunities. All believe that if the chance to sink or cripple the *25 de Mayo* had been taken when it was offered, the war might well have been stopped before it had properly begun, so preventing the death of a lot of men.

This was the reality of the Falklands conflict, the fact that it was a 'hot' war rather than a 'cold' one, and one well expressed by one of *Conqueror*'s junior officers, Narendra Sethia, who later wrote in the *Guardian* of the sinking of the *Belgrano*: 'This was the moment for which we had all been trained, yet a moment which, I believe, few of us really thought we would encounter. Until the moment of firing, it was as if everything in our lives had been a dress rehearsal for a performance that would never happen. But at that moment our lives changed and we knew the dress rehearsal was over.'

The submariners in the Falklands had seen action. If they returned unscathed, they certainly did not return unaffected by their experience. Wreford-Brown played a very straight bat with the media when his identity as the CO who had sunk the *Belgrano* was eventually revealed, presenting an immaculate front of professionalism to the outside world. 'The Royal Navy spent thirteen years preparing me for such an occasion,' he said. 'It would have been regarded as extremely dreary if I had fouled it up.' The conviction with which he pressed home his attack suggests that such a view would have been echoed by the commanders of British SSBNs if they had ever been called upon to fire their Polaris missiles. It was also characteristic of Wreford-Brown that he chose to fly the Jolly Roger in *Conqueror* on his return to Faslane, a tradition initiated by Max Horton during the First World War. His doing so was an action regarded as tactless or even provocative by those who cared to forget the essence of Wreford-Brown's job. Nevertheless, those who knew him well thought he was scarred by the experience, just as James Taylor had certainly been by the deaths at Loch Long. Arguably, he would not have been human if it had been otherwise, and he would not have been a thoroughly trained submarine commander if he had not been able to take the responsibility more or less in his stride. This, it has to be said, is not Wreford-Brown's own reading. It is his misfortune – or fortune – to be for ever associated with a sinking that he regards as a significant part of his naval career but by no means its pivot. While scarcely careless of the fate of the Argentinian sailors, and scarcely ignorant of the political and media furore that followed the sinking and continued long afterwards, he certainly does not see himself as scarred. There is an interesting passage in *One of Our Submarines* where Edward Young describes a CO as possessing the 'crust of emotional indifference towards his targets which would have been natural in one whose business was war'. Perhaps it was this that the Navy had successfully inculcated in Wreford-Brown; or perhaps it was something more personal to a determined, self-contained and enigmatic man.

Though the Falklands conflict was in some respects an anachronism, it had ramifications that were of some consequence on another stage. In America, in particular, the feat had been regarded as unachievable, and there was a great deal of professional admiration expressed for the job done, not least by the submariners. As to the 'opposition' in the Cold War, years later a Russian general told Mrs Thatcher that 'the Soviets had been firmly convinced that we would not fight for the Falklands, and that if we did we would lose'. The Prime Minister continued, 'We proved them wrong on both counts, and they did not forget the fact.' Sandy Woodward, though, perhaps deserves the last word.

We must ask ourselves, was it right that we should have gone to the South Atlantic and fought for the Falklands almost as if we were defending the coast of Hampshire? It will always come down to a point of principle. Our response was a fundamental part of the British character. Those who die in battle always pay too high a price, but in the South Atlantic, as in so many other wars, they died for the ideas we stand for. Expressed more formally, they died because we believe in the rule of law for the guidance of human behaviour. But they also died because we, as a nation, wherever we may be, take a perverse pride in that dogged streak of British truculence. And so, in a sense, they died for the very Britishness of us all. Thus, for the final time, was it right to fight that grim battle down in the South Atlantic? I expect, before I am finished, I will be asked that question many times more. And each time the memories of lost friends stand before me. But the answer will always be, yes.

Chapter 12
Head to Head

'All attempts at achieving military superiority over the USSR are futile. The Soviet Union will never let it happen. It will never be left defenceless by any threat, let there be no mistake about this in Washington. It is time they stopped devising one option after another in the search for the best ways of unleashing nuclear war in the hope of winning it. Engaging in this is not irresponsible. It is insane.'

Yuri Andropov, March 1983

Seventeen months after the end of the Falklands War, in November 1983, Nato forces staged a massive exercise called Operation Able Archer that involved going through all the stages of alert that would culminate in the release of tactical nuclear weapons. In the past the Soviets had frequently speculated that such manoeuvres might mask more serious ambitions. So fraught now were international relations that on this occasion the Kremlin convinced itself that a pre-emptive Nato strike on the Soviet Union was imminent. The Cold War, it seemed, was about to ignite.

Leonid Brezhnev had died in November 1982 and had been replaced by a former head of the KGB, Yuri Andropov. Like his predecessor, Andropov was old and ill. Yet he surprised all his listeners, both at home and abroad, by his proposal at a Warsaw Pact meeting in January 1983 that the alliance should form a non-aggression agreement not only with Nato but also with its own members. This constituted a remarkable break with the eighteen years of Brezhnev's rule, a repudiation of the Brezhnev Doctrine that had permitted

Soviet interference in the internal affairs of member states, most memorably the invasion of Alexander Dubček's Czechoslovakia in 1968. Andropov's timing, too, was curious, for the democracy movements within Eastern Europe were gathering strength. In Poland, still under General Jaruzelski's military rule, the leader of Solidarity Lech Walesa was given the Nobel Peace Prize; in Czechoslovakia the Charter 77 dissidents continued to call for greater human rights; and in East Germany – of all places – there were calls for nuclear disarmament.

Reagan saw Andropov's January announcement as a sign of weakness, and at once pushed home his advantage. A few days later he characterized the Soviet leadership as 'the focus of evil in the modern world'. Then, on 23 March, he made a proposal even more remarkable than Andropov's. Since the explosion by the Soviets of their own atomic bomb in August 1949, relations between the superpowers had been underpinned by the idea of mutual deterrence. The threat of catastrophic destruction – Mutual Assured Destruction – had effectively prevented West or East from embarking upon anything other than conventional conflicts, and these only undertaken through surrogates in Asia, the Middle East, Africa and Latin America. Now Reagan proposed a shield in space that would protect the United States from incoming ballistic missiles. The Strategic Defence Initiative (SDI), as it was called, was dubbed Star Wars, after George Lucas's 1977 science fiction epic, the sequel to which – ironically entitled *The Empire Strikes Back* – had recently appeared. In theory, if the project was successfully implemented, this would derail the notion of Mutual Assured Destruction, making the Soviets alone vulnerable to ballistic missile attack, and rendering their own land- and submarine-based missile force useless. Although there was little evidence at the time that the scheme could actually be put into practice, the pronouncement was in many respects a master-card. The further demands it would place on Soviet defence-spending to replicate the American system would be intolerable. Andropov was forced to revert to simple defiance. 'All attempts at achieving military superiority over the USSR are futile,' he declared.

Still, despite continuing the START talks, the successor to SALT, in Geneva, the Reagan presidency seemed determined to pursue its aggressive policy. Its support of the Mujahideen in Afghanistan increased, it gave considerable help to the anti-Communist Contras in Nicaragua, and in October 1983 it intervened directly in Grenada. A Communist-inspired military coup in this former British colony in the Caribbean raised the spectre of a new Cuba on America's doorstep. Reagan described the new regime as a 'threat to the security of the United States' and acted quickly. The United States invasion of the island, Operation Urgent Fury, overthrew the People's Revolutionary Government in a matter of hours.

The invasion of Grenada was one of several incidents that clouded the otherwise strong friendship between Reagan and Margaret Thatcher, the embodiment of the 'special relationship' between the United States and Britain. Resoundingly re-elected on 9 June 1983 in the aftermath of the Falklands War, Mrs Thatcher had not been informed of US intentions towards a country of which the Queen was still head of state. Infuriated, she made no secret of her feelings to Reagan himself. Moreover, the news broke at a time when huge demonstrations were being staged in London over the arrival at the US air base at Greenham Common in Berkshire of the cruise missiles that were part of the Nato response to the Soviet SS-20.

Mrs Thatcher was similarly wrong-footed by Reagan over SDI. He did not forewarn her of the announcement, and it appeared to contravene the Anti-Ballistic Missile treaty signed by Nixon and Brezhnev in 1972 at the height of détente. As a scientist she was sceptical about the practicality of the scheme. Moreover, even if it did work and provide an umbrella under which the United States could shelter, the implications for Europe did not seem to have been thought through. It might simply lead to the Soviet Union retargeting its missiles at America's Nato allies in Europe. Like other European leaders, Mrs Thatcher regarded SDI as a profoundly destabilizing influence.

Adding to the disquietude of that autumn was the shooting down by a Russian Su-15 fighter of a Korean Air Lines jumbo jet, *en route* from New York to Seoul, that had strayed into Soviet airspace. Two hundred and sixty-nine people died in what Reagan called 'an act of barbarism', Margaret Thatcher 'an atrocity against humanity'. In a speech in Washington on 29 September, Mrs Thatcher went further, declaring that the West was 'confronted by a power of great military strength, which has consistently used force against its neighbours, which uses the threat of force as a weapon of policy, and which is bent on subverting and destroying the confidence and stability of the Western world'.

Amid the tensions that these incidents created, it was hardly surprising that the Soviets should have had profound suspicions about Operation Able Archer. On 7 November 1983 – the eve of the exercise – one of the pretenders to Andropov's throne, Grigory Romanov, remarked 'Comrades, the international situation at present is white hot, thoroughly white hot.' Less than three weeks later, on 23 November 1983, the first of the Pershing missiles reached American bases in Germany, and the Soviets walked out of the START talks. Not long after, Romanov's main rival, Mikhail Gorbachev, declared, 'Never, perhaps, in the post-war decades has the situation in the world been as explosive . . . as in the first half of the '80s.'

Scientists that autumn predicted that a war would lead to a nuclear winter. A huge cloud of dust would spread across the whole planet, cutting the surface off from the sun and causing the temperature over much of the globe to drop to below freezing. Crops and the rainforest would be destroyed. When the cloud eventually lifted, the damaged ozone layer would let in huge quantities of ultra-violet radiation, causing cancers, blindness and genetic mutation. Civilization would be effectively destroyed.

*

Toby Elliott, commanding the SSBN *Resolution*, was among the first to encounter the maritime expression of this unprecedented period of tension. During the Falklands War, British intelligence had assumed that Soviet forces would not much interest themselves in the engagement. Argentina was largely outside the Soviet sphere of influence, and certainly geographically remote from her bases. As it turned out, although Woodward's taskforce was overflown on the way down to the South Atlantic by Soviet long-range maritime patrol aircraft based in Angola, this assessment was essentially correct. Nevertheless, the Soviets were well aware of the opportunity presented by the diversion of the British SSN fleet to the South Atlantic.

Quite how many boats had been dispatched remained a matter for conjecture. The British, of course, had to maintain a balance between giving the Argentinians the impression that the largest number of boats were on station, so threatening their naval forces, and at the same time giving the Soviets the impression that only a few were in the South Atlantic. In practice, the Soviets doubtless assumed that a large part of the British SSN force was either on station off the Falklands, on its way there or on its way back – as was indeed the case, and as their own intelligence-gathering procedures would have confirmed.

However, although the SSN fleet had a number of stand-alone missions, it was also responsible for protecting the nuclear deterrent, the maritime equivalent of a fighter escort for a bomber. It was the job of the SSBN to lose itself in the wastes of the sea, to turn away from any possible Soviet contact, to maintain its principal function of remaining undetected and so protect the credibility of the deterrent. Conversely, it was the role of the Soviet Northern Fleet SSNs to detect and identify Nato SSBNs. Should a Soviet SSN come too close to detecting its Western quarry, the task of the fighter escort was to drive it away. *Resolution* in the course of the Falklands War was obliged to operate largely without SSN protection. The Soviets were not slow to realize that this might be the case. The result was a concerted attempt by a specially constituted Soviet taskforce comprising Victor III SSNs to detect both *Resolution* and the French and American SSBNs on patrol. Four or five years previously such a taskforce would have represented a relatively modest threat. Now, though – largely as a consequence of the Whitworth-Walker ring – the best boats in the Soviet fleet were markedly quieter, and there were still more Soviet boats overall than there were Nato boats. The hunters outnumbered the hunted. Here lay the challenge for an SSBN commander, the game of underwater hide-and-seek on which the credibility of the deterrent rested and – as the *Sceptre* incident suggested – on which the lives of the two opposing crews depended. Though many years have since passed, Toby Elliott will say little about this patrol. 'The Soviet SSN force made a lot of noise as they beat the place up. This helped the intelligence analysts enormously and made our task of remaining undetected that much easier. It was, though, an unusually testing patrol.'

Despite Soviet efforts, there is no evidence that *Resolution* was detected. The Commander-in-Chief, Admiral Sir John Fieldhouse, was relieved to hear from Elliott that nothing 'untoward' had happened when he debriefed him, and the British SSBNs thus retained their unbroken record. The naval writer and former British submarine commander Richard Compton-Hall wrote shortly afterwards in *Submarine Warfare*: 'Although it is claimed that no western SSBNs have yet been trailed to their secret patrol areas or detected while there, a really concentrated Soviet submarine ASW [Anti-Submarine Warfare] effort against one or two British or French SSBNs might well succeed.' Not surprisingly, Elliott disagrees. 'A British SSBN handled with care and provided with first-class intelligence support is an extremely difficult target for even the best anti-submarine forces.'

*

The majority of the SSN fleet was withdrawn from the South Atlantic once the Falklands had been recaptured, although a single submarine remained on station there for some time. Most of the boats could therefore now revert to their normal Cold War duties. Chris Wreford-Brown, Martin Macpherson and Jeff Tall all took their charges into the front line.

For Macpherson, the Falklands had proved a disruption. Following his Arctic patrol in *Valiant*, he had been given the job of taking the first of a new class of British SSNs – the Trafalgars – out of build and into a state of operational readiness. During the conflict some of his officers were temporarily diverted to other tasks. His First Lieutenant was sent to the aircraft-carrier *Hermes*, and his navigator – a fluent Spanish speaker – was dispatched to interview the crew of the crippled Argentinian submarine *Santa Fe*. Indeed, Macpherson himself was involved in an interesting project to discover the sound signatures of Argentina's two German-built submarines, an episode more reminiscent of industrial espionage than the military variety. Added to Macpherson's load was the fact that *Trafalgar*, as the first of her class, had to undergo more extensive and intensive sea-trials than would be the case for later boats of the same design. A new Flag Officer Submarines also made it clear that he would be setting his own demanding standards for the boats under his command. Sandy Woodward would not tolerate anything less.

Eventually commissioned in May 1983, in many respects the £200 million *Trafalgar* represented the culmination of British SSN engineering expertise, building on the experience of the Dreadnought/Valiant class and then the Swiftsure boats such as James Taylor's *Spartan* and Roger Lane-Nott's *Splendid*. Proponents of the Trafalgar class claimed them to be the finest SSN attack boats of the Cold War. The class of seven had the same hull design at the Swiftsures but they were significantly quieter than their predecessors, markedly better equipped by way of sonar, and had more powerful reactors. Toby Elliott, who would take over *Trafalgar* from Macpherson, used to demonstrate the outstanding qualities of his boat to visiting VIPs by taking his guests into his cabin when the boat was meandering along at 4 knots, a couple of hundred feet under the waves. There on a table he would stand a pencil on its end. He would then make his way to the control-room, where he would order maximum revolutions to be set in the full power state, the nuclear equivalent of full-steam ahead. Within sixty seconds, the 4,500-ton submarine would be thundering along at over 30 knots. Returning to the CO's cabin, the VIPs would be shown the pencil, still standing. Elliott likened the submarine to a racing Bentley. He adds that Admiral Gorshkov himself had been recorded as commenting that he knew when *Trafalgar* was at sea because over-flying Soviet satellites revealed an empty berth at Faslane, but he had absolutely no idea where she had gone. On leaving her base, she simply vanished into a black hole.

This was not the experience of a Soviet Natya-class ocean minesweeper encountered by Macpherson when he was conducting the boat's early torpedo trials off Gibraltar. This was at a time when both sides made every effort to retrieve each other's hardware. Firing from a variety of depths, *Trafalgar* surfaced after each firing to retrieve the Mark 24 Tigerfish torpedo, only to discover on one occasion that the minesweeper had already got a line on the torpedo and was preparing to get it on board. Macpherson remarks: 'I told them to put it back. And they did.'

It was also while in Gibraltar that Macpherson was ordered to pick up and trail a couple of Meko-class frigates. These had been built by Blohm and Voss in West Germany for the Argentinian government, and they were being delivered to the South Atlantic. Picking them up in the Bay of Biscay, *Trafalgar* trailed the frigates hundreds of miles south, all the while collecting acoustic and electronic intelligence for the Nato database. Finally, in 1984, he took the SSN on her first operational patrol in the Norwegian Sea, where he picked up and trailed a Victor SSN using *Trafalgar*'s new type 2020 sonar. The Victor was one of the second-generation Soviet attack boats, at 5,300 tons rather larger than *Trafalgar*, but also noisier. He was then put on to a Yankee SSBN on her way home to Murmansk. This he followed up to Bear Island before switching to even more interesting prey, an Alfa, the small, high-speed Soviet SSN that so concerned the West. She was operating in a thermal front, an area where two streams of sea water of different temperature pass each other. These provide masking qualities for sonar, and enable adroit COs to gather intelligence about the opposition without the same thing happening to them. Like James Taylor's first patrol in *Spartan*, Macpherson's was something of a triumph. 'Martin was a fine intuitive CO,' says Marcus Fitzgerald, who served with him as a weapons officer. 'But there were a few others more or less as good. The remarkable thing about Martin was that when the game became infinitely more technical, he found he had an enormous gift for that too.' For this patrol and his work in getting *Trafalgar* operational, Macpherson was awarded the OBE.

Macpherson was joined that year in the SSN front line by Jeff Tall. Following the Falklands he was promoted to Commander in December 1982 and had a spell as officer in charge of the submarine tactics and weapons group at Faslane. One of the problems to be sorted out was the long-standing deficiency of the Mark 24 Tigerfish torpedo that Macpherson had been testing. The torpedo made enough noise on discharge from its parent submarine to alert the increasingly sophisticated counter-measures carried by Soviet submarines. Tackling this sort of task put Tall on his mettle, and he came to be highly regarded in tactical development.

His relationship with his new Flag Officer Submarines, Woodward, was nevertheless equivocal. They had worked together closely in the Falklands on *Hermes* but not invariably harmoniously. Says Tall, 'I remember being called down to Northwood to see him, and at once we started arguing about the weather – arguing!' Yet despite criticizing certain aspects of Tall's performance, Woodward had good news for him. He was to be given the SSN *Churchill*. Although he had been Executive Officer in the SSBN *Renown*, Tall had not enjoyed a sea-command since the SSK *Finwhale*. He was delighted, for in a community that was both deeply fraternal and intensely competitive, he had begun to feel that he was being left behind by his contemporaries. *Churchill*, an improved Valiant-class boat now ten years old, had a good reputation as a reliable and happy boat. To Tall, too, she was familiar, for he had served on her as supply officer ten years previously. Now he would return in command, at last getting the chance to put his stamp on a nuclear-powered submarine.

By the time he had undergone the various refresher courses run for officers returning to sea command, the opposition had taken strides even beyond those encountered by Elliott. Variously deployed in the Mediterranean, the GIUK gap, and the Norwegian Sea, Tall found himself up against the Soviets in their usual numbers but now with technology every bit the equal of a design only one step on from *Dreadnought*. Leaving aside the extraordinary Alfa, the third generation of Soviet SSN attack boats had started to come on stream in 1983. These were designated Sierras, and were assumed to be a replacement for the Victors, the last of which had appeared in 1978. At almost 8,000 tons, a Sierra displaced twice as much as *Churchill*, was probably 10 knots faster, and was considerably more heavily armed. Another class of attack boat, the Mike, was even larger, a 10,000-toner with a twin nuclear reactor and – like the Alfas – a titanium hull. This gave her a greater diving depth than the Sierras and considerably more than *Churchill*. Tall accordingly had his work cut out. 'It was an incredibly demanding schedule. You couldn't breathe before the next bit of intelligence would come through, wanting you to do this, that or the other.' There were rewards, however. Given the opportunity, Tall proved a master at establishing good relationships with and motivating his crew. There was little doubt as to who was in charge, but he was sympathetic to those who served under him, and his style of command contrasted with the *de haut en bas* approach of one or two of his generation. 'After all,' says Tall, 'you're looking after what amounts to a whole community at sea. You owe it to them.'

It was while on the trail of one of the older Soviet boats, a Charlie-class guided-missile SSGN coming out of the Mediterranean, that Tall was pulled off his quarry and dispatched on another, grimmer task. It was 23 June 1985, a week after the huge Live Aid concerts in London and Philadelphia for African famine victims. An Air India 747 flight from Toronto to Delhi via Heathrow had blown up in mid-air off the coast of Ireland, and *Churchill* was sent to attempt to locate the black box flight recorder. Having done so, the submarine rose to periscope depth among the flotsam and jetsam of overhead lockers, personal belongings and lifejackets. 'There was a sense of profound sadness,' recalled Tall. 'The experience brought home what tyranny was all about, be it terrorism or totalitarianism. Not that I had any doubts, but I knew then that I was on the side of the good guys.'

Following the Falklands, Chris Wreford-Brown had taken *Conqueror* into refit. He had then been given *Valiant*, just coming out of refit, as a replacement. This was the first of the all-British SSNs, commissioned in July 1966, and the submarine that had seen action in the Falklands under the command of Tom Le Marchand. Some COs did not progress beyond their first command after Perisher, and some COs progressed no further than a first nuclear command. The best were given a second nuclear boat.

One of *Valiant*'s first tasks was a group deployment to the United States, where large-scale exercises with the US Navy were to take place. These Wreford-Brown found relatively easy, for his ship-handling skills and confidence had been honed by the battle experience of the Falklands. When he took *Valiant* into the giant US naval base in Norfolk, Virginia, he was aware that US attack boats always had a couple of tugs to take them alongside. Wreford-Brown, more competitive than his manner might suggest, decided to do it himself. This requires nerve and skill, as Edward Young observed when watching Jeremy Nash, the CO from whom he was to take over his first command, perform the same manoeuvre:

> *P.555* came in first. Turning gradually in a wide starboard sweep, she was approaching with an impressive air of confidence and efficiency . . . the seamen were already on the deck-casing in the usual harbour stations rig of bellbottoms and white jerseys, hauling out the berthing wires and ropes from

their storage inside the casing. Among the men on the bridge I could now make out the figure of Jeremy Nash, tall, erect, concentrated on making a good approach. With enough way on, he stopped engines and glided in until he was nearly opposite his berth, going astern on his motors to halt her exactly where he wanted her, almost parallel to the quay and only a few feet off. Heaving lines shot out, the bow and stern lines were secured, the spring wires followed, and with a touch ahead on his inside screw and a touch astern on the other, Jeremy snugged her in and came neatly alongside. Not until he had passed the order, 'Fall out harbour stations, finished with main motors', did Jeremy look up to where I was standing.

Valiant, however, was several thousand tons larger, and she carried a nuclear reactor.

Then, in May 1983, Wreford-Brown took his boat on a ninety-day patrol back to the Falklands. The voyage brought back memories of the conflict, and Wreford-Brown went out of his way to ensure that all the crew got a chance to go ashore, for despite their proximity a year previously, very few of them had actually seen the islands, let alone met the islanders whose freedom they had played a part in restoring. For Wreford-Brown himself, it was also moving to see the community for which he had so successfully fought.

At the end of the patrol, *Valiant* returned to Faslane, and it was from there, towards the end of his time on her, that he was scrambled to intercept a Victor III SSN that had been detected in the North-Western Approaches. Although not as good a boat as its successor, the Sierra, the Victor III was more than a match for the ageing *Valiant*.

The Victor was an intruder in British home waters and might or might not intrude into British territorial waters. She might be also be probing general operational capability or be specifically after an SSBN. Normally only passive sonar was used against such a target. Now, unusually, Wreford-Brown was dispatched to find the intruder and advised to use active sonar in order to make it clear to the Victor's CO that he had been detected. In these circumstances, as Wreford-Brown delicately remarks, 'It was known that the Russians sometimes did funny things.' Active sonar is a double-edged sword, for though it reveals the precise range and bearing of the hunted to the hunter, it also does precisely the reverse. Once detected, some Soviet COs would turn abruptly on the submarine trailing them and head straight towards the sonar source. Such reversals in course could be gentle turns, easily tracked. They could also be abrupt and violent. In either case, such a reversal was a severe test of the reliability and accuracy of the sonars on each submarine, not to mention the nerves of the respective COs. A sudden and violent reversal of course was, with good reason, known as a 'crazy Ivan'.

By the time Wreford-Brown made contact with the Victor, the order to use active sonar on her had been rescinded. He had, though, still to keep *Valiant* in touch with the Victor – without the Victor knowing. Like any submarine CO in the Cold War, the commander of the Victor would be on the look-out for a shadow and would act accordingly. Rather than follow a fixed bearing at a fixed speed for a reasonable period of time, he would change course, speed and depth on a more or less random basis – sometimes at the throw of a dice kept just for this purpose. Then, because his propeller noise rendered his own passive sonar ineffective directly behind him, from time to time he would turn around completely. *Valiant*, following not in the Victor's wake but slightly to one side, would follow him round, being careful to stay in the area in which she could not be heard. Meanwhile, Wreford-Brown tried to second-guess the Victor's CO, to predict what he would do and when. It was like a game of three-dimensional chess, with the lives of a couple of hundred men at stake. As James Taylor puts it:

During a trail you will build up a picture of your target, how he operates, when he goes to periscope depth, what discernible pattern there is in his operations, where he is going, what other forces are involved. You will observe shifts in bearing, bearing rate and frequency; all the time, you're turning these mathematically into possible courses and speeds, always looking for the most dangerous one – his closing you at high speed, or his being a good deal closer than you think. Detection may be lost from time to time, as he alters course or depth, or you alter course or depth to take your own broadcast [radio traffic] or to sprint to get ahead of him. You may also lose contact as he or you pass through an ocean front, and at the back of your mind is the knowledge that the Soviets invest a whole lot more in oceanographic research than we do.

Valiant detected the Soviet submarine in the North-West Approaches and classified it as a Victor II, a less challenging target. Thereafter, for a period of three weeks, the submarine patrolled slowly to the west and north-west of Ireland in the vicinity of the Continental shelf, maintaining intermittent passive contact with the Victor, sometimes on her towed array sonar, sometimes, when closer, on her 2001 bow sonar. To maintain a trail for so long was both a challenge and a real achievement, one that, for Wreford-Brown at least, outstripped his experience in the Falklands.

*

While the pressure on the Nato submarine force continued to grow, plans for reinforcement of the UK submarine service were in hand. Following the announcement of the acquisition of the Trident missile system in June 1980, the Ministry of Defence had crystallized its plans for a new deterrent submarine. Like its American counterpart, the Ohio-class SSBN, it would be built around the Trident missile system. Both classes of boat carried sixteen missiles, as had the Polaris boats. But the sheer size of the Trident missiles meant that an altogether larger submarine was needed, especially when it was decided that it would be fitted with the second-generation Trident II, which was 3.6 metres longer than its predecessor. Although what would be called the Vanguard class of British boats would weigh in at rather less than the 18,700-ton Ohios, at 16,000 tons they were nevertheless almost twice the size of the Resolution-class SSBNs that they replaced. The range of the Trident IIs and of the submarines in which they were installed meant that anywhere in the world could be attacked at any time, from any place, virtually without warning.

Like *Resolution*, the Vanguard submarines also used an SSN class as their basis, in this case the new Trafalgars. The SSBNs would comprise the bow and stern sections of the Trafalgars, with an extra central section acting as a missile hangar. This gave them a length of nearly 500 feet, a hundred foot longer than *Resolution*. To power such a monster a new generation of nuclear reactor was designed, the PWR2. At 27,500 horsepower, this was almost twice as powerful as the PWR1 used in the Trafalgars. Despite the pressures placed on the Polaris crews, the record of the patrols over the preceding fifteen years had proved that it was possible to keep at least one deterrent submarine at sea continuously with a total complement of four submarines. The intention was accordingly that four of the new SSBNs should be built, to supersede the ageing Resolution class as they became operational. Besides carrying the considerable fire-power of the Trident missiles (Sandy Woodward wrote that they made 'Polaris look like an up-market firework'), the class would be markedly quieter than the Resolutions and would be equipped with the very latest sonar. This theoretically made them the equal of the Ohio class in their ability to avoid detection, and the superior of the Soviet Delta IV, the last in the line of Deltas that dated from February 1984. The first of the class, *Vanguard* herself, was laid down in 1985. At the same time, a great deal of work was going into plans for the expansion of HMS *Neptune* at Faslane to provide facilities for these very large submarines, approval for the work finally being granted on 7 March 1985. Soon the works would be second in size only to those on the Channel Tunnel.

Simultaneously, efforts were being made to complement the new Trafalgar SSNs with a new class of SSK. The Navy had publicly announced its intention to replace the old Porpoise/Oberon class in 1979, for these boats were now obsolescent if not positively obsolete. In fact, plans to update them would bear fruit in the next few years, but what was really needed was a brand-new submarine. Diesel-electric boats are – generally speaking – a good deal cheaper and quicker to build than their nuclear counterparts, so that for each nuclear submarine, perhaps two diesel-electrics might be afforded. Moreover, such qualities as speed of passage that *Spartan* had demonstrated spectacularly in the Falklands were of less importance for the sort of role which the Navy envisaged for a new SSK. This was publicly identified as guarding the GIUK gap, although doubtless in practice the submarines would also have been deployed further north, and in the Baltic. Moreover, as the deployment of *Onyx* to the Falklands had indicated, there were still certain submarine operations on the

Royal Navy's roster to which SSKs were best suited, particularly the landing and recovery of Special Forces.

At first the Navy's requirement was for a submarine no larger than the Porpoise/Oberons she would replace. However, bearing in mind that the considerable design and development costs of that class had been amortised against foreign sales to the Canadian, Australian, Brazilian, Chilean and Israeli navies, the Ministry of Defence took the view that there was a better chance of selling a larger, more sophisticated vessel abroad, and the set tonnage was therefore raised to 2,400. Designed by Vickers in conjunction with the Navy's design facility in Bath, the resulting boat was larger than most contemporary SSKs, with greater endurance – about 8,000 miles – and more heavily armed. Moreover, because of the high degree of automation that the development of computers now permitted, she could operate with a crew of only forty-seven, two-thirds that of the Oberons.

The ordering of these submarines on 3 January 1986 indicated that, in the aftermath of the Falklands, there was no lack of political will in prosecuting the Cold War. Neither was there as yet any serious indication in international relations to suggest that that will was misplaced.

As to public perceptions of the Cold War, the immense popularity of Tom Clancy's submarine thriller *The Hunt for Red October*, first published in 1984, suggested that fears of a nuclear holocaust were still widespread. The book tells the story of the defection of a new Soviet SSBN to the West and is loosely based on an attempt by the Soviet Krivak-class frigate *Storozhevoy* to run from Riga to sanctuary off the Swedish island of Gotland on 8 November 1975. Submariners themselves were also fascinated by the book which divulged a good deal of operational detail about their profession that was often – though incorrectly – assumed to be classified. (They were even more intrigued by the film, starring Sean Connery, that came out in 1990. 'Of course we all like to think well of ourselves,' says Jeff Tall, who in height resembles Tom Cruise rather than Commander Bond. 'But I don't think any of us quite cast ourselves in the mould of Sean Connery.')

*

In the summer of 1985 Martin Macpherson relinquished command of *Trafalgar* to Toby Elliott and was posted Commander S/M of the Second Submarine Squadron in Devonport. Now aged 40, he had been on the Navy's fast track since Perisher, and with *Onslaught* and *Trafalgar* he had two highly successful commands to his credit. He had also served successfully as Teacher. In the opinion of some, it was a great pity that he had not been to hand with an up-and-running SSN at the time of the Falklands – some called him the best wartime submarine CO the nation never had – but the unexpected nature of the crisis had not provided much opportunity for forward planning. In any event, to date Macpherson had been required to be no more than a highly successful submarine commander. Now, as Commander of the Second Squadron, he would face greater responsibilities. In Devonport he had a group of COs to manage, encourage, teach and discipline. He had also to give some thought to the wider aspects of the submarine war with the Soviets.

Macpherson had joined the submarine service at a time when the advantage lay definitively with Nato. The US and British SSBNs and SSNs were markedly superior to their Soviet counterparts, particularly in their levels of quietness and in their ability to use their sonar to detect the opposition at a distance. Since that time, no British SSBN had ever been detected. Moreover, the Soviet equivalents, travelling to the North Atlantic to threaten the US eastern seaboard, generally – if not invariably – had been detected. As John Coward, who had now taken over *Valiant* from Chris Wreford-Brown, magisterially remarked, 'We meet the opposition, they do not meet us.'

In the critical area of the deterrent, therefore, Western political leaders probably assumed that their Soviet counterparts were unlikely to risk a first nuclear strike on the grounds that in so doing they would be signing their own death warrants, and those of large swaths of the Soviet population. This of course assumed a reasonable degree of logic on both sides. It also assumed that the horror of an unintentional war triggered by a renegade military unit or computer malfunction would not occur. Neither was beyond the bounds of possibility. As has been remarked, *The Hunt for Red October* was based on a real incident, and there were various computer malfunctions throughout the Cold War, including one on 3 June 1980 when the North Atlantic Defence Command computer indicated that a Soviet ICBM launch had just taken place. Nevertheless, the overall assumption did not seem unreasonable.

Gradually, though, the basis on which those assumptions were made – certainly in terms of the superiority of the Nato submarine force – was eroded. The Soviets under Admiral Gorshkov had made enormous progress in terms of their sonar and quietening technology. As John Moore would write in 1986 in *Submarine Warfare*: 'For many years it was the custom in the West to speak of the Soviet Navy as having a ten-year technology gap compared with the more modern ships and submarines of Nato. Nobody was very specific about the areas in which this gap existed, but developments over the last ten years have shown that, if it really did exist, it has been firmly and effectively bridged.'

The reality of the situation was brought home to Macpherson in his new position when, periodically, he visited Northwood. There, in a bunker deep beneath the mock-Tudor villas beloved of stockbrokers from a gentler age, was the war-room of popular fiction, the nerve-centre that brought together intelligence from SOSUS, SURTASS, satellite and aircraft surveillance and a range of other data to provide an overview of Soviet submarine activity in the Nato area. On the wall was a huge electronic map displaying the whole of the North Atlantic, the Arctic and Barents Seas, the North Sea and the Western Approaches, the Channel, the Bay of Biscay, the Mediterranean and the Baltic. From here, in co-ordination with the office of Commander Submarine Atlantic (COMSUBLANT) in Norfolk, Virginia, the Nato submarines were directed.

The first indication that a Soviet submarine or surface unit had been detected might come from any number of sources but would generally originate from SOSUS. Depending on how close the submarine was to the SOSUS hydrophones, this might place it in a box of anything up to 100 miles square. To narrow the area of search, maritime reconnaissance aircraft such as the RAF Nimrods would be directed to overfly the box and drop a series of sonobuoys or to use Magnetic Anomaly Detection. In this way the box was quartered and – normally – the location of the vessel narrowed down. From the library of vessel sounds collected by Nato anti-submarine forces the submarine would probably be identified. If she was approaching a recognized choke-point – the GIUK gap or the Skagerrak – the sentinel submarines guarding these points would be alerted: if not, one of the Nato SSNs or SSKs might be deployed to trail her, as had Chris Wreford-Brown on *Valiant*. Sometimes the trail would be just that, an opportunity to follow the Soviet vessel and discover as much as possible about her technological and operational parameters: how fast could she steam, how deep she could dive, the range of her torpedoes and missiles. What was critical, however, was that at any given moment, the location of all operational Soviet units should be known as precisely as possible, and that a Nato unit of one sort or another should be within reach of a fair proportion of them. Now that the Soviets had caught up technologically, those responsible for the conduct of this game of hide-and-seek had their work cut out.

Not surprisingly in the circumstances, British tactics to counter the threat became more aggressive. In recognition of his efforts in the Falklands, James Taylor had been given the position of Commander Sea Training, based in Faslane under Michael Boyce, former CO of *Superb* and now Chief of General Staff. His job was to work up British and other Nato submarines into a high state of operational readiness. Says Taylor:

> We went through all sorts of contingencies on those boats, loss of steering, loss of hydraulics, fire, flood, casualty, collision. All this was done alongside at Faslane. Then we went and did it at sea. This could be quite tricky. In one case a boat broached the surface unintentionally and then slid backwards down to her test depth with no propulsion and no compressed air in the ballast tanks to get her to the surface. It was all character-building stuff. Short of sea command, Commander SST is one of the very best posts the Navy can give you. The excitement lies in letting a captain and crew explore the limits of what they can do, what they can get away with and what they cannot. By 1985, the Submarine Flotilla was better prepared professionally than at any time in its operational history.

Above all, under Boyce and Taylor the tactic became not simply to trail the opposition but to close on it sufficiently to achieve a firing solution. As a consequence of the twin forces of political events and the fast advancing Soviet submarine technology, Soviet and Nato submarines were now head to head.

If war had actually broken out, it seems likely that Nato would have attempted to hold the line in Germany while North American reinforcements were convoyed across the Atlantic. The Warsaw Pact in turn would have attempted to conquer Nato's army in Europe and to sever the supply line across the Atlantic by massed submarine attack. In order to prevent such an attack, Nato's navies would have had to try to block various choke-points that it had spent the Cold War guarding, in an attempt to prevent Soviet submarine and surface units from reaching the Atlantic. The patrols in forward areas such as the Barents Sea would have been sent in to tackle the Soviet SSBNs in their bastions. Ten years earlier, Nato's navies might have been confident of success in such a war, but by the mid-1980s the forces of East and West were so finely balanced that the outcome would have been too close to call.

*

Yuri Andropov, long ailing, had finally died in February 1984. There had been hopes both in the USSR and in the West that he would be replaced as General Secretary by one of the new generation of Soviet leaders, but it was not to be. Andropov's successor was Konstantin Chernenko, a 72-year-old who suffered from emphysema and who was a member of the old guard. It seemed unlikely that he would usher in an era of change. Soviet embroilment in Afghanistan continued, with 140,000 troops now based in the country. Tolerance of dissidents within the Eastern bloc remained minimal. In Poland, the authorities arranged the murder of the Catholic priest Father Jerzy Popielusko, who had preached in support of Solidarity: 300,000 Poles attended his funeral. In Czechoslovakia repression of the activities of Charter 77 continued.

Chernenko's period of leadership was brief. The General Secretary died on 10 March 1985 after only a year in office. His replacement, aged 54 and by some years the youngest member of the Politburo, was a man with a reputation for radicalism. Mikhail Gorbachev was already known to the West and had been publicly applauded by Mrs Thatcher when he had led a thirty-strong delegation to London in

December 1984. It was seventeen years since a senior Soviet politician had visited Britain, and the first time that Gorbachev had visited a major Western power. He proved himself clever and reasonably open to argument. 'I like Mr Gorbachev,' Mrs Thatcher told the world. 'We can do business together.' Within six weeks of taking office, Gorbachev presented his plans for the modernization of the Soviet Union to the Central Committee. He regarded defence as the black hole that consumed much of the economy and a vast amount of the technological and scientific expertise of the Soviet republics. Social change within the USSR was not possible without an end to the arms race. The lever he intended to grasp was therefore nuclear disarmament, and one of his first ambitions was to rekindle Western enthusiasm for the stalled START talks.

It was to this end that in November 1985 Gorbachev and Reagan met at a summit in Geneva. Predictably the pair found much to disagree about, most significantly the US Strategic Defence Initiative. On a personal basis, the 74-year-old leader of the Western world seemed no match for his intelligent, cultured and vigorous counterpart, who described Reagan as 'a cave man, a political dinosaur'. Nevertheless, a level of mutual understanding was reached over disarmament, with a commitment to re-energize the START talks. In a communiqué the two agreed that 'a nuclear war cannot be won and must never be fought'. And at the press conference that followed the summit, Gorbachev declared, 'The world has become a safer place.' In Czechoslovakia, though, where enthusiasm for the new Soviet leader was muted, the Communist Party expressed official doubts over the hopes generated by the summit. Likewise in Barrow-in-Furness, work on the new SSBN *Vanguard* and the first of the new SSK class, to be called *Upholder*, proceeded apace. The Cold War was not yet over.

Chapter 13

Return to Berlin

'Of all the titles in the armed services, I suppose that of Captain is the most romantic, the one most likely to evoke images of swash-bucklers and daredevils of the high seas. For it is a rank which has inspired maritime folklore to blur inseparably the line between fact and fiction, between buccaneers and king's officers, pirates and plain adventurers. The very mention of a few names – Bligh, Cook, Ahab, Kidd, Morgan and Hornblower – there's legend for you.

Sandy Woodward, *One Hundred Days*, 1992

On 12 October 1986 the most extraordinary agreement of the twentieth century came within a scintilla of being reached. Mikhail Gorbachev, eighteen months into his term as General Secretary of the Soviet Communist Party, at short notice called for a meeting with Ronald Reagan, now two years into his own second term as US President. The pair would meet in the capital of Iceland, Reykjavik, half way between the Soviet Union and the United States.

The first day of the meeting – 11 October – saw Soviet proposals for major reductions in both strategic and intermediate-range weapons. Further proposals were made by the US and Soviet team through the night. The following morning, Gorbachev and Reagan themselves made more progress. The SS-20s and the US Pershing and cruise missiles – now called Intermediate-range Nuclear Forces (INF) – based in Europe would be removed, and the number of ICBMs and submarine-launched SLBMs would be cut by half over the following five years. This was striking enough, the most rapid progress that had ever been made on arms reduction during the twenty-year history of such talks. Over lunch, the Americans went even further, proposing the destruction over the following decade of all strategic, longer-range missiles. Reagan recalled, 'We were getting amazing agreements. As the day went on, I felt something momentous was occurring.' Gorbachev, sensing his chance, made an astonishing counter-proposal. Why not eliminate all nuclear weapons?

'All nuclear weapons?' responded an astonished Reagan. 'Hell, Mikhail, that's exactly what I've been talking about . . . get rid of all nuclear weapons . . . that's always been my goal.'

'Then why don't we agree on it?'

Ignoring the fact that the Chinese, the Israelis and others had nuclear weapons that they were unlikely to give away at America's request, Reagan replied: 'We should, we should.'

Yet the stumbling block to this agreement which would have changed world history in a matter of days was the Strategic Defence Initiative. Gorbachev knew that Reagan's Star Wars project would bankrupt the Soviet Union. For Reagan it had become a cherished dream. Both sides seemed immovable. When Reagan was pressed – pressed very firmly – by the Soviet leader on this point, he turned to his Secretary of State George Shultz for advice, scrawling him a note that read, 'George, am I right?' Shultz replied: 'Absolutely.' With this the talks collapsed. Yet as Shultz himself said, 'We made more headway on limiting [nuclear weapons] there than in any two days in the history of man.' And Gorbachev concluded: 'In spite of all its drama, Reykjavik is not a failure; it is a breakthrough which for the first time enabled us to look over the horizon.'

In the shorter term, though, confusion reigned over what exactly had been proposed and agreed. The President had apparently been prepared to barter away the American nuclear weapons based in Europe, and ultimately to rob the continent of her nuclear umbrella, thereby leaving Europe and Britain vulnerable to the superior Soviet conventional forces. Although nothing of substance actually seemed to have been settled – certainly nothing was signed – to many European leaders the very proposal was horrifying. Submariners were scarcely more enthusiastic. On hearing the news, James Taylor told Douglas Littlejohns, sometime CO of *Sceptre* and now Assistant Director of Naval Warfare, that 'Reagan has just offered to make you redundant.' In his official capacity Littlejohns wrote a brief for the Prime Minister on the strategic implications of such a move, presented to her by Admiral Fieldhouse, by then the Chief of the Defence Staff. Within days Mrs Thatcher flew to Washington to remonstrate with Reagan. She is understood to have said or implied that it was 'not his deterrent to give away'.

This was a game played for the highest stakes, and Gorbachev knew it. For he now realized that only the most drastic of reforms could save the whole Marxist-Leninist experiment. In December 1984 he had set out his vision for the Union of Soviet Socialist Republics in a speech introducing two words that were to change the face of the twentieth century, *glasnost* and *perestroika*. 'Profound transformations must be carried out in the economy and the entire system of social relations, and a qualitatively higher standard of living must be ensured to the Soviet people . . . *Glasnost* [openness] is an integral part of a socialist democracy. Frank information is evidence of confidence in the people and respect for their intelligence and feelings, and for their ability to understand events for themselves.' *Perestroika* – reconstruction – he regarded as equally essential. Soon he would be obliged to call for *uskorenige*, or the acceleration of reform. As his right-hand man he appointed as foreign minister Edward Shevardnadze. Together, as James Taylor – now promoted Captain – remarked, they were curiously reminiscent of two other highly intelligent, strong-willed reformers determined to change the nature of East-West relations, Richard Nixon and Henry Kissinger.

The root of Soviet problems remained essentially economic, with two particular areas constituting a vast drain on the resources of the system. Aid to Communist surrogates such as Vietnam, Cuba and Iraq relieved the USSR of billions of roubles, as did support for her Warsaw Pact allies by way of such things as oil subsidies. This particular deficit was also exacerbated in the early 1980s by falling oil prices. In the same period, Vietnam alone was receiving the equivalent of US $1billion a year. Like the West, the Soviets also found the increasingly sophisticated technology of defence a burden on the budget. Reagan had increased the US defence budget to 7 per cent of the country's gross domestic product during his first term. Though America was immensely richer than the USSR, this nevertheless represented a very substantial sum. The Soviet figure is less easy to identify, and was certainly never accurately measured even by the Soviets themselves, but Shevardnadze once suggested that by the mid-1980s it had risen to an astonishing 50 per cent of GDP. The result of this was perfectly simple. It impoverished the Soviet people. In the West the issue of defence spending was to a greater or lesser extent a matter of choice for an electorate voting for a democratically elected government. In the totalitarian Communist world, there was no such choice. In a one-party system the people had no option, and in the absence of freedom of expression and freedom of the press, there was little informed debate about the matter.

Nevertheless, a level of dissent was inevitable, and it showed no signs of decreasing under Gorbachev. Indeed, quite the reverse. If there had since Tsarist times been a tradition of dissent and the repression of dissent, it was also the case that the Soviet people increasingly had more to complain about, and that increasingly they were encouraged to complain. As Gorbachev himself told the Party Congress on 25 February 1986, he had come 'to tell the Party and the people honestly and openly about deficiencies in our political and practical activities, the unfavourable tendencies in the economic and social and moral sphere, and about the reasons for them'. Like Khrushchev before him, Gorbachev was obliged to find fault with his predecessors. A 'peculiar psychology' had characterized the Brezhnev era, he declared. It was 'how to improve things without changing anything'. With the world evolving rapidly outside the Soviet Union and – thanks to *glasnost* – the Soviet peoples now increasingly aware of that world, stasis was untenable. Addressing a group of writers four months later, Gorbachev asked, 'If not us, who? And if not now, when?' The beginning of the end of the Soviet Union was at hand.

On 26 April 1986 two explosions wrecked one of the four nuclear reactors of the power station at Chernobyl in the Ukraine. A radioactive cloud drifted across Eastern Europe, reaching Britain on 1 May. There was a certain irony in the fact that the leader of a country so busily calling for openness avoided informing the world of the accident until after the damage was done.

*

Yet while seismic shifts in global relations were being discussed in Reykjavik, the war beneath the sea – much of which was taking place in the immediate proximity of Iceland – still showed little signs of a thaw.

The days preceding Reykjavik had seen an extraordinary drama take place when an early Soviet Yankee-class SSBN suffered an internal explosion of missile fuel in a missile tube. The American SSN *Augusta* was close at hand, and in *Hostile Waters*, a film later made of the incident, was depicted as having caused the explosion by colliding with the Yankee. Three Soviet crew members were killed, and the Yankee eventually sank east of Bermuda on 6 October. Though the incident might be taken as reflecting the poor safety standards aboard Soviet submarines, two new Soviet vessels just coming into service gave Nato cause for concern: the Akula SSN attack submarine and the extraordinary Typhoon SSBN missile submarine.

It had for some time been Soviet practice to design its submarines in tandem, the design briefs being given to different shipyards which – typically – developed in parallel one conservative and one more radical design. The Akula (the word means shark in Russian) was the twin of the titanium-hulled Sierra, a 370-foot-long, steel-hulled vessel of 10,000 tons. After the first hull was launched in July 1984, her sound trials were monitored by Nato submarines. The level of sophistication that they revealed, a level that Western intelligence had not predicted from the Soviets for another decade, caused consternation in the West. She was capable of more than 35 knots, she had a highly sophisticated sonar array, and she was described by the Armed Services Committee of the US House of Representatives as 'the best submarine in the world today'. The less diplomatic, mindful of the successes of the Walker-Whitworth spy ring, dubbed the Akula the Walker class. Douglas Littlejohns's comment was, 'Christ, they've caught us up.'

Equally alarming was the Typhoon. In 1966, Britain's 8,500-ton *Resolution* had been the largest submarine yet launched by either the West or the Soviets. Fourteen years later, in 1980, the Soviets launched a monster at least twice and some supposed three times the size of *Resolution*. The Typhoon was 516 feet long, and she was powered by two nuclear reactors producing something in the order of 80,000 horsepower, giving her an estimated dived speed of 25 knots. She was armed with twenty SS-N-20 ballistic missiles, with ten warheads apiece, and six torpedo tubes. Thus equipped, she was assumed to be the first submarine to be designed exclusively for the sort of Arctic deployment that Martin Macpherson had investigated aboard *Valiant*. Whereas the existing Soviet SSBNs had generally established sanctuaries or bastions in the Barents Sea and the Sea of Okhotsk, the Typhoon, with her reinforced fin, forward diving planes that could retract into the hull, and shielded propeller shaft, was apparently designed specifically to shelter under the Arctic ice. She was even rumoured to have a swimming-pool to provide her crew members with exercise. Above all, she was thought to be intended as a final riposte in the event of nuclear war, sitting out the nuclear exchange under the ice and firing her missiles only when the West was beginning to recover. She was, in short, the 'doomsday machine' of popular fiction. The first Typhoon entered service in 1983, and by 1986 three or four of a class of six were operational. James Taylor remarked that the Akula was seen as 'the precursor to a great event' and – in an interview with John Dunn on BBC Radio 2 – observed that the Typhoon was too wide, too long and too high to fit into Winchester Cathedral. Reykjavik or not, he says, 'Every now and again the Russians would come up with something that would be seen as setting all our efforts at naught.'

*

Now Assistant Director of Naval Warfare, Taylor was based at the Ministry of Defence. Also in Whitehall now were Roger Lane-Nott as Assistant Director of Defence Concepts, and Chris Wreford-Brown as Director of Naval Plans. Just turned 40, all three had also just been or were just about to be promoted Captain. Woodward comments: 'Achieving the rank of Captain in the modern Royal Navy requires a fairly stringent piece of career assessment. The general rule is that you will be offered four or perhaps five jobs during the next eight or nine years, after which they will either make you a rear-admiral or thank you perfunctorily for all you have done and dispense with your services. It's known as "Falling off the Captain's List," and represents bad news for most.' Together with Tall,

Macpherson and Elliott, the three had come a long way since Dartmouth. The question now was how much further they might go.

As Whitehall warriors, they were also beginning to learn the ways of bureaucracy. Lane-Nott's job involved speculating on the nature of maritime warfare and operations in the future, in some instances as distant as 2015. In a way he found it fascinating, and he also discovered that some of the political skills necessary for survival in the huge faceless block on the east side of Whitehall, imaginatively known as Main Building, came naturally. At the same time, he was unused to waiting six months for a decision on something he had proposed should be accepted or rejected. Taylor was responsible for more short-term planning, making sure all the contingencies were in place for a Soviet naval deployment – or in layman's terms, that the submarine service was ready for war. He was perfectly capable of the necessary political and intellectual cut-and-thrust but was too impatient and plain-spoken to be entirely comfortable in such an environment. He commented:

> As a captain you're a small and sometimes disregarded cog in an incredibly big machine, and it's very difficult to change the status quo without offering concurrent money savings or soothing the egos of those responsible for the existing arrangements. For many of us in the MoD at the time, it was all a little too close to *Yes, Minister.*

Similarly Wreford-Brown, thoroughly at home beneath the sea, found Whitehall an alien environment. 'It was my first time in Main Building, and it took time to settle in, to understand where the influence lay, and how to manipulate it.'

Yet Whitehall gave all of them some idea of the wider strategic and political significance of their work as submariners. As Toby Elliott says of his spell in Whitehall slightly earlier on: 'It was the first time I had worked outside the confines – the very narrow confines – of the submarine flotilla, not just pushing a black tube around the oceans.' He had taken a flat in Pimlico, and he would leave his office in Whitehall most evenings at about 7 p.m. and walk back towards the river. His route took him past Downing Street where, several evenings running, he encountered a student protester. Round his neck the student had a placard that read 'I am sitting here until Maggie removes the cruise missiles.' At first Elliott tried to engage him in conversation. Finally he tempted him with a beer. On each occasion, pointing to his placard, the protester declined. For Elliott, this freedom of speech was precisely what he had been fighting for under the sea. 'I was delighted to witness it being exercised so demonstratively right in the heart of London.'

*

At a Central Committee meeting on 27 January 1987, Gorbachev pushed for greater modernization within the fifteen Soviet republics. He called for 'democratization' of the Party, deplored the economic and social failures of the system, and declared, 'We must not retreat.' *Glasnost* permitted much more direct and honest reporting of the Soviet imbroglio in Afghanistan, and the Soviet media – unprecedentedly – began to call for withdrawal. In Moscow itself Gorbachev announced his intention to eliminate the Soviet intermediate-range nuclear forces in Europe, this time without any preconditions on SDI. At stake, said Gorbachev, was 'the survival of humanity'. Reagan, embroiled in the Iran-Contra scandal, nevertheless saw Gorbachev's pronouncement as an opportunity. Soon he would challenge the Soviet leader on the most powerful of the Cold War's symbols, the Berlin Wall. 'If you seek peace, if you seek prosperity for the Soviet Union and Eastern Europe, if you seek liberalization, Mr Gorbachev, tear down this wall.'

Working in tandem, Mrs Thatcher attacked the Soviets on the issue of human rights. In March 1987 she visited Gorbachev in Moscow and stated unambiguously, 'If a country persists in putting people in prison for their religious and political views, that's something you've got to take into account when you're gauging whether they are going to keep any agreements you make on arms control.' Re-elected for a third term that May, she saw Gorbachev again the following December. The Soviet leader was on his way to the Washington summit that would see the signing of the Intermediate-Range Nuclear Forces Treaty. Gorbachev spoke of 'planting this sapling which may one day grow into a mighty tree of peace'.

Still, little of this filtered down to the submarine squadrons. In

Faslane work was proceeding on the extensions to the base to accommodate the Vanguard submarines, while in Barrow *Vanguard* herself was beginning to take shape in the vast building hall specially erected for the purpose. The first hull of the Vickers 2400 SSK was launched on 2 December 1986 and named *Upholder*. Soon Commander Geoff McCready, a Dartmouth graduate of the class of 1970 who had taken his Perisher ten years later and gone on to command *Orpheus*, James Taylor's old SSK, would be appointed as her CO.

On the operational front, at the beginning of 1987 Martin Macpherson had been transferred from the Second Submarine Squadron to Northwood. Here he was working with his former Teacher Toby Frere as Staff Officer Operations supporting the Flag Officer Submarines. The position as far as Macpherson was concerned was now simple: 'A hell of a lot was going on and, of course, we'd lost all our advantage. Despite the fact that there were fifty US SSNs in the Atlantic, and sixteen British, we were still very stretched.' By comparison the Soviets had at their disposal worldwide in the order of ninety SSBNs and almost a hundred SSNs. Macpherson's particular area of responsibility was the North-east Atlantic and the Norwegian and Barents Sea, in which his principal task was to ensure all Soviet submarines were accounted for. 'Every day you'd head-count the subs in the Barents, and if they weren't on the wall [in harbour] it was your job to make sure you knew where they were.' Critical of course was the 'surge deployment' that might signal war. For this purpose SSN patrols continued to be conducted in the Barents to provide 'indications and warnings' of such deployment. Indeed, on 1 February 1987 *The Times* reported a story that had run in a Sunday paper about a collision between a Soviet Typhoon SSBN and a British SSN. This proved to be Roger Lane-Nott's old charge, *Splendid*, that had managed to entangle her towed array with the Typhoon in the Northern Fleet's training area in the Barents Sea.

Then, one Friday afternoon later in the year, when all seemed reasonably calm, Toby Frere set off on the four-hour drive that would take him to his West Country home. At 1500 Macpherson called him up on his secure mobile and told him that SOSUS had picked up a Victor III SSN coming round North Cape, the northern tip of Norway. No sooner had he put the phone down than another was registered. By the time Frere stopped again at the M4 motorway services station outside Bristol, there were three on the electronic plotting board in the Northwood bunker. 'Well,' said Frere, 'I'd better come back.' By the time he returned to Northwood, Nato had detected five Victor IIIs on the loose who, in Macpherson's words, 'very clearly meant business'. It was a classic Cold War exercise to test the ability of the opposition to deploy in the face of an unexpected threat, and a clear message from the Soviets that, *glasnost* or not, their military machine was still to be reckoned with. Their objective was to detect a British SSBN. This, at a time when the Trident debate was still continuing, was an overtly political act, for any successful detection of the existing deterrent would have been catastrophic.

In response to the Soviet challenge, Frere had to lay on boats to mark the Soviet submarines. Among those at his disposal were Jeff Tall's *Churchill* and Toby Elliott's *Trafalgar*. Tall remembers receiving an unofficial message from Macpherson alerting him to the possibility of *Churchill* taking up the chase. The SSN was alongside one of her American counterparts in Lisbon. 'Basically Martin told me to stay flashed up' – in other words, to maintain the reactor at critical to allow for a swift departure. Tall was due to dine that evening on board his American opposite number. Despite the fact that the US Navy and the Royal Navy worked very closely as allies throughout the Cold War, there were nevertheless certain pieces of information that were not exchanged. Tall remembers going aboard the US submarine that evening and thinking, 'He's flashed up, I'm flashed up, he knows that I know, and I know that he knows, and neither of us will say.' Toby Elliott remembers the long haul back across the Atlantic at high speed. Unfortunately *Trafalgar*'s towed array sonar failed under the strain, and a change in equipment had to take place in a Plymouth backwater before she could join the operation. The Victors were out for ninety days, ranging right across the Atlantic and providing the Nato crews concerned with a vivid foretaste of submarine warfare in the nuclear age. Tall judged the outcome to be 'US/UK 4, Soviets 1'. Even so, it was apparent that Nato resources had been thoroughly stretched by some very good submarines run by entirely competent crews. Comments James Taylor, 'It also focused the attention in the Naval Staff at the MoD!'

That year, 1987, saw Toby Elliott completing his term as CO of *Trafalgar*. Selected for promotion to Captain, he was then posted to the

Joint Services Defence Course, an indication that his career in the Navy was by no means over. *Glasnost* had now reached such heights that one of the visiting lecturers was the Soviet Ambassador. When Elliott had completed the course he was sent to command the Tenth Submarine Flotilla in Faslane, which comprised the four Polaris boats. As his next-door neighbour in the married quarters section of HMS *Neptune* he found his old friend Martin Macpherson. Now also promoted, Macpherson had been appointed Captain Submarine Sea Training. Elliott and Macpherson took a similar line on most matters and found little on which to disagree. There was, though, now sufficient talk in the air about the Soviet willingness to prosecute a conflict that they were jointly charged by the then Flag Officer Submarines, Rear-Admiral Frank Grenier, to ensure that the Squadron's sense of purpose should not be diluted. One of Elliott's first actions was to get a large board made up and placed outside his office. It bore the old motto of the Tenth Submarine Flotilla, derived from its record in the Mediterranean during the Second World War, 'the Fighting Tenth'. By this stage, the four SSBNs had maintained the national deterrent continuously and without any break for twenty-one years. 'It was quite a record,' says Elliott, 'one of achievement by the four boats, their crews and the many thousands of servicemen and civilians in support – one which deserves to be recognized.'

Beyond their official duties, Macpherson and Elliott took a considerable interest in the periodic visits made by Geoff McCready in the SSK *Upholder*. As old diesel-electric COs, they were fascinated to see how the new submarine was shaping up. McCready, having knocked together the crew, was in fact experiencing teething problems with the boat. The first involved the torpedo tubes. It was the opening of a rear torpedo door when the bow cap was open that had caused the *Thetis* disaster in 1939. In the new *Upholder*, an elaborate series of hydraulic interlocks was intended to prevent both outer and inner doors being open at the same time. Should any of the valves in the system fail, they were supposed to revert to the shut position. McCready's weapons officer was sharp enough to notice that one or two of the valves could fail in the open position, thus rendering *Upholder* and her crew vulnerable to the fate of *Thetis*. The second was a problem with the drive train, the whole system comprising electric and diesel motors linked to the propeller shafts. This manifested itself when McCready was conducting speed trials on the submarine close to the Isle of Jura, off the west coast of Scotland. It was a calm clear day with – fortunately as it was to turn out – little shipping. He was 60 metres deep when, as part of the trial, the drive train was switched from forward into reverse to test the submarine's ability to come to a rapid stop in an emergency, going from half-ahead to half-astern.

> *Upholder*'s First Lieutenant was standing at the helmsman's console, the Engineer Officer monitoring close by, and I was in the 'Command Chair'. This is a luxury not normally granted to an SSK CO, and I made great show of doing up my safety belt in expectation of the speed we were hoping to achieve. With the submarine going forwards at about 17 knots, I ordered 'half-astern'. At first all seemed well, as the astern revs came on. But just then the First Lieutenant began to notice the tachometer building up beyond the range expected. Then there was a bang and all the lights went out. The Engineer Officer asked for permission to go aft, to which I replied 'Yes please, Engines.' By then the crew's training had kicked in and the First Lieutenant began issuing orders by voice to be relayed to the various emergency positions to regain control of the submarine – all of this in the pitch dark and without any power. The submarine began to take a bow-up angle which I was happy with as I felt the surface picture was sufficiently fresh in my mind to enable me to extend my 'all round look interval' – the personal prerogative of a CO as taught on Perisher. It was then that I cursed the fact that I'd fastened my seat belt – I couldn't get the bloody thing undone for several seconds and was glad the dark hid my embarrassment! The crew forward had control of the foreplanes and the helmsman had control of the after planes, and therefore we made a reasonably controlled return to periscope depth where indeed – and pretty luckily – nothing was close. We sat for some time wallowing on the surface, safe, while things were sorted, and we eventually made it back to Campbeltown.

Meanwhile, Chris Wreford-Brown returned to sea as CO of the brand-new Type 22 frigate *Cornwall*. She was the first of a batch of vessels that had been improved as a result of the Falklands experience, and she now had a close-in weapons defence system capable of firing 5,000 rounds a minute, and improved damage-control arrangements. She was also the first Royal Navy surface ship to be equipped with the Sub-Harpoon anti-ship missile that Rupert Best had taken to the Falklands in the SSN *Courageous*. Like the French Exocet, this is a sea-skimming missile that is very difficult to detect and that has a range of almost 100 miles. Wreford-Brown took *Cornwall* over in build and then raised £27,000 of private money to make her the first Royal Navy ship ever commissioned outside a naval port. He chose the Cornish port of Falmouth, where he and Macpherson had memorably spent a weekend more than twelve years previously, for the ceremony. *Cornwall* was commissioned by the Duchess of Cornwall, the Princess of Wales, on 24 April 1988.

Cornwall was the first surface ship that Wreford-Brown had served in for more than a decade, and – like John Coward on *Brilliant* – he brought the perspective of a submariner to the job. Indeed, it was for this very reason that submariners showing outstanding qualities as COs were transferred to surface commands. The sheer physical proximity of people in a submarine inculcates the sort of close comradeship that generally produces highly efficient operating units, at its simplest leaders who get the best out of their men. The proximity of the submariners to the front line of the Cold War also inculcated certain attitudes and states of mind to a greater extent than did surface ship commands. As Wreford-Brown puts it: 'There was a tendency to regard frigates as defensive platforms in Anti-Submarine Warfare. With her improved capability, weapons and sensors, I considered *Cornwall* to be an offensive weapon platform and trained her operations team accordingly. I'd also forgotten what it was like on frigates. On *Conqueror* or *Valiant* all your heads of department were to hand if not actually in the control-room. On *Cornwall* if I made a decision I then had to find someone to listen to it.'

Having worked the frigate up into a state of operational readiness, Wreford-Brown was then selected for the Royal College of Defence Studies. Among the eighty members from forty countries were eight from the Navy, including Roger Lane-Nott. 'It was a time', remembers Wreford-Brown, 'when the world was changing very rapidly.'

*

By the end of 1988 the speed of political change in the Soviet Union was undeniable. Gorbachev's problem was that the social and above all the economic change that he needed to go with it were not keeping pace. The failure of a command-and-control economy, where all enterprise and industry lie in the hands of the state, was all too evident. Replacing the system with a market-led economy was, however, a very different thing, particularly in a community that had known nothing of market economics for three generations. Within the Soviet Union, resistance to reform grew. Nevertheless, as both master and servant of events, Gorbachev pressed on. With Reagan's second term drawing to a close, and George Bush now President Elect, the opportunity arose for one last summit with the American President. It took place on 7 December 1988, and saw the signing of further arms control agreements. Gorbachev's speech that same day to the General Assembly of the United Nations was more remarkable: 'This new stage [of world history] requires the freeing of international relations from ideology.' Accordingly, he announced a unilateral cut in Soviet armed forces of 500,000 men, and the withdrawal of 10,000 tanks, 8,500 artillery pieces and 800 aircraft from Eastern Europe. Simultaneously, he repudiated the Brezhnev Doctrine and declared Soviet commitment to 'freedom of choice' for nations, claiming that there would be no exceptions to such commitments. The *Washington Post* commented that it was 'a speech as remarkable as any ever delivered at the United Nations ... Gorbachev invited the world literally to beat its swords into ploughshares.' A speech that would change the history of the world, it was also in effect the closing speech of the Cold War.

Five months later, the first crack in Churchill's Iron Curtain began to appear. In Hungary – the scene of the Soviet invasion in 1956 – the barbed-wire border with Austria began to be dismantled. At the same time, in Poland General Jaruzelski opened talks with Solidarity. It was agreed that elections would be held in June. These gave Solidarity a majority in the lower house, and 99 out of 100 seats in the Senate. To form an administration, the Communists had to join a coalition with Solidarity, something akin to the Devil signing a pact with God. On 22 August, Mieczyslaw Rakowski, Secretary-General of the Polish Communist Party, phoned Gorbachev for counsel. He was told that 'the time has come to yield power'. Only hours later the

Hungarian foreign minister Gyula Horn also sought advice from the Kremlin. With the border now open between Austria and Hungary – and therefore between East and West – thousands of East Germans were travelling to Hungary via Czechoslovakia to escape their own regime. However, Hungary had signed a treaty with East Germany in 1968, agreeing not to allow East Germans to leave for the West through Hungarian territory. Horn now sought to abandon the treaty, and the Kremlin acquiesced. On 10 September 1989, the Hungarian border was opened to the East. 'It was', said Horn, 'quite obvious to me that this would be the first step in a landslide-like series of events.' Soon, thousands of East Germans were fleeing to the West.

These events coincided with James Taylor's return to sea with his own command for the first time since *Spartan*. Like John Coward and Chris Wreford-Brown before him, he was given a surface ship, in this case the Type 22 frigate *London*. Maintaining the fraternity of the service, he took her over from Douglas Littlejohns, back at sea after his desk job. *London*, displacing 4,400 tons and with a complement of 286, could carry either two Lynx helicopters or one Sea King and was equipped with a mass of special surveillance technology. 'She was 500 feet long and my first surface command,' remembers Taylor. 'It wasn't the same as taking over *Spartan*, but it was still a huge responsibility. I found, as did Chris Wreford-Brown, that the chain of command was less immediate. At the same time, I did not have the deep technical grasp of the ship's systems that I had acquired over years in submarines. This meant a different approach, sifting information rather than acting directly on it. But I very much enjoyed the challenge, not least of increasing the involvement between me, as Commanding Officer, and the rest of the ship's company.'

London was in fact the surface equivalent of the submariner's 'sneaky boat', and it was for just such purposes – surveillance – that Taylor was dispatched to the Barents Sea in the company of a Royal Fleet Auxiliary, similarly prepared for intelligence-gathering with equipment that included two specially adapted Sea King helicopters. Such missions were essays in brinkmanship, each side still intent on laying down a marker. As it turned out, the two ships were treated to a display of Soviet maritime units and weaponry that almost amounted to a review of the Soviet Northern Fleet. Gunnery shoots, missile firings, joint manoeuvres of Soviet surface units with Backfire bombers and Foxtrot fighters, and sightings of Zulu, Charlie, Victor I and II, Sierra and Akula submarines culminated in an encounter with the monster Typhoon, the submarine about which Nato's inquiries were still far from complete. Catching her on the surface, Taylor ended up with one of his Sea King helicopters hovering twenty feet above the Typhoon's missile space, sucking in intelligence like the sensors on the fictitious star-ship *Enterprise*. In international waters, the Soviets could do very little about this piece of audacity. There was also an incident with a torpedo that was reminiscent of Martin Macpherson's experience in *Trafalgar* in the Mediterranean. 'In a mirror image of Martin's experience,' says Taylor, '*London* got into a torpedo-firing exercise by a Victor-class SSN and secured a line on the latest Soviet heavyweight torpedo. This was very high on the intelligence shopping-list I had been given, but my instructions were only to remove hardware if I was unobserved. A Soviet destroyer was sitting almost alongside me. While he invited me to let the torpedo go, and I feigned deafness, our ship's diver gave it a thorough examination under water before we slipped the line.' Then, as the manoeuvres wound down with the approach of autumn, *London*'s wardroom became more and more intrigued by the events taking place in Eastern Europe. The frigate had long been scheduled to pay a courtesy visit to the German North Sea port of Wilhelmshaven. Now it appeared as though there might be an opportunity to see history unfolding.

The Soviet Foreign Minister Edward Shevardnadze had visited Washington in September, and had met at some length with the new Secretary of State James Baker. From this meeting emerged positive indications on further arms reductions and particularly on a START treaty. More importantly, the Bush administration began to take seriously the Soviet conviction that radical change was needed. As Baker said: 'The situation has got the makings of a whole new world.' The following month, Hungary abandoned Communism and dropped the term People's Republic. On 6 October, Gorbachev visited East Germany, which had closed its border with Czechoslovakia in an attempt to stem the exodus to the West. In a bizarre, Alice-in-Wonderland confrontation, the East German hardliner Erich Honecker was given a dressing-down by Gorbachev, who urged him to adopt *perestroika*. Vast crowds assembled on the Unter den Linden, where East met West at the Brandenburg Gate close to the Wall. On 8 October Honecker ordered the police to fire on 70,000 protesters in Leipzig. When they refused, the ensuing upheaval led to Honecker's replacement by the reformist Egon Krenz.

By now, though, the East Germans were demanding not reform but the repudiation of Communism. At the end of the month huge demonstrations took place in Dresden and Leipzig, and the border with Czechoslovakia was reopened. Within days, 50,000 people had fled to the West. Then, following a demonstration of half a million people in East Berlin, on Saturday, 4 November, Krenz was left with little choice. It was precisely the situation that Khrushchev had faced twenty-eight years previously, when the German Democratic Republic was fast losing East Berliners to the West. Now, though, the tide could no longer be contained. On 7 November the government resigned, to be followed on the 8th by the entire Politburo. On the 9th the Central Committee of the East German Communist Party announced that visas would be granted to East German citizens to visit the West.

By now *London* had docked at Wilhelmshaven, and Taylor and five fellow officers took the military train into West Berlin, travelling along the narrow corridor through East Germany that Stalin had blocked on 24 June 1948 in the build-up to the Berlin airlift. That night crowds gathered on both sides of the Wall, the structure that had divided the city for twenty-eight years. They viewed it with some caution. Nearly two hundred people had been shot trying to cross it, and no one knew how the border guards would react to crowds of an unprecedented size. At the eight crossing-points, a few East Berliners with visas were allowed to venture across. The crowds then demanded that those without visas should also be allowed to cross. Headquarters could give the guards no clear instructions. Eventually the gates were opened at all the crossing-points. A trickle went through; the trickle became a stream, the stream a flood. The Wall having been breached, both East and West Berliners then turned on what had long divided them, what had long divided East and West. They used stones, hammers, pickaxes, anything that came to hand. Taylor, at the Wall itself, remembered 'a man in a T-shirt and jeans wielding a sledgehammer, shouting, "I just hate this bloody thing." '

It was John F. Kennedy who had invited those who didn't really understand the 'great issue between the free world and the Communist world' to come to Berlin. It was Kennedy, too, who in that great speech had foretold the fall of the Wall, and who had told the German people that when that day finally came the people of West Berlin would be able to take 'sober satisfaction' in the fact that they had been in the front line for almost two decades. As it turned out the Berliners had manned the front line for almost forty-five years. Finally though, that night, their time had come. Taylor, too, took some sober satisfaction – and some less sober – in that night's events. As a close student of Soviet affairs, he realized that there was more than mere symbolism to the destruction of the Wall; that it was the clearest indication yet that the days of Communism were numbered. Taylor had long understood the issue represented by Berlin; indeed it had been his job to do so. He had come to Berlin to see the fruits of his labours in the destruction of the Wall.

Epilogue

'Our deterrent, as part of the Atlantic Alliance, has helped to prevent war in the past. It will help to do so in the future. That is what it is for. All those concerned, many of whom are present today, can take pride in that.'

John Major, 28 August 1996

On 28 August 1996 the Prime Minister John Major visited the Clyde submarine base of HMS *Neptune* at Faslane. He was there to preside over the ceremony to mark not only the decommissioning of the SSBN *Repulse* but also the end of the whole Polaris programme, a programme that had seen a Polaris boat on patrol continuously since Mike Henry first took *Resolution* out of Faslane on 14 June 1968. Despite the continuation of the seaborne nuclear deterrent in the form of the Vanguard submarines carrying Trident, the ceremony marked the end of an era.

Since the fall of the Berlin Wall almost seven years previously, the complexion of international relations had changed almost unrecognizably. On 11 March 1990, the Soviet Union's Communist Party had broken the totalitarian system that had reigned for nearly three-quarters of a century by accepting the creation of political parties other than its own. Within the week, the Baltic state of Lithuania declared its independence, to be followed in due course by Estonia and Latvia. In May, in Romania, the first open elections for fifty-three years were held, while at the end of that month the radical Boris Yeltsin was elected President of the largest of the Soviet republics,

Russia. That autumn there occurred the extraordinary spectacle of the reunification of Germany as a member of Nato. The following year saw an equally remarkable rapprochement in the form of the Bush-Gorbachev summit on the Gulf crisis. A joint statement was issued from the leaders of East and West to the effect that they were 'united in the belief that Iraq's aggression must not be tolerated'.

Following the successful prosecution of the Gulf War, in the Soviet Union Yeltsin began to press for more rapid reform than even Mikhail Gorbachev was prepared to accept. On 1 July 1991 the Warsaw Pact was dissolved. Then, following the failure of a Communist coup on 19 August in Moscow, Gorbachev himself resigned as party leader. On 29 August the Soviet Union's Communist Party was suspended. Before the end of the year, the Commonwealth of Independent States (CIS) had replaced the Soviet Union, with Yeltsin as its president. By 1994, it was necessary for Nato to redefine its role as a Pan-European peacekeeper, to consider the inclusion within its ranks of the former states of the Soviet Union and members of the Warsaw Pact, and to concern itself with the control and disposal of the former Soviet nuclear arsenal. The new American President, Bill Clinton, met his Russian counterpart on 12 January 1994 in the Ukrainian capital of Kiev. His purpose was to urge Yeltsin to destroy nuclear weapons still based on Ukrainian soil. That autumn British, French and American troops, stationed in Berlin since 1948, were finally withdrawn. While the Balkans remained a running sore, on 28 November 1995 Russia accepted that its own peacekeeping forces in Bosnia – part of the United Nations Protective Force – would come under American control. Then, on 3 July 1996, Yeltsin became the first democratically elected President of Russia.

In many respects the audience in Faslane that day in 1996 was too close to these events to realize quite how extraordinary they were. The lowering of the Soviet flag over the Kremlin symbolized little less than the fact that a second great Russian revolution had occurred. Despite the continued existence of a Communist regime in China, it was an indication that revolutionary socialism, which many had thought would engulf the world, had had its day. It demonstrated, too, that the Cold War was over. Even the best informed and most prescient had hardly envisaged such an event. It was assumed that the Communist bloc was a permanency, the *doppelgänger* of capitalism in the balance of power that had obtained since the Second World War. In 1979 when Margaret Thatcher came to power and détente collapsed, to many it looked as though the Third World War was just around the corner; even in early 1989 no one imagined what the revolutions in Eastern Europe would achieve; only six years before that, many had believed that global war was imminent. As it turned out, however, the economic burden imposed on the USSR principally by the arms race caused its implosion; and if the Soviets had ever seriously considered waging an aggressive war, the activities of Nato air, land and sea forces had persuaded them that such a war could not be won. As Harold Macmillan had thought as long ago as 1957, by combining its resources the West, although it might not defeat the Russians, 'will wear them out and force them to defeat themselves'. Things had fallen apart: the centre could not hold.

Thirty-three years before John Major arrived at HMS *Neptune* to preside over the decommissioning ceremony, 300 naval cadets had assembled at the other end of the country, in Dartmouth. The Second World War was then still a very recent memory. Rationing had ended less than ten years previously, and the British Motor Corporation's Mini was a stripling. The previous autumn had seen the Cuban missile crisis and a plethora of arrangements for the civil defence of the country in the face of nuclear war. Five years later, when the Polaris patrols began, the Soviet Union had invaded Czechoslovakia and – as John Major pointed out in his address – the Vietnam War still raged. By the time the cadets had progressed to the commanding officers' qualifying course, Yom Kippur seemed quite likely to be the starting-point for global war. By the time they were given their nuclear commands, the quality of the Soviet submarine threat nearly matched that of the West. Then came the Falklands conflict that saw them blooded, and the needle-point political and military confrontation of the mid-1980s that might again have led to nuclear war.

Now, though, it was over. Thirty-three years on, their job was done.

As the Cold War wound down after the fall of the Berlin Wall, the class of '63 had continued in their service. Jeff Tall at the age of 47 was first given command of the SSBN *Repulse* and later posted as

Fleet Trials Officer on the CinC Atlantic Fleet Staff, for which he was awarded the OBE. Chris Wreford-Brown was posted CO of the Second Submarine Squadron in Devonport. Toby Elliott saw action as CO of John Coward's old frigate *Brilliant* in the Gulf War, Roger Lane-Nott commanded the frigate *Coventry* and was captain of the First Frigate Squadron. James Taylor, now a Commodore, served as Chief of Staff to the Flag Officer Submarines, by then Coward himself. Coward was succeeded by Toby Frere, and Roger Lane-Nott then replaced Taylor as his Chief of Staff. Frere's own successor was Lane-Nott, the man from the class of '63 who reached the pinnacle of the British submarine service. As his own Chief of Staff, he chose Martin Macpherson. Between them the pair ran the country's submarines from 1993 to 1996.

To those present that day in August 1996, John Major suggested that this was a moment for the expression of gratitude. With Vice-Admiral Hugh Mackenzie, the man who had masterminded the Polaris programme, at his side, the Prime Minister said that the country could give thanks for those whose 'continuous patrols that have been vital to ensure this country's peace and security, [making] a unique and invaluable contribution to the remarkable record of maintaining a Polaris submarine at sea . . . on deterrent patrol, undetected by friend or foe, every minute of every day of every year from 1968 until May of this year'. He might have added more. John F. Kennedy had talked of the horrifying threat of nuclear conflict, indeed of global destruction, that had hung over the post-war generation. With the end of the Cold War and the collapse of the Soviet Union, that shadow was very largely lifted.

*

The ceremony at Faslane naturally focused on SSBNs – hence the absence that day of the likes of Martin Macpherson, Chris Wreford-Brown and James Taylor. Nevertheless, for two reasons the complementary work of the remainder of the submarine flotilla, the SSN and SSK fleet of attack submarines, should not be forgotten. The centenary of the submarine force in 2001 is a fitting point at which to assess its achievements; and the tragedy of the sinking of the Soviet Oscar-class *Kursk* on 12 August 2000, and the loss of her 118-man crew, is a vivid reminder of the intrinsic dangers of submarine operations.

The constraints of national security have inevitably meant that this book has not been a comprehensive survey of the activities of British SSKs and SSNs during the course of the Cold War. It gives a flavour, though, of the way in which the Soviet SLBM submarine deterrent was compromised by the activity of the British attack boats working with their Nato counterparts, both in their constant surveillance of the Soviet fleet and on the intelligence-gathering missions in the Barents Sea and elsewhere; and the way in which the Soviets' own attack boats were kept at bay by their Nato opposite numbers. They were the 'thin black line' that convinced the Soviets that they would do no better than the Germans had in attempting to sever Europe's transatlantic lifeline to the United States, convinced them that the submarine battle could not be won.

In the aftermath of the Cold War, however, the force of attack boats has been considerably run down. In 1986 the United Kingdom boasted fifteen SSNs and twelve SSKs. Today, it can muster twelve SSNs and no SSKs whatsoever: the remaining Oberons have been scrapped and the four brand-new Upholders are in the process of being sold. 'What, if any, other branch in this country's offensive forces has taken a 50 per cent cut?' asks Sandy Woodward. Although the US Navy has seen comparable reductions, this may suggest that the value of the force as a highly flexible means of both power projection and weapons delivery is insufficiently appreciated – this despite the fact that the Navy has spent the past ten years developing a number of capabilities that inevitably took a back seat during a conflict that was principally an anti-submarine operation. The most dramatic of these is the ability to attack targets up to 1,000 miles inland with the Tomahawk cruise missile, and the most important the integration of the SSN into RAF and even Army joint operations to the extent that – in Martin Macpherson's words – 'the SSNs have become even more indispensible to the defence of the realm'. Despite the fact, too, that the world still bristles with nuclear and conventional threats. If the threats are – currently – less obviously identifiable, they are no less real. China, India, Iraq, Israel and North Korea are known to possess or strongly suspected of possessing nuclear arsenals and the means of delivering such weapons, and it would be a bold man who predicted an age of prosperity and stability for the next twenty-five years. As was once said, those who fail to learn the lessons of history are destined ever to repeat it.

It is of course the task of history itself rather than contemporary comment to try to assess objectively the full and precise contribution made by British submarines and submariners – both the Polaris boats and the attack boats – to the Cold War. This is something that will doubtless be undertaken at a later date, when the passing of time has bestowed perspective on recent events. The submariners themselves, though, are very clear about what they did. Toby Elliott, commander of both the SSN *Trafalgar* and the SSBN *Resolution*, best summarizes their feelings. 'The submarine flotilla fought the longest battle of the whole bloody lot. Every patrol we did was a contribution to that end, and whatever type of hull it was, we achieved an awful lot for our country and for world peace.' John Coward is equally trenchant. 'There was a war,' he says. 'And we won it.'

On a more personal note, too, something may be added. In his own book on British submarines, Jeff Tall reminds his readers that for maritime nations on the navy 'doth the well-being of the state depend'. Tall and his contemporaries were the lifeblood of the Royal Navy at the height of the Cold War, as were those who came before and after the class of '63. At a time when the nation is looking back on its achievements in the last century, it is often remarked that the country's Battle of Britain fighter pilots – the Few – were ordinary people doing extraordinary things. The sons of that generation, the Dartmouth class of '63, the likes of Elliott, Lane-Nott, Macpherson, Tall, Taylor and Wreford-Brown, cannot accurately be described as figures 'seven feet tall and made of high-grade steel' that I had once imagined; indeed, they were – and are – human enough. But through a combination of native talent, the Navy's training and ambition they became submarine COs. Like the Few, Britain's Cold War submariners were also ordinary people doing extraordinary things.

Appendix I

SSKs, SSNs and SSBNs of the Royal Navy

Class	Submarine	Date of Commissioning
Porpoise/Oberon SSKs	Porpoise	17 April 1958
	Rorqual	24 October 1958
	Grampus	19 December 1958
	Narwhal	4 May 1959
	Cachalot	1 September 1959
	Finwhale	19 August 1960
	Orpheus	25 November 1960
	Walrus	10 February 1961
	Oberon	24 February 1961
	Sealion	23 July 1961
	Odin	3 May 1962
	Olympus	7 July 1962
	Onslaught	14 August 1962
	Otter	20 August 1962
	Oracle	14 February 1963
	Otus	5 October 1963
	Osiris	11 January 1964
	Ocelot	31 January 1964
	Opossum	29 February 1964
	Opportune	28 December 1964
	Onyx	20 November 1967

Class	Submarine	Date of Commissioning
SSNs	Dreadnought	17 April 1964
	Valiant	18 July 1966
	Warspite	18 April 1967
	Churchill	15 July 1970
	Courageous	16 October 1971
	Conqueror	9 November 1971
	Swiftsure	17 April 1973
	Sovereign	11 July 1974
	Superb	13 November 1976
	Sceptre	14 February 1978
	Spartan	22 September 1979
	Splendid	31 March 1981
	Trafalgar	27 May 1983
	Turbulent	28 April 1984
	Torbay	7 February 1985
	Tireless	5 October 1985
	Trenchant	14 January 1989
	Talent	12 May 1990
	Triumph	12 October 1991
SSBNs	Resolution	30 October 1967
	Repulse	28 September 1968
	Renown	15 November 1968
	Revenge	4 December 1969
	Vanguard	14 August 1993
	Victorious	7 January 1995
	Vigilant	10 December 1996
	Vengeance	27 November 1999
Upholder SSKs	Upholder	9 June 1990
	Unseen	7 June 1991
	Ursula	8 August 1992
	Unicorn	25 June 1993

Appendix II

Flag Officers Submarines, 1946–2001

1 November 1946	Vice-Admiral M. Mansfield, CB, DSO, DSC
8 April 1948	Commodore B. Bryant, DSO, DSC
23 August 1948	Rear-Admiral G. Grantham, CB, CBE, DSO
20 January 1950	Rear-Admiral S.M. Raw, CB, CBE
4 January 1952	Rear-Admiral G.W.G. Simpson, CB, CBE
9 February 1954	Rear-Admiral G.B.H. Fawkes, CB, CVO, CBE
7 December 1955	Rear-Admiral W.J.W. Woods, CB, DSO
12 November 1957	Rear-Admiral B.W. Taylor, CB, DSC
24 November 1959	Rear-Admiral A.R. Hezlet, CB, DSO, DSC
31 July 1961	Rear-Admiral H.S. Mackenzie, CB, DSO, DSC
23 January 1963	Commodore F.J.D. Turner, DSO
28 May 1963	Rear-Admiral H.R. Law CB, OBE, DSC
27 May 1965	Rear-Admiral I.L.M. McGeoch, DSO, DSC
28 December 1967	Vice-Admiral M.P. Pollock, CB, MVO, DSC
10 November 1969	Vice-Admiral J.C.Y. Roxburgh, CB, CBE, DSO, DSC
2 September 1972	Vice-Admiral J.A.R. Troup, DSC
2 July 1974	Vice-Admiral I.G. Raikes CBE, DSC
22 November 1976	Rear-Admiral J.D.E. Fieldhouse
5 December 1978	Rear-Admiral R.R. Squires
14 December 1981	Vice-Admiral P.G.M. Herbert, OBE
12 May 1983	Rear-Admiral Sir John Woodward, KCB
23 November 1984	Rear-Admiral R.G. Heaslip, CB

19 May 1987	Rear-Admiral P.F. Grenier, CB
26 September 1989	Vice-Admiral J.F. Coward, DSO
19 September 1991	Rear-Admiral R.T. Frere
14 December 1993	Rear-Admiral R.C. Lane-Nott, CB
12 February 1996	Rear-Admiral J.F. Perowne, OBE
4 August 1998	Rear-Admiral R.P. Stevens, CB

Bibliography

All books were published in London unless otherwise stated.

Max Arthur, *The Navy: 1939 to the Present Day* (Hodder & Stoughton, 1997)

Kit L., Kermit and Carolyn Bonner, *Cold War at Sea* (Osceola, Motorbooks International, 2000)

Ben Bryant, *One Man Band* (William Kimber, 1958)

Buchheim, Lothar-Gunther, *Das Boot* (Munich, Piper Verlag, 1973: English translation Cassell, 1999)

Eric Bush, *How to Become a Naval Officer* (Allen & Unwin, 1963)

Peter Byrd (ed.), *Foreign Policy under Thatcher* (Oxford, Philip Allan, 1988)

James Calvert, *Surface at the Pole* (Hutchinson, 1961)

John Campbell, *Margaret Thatcher* (Jonathan Cape, 2000)

Don Camsell, *Black Water* (Virgin Publishing, 2000)

William Guy Carr, *By Guess and by God* (Hutchinson, 1919)

Tom Clancy, *The Hunt for Red October* (HarperCollins, 1984)

— *Submarine* (HarperCollins, 1993)

Andrew Cockburn, *The Threat* (Hutchinson, 1983)

Richard Compton-Hall, *Submarine versus Submarine* (Newton Abbot, David & Charles, 1988)

John Coote, *Submariner* (Leo Cooper, 1991)

Chris Craig, *Call for Fire* (John Murray, 1995)

Jonathan Crane, *Submarine* (BBC Publications, 1984)

George Crider, *War Fish* (New York, 1954)

Michael Dockrill, *British Defence since 1945* (Oxford, Blackwell, 1988)

Nigel Fisher, *Harold Macmillan* (Weidenfeld & Nicolson, 1982)

Norman Friedman, *The Fifty Year War* (Chatham Publishing, 2000)

S.R. Gibbons, *The Cold War* (Harlow, Longman, 1987)

Martin Gilbert, *The History of the Twentieth Century Vol. 3: Challenge to Civilization* (HarperCollins, 1999)

S.G. Gorshkov, '*Navies at War and Peace*' trans. in *Red Star Rising at Sea* (Annapolis, US Naval Institute Press, 1974)

Edwyn Gray, *Few Survived* (Leo Cooper, 1986)

Sean Greenwood, *Britain and the Cold War* (Macmillan, 2000)

John Hackett, *The Third World War* (Sidgwick & Jackson, 1978)

Max Hastings and Simon Jenkins, *The Battle for the Falklands* (Michael Jospeh, 1983)

Denis Healey, *The Time of My Life* (Michael Joseph, 1989)

Edward Heath, *The Course of My Life* (Hodder & Stoughton, 1998)

John Hervey, *Brassey's Sea Power: Submarines* (Brassey's, 1994)

Michael Heseltine, *Life in the Jungle* (Hodder & Stoughton, 2000)

Richard Humble, *Submarines* (Birmingham, Basinghall, 1981)

Jeremy Isaacs and Taylor Downing, *Cold War* (Bantam, 1998)

Jane's Fighting Ships (Jane's Information Group, various editions)

Rebecca John, *Caspar John* (Collins, 1987)

John Keegan, *Price of Admiralty* (Hutchinson, 1988)

Peter Kemp, *The Oxford Companion to Ships and the Sea* (Oxford, Oxford University Press, 1988)

Nikita Khrushchev, *Khrushchev Remembers: The Last Testament* (André Deutsch, 1974)

Jack Kneece, *Family Treason: The Walker Spy Case* (New York, Stein & Day, 1986)

Chuck Lawliss, *The Submarine Book* (New York, Burford Books, 1991)

William M. Leary and John H. Nicholson, *Under Ice* (Texas, Texas A & M University Press, 1999)

F.W. Lipscomb, *The British Submarine* (Conway Maritime Press, 1975)

Harold Macmillan, *At the End of the Day* (Macmillan, 1973)

John Marriott, *Submarine* (Ian Allan, 1986)

Alastair Mars, *Unbroken* (Corgi, 1975)

Martin Middlebrook, *Task Force* (Penguin, 1987)

David Miller, *The Cold War: A Military History* (John Murray, 1998)

John Moore, *Sea Power and Politics* (Weidenfeld & Nicolson, 1979)

— (ed.), *The Impact of Polaris* (Huddersfield, Richard Netherwood Ltd, 1999)

— and Richard Compton-Hall, *Submarine Warfare* (Michael Joseph, 1986)

Kenneth O. Morgan, *The People's Peace* (Oxford University Press, 1990)

John Newhouse, *The Nuclear Age* (Michael Joseph, 1989)

David Owen, *Face the Future* (Jonathan Cape, 1981)

Peter Padfield, *War Beneath the Sea* (John Murray, 1995)

Norman Polmar and Jurrien Noot, *Submarines of the Russian and Soviet Navies, 1718–1990* (Annapolis, United States Naval Institute, 1991)

Bryan Ranft (ed.), *Ironclad to Trident* (Brassey's, 1986)

Patrick Robinson, *Nimitz Class* (Century, 1997)

— *HMS Unseen* (Century, 1999)

Sherry Sontag and Christopher Drew, *Blind Man's Bluff* (Hutchinson, 1999)

J.J. Tall and Paul Kemp, *HM Submarines in Camera* (Sutton Publishing, 1998)

Margaret Thatcher, *The Downing Street Years* (HarperCollins, 1993)

Dan van der Vat, *Stealth at Sea* (Weidenfeld & Nicolson, 1994)

— *Standard of Power* (Hutchinson, 2000)

John Wells, *The Royal Navy: An Illustrated Social History, 1870–1982* (Stroud, Alan Sutton, 1994)

Nigel West, *The Secret War for the Falklands* (Little, Brown, 1997)

Harold Wilson, *Final Term: The Labour Government, 1974–1976* (Weidenfeld & Nicolson, 1979)

John Winton, *The Submariners* (Constable, 1999)

Richard Woodman, *The History of the Ship* (Conway Maritime Press, 1997)

Sandy Woodward and Patrick Robinson, *One Hundred Days* (HarperCollins, 1992)

Edward Young, *One of Our Submarines* (Rupert Hart-Davis, 1952)

Hugo Young, *One of Us* (Macmillan, 1990)

John Young, *Cold War in Europe, 1945–1991* (Arnold, 1991)

Philip Ziegler, *Mountbatten* (Collins, 1985)

— *Wilson: The Authorised Life* (Weidenfeld & Nicolson, 1993)

Acknowledgements

This book was in the first instance the suggestion of Simon Anderson, without whose enthusiasm it would not have been written. Subsequently, the principal subjects of the book were generous with their time: Toby Elliott, Roger Lane-Nott, Martin Macpherson, Jeff Tall, James Taylor and Chris Wreford-Brown all gave me a series of interviews over a period of more than two years. I am also grateful for interviews provided by other British submariners, among them Sir John Coward, Marcus Fitzgerald, Sir Toby Frere, Phil Higgins, Doug Littlejohns, Fred Scourse and Sir Sandy Woodward.

As background to the book, I visited both the United States and what was the Soviet Union. In the States, Admiral Hank Chiles was instrumental in introducing me to the American counterparts of the class of '63 and a series of experts including Richard Boyle, Bruce DeMars and the Commander of the US Atlantic submarine force, Admiral Edmund Giambastiani. In Russia Geoff McCready was kind enough to perform a similar office. Marcus Fitzgerald also arranged for me to be present at the Demonstration and Shakedown Operation for *Vengeance*.

Finally, a great deal of work in shaping the book was undertaken by John Moore, formerly editor of *Jane's Fighting Ships* and a distinguished submariner, and Gail Pirkis. John has been my tutor and mentor in submarine matters, Gail – the book's editor – an unfailing critic of English prose and Cold War history. And the book would certainly not have been completed without the uncomplaining and unfailing support of my wife Kate, who has done rather more than tolerate its demands.

Index